Arden whirled to look at him. "You want me to marry you?"

"Well, actually, I'd like you to pretend to want to marry me. And I'll pretend to want to marry you."

"It's a ridiculous idea. I can't pretend to be in love."

"Am I so repulsive?"

"You're a very attractive man, Griff. I just—"

Immediately, he stepped closer. "You don't have time for an all-expenses paid vacation in sunny Georgia?"

"I don't think..."

Once more, he came close, laying his warm hands on her bare shoulders.

"Is there something you want or need, Arden? Something I can give you?"

An idea popped into her mind, burrowing up from somewhere deep in her subconscious, a suggestion so outrageous that he would no doubt turn her down immediately and walk out of her life without a backward glance.

"There is something I want, Griff. I want a child."

A Secret Arrangement

Lynnette Kent & Cathy Gillen Thacker

Previously published as *A Convenient Proposal*
and *The Secret Seduction*

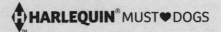

ISBN-13: 978-1-335-69093-7

A Secret Arrangement

Copyright © 2011 by Harlequin Books S.A.

First published as A Convenient Proposal
by Harlequin Books in 2011 and
The Secret Seduction by Harlequin Books in 2004.

The publisher acknowledges the copyright holder
of the individual works as follows:

A Convenient Proposal
Copyright © 2011 by Cheryl B. Bacon

The Secret Seduction
Copyright © 2004 by Cathy Gillen Thacker

PLEASE RECYCLE · THIS PRODUCT IS RECYCLABLE

Recycling programs
for this product may
not exist in your area.

Printed in U.S.A.

HARLEQUIN®
™ www.Harlequin.com

CONTENTS

Lynnette Kent lives on a farm in southeastern North Carolina with her six horses and six dogs. When she isn't busy riding, driving or feeding animals, she loves to tend her gardens and read and write books.

Books by Lynnette Kent

Harlequin American Romance

Smoky Mountain Reunion
Smoky Mountain Home
A Holiday to Remember
Jesse: Merry Christmas, Cowboy
A Convenient Proposal

The Marshall Brothers

A Wife in Wyoming
A Husband in Wyoming
A Marriage in Wyoming

Harlequin Superromance

The Last Honest Man
The Fake Husband
Single with Kids
Abby's Christmas
The Prodigal Texan

Visit the Author Profile page at Harlequin.com.

A CONVENIENT PROPOSAL

Lynnette Kent

To Murphy, with thanks for introducing us to banjos, bluegrass and the Georgia mountains.

And, as always, to Martin, adventurer and banjo player, with love.

Chapter 1

Cool sand beneath his feet. A salty breeze off the ocean. Midnight stars overhead and cold champagne to drink. What better way to celebrate New Year's Eve?

Not that Griff Campbell was looking forward to the new year. Or even the new week, since tomorrow morning—New Year's Day—would see him returning to his Georgia hometown after a six-month exile. Self-imposed exile, actually.

Some people might call it running away.

For tonight, however, he'd tied his rented speedboat to an abandoned pier on the most deserted beach he could find—a little chunk of sand and live oak trees just a few miles off the Miami coastline, where nobody could find him and he could, he hoped, dredge up the enthusiasm to go home.

Two bottles of champagne down, and all he'd dredged up so far were the seashells rattling in the pockets of his shorts. Griff took a swig of Taittingers, then swiped his shirtsleeve across his chin to catch a dribble. Champagne was almost too easy to drink, sometimes. He'd popped this cork only a few minutes ago and now it was…how far gone?

Lifting the bottle as he walked along, he peered into the dark glass, trying to judge the level of liquid within. The moonless night offered no contrast to see by, but the light weight told its own tale. He'd better slow down, or he wouldn't have a toast left at the stroke of twelve.

When he let his arm fall back to his side, however, the curvy shape lingered in front of him, like a white shadow of the bottle he'd been staring at.

It was a woman, he realized. She stood about a hundred yards farther along, facing away from him. Her light-colored dress contrasted starkly with the indigo water and sky. She didn't turn around as he advanced, or seem to take any notice of his approach. He might as well be invisible.

Her obliviousness—her very presence on this deserted island—intrigued him. Griff walked up until he stood just a breath away, then tapped her on the shoulder as he said, "Happy New Year."

The woman jumped about six feet off the sand and spun to face him. "What—? Wh-who are you?" Her face was as beautiful as her slender figure and as pale as her white dress. "What do you want?"

Now he felt like a rat for shocking her. "Sorry. I didn't mean to scare you."

"This is a private island," she told him fiercely. "You're trespassing."

"I must have missed the sign. I just wanted someplace quiet tonight." He backed away several steps, holding up his hands, and thus the champagne, in a gesture of surrender. "I'm not dangerous. I swear."

She looked at the bottle and then back to his face. "Are you going to hit me with that?"

"God, no. I could offer you a drink—" he glanced at his watch "—in about ten minutes. I would never hit a woman." If ever he'd been tempted, it was six months ago. But the past was just that. Past.

Without warning, a glowing rocket streaked across the sky beyond the woman's right shoulder, bursting into a flower of white sparks overhead. An instant later, a loud boom shook the leaves on the nearby live oak trees.

"So much for quiet," Griff said.

"That's the fireworks in Miami." She turned away again, facing north. "They start at eleven-fifty."

But Griff's gaze lingered on the graceful length of her spine, the supple muscles in her shoulders revealed by the low-backed dress and the sweet curve of her hips.

"Nice," he murmured. If she heard, she didn't respond.

Then a series of red, green and blue explosions jerked his attention back to the horizon. Every second sent new bombs streaking skyward, splashing brilliant colors into the air and across the water. The night became filled with noise, from bass booms to whirling squeals and everything in between, as the old year received a hearty send-off and the new one arrived with rambunctious glory.

A thunderous finale concluded the program. Only trails of smoke remained, a crowd of gray ghosts drifting over the sea.

Griff's companion blew out a deep breath. "Fantastic." She glanced at him over her shoulder. "I gather you're not planning to assault me, after all."

Griff shook his head. "The thought never crossed my mind. Although…"

She turned to face him. "Yes?"

He'd consumed enough champagne to say what he was thinking. "We'd better keep up the old tradition if we expect to have a good new year."

"What tradition is that?"

Griff let the champagne bottle fall to the sand at his feet, then took the two steps separating him from the woman in white. Curving one hand around her upper arm, he used the other to bracket her chin with his fingers and tilt her head to the perfect angle.

"This," he said, and bent to kiss her.

She stiffened, but didn't jerk away. Encouraged, he increased his pressure, molding their mouths more firmly together. She tasted cool and sweet, like ripe melon. After a moment, her generous lips softened, inviting him to explore their curves and the way his angles fit against them. Her hand fluttered to his shoulder and he slipped his arm around her waist. A heartbeat later, the tip of her tongue touched the edge of his upper lip.

The fireworks started up again, inside Griff this time. Desire exploded in his belly, flashed through his veins. He was breathless and light-headed and pumped up all at the same time. He could have kissed this woman forever.

And he didn't even know her name.

The thought steadied him, allowed him to slow the kisses and return both of them to ground level. There were a couple of things they needed to get straight before taking off for wonderland…paradise…wherever she wanted to go.

"Who are you?" he murmured, loosening his arms and using one hand to brush her hair back from her face.

"Arden." Her voice was as hushed as his. "Arden Burke."

"I'm Griff Campbell." He smiled at her. "Will you marry me?"

Rendered speechless, Arden stared into the shadowed face of the stranger she'd just kissed. Her mind reeled in delighted response to the feelings he'd stirred up, and in amazement at the fact she'd allowed him to touch her at all.

Finally, she found her voice. "Oh, of course. Right away."

His eyes crinkled as he laughed. "Excellent. Let's toast to our wedding." He surveyed the sandy beach around their feet, then danced both of them sideways two steps to pick up the champagne he'd dropped. After polishing the mouth of the bottle with the hem of his gold-and-blue shirt, he extended it to her. "You first."

Why not? Arden tilted back her head and poured a long stream of the wine down her throat. "Wonderful," she said, handing back the bottle. "Your turn."

He—Griff—tipped it in her direction. "To us." Then he took his own drink, upending the bottle. She noticed he didn't wipe off the mouth this time. "And a happier New Year."

She walked beside him as he trudged toward a trash can at the top of the beach. "Amen."

He might be drunk, but he was listening. "Has your year been unhappy?"

Arden expelled a short breath through her nose. "Some parts. Has yours?"

"I can't remember a worse one." He tossed the bottle into the can.

Neither could she, as a matter of fact. "What happened?"

Without answering, he headed back to the water's edge. He'd linked his right hand with her left, so they walked side by side like a pair of lovers. His palm was surprisingly warm, dry and comfortable.

"I was supposed to get married six months ago—June fourth, to be exact. On June first, my fiancée and my best buddy since second grade informed me they were in love and she couldn't go through with our wedding."

"That would make for a bad year." Arden glanced at him, but he was staring up, telling his story to a star. "What an awful thing to do to you."

Griff nodded. "I thought so. We'd been engaged for two years. You'd think she could have figured it out before the week of the wedding." Beneath the surface of his calm tone, pain roiled like an undertow.

Arden squeezed his hand. "Surely you didn't wait six months to take a vacation."

"Nope. I left that night and caught a fishing boat out of Tampa a few days later. I've been working my way through the islands ever since."

"The new year is supposed to be a chance for a fresh start. Are you planning one?"

"Well, I'm going home tomorrow. Does that count?"

"And home is...?"

"Sheridan, Georgia, where they like to pretend the

Civil War—hell, the whole second half of the nineteenth century—never happened."

"You don't sound exactly nostalgic."

He shrugged. "It's a nice place. Just…suffocating."

"Why go back?"

"My boss, who also happens to be my dad, says he'll replace me if I don't show up this week."

"So you have family who would like to see you home again."

"Parents and three sisters, to begin with. But…" He drew a deep breath. "Zelda and Al are getting married on Valentine's Day."

"You still love her?"

"No. No, I'm over her. I think."

Arden let the indecision pass. "But being there when everyone is celebrating will be hard."

"You have a gift for understatement." His grin flashed in her direction. "There will be a slew of parties. Half the town belongs to the country club, and everybody wants to host the happy couple, even if they're only inviting the same people they saw at last weekend's barbecue and last night's open house."

He stared into the distance, as if he could see all the way to Georgia. Darkness hid the color of his eyes, but she could appreciate the strong bone structure of his face, the cleft in his chin and the curls in the hair he obviously hadn't cut for six months. He looked like a romantic poet. Arden found it hard to believe a woman would leave him for someone else.

Especially after he'd kissed her.

"Maybe you need some camouflage," she said, trying to be helpful. "Another girlfriend to prove you're over being left at the altar."

Griff halted suddenly, as if he'd run into a brick wall. He wore a bemused, amazed expression. "A beautiful woman," he said, in a wondering voice, "who I'm obviously in love with."

Arden nodded, going along with the joke she'd started. "Definitely a plus. Do you have one of those?"

He ignored the question. "And who is obviously passionately in love with me."

"That would certainly show them, wouldn't it?"

Turning toward her, he drew her close, holding her hands against his chest. His eyes, black in the night, fixed on her face. "Would you be that woman? Could you be obviously, passionately, devotedly in love with me?" He kissed one set of her knuckles, and then the other.

The touch of his mouth set off thrills inside her—a fact both enticing and embarrassing. She was desperately tempted to do exactly what he asked.

But the idea was crazy, and she shouldn't be so easy to sway. "I don't think so, Griff. Sorry."

His hands loosened and she pulled free, then began to walk south, away from him.

"But you said you'd marry me." Having him behind her muffled the words.

Looking over her shoulder, she scowled at him. "How much champagne have you had tonight?"

"Two bottles, before the last one." He came closer. "But that's irrev-irrelevant."

"It's perfectly relevant. You're too drunk to know what you're saying."

"Not true. And you said yes. 'Right away,' you said."

"I didn't mean it. You didn't mean it, either."

"I do now."

She whirled to look at him. "You want me to marry you?"

"Well, actually, I'd like you to pretend to want to marry me. And I'll pretend to want to marry you. We don't have to do anything permanent." His smile vanished. "I'm not planning on going through that hell again."

Arden knew exactly how he felt. "But won't people in your hometown want to throw all those same parties? Won't they be expecting a wedding?"

"We won't let it get that far. All we have to do is stay happy through Zelda and Al's wedding. Then we'll have a big fight, break up and never see each other again. It's a brilliant plan."

"It's a ridiculous idea. I can't pretend to be in love." Though some people could, she'd discovered in the recent past.

"Am I so repulsive?"

He stood about ten feet away, swaying as if a stiff breeze might knock him down. Hearing the despair in his voice, Arden could barely keep from going over and demonstrating exactly how far from repulsive he was.

"You're a very attractive man, Griff." She wouldn't do this. She couldn't. "I just—"

Immediately, he stepped closer. "You don't have time for an all-expenses-paid vacation in sunny Georgia?"

She had nothing but time. "That's not the problem."

"You're already involved?"

"No." She gave the word more emphasis than it deserved. "I have no demands on my time or…or my affections."

"But you won't do me this favor? I know it'll take a couple months. Well, six weeks, anyway. Maybe seven.

And then you'll be free to come home. Would it be so bad to spend a little time on the mainland, eating good Southern food?"

"Of course not." Trying to explain why this was a bad idea would expose too many scars she didn't like to think about, let alone reveal to a stranger. "I simply... I don't think..."

Once more he came close, laying his warm hands on her bare shoulders. Until that moment, Arden hadn't realized how chilly she'd gotten in the late night breeze.

"Is there something you want or need, Arden? Something I can give you? I'm not filthy rich, but I could probably grant most reasonable requests. Jewelry?" He looked her up and down, then shook his head, because she wasn't even wearing earrings. "Clothes? A car? Land? My family owns some nice property on the Georgia coast and in the mountains, up near Lake Lanier. Tell me what you want. Let's see if somehow I can make it happen."

Instead of looking at his all too tempting face, Arden stared down at the sand between her bare feet and his. An idea popped into her mind, burrowing up from somewhere deep in her subconscious, a suggestion so outrageous that he would no doubt turn her down immediately and walk out of her life without a glance backward.

And that was exactly what she wanted, wasn't it?

Lifting her head, Arden kept her face stern. "There is something I want, Griff. Something I think you could give me."

His hands tightened on her upper arms. "Great. Just spare me two months of your life and I'll do whatever it takes to make your dream come true."

She hesitated again, then looked him in the eye. "What I want from you, Griff, is simple.

"I want a child."

Griff's brain wobbled inside his skull. "*What* did you say?"

Arden's gaze didn't falter. "A child. I want you to make me pregnant."

The champagne he'd been drinking nonstop kicked in at that moment, driving his mental wobble into a full-blown, three-hundred-sixty-degree tilt. With the world spinning, Griff stepped away, dropped heavily onto the sand, then collapsed backward to lie spread-eagle on the beach.

"Oh, man," he groaned. "I drank too much. I'm having hallucinations."

"You heard me correctly," the serene voice said from high above him. "But if you're not interested, I understand. Happy New Year."

He opened his eyes and saw that she had turned to leave. "Wait." Flailing a hand sideways, he managed to snag the hem of her dress between two fingers. "Don't go."

She could've pulled free with one step, but she didn't.

So Griff tugged at the dress. "Sit down. I can't talk to you way up there."

To his surprise, she folded her lithe body into a compact package just out of his reach.

"Thanks." He let his head drop back, and put an arm over his eyes. The whirling in his brain didn't stop. "Let me see if I understand. You want me to marry you and make you pregnant?"

"No."

"I thought—"

"I want a child. I don't want a husband."

That stopped him cold, and the gyrations in his head slowed down a little. "So…we'd be lovers?"

"Briefly. Until I got pregnant." After a pause, she said, "I would, of course, stay until the, um, favor I'd be doing for you was completed."

"Right." His mind drifted back to the New Year's kiss they'd shared. Powerful incentive, that kiss. He turned his head on the sand to look at her. "Then what?"

She lifted a shoulder. "Then I would come back here, to my home. And you would do whatever you plan to do after the wedding."

There was a problem with that scenario, but he was having trouble chasing down the specifics. A man would have to be made of stone if he failed to react to the sight of Arden Burke on the beach beside him, with hair like a fringe of black silk along her jawline, her skin as smooth and creamy as magnolia blossoms and her lips the color of a rosy dawn. She was slender but not shapeless, as revealed by the low neck of her dress and the curves of her calves and ankles.

Griff was not made of stone. In fact, at this moment his blood surged through him like waves of liquid metal—iron, maybe, heated to its boiling point, burning from the inside out.

And he was getting dizzier by the minute, sleepier by the second. "It's a deal," he said with a yawn. "We'll leave in the morning." With the decision made, he rolled onto his side, pillowed his head on his arm and gave in to sleep.

Arden got to her feet and stood surveying the man snoring in the sand. It would serve him right if she left him there to spend the rest of the night. He'd be miserable enough. And that was before the crabs started to nibble.

She actually walked away, getting as far as the sea grass on the primary dunes. There, she stopped to look back.

He could hardly be seen in the darkness, just a long shape that might be a piece of driftwood or a mass of seaweed. He'd get five hours of sleep before the sun rose. As drunk as he was, he wouldn't even remember what he'd offered, what she'd said…what they'd agreed to do. And that was for the best.

So why was she going back to him? Why should she care what happened to this stranger on the shore?

He'd turned onto his back again. Kneeling beside him, she studied the strong face and neck, the muscled shoulders and chest, the narrow waist and hips and really, *really* great calves. Not many men had such slim, straight legs. His tan testified to six months in the Caribbean sun and his hair, probably a light brown in Georgia, was a tangle of gold and silver waves. He would make beautiful babies.

Or maybe not. Arden shook her head at her own foolishness. Maybe he was sterile. She should have him take a fertility test, not to mention other important examinations, before she committed to sex with a man about whom she knew nothing at all.

A sudden ache constricted her chest and throat. Her own ability to conceive wasn't in question. She knew she could *make* a baby. But could she carry it full term this time?

Shaking her head again, she got to her feet. Whatever she decided tomorrow, whatever Griff did or didn't remember, she couldn't let him spend the night on the beach.

Too bad she didn't have the violin handy. She could make some pretty awful noises, enough to wake the dead, let alone the drunk. Her music was yet another loss she'd dealt with during this last year.

So she kicked him. With the side of her bare foot, again, and again. Not hard enough to hurt, just enough to irritate him thoroughly. After an amazing amount of abuse, Griff woke up, swearing and yelling even after he recognized her. He fell when she tried to help him up, and during their climb across the beach toward the dunes.

"How far?" he panted, as they stepped onto the path leading inland. "Are you trying to kill me?"

"Not far. No." She barely found the breath to speak. He was leaning on her, his arm over her shoulders, and she felt as if she was bearing at least half his weight. "Just put one foot in front of the other." That was the most she could manage at this point.

As live oak trees started closing in overhead, the darkness became complete. All she could see was a swath of white sand leading into the jungle. Had she gotten them lost?

No. With relief, she saw the side trail branching off to the left and the signpost for the cottage.

"A few more minutes," she told Griff. "And we'll be home."

Home was a small stucco bungalow in a clearing within the dense grove of trees—one bedroom and one bath under a red tile roof. She'd left the porch light on during her walk to watch the fireworks. The yellow glimmer guided her back.

Griff straightened up as he saw it, and blew out a deep breath. "I was beginning to wonder if you were planning to maroon me in the wilderness."

She slipped out from under his arm and stepped up to open the door to the screened porch. "I will, if you don't behave."

He followed her inside. "I hear you." Then he swayed and yawned at the same time. "At this point, I'm too incapacitated to make trouble for anybody."

"I'll hold you to that." Arden pushed open the door into the house, then gasped as a furry shadow raced past her.

In the next instant, Igor pinned Griff Campbell against the wall.

Chapter 2

Crouched within biting distance, hackles raised, teeth bared, the black-and-brown collie mix made no sound, not even a growl. But the grim look in his eyes promised attack.

Pressed against the wall of the screened porch, Griff cleared his throat. "Arden? A little help here?"

She took hold of the dog's collar. "What in the world is wrong with you, Igor? Is this how you say welcome home?"

Igor waved his fluffy tail back and forth. But he didn't change his stance, and his glare stayed on Griff.

"I don't usually get this reaction," he said quietly. "What's going on?"

"I'm not sure. I've never seen him behave this way. Then again, I haven't seen him with another person since I took him from the shelter." Shaking her head, Arden started backing up, holding on to the dog. "I'll put him away."

"No, wait. Let's see if we can call a truce first. He's a rescue?"

She nodded.

"Let me guess…his owner was a guy?"

"Yes."

"Abusive, probably." Griff relaxed slightly. "Igor might think all men are out to hurt him."

"That could be true." She went down on her knees beside the dog and put her arm around his neck. "It's okay, Igor. Griff won't hurt you. He likes dogs."

"I don't like dogs that bite." But he said the words in a pleasant, nonthreatening tone. "I didn't hear him barking as we came up. I would have been better prepared."

"He doesn't bark. His larynx has been removed. He 'barked too much.'" Her tone made the words a quotation.

"The bastard. Sometimes I'm ashamed to be human." Moving slowly, Griff sank into a squat. "Right now, I'm ashamed to be a veterinarian."

Arden nodded. "I know what you mean." At the sound of her calm voice, Igor lowered his hackles a fraction. "Should I leave, do you think? Will he be worse or better with me here?"

Griff ran his gaze over her, from her sleek black hair to the tips of her pink-polished toes. "You won't be able to stop him, whatever he decides to do. Maybe without you to protect, he'll calm down."

"Okay." She petted the dog again, then straightened up and retreated toward the house. When Igor didn't move, she gave Griff a smile and a thumbs-up, then stepped inside and closed the door.

Releasing the breath he'd been holding, Griff made his posture as unthreatening as possible. He didn't want to sleep on the concrete floor of the porch, and the wicker chairs and love seat all looked creaky. The dog would have to let him into the house.

"Good boy, Igor. Let's be cool, okay?" He lowered his hands to hang between his knees, in full sight. "Sounds like you're a good dog. I used to be a good dog. And I guess I'm going home to be a good dog again. So we're going to be good dogs together, all right?"

As far as Igor was concerned, he might have been saying, "Blah-blah-blah." The tone mattered, though, and Griff kept it calm. "That's it," he said, as Igor's lips lowered to cover his teeth. "No threat here. Just two good dogs, hanging out."

Pottery and metal clinked inside the house, and the aroma of coffee soon filled the air. Step by step, Igor drew closer to Griff, who stayed motionless as the dog reached out to sniff at his toes, his fingers, his wrists.

"Good boy." He lifted a finger to stroke the floppy ear.

Igor scooted backward. His upper lip curled again, revealing those bright white canines.

"Bad boy," Griff told himself. "At this rate, the floor's beginning to look pretty good." The dizziness had evolved into a headache. His eyes burned and his stomach growled. "Terrific. I'm getting to enjoy the hangover without waiting for the morning after."

"This will help." Arden stepped forward and set a cup of coffee on a nearby table, along with three white pills. "I'm going to put Igor in the bedroom. Then you can come in and sleep on the couch."

"That's one way to protect your virtue," Griff muttered as she led the dog away. "I'll never get past Igor the man-eater."

Not that he had any inclination to ravish the fair maiden. At this point, he could generate sufficient passion for only one pursuit—sleep.

After swallowing the aspirin, he left the mug of coffee half-finished and followed his desire onto the cushions of the gray leather couch in the living room. A pillow covered in soft pink cradled his head and a blanket in the same shade warmed his legs and shoulders.

Should've brushed off my feet, he thought hazily. *Sand everywhere...*

I wouldn't dread going home, if she came with me....

Arden returned to the living room to find her stranger passed out again, on the couch this time. There would be sand everywhere, but vacuum cleaners existed for just that reason. In the morning they'd clean up the mess, have some breakfast, then she'd point him toward the pier and send him on his way. No sense in recalling the craziness they'd talked about. He'd already forgotten.

And she would, in time. She and Igor were quite satisfied with their routine here on Chaos Key, just the two of them. Water and sun and sand, an occasional trip to the mainland and, always, the sound of the waves on the shore—the only music she wanted now, the last music she would know. The last *sound* of any kind.

Bringing up a baby would only complicate her life. A child needed experiences, people and places Arden had determined to avoid. She could have one or the other. Not both.

Let that dream go. She settled into her bed with Igor curled up against the backs of her knees, a little more tensely than usual. *You chose this path. Now honor it.*

A strangled snore reached her from the living room,

and Arden sighed. Letting go would have been much easier only a day ago. Even an hour ago.

Last year, that would be. Before she'd met Griff Campbell.

He was still asleep, with the pillow over his head and the rest of him covered by the blanket, when she got up at seven. He'd roused at some point, because the coffee mug she'd given him had been emptied and set in the sink. Would a single cup be sufficient to ward off the headache he'd earned?

Arden made a fresh pot, gave Igor his breakfast and took her own mug out to the porch, where she usually spent her mornings. No doubt the smell of coffee would awaken her guest soon enough.

When an hour had passed and the growling in her stomach had begun to make Igor nervous, she went back to the kitchen for breakfast. She finished off her bowl of yogurt with nuts and honey, and Griff still hadn't stirred. Igor now sat beside the porch door, anxious for their daily walk on the beach.

Arden hesitated, then stepped outside and let the screened door slap shut behind her. This was one reason she didn't want a man in her life, let alone a husband. A woman in a relationship had to cater to *his* demands, *his* expectations and *his* schedule. *His* plans and *his* goals would take over, while what she wanted and needed drifted away like a leaf on the ocean. Arden had never met a male of the species who didn't think of himself first.

Walking the beach under a bright blue sky and throwing a piece of driftwood for Igor to retrieve, she saw no reason to revoke her decision. The only thing she wanted from anyone these days, especially men, was distance—even a man as seductive and engaging as Griff.

Or maybe *especially* one as seductive and engaging as Griff.

But would there really be a drawback to doing him the favor he asked? To judge by his attitude, he still had feelings for his ex-fiancée, which would surely minimize any complications. Arden didn't doubt she could keep her own emotions under control—between them, her father and her ex-fiancé had demonstrated the utter faithlessness of men. Not only were they too much trouble, they couldn't be trusted any farther than you could throw them.

But a baby...ah, a baby would give her a reason to live. A child—boy or girl, it didn't matter—would be all she could ask as a replacement for the loss of her hopes and dreams. A year ago, her belly had just started to become rounded when her entire world came crashing down. No more music, no marriage, no connection with her mother. And no baby.

Now Griff offered her a second chance. And though she could afford artificial insemination, she preferred the old-fashioned method of procreation, especially with Griff Campbell as the official candidate—a man who, to her surprise, she liked and desired. If she agreed to his proposal, he could keep his pride intact and she would get the family she'd always wanted.

What do I have to lose?

The answer struck her like a slap in the face. By connecting so intimately with Griff Campbell, she would give away the independence she'd waited so long to enjoy. The solitude she valued. The anonymity required to cope with her new life.

"Good morning!"

She turned at the call to see him sauntering over the sand in her direction. He had a lazy way of walking, with a little bit of a slouch to his lean body, completely at odds with the energy she could see in his bright blue eyes. Though he wore the same clothes as last night, he looked neat and presentable. And far too appealing to resist.

"Good morning," he said again. "Sorry to be such a lazybones. That couch of yours is way too comfortable."

"Not a problem," she lied. Seeing him again awakened all her anxieties, as well as her yearnings. "Igor and I just followed our usual schedule."

"Stick chasing is a great way to start the day." Griff stretched down a hand to Igor, who had parked himself, stick in mouth, at her feet. "Want me to throw for you, son?"

Igor bared his teeth.

Griff straightened up. "I'm guessing that's a no."

Arden stopped herself from apologizing. "Are you feeling okay? No hangover?" *No memory of the crazy plan we talked about last night?*

"Nope. You make great coffee. The perfect antidote for the morning after." His grin revealed even white teeth and showed off the lips she remembered tasting last night.

"Well, you must be starving. Let's go back to the house and I'll make some eggs and toast. I don't have bacon, I'm afraid."

He held up a hand. "Not necessary. I saw you had some yogurt in the fridge, so I added nuts and honey and made a meal. Couldn't do much about my clothes except shake them out, but I did borrow a towel and take a shower." He scratched his fingers over his stubbly chin. "Not your razor, though. I look pretty rough."

"Oh. Well…well, good." Stunned by the idea of a man who ate yogurt and didn't steal her razor, Arden started up the beach toward the cottage path. "You're planning to fly back to Georgia today, is that right? From Miami?" The sooner he left, the better. Even more than last night's drunk, this morning's version tempted her into fantasies that would destroy her peace of mind.

"I *was*. My flight left—" he squinted at his watch as they stepped under the palms at the start of the trail "—twelve minutes ago."

She walked ahead of him, preparing herself for the worst. "What will you do now?"

"That," Griff said, "is what we have to talk about."

The silence in place of her reply said all Griff needed to know. Arden had reconsidered last night's agreement and wanted to back out. As a gentleman, he should allow her that option.

But he simply didn't want to. Standing in her neat little cottage, holding a cup of coffee to fight the headache he'd pretended he didn't have, Griff decided he wasn't ready to let this woman escape so soon.

She faced him from the other end of the kitchen, standing with her back to the window above the sink, which left her face shadowed. Now that he could see her in daylight, he recognized shadows in her eyes, too. The lady owned a troubled past.

He leaned a hip against the counter and took a long draw from his mug. "I gave you the high points of my life last night—or low points, depending on your perspective. You've got some mystery going on, though, and I'm curious. Are you on vacation down here, escaping the cold and snow up north with a few weeks in the Florida sun?"

She sipped from a delicate china cup. "I've lived here full time for the last year."

"Alone?"

"I have Igor for company." She'd left the dog outside when they came in.

Griff was grateful to be free of the canine's disapproval, at least temporarily. "So this is your own private piece of Florida?"

After a pause, she shook her head. "The island belongs to…a friend of mine. I'm the—the caretaker."

"You're here to keep an eye on the place, chase off trespassers, that sort of thing?"

"Exactly that sort of thing." She frowned into her coffee. "Obviously, I need more practice at the chasing off trespassers part of the job description."

He didn't believe her, but he let the lie pass. "My mother always said I was obstinate."

"I believe that."

"Good. Because I'm asking you again this morning if you'll come back to Sheridan with me and pretend to be my girlfriend for a couple months."

Now she frowned directly at him. "It's a ridiculous idea."

"For that reason alone, it'll work. Nobody would expect me to do something so…so—"

"Ridiculous."

"I was trying for a synonym. But okay. People won't be looking beyond how beautiful you are and how lucky

I am. That's all I ask—the chance to ease back into my life without a bunch of fanfare. You can make that possible."

She gazed at him for a long moment, but he couldn't tell what she was thinking until she said, "And in return you'll give me a baby?"

Griff swallowed hard. "I can do my best. There aren't any guarantees on that kind of thing." Boy, could he do his best. He'd be more than willing to make love to her morning, noon and night, given the opportunity.

The baby part, he wasn't nearly so sure about. His head wasn't clear enough to consider the inevitable complications.

Still, how many couples actually got pregnant right away? Most of the time it was months before a woman conceived, if not years. He could even do a little cheating, figure out her monthly cycle and avoid the most dangerous times…if things got that far.

"What do you think?" Setting his mug down, he crossed to stand in front of her in the narrow aisle. "Anything I can do to help you decide?" Watching her stormy eyes, he removed the cup from her hands and put it gently on the counter. "For instance, just in case you thought last night was a figment of your imagination…"

Propping his hands on the sink rim behind her slim waist, Griff lowered his head to kiss her again. She was shorter than he'd realized last night on the beach.

Her lips were just as smooth, though, her taste every bit as potent. Forget champagne…he'd be more than satisfied to sip this ripe, mellow flavor over and over again.

She gave a little moan and slid her arms around his neck. He caught a whiff of scent from her skin, as clean and clear as the sea itself. The kisses went on and on, deeper, wilder, while her breasts nestled against his chest and her bare knees hugged one of his. A wave of lust broke over Griff. He was desperate, drowning, totally aroused and barely hanging on to the edge of sanity…and the kitchen counter.

With a gasp, he dragged his mouth free and set his chin on top of her head. "Um, yeah… I think that answered all my questions." He blew out a breath, took another one. "What do you say? Are you coming with me to Georgia?"

Stepping back, he eased his knee away from the provocation of hers, then blinked a couple of times to bring his eyes into focus.

Her perfect cameo face looked as befuddled as he felt. Her troubled green-gray eyes were the color of the ocean just before rain starts to fall. He saw need and pain and doubt chase like lightning across that horizon.

"Come with me," he urged. "You've got Igor to keep me in line."

The mischievous delight in her smile socked him right in the gut. "True." She hesitated a moment longer…or was it a lifetime?

"Okay," Arden said, finally. "Give me an hour to pack."

"You pack faster than any woman I know."

Arden eyed him with amusement as she carried her bag into the living room. "Are we talking about vast numbers?"

Griff grinned. "Three sisters and two grandmothers, one mom, assorted cousins. And the ex-fiancée who brought her entire wardrobe every time she visited me at school."

Arden picked up the dog's bowls and went to the kitchen sink to wash them. "Plus assorted friends, I imagine." Her emphasis on "friends" gave the word a different meaning.

He waggled a flattened hand. "Maybe one or two. That's ample, if not strictly vast."

"You're right." The bowls went into a duffel bag along with a small bag of food and a liter bottle of water. The dog's suitcase, Griff assumed. "I don't keep all my clothes here on the island. I'll need to stop in Miami to pick up a few more things." With her duffel in one hand and Igor's in the other, she stopped in front of Griff. "Will that lump me in with the rest of your women?"

He stared down at her a moment, considering the question. "No," he said at last, moving to close the door behind them. "No, I think you're in a class all by yourself."

At that, the bags thudded down on the porch's cement floor. She whirled to glare at him. "There are rules to this arrangement," she said in a stern voice. "We both have to remember them."

Griff crossed his arms and braced his shoulders against the door. "Rules?"

She held up one finger. "This is a business deal, not a romance."

"Okay." He had to agree. She wouldn't come, otherwise.

The second finger came up. "This engagement exists in public only. When we're alone, we don't need to maintain displays of affection."

"No?" He shrugged, looking at the bead board ceiling. "Then you won't be getting pregnant."

"That is part of the contract." The squeak in her voice told him more than she would want him to know.

Griff lowered his eyes to meet her gaze. "Last I knew, getting pregnant required a certain level of, uh, affectionate display."

She actually stood there pondering the issue, while he did his best to hide a smile.

"Well, yes," she finally agreed. "But it's just sex. No...no—"

"Feelings?" What in the hell was *just sex?*

"Emotions," she corrected. "No emotions involved. We're not planning a life together. This is strictly an engagement of convenience."

"Right." He lowered the shades on the porch and held the door for her to exit. Her "rules" sent a chill down his spine. But he'd worry about that after they got past the first hurdle—meeting his family.

As they walked along the path to the other side of the island, Igor darted into the brush under the tall trees, always checking back after a few moments to be sure they hadn't gotten lost. At least for now, he didn't seem to object to another male's presence on the journey.

"Does your friend who owns the island come down fairly often?" Griff slipped his fingers into the handle of her heavier bag. After a short tussle, she conceded and let him carry it.

"Never. The main house is old and falling apart. Only the cottage is livable, but it's not big enough for more than two people."

"So your friend has a family?"

An annoyed glance flashed his way. "You're being nosy, aren't you?"

He tilted his head to the side. "I call it making polite conversation."

"The kind I—your adoring fiancée—will have to parry at all these parties we'll be attending?"

"Exactly."

She nodded. "I'll be prepared."

But she hadn't, he noticed, answered the question.

As the path led them past the ruined glory of the island mansion, Griff stopped for a moment to stare. "That place doesn't need a caretaker—it wouldn't provide shelter for a drenched rat. So why does your friend want someone living on this pile of sand?"

"I think I told you last night—to warn strangers away. To watch out for the wildlife, pick up trash and take care of the cottage. That sort of thing."

From the high point where the house stood, the path began a gentle slope down toward the water. Griff cupped his free hand loosely around Arden's elbow, just in case.

"Considering I didn't see a trace of you until I'd been here several hours," he said, "and then you let me spend the night, I have to say I'm wondering about your job performance."

During the long pause following his comment, they stepped out from under the trees onto the beach, barely a hundred yards from the dock where his rented speedboat bobbed on the waves.

Then Arden put the dog's bag on the ground, unzipped a pocket on the side and withdrew a cell phone, which she held up in front of his face. "My performance, as you put it, consists of calling the police. I didn't expect to have visitors after dark last night, so I didn't take the phone with me to watch the fireworks. Most people come during the day to sunbathe and swim."

Griff raised a skeptical eyebrow. "Drug runners and smugglers might appreciate having a base on a small, out-of-the-way place like this. And they like working in the dark."

"That's why the Coast Guard patrols at random times every day. That's why there are motion detectors posted in the ruins and throughout the woods, linked to a monitoring system in the cottage and an alarm on the mainland. I don't know how you bypassed them."

"Beginner's luck—I walked along the shore. Your friend must have deep pockets."

"Plus…" Ignoring his comment, she bent to Igor's kit again, and this time came up with a shiny, businesslike pistol. "I do know how to use this, should the occasion arise."

"Whoa. That's not your standard hunting rifle." He held his hands in the air as he backed up a step. "You didn't have that at the beach last night, either. Did you bring it along today in case Igor couldn't keep me under control?"

"I thought I would put it in storage while I traveled. There's no sense leaving a weapon for someone to find."

"Good point." Griff blew out a long breath. "You're quite a puzzle, Arden Burke. And very good at avoiding questions."

She gave him a serene smile, then bent to replace the pistol and close the zipper. "I think I've just given you quite a lot of information. Besides, I should be asking the questions, since I'm supposed to know you well enough to want to marry you. For instance, can I trust you to pilot us to the mainland without sinking? How long have you been driving boats?"

"Hah." Grabbing up the dog's bag, he started toward the dock, leaving her to follow empty-handed. "I've been fooling around with boats since I was ten, maybe even younger. We have a summer place at Lake Lanier, and we always had ski boats."

He climbed onto the prow of the speedboat and transferred her bags into the bottom, then pulled the small craft sideways against the pier. "Does Igor need help?"

Arden shook her head. "Igor, jump." She pointed at the boat. "Let's go."

The dog gave her a skeptical look, but after a moment of hesitation, he hopped in.

"Good boy," she told him. "Good dog."

Griff held up a hand. "Your turn."

The boat dipped and rose slightly with the waves washing into shore, but Arden boarded gracefully, with just the slightest dependence on his hand for balance.

"I've never known anybody so good at changing the subject," he declared. "Will I ever get a straight answer from you on a personal question?"

"That's another rule. No prying." She unrolled a broad-brimmed hat and set it on her head, then took a seat at the bow, next to the dog. "Now, are you planning to bring the dock with us, or shall we untie the rope before you turn on the engine?"

Chapter 3

In Miami, they took a cab from the marina to one of the high-rise buildings overlooking the waterfront. Igor was completely at home in the car and then in the elevator.

Griff was not. "The ride up is taking longer than the trip over here."

Arden looked at him in surprise. "Are you claustrophobic?"

"No…well, maybe a little." He hunched his shoulders, rolled his head around and then rubbed a hand over his face. "I haven't been in an elevator, or a building more than two stories high, in months. That's all."

"We won't be here long." They stepped into a quiet hallway with closed doors and a deep green carpet. Arden turned left and led him to the last door on the right, where she put her key into the lock of number 3209. "If the height bothers you—"

"Not height," he corrected, stepping in after her. "I'm just not used to being...wow."

The wall facing the apartment entrance was a panel of glass from floor to ceiling, offering a panorama of the Florida coastline and the Keys beyond. Griff crossed to the wide expanse of window. "Talk about million-dollar views!"

She stood beside him a moment, gazing out into the sunny afternoon. "You can see storms coming from beyond the horizon. I've spent whole afternoons just watching the weather change."

He turned his head to look at her, a new understanding in his eyes. "I wouldn't be able to offer you anything you couldn't buy for yourself, would I?"

Arden decided to answer the question. "Probably not."

"And the island—Chaos Key, right?—belongs to you."

"Yes." Before he could continue the conversation, she hurried toward the bedroom. "I'll just be a few minutes. Make yourself at home—there are drinks in the refrigerator and snacks in the cupboard."

She sighed in relief when the snap of a pop top and the rustle of chips assured her he'd accepted the invitation. Given what she'd learned about Griff Campbell already, she wouldn't have been surprised if he'd followed her to the bedroom to pursue the conversation he'd tried to start and she didn't want to finish.

Igor claimed his usual spot on the king-size bed while she stowed the pistol and ammunition in her wall safe. Then, with a hiss of cold air, Arden opened one side of the hermetically sealed closet she'd installed for storing most of her wardrobe. Choosing casual wear to take with her posed no real fashion dilemma. A couple of cold-weather dresses, a few classic shirts and skirts, plus jackets and sweaters for outdoors… New jeans and shoes would be required, but shopping would give her something to do with her acquaintances in Sheridan, Georgia.

That plan called up yet another rule: no attachment to the natives. She would have to be friendly without developing friendships—an art she'd practiced nearly as often as she practiced the violin. In any event, the chance that she would share interests with the residents of a tiny, backwoods Georgia town seemed more than remote.

Thinking about the parties Griff had mentioned, Arden exposed the second half of the closet…and immediately wished she hadn't. Her pulse rate quickened and tension cramped her stomach as she caught sight of evening gowns covered with red or navy or emerald sequins, plus the thousands of tiny black beads sewn onto party frocks and formal dresses she'd once considered her work wardrobe.

Worse still was the corner of a white gift box peeping out from beneath a black skirt hem. She didn't have to lift the lid to remember the contents—tiny caps knitted from soft pastel wools, cotton blankets and towels in pale green and yellow, a small rattle carved from walnut. In a year's worth of free time, she'd failed to dispose of her last ties to that fragile, lost soul.

Arden squeezed her eyes shut. *Stupid*—she should have planned to buy new dresses rather than subject herself to this ordeal. God knew she would never wear any of these clothes again. Why call up her worst memories?

Definitely not because she intended to share them

with her *fiancé*. "No confessions" would join the list of rules for this engagement, she decided as she closed and resealed the closet. Her past didn't affect Griff Campbell in any way.

As for her hearing loss, she would keep that a secret, too. The whole point of this exercise was to present a lovely, desirable woman to his hometown. Showing up with a deaf, unemployed musician would not create the same impression.

Anyway, Arden hated being the object of pity. She'd retired from the music business so she wouldn't have to face the sympathy of her colleagues…and the smugness her rivals.

With her choices made, she snapped her fingers at the dog. "Come on, Igor. Let's go for a ride." Alert and ready for adventure, as always, he hopped off the bed and pattered down the hallway. With the few clothes she'd chosen folded into a suitcase, Arden took a deep breath and followed. The rest would go to charity when she returned. An empty closet. A new life.

"I'm ready," she called, returning to the living room.

Griff didn't answer, because he'd fallen asleep on the couch. Again. He had certainly taken to the Hispanic tradition of the siesta.

Leaving her luggage with the other bags by the door, she crossed the room to shake him awake, but paused at the end of the sofa, observing the man to whom she was now *engaged*.

Though his clothes needed changing and his jaw remained stubbled, this morning's shower had revealed just how attractive he was. His clean hair was a lighter blond than she'd realized, his eyelashes longer, darker and thicker. The fullness of his mouth explained a lot about the power of his kisses.

Remembering that encounter in her kitchen this morning, she found herself holding her breath. Not since she was a teenager had she experienced such an intense, immediate desire for a man she didn't know. She'd never before indulged the feeling, as she was preparing to do now.

In the past, she had proceeded with care, slowly developing what she thought was a solid relationship. Despite such caution, love had ruined her life—one lesson she didn't want to repeat.

"Hey." The long lashes lifted and Griff's bright blue eyes focused on her face. "I didn't intend to fall asleep. You ready to head north?"

"Yes." She turned away from him to hide her blush. "I need to leave a note for the housekeeper and then we can go."

"Take your time."

When they met by the door, he shook his head at her single suitcase. "My sister Kathy needs one that size for just her shoes."

"I'm not bringing many shoes." Arden wrestled with him for a moment over who would wheel the case along, then gave in and picked up Igor's bag. "There will be shopping going on, I assure you. Most of my clothes here are out of style."

"You should let me pay for your new clothes," he said, in the elevator. "You wouldn't be buying them if I hadn't asked for a favor."

"But then I'd have to think about how much everything costs, and that wouldn't be any fun."

"You don't consider prices when you go shopping?

You must be wealthier than I'd imagined, having a condo like this." He looked at her out of the corner of his eye. "Or is it your 'friend' who doesn't think about prices?"

"I consider value before cost." She tried not to sound defensive. "If you tried to sell me a car for sixty thousand that I knew was worth only forty, I'd balk. And I don't like buying two-hundred-dollar jeans if fifty dollars buys the same comfort."

"Got it." The elevator doors opened at the garage level, and she held the door while he stepped out. "That makes me anxious to see what kind of car you do drive."

"The car was an indulgence, I admit." She led the way down the aisle of vehicles. "But I've kept it for six years now, and it still moves like there's a wild animal under the hood."

Griff stood motionless, an expression of reverence on his face, when she indicated the gold Jaguar and popped open the trunk. "I was hoping this would be yours." He set the suitcases and Igor's bag inside, along with the small bag he'd retrieved from a locker when returning the rental boat. "Do I get to drive?"

Arden held out the keys. "Be my guest."

Before he went to the driver's side, he opened the passenger door for her. But she hadn't even started to move when Igor jumped in and took his usual place on the right front seat.

Griff looked from her to Igor and back again. "I have a feeling he won't appreciate any effort on my part to move him to the back."

The warning light in the dog's eyes confirmed that assumption. "Get in the back," Arden told him. "Go, Igor. In the back."

Instead, he curled into the tan leather seat and put his chin on his paws.

"No, Igor." She snapped on the leash. "I'm riding there." She tugged. "Down. Get down."

Expressing reluctance with every line of his body, Igor climbed out of the car. Arden opened the back door and indicated the seat with her leash hand. "Get in, Igor. In the car."

He jumped in easily enough. As she started to close the door, though, he climbed over the console to reclaim his place in the front passenger seat.

Griff laughed as Arden stamped her foot. "Igor, no."

She went through the process twice more, with the same result each time. "Igor!"

"Maybe you ought to drive for a while," Griff suggested. "I'll ride in the back."

Appalled at the idea, Arden gazed at him for a long moment. "What did you say when your fiancée told you she couldn't go through with the wedding?"

With his hands in his pockets, he shrugged one shoulder. "Um...not much."

"You didn't argue? Try to change her mind?"

"I doubt that would have been worth the effort. She and ol' Al looked pretty good together." He rubbed a hand over his hair, rumpling it into curls. "I'd never noticed that before, in all the time we spent together. Maybe I should have."

"You just left town?"

"Ran away. Yeah." He avoided her gaze, turning his head to look at the cars on either side of them. "I couldn't stay to have people feel sorry for me."

Arden didn't tell him just how well she understood that perspective. Griff would want to know why. "Well, *you* are driving, so Igor and I will simply have to come to some kind of agreement about the other seats." Keeping a tight hold on the leash, she sat down quickly in the front, pushed a button to move the seat as far back as possible, then allowed the dog to jump in at her feet.

"We're set," she said. "Ready to go?"

"Sure." But the shadows hadn't left Griff's gaze. He closed the passenger door and rounded the back of the car, then slid into the driver's seat. "Georgia, here we come."

His rich voice conveyed no enthusiasm whatsoever.

Thanks to the holiday and New Year's Day football games, the lanes on Interstate 95 were practically empty of traffic.

"The only problem is holding down the speed," Griff remarked. "This baby wants to go fast."

Arden smiled. "That's why I bought it."

"Eighty feels like forty. We could be in Jacksonville in time for dinner if I let her run full throttle."

"With only two or three speeding tickets to show for the trip."

"True." He eased his pressure on the gas pedal and set the cruise control. "I'd have a hard time getting back to work with a suspended driver's license."

She turned her knees so she could sit sideways in the seat. "You said you're a veterinarian. Do you work in an office?" Igor huffed as she changed position, then wiggled himself into another arrangement of legs and head and bushy tail.

"We see small animals in the office in Sheridan. But we also see large animal clients, usually at their farms, and for those we take an SUV with the equipment and supplies we need."

"Which do you like better, dogs and cats or horses and cows? Medically speaking."

"That depends on whether or not it's raining." His cheek dimpled with a grin. "Examining a sick horse in the cold rain is nobody's idea of fun."

"I guess not. Do you have horses and cows yourself? Dogs and cats?"

"My dad and mom have about a thirty acres, and they've kept horses all my life. Lots of cats live at the barn. And there are always dogs hanging around."

"But what about you, personally?"

The answer came after a pause. "I was at school for eight years, mostly living in student housing, so I didn't have a pet. Since I've been working, there just hasn't been time. I thought, when I bought the house for us to live in after the wedding, that we'd get a dog, too. But…" Griff shrugged.

"Did you sell the house?"

"I've been living on the money." He chuckled. "Pissed most of it away, I guess you'd say. But I had a good time."

Without commenting, Arden sat straight in the seat again. The next time he glanced over, she'd put on a very big, very black pair of sunglasses, effectively shutting him out. Or herself in, depending on how you looked at things.

Griff would have preferred to continue the conversation, but he'd already said more than he should have. Arden's questions had led him into revealing how much of a coward he was, how totally he'd messed up his life at home. She probably regretted ever agreeing to this escapade in the first place, and was halfway to dropping him out on the side of the road before she turned around and headed back to her island.

Worst of all, she'd left him alone with his thoughts, a meeting he'd avoided with great success since last June. The Jag required no effort to drive, and the empty road demanded little concentration beyond staying between the lines. All he had to do was think, unless…

With the push of a button, the car's radio came on, tuned to a classical station where a solo violin screeched like a lonely bird in a deserted forest. Griff winced and used the steering wheel button to search for his kind of music, a place where the violins were called fiddles, where banjos and mandolins created that mountain sound.

The satellite system installed in the Jag gave him just what he wanted. He sat back with a contented sigh, nodding his head and tapping his fingers on the wheel to a kicking rendition of "Orange Blossom Special."

Two of Arden's slender fingers touched a button and lowered the volume. When he glanced in that direction, she was staring at him over the top of those black lenses. "This is your music preference?"

"Bluegrass? Definitely." When she didn't respond, he reached toward the control panel. "I can turn it back. This is your car—"

"No." She put her hand over his. "You're driving, so you should play whatever music you enjoy."

"Driver's choice," Griff said. "It's a deal."

But with the bargain struck, neither of them moved for a moment. The warmth of Arden's palm against his skin sent heat flaring through Griff's chest and straight into his belly. Without effort, he could imagine her stroking his bare shoulders, could almost feel those smooth palms sliding along his ribs and driving him crazy.

Breathing fast, he kept his eyes on the road, though his eyes ached with the effort.

Finally, she lifted her hand. He pulled his arm back to rest on his thigh. Time for a little camouflage.

"The musicians do have remarkable technique," Arden said after a few minutes. "Some of those passages aren't easy to play, especially at such a quick tempo."

He welcomed the change of subject. "You sound like you know what you're talking about. Do you play an instrument?"

"Oh…no." This time she turned her knees away from him, requiring the dog to move again. "Not anymore, that is." She paused barely a second before saying, "I've developed a headache. I think I'm going to try to nap a bit, if you don't mind. Then I can drive whenever you're tired."

"Go right ahead. I'm good for hours yet."

Propping her head against the door frame, she withdrew as far as possible without leaving the car. After a few minutes, Griff saw her hand, which had been tightly fisted in her lap, loosen to a gentle curve. Her deep breathing signaled that she had, in fact, fallen asleep.

But not before leaving him some interesting points to consider.

The lady had evaded nearly every question he'd asked. She denied playing an instrument—"not anymore," she'd qualified. But he'd spied a well-worn violin case leaning in one corner of the cottage.

She lived alone on a sandbar, but owned a million

dollar condo across the bay. Why would she maroon herself in the middle of the ocean?

Now she was heading back to civilization with him. Because, she said, she wanted a baby. Did she really plan to raise a child by herself on the island? That sounded like a new twist on the Tarzan plot. At least the condo, with its housekeeper, would make their lives comfortable.

But that huge space had been empty of any personal touch. No pictures on the walls or memorabilia lying around to reveal who lived there. How could such a desirable woman exist all alone in the world...alone except for the mute dog she'd rescued?

As they passed Naples, Florida, Arden stirred a little in her seat. Griff glanced over and saw that the sunglasses had slipped down her nose. He reached out, carefully took them off and put them in her lap.

The monotonous miles of Interstate 95 offered few diversions, so he found himself looking back fairly often at the fan of long lashes against her rosy cheeks and the shiny wing of black hair curving against her chin. She wore another linen dress today, pale green, with the swell of her breasts just visible under the soft cloth.

Blowing a long, silent whistle, Griff fixed his gaze on the road again. The woman turned him on, no question about it. He could blame six months of celibacy, at least in part—he wasn't stupid or suicidal, and drinking his way around the Caribbean had not entailed indiscriminate sex. His ex-fiancée had been his last partner.

His body was definitely ready, willing and able to launch Arden toward her goal of motherhood.

That would make him the father of a child living more than five hundred miles away. The image didn't fit with his definition of parenthood. Could he let his own flesh and blood grow up without him in the picture?

And this might be his only chance for a kid, given his current opinion of the marriage process. Maybe Arden would let him visit, at least. But he'd promised her no ties, after this escapade....

As he drove, his brain seethed with questions, not least of which was an explanation for the isolation she had imposed upon herself. He would get the answers, too, just as soon as his Sleeping Beauty opened her eyes. He needed to understand her life, her personality. Then they could set about consummating, as it were, the second part of the program.

Satisfied with his plan, Griff turned the volume on the radio up one notch and settled back in his seat.

An hour or so later, he glanced at his passenger to find tears coursing down her cheeks. Before he could react, she threw an arm across her eyes. A sob broke free from her throat, then another, even more anguished.

At the same moment, flashing lights in the rearview mirror caught Griff's attention—flashing *blue* lights, coming up behind him. He looked at the speedometer and realized he'd forgotten about cruise control. "Shit."

Moving his right foot to the brake pedal, he swore for the length of time it took him to slow the Jag down and pull over.

The change in motion woke Arden. She let her arm fall and sat up straight. "What's going on?"

"Turns out ninety-five is the route we're on, not the speed limit sign."

Wiping tears from her cheeks with her fingers, she frowned. "I don't understand."

Griff rolled down his window. "I'll let the nice officer here explain it to you."

Twenty minutes and two hundred dollars later, Griff eased the car back onto the highway. He had turned the radio off and they rode in silence for a few miles.

"I appreciate the loan," he said at last, in a stiff voice. "I'll pay you back when we get home."

"That will be fine." Arden wasn't sure what she could safely say—men didn't like to be reprimanded. "You might try to stay within the speed limit from now on," she ventured. "I have only three hundred dollars left."

His warm chuckle eased the tension between them. "Now, that's just about the last response I expected. Thanks for not throwing a fit. I'll be careful to stay legal for the rest of the trip."

Releasing a deep breath, she let her head drop back against the seat, and wished the drive would end so she could lie down in a dark room with a cool cloth over her face. Her temples had started to pound and her eyes felt itchy and swollen. Slipping her dark glasses on again, she was thankful for somewhere to hide.

"Why were you crying?"

She jumped at the sound of his voice in the quiet car. "I wasn't. I mean…"

Griff was shaking his head. "I was speeding because I was watching tears roll down your cheeks, and wondering what was wrong."

Arden squeezed her eyes shut and clasped her hands together in her lap. "I—I must have been dreaming."

"Yeah, I figured that out. Must've been a sad dream. Or scary."

"I don't remember."

"I don't believe you."

She glared at him. "My dreams are none of your business."

He shrugged. "As your fiancé, I disagree."

"You're not really my fiancé."

"For the time being, I'm considering this a real engagement. Especially given what you expect as, um, payment for services rendered. So I'd like to know what sort of dream makes you cry."

Maybe he wasn't as easygoing as she'd thought. "I really don't remember much. Just an overwhelming sorrow." She added truthfully, "I didn't want to be left."

"Someone was leaving you?"

Arden shrugged. "That's what it felt like."

"I guess you've lost people in your life. Your parents?"

Damn his insight. "My father, actually. He left my mother and me when I was five." Funny how this had become the least vulnerable of her wounds.

Griff used a vulgar word to characterize the man. "But your mother stayed. She's still with you?"

"We're estranged," Arden snapped. "So I was crying about my parents in the dream. Will you let it go now?"

He didn't react to her peevishness. "I doubt it. But I'll give you a break." The next moment, he punched the radio on, then turned the dial. A Bach fugue, played on the harpsichord, flowed into the car, filling every crevice like ocean waves swirling around each shell and pebble on the beach.

Arden could hardly breathe. "Turn it off," she choked out. "Please."

The sound stopped. "Sorry," Griff said. "I thought you would like classical."

Swallowing hard, she shook her head. "I don't need music. I'm good with silence, if you are. Or...or the bluegrass." She didn't feel at all connected to such a foreign style of playing, which made it bearable. "Whatever you want."

He gave her a sideways glance. "Let's go with silence." Just as she started to relax, he said, "We can tell each other our life histories. That's what engaged people do, right?"

Arden reached for the radio. "I'd prefer bluegrass."

Chapter 4

The whining vocals and jangling instruments created an excellent barrier between the two halves of the front seat. Arden sat with her eyes closed and her head back, hoping to relax and dull the knives stabbing through her skull. By the time they'd reached Daytona Beach, however, she could only surrender.

She turned the radio off. "Could we stop for the night? I really don't think I can ride much farther without being sick."

Griff flashed her an assessing glance. "No problem. There's a good place to stay just two exits from here. Give me ten minutes and we'll have a room."

"No speeding," she reminded him.

"Strictly under the limit," he agreed. "And it'll still be ten minutes."

She stumbled across the grass beside the parking lot

with Igor while Griff registered, then followed the Jag on foot as he drove around the building to the space nearest a door.

"I'll bring the bags in," he said, when she stopped beside the trunk. "I want you inside and lying down."

"But—"

"No arguments." He clasped her arm with one big, warm hand and drew her toward the door. "My ten minutes are almost up."

Arden abandoned the argument because the afternoon sunlight jabbed viciously at her eyes. Even the elevator lighting seemed too bright. In the room, she unclipped Igor's leash, then headed for the double bed nearest the air-conditioning unit.

"I'm sorry," she mumbled, crawling to the center of the mattress. "I would help..." The pillow muffled her voice as she buried her face in its softness and succumbed to agony.

When she opened her eyes again, the world—though still painful—had become at least bearable again. She was lying on her side, covered by a soft blanket in a very cool room, with Igor curled in his usual place along the backs of her legs. The only light came from behind a mostly closed door, and the only sound was the soothing hum of air-conditioning. Focusing on that monotonous drone, refusing to ask herself any questions, Arden fell back into sleep.

A slight clink of glass woke her the second time. "Sorry," a man whispered nearby. "I thought you might want something to drink when you woke up."

Memory flooded through spaces vacated by the headache. Griff. The engagement. A baby. "That sounds good," she murmured. "A cold drink would be wonderful."

"Water or tea?"

She moved her head slightly, and it didn't hurt too much. "Tea?"

"Coming up."

Propping herself against the pillows required more effort than it should have, but she managed the feat in time to accept the glass of iced tea Griff offered. "Thank you so much." The first taste was heaven. "Perfect."

He hovered between the beds, as if he couldn't decide whether to sit or stand. "I bought pain medicines, if you want something."

"Right now I'm just thirsty."

After she'd downed the glass and he'd brought another, Griff asked, "Do you get migraines often?"

Arden sipped, sighed, then frowned at him. "Do you always ask so many questions?"

"An occupational hazard, I guess. The animals can't tell me what's wrong, so I have to get as much information from the owners as I can. And that usually means asking questions."

"Could you bring me my bag? I have some pills...."

"Sure."

With the tablets swallowed, she set her empty glass on the table between the beds and slid down to rest her head on the pillows. She remembered that she hadn't answered his question. "I haven't had a migraine in months. But before I moved to Chaos, I was enduring at least one a week. Stress, the doctors said."

"I'm sorry." Griff sat down on the other bed, propping his elbows on his knees. "I didn't intend to bring stress and pain into your life with my proposal."

"Of course not." The medicine was beginning to take effect, making her sleepy and a little drunk. She stretched out her arm to drop her hand onto his wrist. "I'll be fine tomorrow. Just need…sleep."

She wasn't sure, but she thought she felt him kiss her fingers before the world faded away.

Once convinced that Arden was fast asleep and would stay that way, Griff left Igor on guard and went to the hotel lobby to make a phone call. His first act upon reaching the ocean six months ago had been to throw his cell phone as far as possible—and considering he'd played right field for his high school and college baseball teams, that was far enough to be sure the phone never washed up on shore.

Now, he had to call collect. Fortunately, his mother answered. "Yes, of course we'll accept the charges. Griff? Is that you?"

"Hey, Mom. Happy New Year." Hearing her Southern belle accent exposed a soft place in his chest. "How are you?"

"I'm fine. We're all just fine here. When are you coming home?"

Somewhere in the house, his sister Dana screamed, "Griff? Griffith Major Campbell, you get your butt home right now!"

He chuckled. "That was clear enough. As a matter of fact, Mom, I guess I'll be there sometime tomorrow afternoon."

"Oh, Griff, that's wonderful." Now she sounded a little teary, too. "Can we have the family over for dinner? Is that too much for your first night back? Where are you planning to stay? I'll air out the guest cottage—no one's lived there since last summer, but I can have it ready in a jiffy."

"That would be great, Mom." The moment was on top of him before he'd planned how to deal with it. "Um… I'm bringing someone with me."

"That's nice, son. You know friends of yours are always welcome." Her words slowed, then stopped for a second as she interpreted his tone of voice. "Do you mean a girlfriend?"

"That's right. Arden Burke is her name."

"Is this an important relationship?"

"As a matter of fact…" He took a deep breath. "We have been talking about getting married."

Which wasn't a lie—he and Arden *had* discussed pretending to be engaged to be married.

A long pause followed his announcement.

"Mom? You still there?"

"Yes. Yes, I'm here. Just surprised, is all. You haven't mentioned meeting someone. When you called." *Which wasn't nearly often enough,* her tone implied.

"It happened pretty suddenly." Now he felt guilty. His family didn't keep secrets more important than surprise parties, or birthday and Christmas presents. "But I'm sure you'll like her. She's terrific." He sounded like the dumb hero in a two-star romantic comedy. "I thought Arden could stay in the guest house and I could sleep at the house, in my old room."

"Of course. That will work out perfectly." Her voice had cooled from its usual warm tone. "Here's your dad. I'll see you tomorrow, son. Oh, I'm so glad to be able to say that!"

In the next instant, his father said, "It's about time you called to say you're coming home."

Griff grinned, at the same time shaking his head over the familiar, irascible voice. "Better late than never."

"You're way past late. I'm too old to be working this hard."

"Right, Dad. You're so ancient."

"Without a second vet in the practice, I'm feeling ancient. Be prepared to do some serious overtime, 'cause as soon as you get home, your mother and I will be taking a long vacation."

"I'll believe that when I see it. But we'll show up tomorrow afternoon sometime."

"We?"

"Mom will explain. See y'all then."

"Griff—"

"Kiss the girls for me. Bye." He hung up without letting his dad get another word in. Jake Campbell always knew when his children weren't telling the truth. Griff didn't want to risk blowing his cover before he'd even crossed the Georgia state line.

Walking back to the hotel room, he endured second thoughts about his "brilliant" plan for going home. Could he and Arden convince his family that they had fallen in love and decided to get married? Exactly what kind of charade had they agreed to perform?

He entered the room as quietly as the lock would allow. Igor's hackles raised as Griff came near, but subsided when he stretched out on the empty bed. Turning onto his stomach, Griff studied the woman across from him, now curled on her side and smiling slightly—sure signs she'd fallen into a deep, restorative sleep. The thought allowed him to relax, too.

He wouldn't have any trouble demonstrating physical attraction to his "fiancée." Even knowing she needed her rest, he could easily have become aroused enough to wake her up to make love. And he had a feeling she'd be fun to talk to, if she would ever answer his questions.

But she obviously wanted to keep her life—past, present and future—a secret. Griff had to wonder why. Was she a criminal, hiding from the law? Did all that money come from a bank robbery or an investment scam? Embezzlement?

More likely, Arden was a victim hoping to avoid pursuit, perhaps even threats against her life. That would explain the pistol and the dog. Had she witnessed a crime? Or was a jealous ex-boyfriend—*husband,* maybe?—refusing to let her go?

Griff flopped onto his back. *Jeez.* He was going to have to get a few answers from the lady, if only so he could stay alert and protect them both.

During tomorrow's drive they would have to talk about the information lovers tended to share, so they wouldn't be surprised when questions popped up. With his mother and three sisters at the dinner table, an interrogation would definitely be on the menu.

Meanwhile, Dr. Jake would scan their faces with his sharp blue eyes and register every hesitation, every panicked gulp, every blank-minded pause. Griff might not reveal his thoughts right away, but he had never successfully lied to his dad.

He was pretty sure tomorrow wouldn't be any different.

The next morning, Arden swore she had recovered completely, and left Griff no choice but to believe her when she downed a huge country-style breakfast.

"I'm always famished after a migraine," she said, spreading jam on a corn muffin. "And we didn't really eat yesterday, did we?"

"I had a sandwich last night. But I'm glad you feel better." Griff had done a reasonable job of finishing his own platter of food. "So we're ready to go?"

Her nod set her hair swinging. "Definitely."

They stopped for lunch at an outlet mall just over the Georgia–Florida line. "First we eat," Arden declared. "Then we shop."

Seeing the excitement in her face, he chuckled. "Lead the way."

He followed her into the most upscale stores and watched her browse the racks with a critical eye. Then she would disappear into a dressing room with an armful of clothes, finally emerging with a select few items.

Only once did she ask for his help. "Stay there," she told him, heading in with a pile of jeans. "I'm going to want a second opinion."

Slouched in a chair near the dressing area, Griff waited with the resignation of a man who had spent too many hours watching sisters try on clothes, and who had all too often been asked for his appraisal, only to be told he didn't know what he was talking about.

He would just tell Arden she looked great in everything, then let her choose. No sense getting into an argument over jeans.

Then she walked out in the first pair. "Wow," he said sincerely. "Those look great." The jeans rode low on her hips and fit tight in all the right places. She had put on a snug T-shirt, which revealed her slender waist and rounded breasts. Griff wholeheartedly approved.

Arden frowned as she examined her mirror image. "Not bad. Maybe a little wide in the leg?"

He tilted his head and considered. "Don't think so."

She nodded. "Right. I'll be back."

He shook his head when she reappeared. "Too big." By which he meant *not tight enough.*

"Comfortable," she replied. Then she pulled at a fold of fabric over her hip. "But you're right. Too big."

In the end, she chose the first jeans he'd liked, plus an even slimmer, tighter pair that left him shifting in his seat.

"Nice," he managed to say. "Very nice." He doubted she would appreciate being told those jeans were "hot."

In the next store, Arden browsed through the coats and jackets while Griff went to the men's department for clothes and shoes he could wear to dinner at his mother's table. As he changed in the dressing room, an announcement came over the sound system. "Shoppers, be aware that we have a lost child in the store. If you see a little girl wandering alone, please inform a salesperson immediately. Thank you."

As he left the changing area, Griff checked behind each door, but all the booths were empty. With his old clothes in a shopping bag, he went back to the women's department.

He couldn't see Arden anywhere. Lingerie, dresses, sportswear, makeup...no slim, dark-haired beauty was to be found. Returning to the coat section, he walked slowly among the displays, wondering if he should stay put and allow her to find him. Had she decided to ditch the plan, after all?

In the end, he almost tripped over her where she sat

on the floor, head bent to look beneath coats hanging from a rack.

"Can you come out now?" Her low, sweet tone made the words sound like a lullaby. "Your mommy is wondering where you are."

The child didn't answer.

Arden extended her hand a short way. "I can take you to your mommy, if you want." Still no response. "Or your mommy can come to you."

Griff took the hint and notified the nearest saleswoman. Then he went back to serve as a marker for the child's location.

Moments later, a blonde woman with a tear-streaked face dropped to her knees beside Arden. A crowd of security officers, store managers and salespeople hovered behind them.

The mother stretched out her hands. "Kristy? Kristy, honey? Come to Mommy."

The little girl spoke this time. "Unh-uh."

"Sweetie, you can't stay here. We have to go home."

"No."

The mother's cheeks flushed, and annoyance replaced some of her panic. "Come on out, sweetheart. We'll go get that ice cream you wanted."

Arden looked up at Griff. "We need a toy," she said softly. "Can you find one?"

A glance around showed him the children's department across the store. "Be right back."

He sprinted as if he'd hit a double, grabbed a stuffed duck off a shelf and raced back like he was stealing home. Panting only slightly, he dropped the toy in Arden's lap.

"Quack, quack," she said immediately, sounding like an authentic bird. "Quack, quack, quack."

She made the duck waddle forward, as if taking a peek at the little girl, and then retreat, still quacking. The second time, a small hand followed. Finally, a child's head emerged from among the hanging garments. Kristy reached for the duck as her mother reached for her.

"There you are." The woman got to her feet with her daughter in her arms. "Naughty girl, hiding from Mommy."

Arden had released the stuffed duck into the little girl's hold. Kristy put the toy under her chin and hid her face against her mom's neck.

"Thank you so much." The mother gave Arden a grateful look. "We'd been searching for an hour when they made the announcement. I was so afraid someone had taken her." Tears spilled onto her cheeks again. She kissed Kristy's forehead. "So afraid."

Arden set a hand briefly on the child's back. "I'm glad I could help. I just happened to hear her singing to herself." She gathered her shopping bags and backed up as she spoke. "Let her keep the duck as my present."

"Oh, no–"

But Arden turned at that moment and began to walk away. Catching a glimpse of her face, Griff pulled a couple of twenty dollar bills from his pocket and dropped them beside a register, then hurried after her.

He caught up in time to open the outside door before Arden could. Once they'd cleared the exit, he stopped her with a hand on her arm. "Are you okay?"

Tears sparkled in her long lashes as she looked up at him. "Yes. Yes, I'm fine."

"Forgive me for saying so, but you don't look fine. You look…devastated."

"Not at all." Setting down her bags, she wiped her fingers over her eyes and cheeks. No mascara smeared, proving that her long lashes were natural. "Really, I'm okay."

Griff took the opportunity to pick up the shopping bags himself. "She was a cute little girl."

"All those blond curls." Arden sighed and nodded. "But evidently a handful for her mother."

"Most kids are, at one time or another. I'm sure my mother will tell you stories about my escapades. One of the drawbacks to this charade, I guess. You'll know more about me than you ever wanted to."

"And we should be on the road, shouldn't we?" Arden started walking briskly toward the parking lot. "We wouldn't want to be late for dinner."

Surprised that she hadn't argued about carrying the bags, Griff followed. Igor greeted them at the car windows, and Arden took him for a brief walk in the chilly fresh air before they resumed the trip.

With her sunglasses back in place and her face turned toward the window, she couldn't have signaled more clearly that she wasn't in the mood to talk. Griff left her alone and even left the radio off as he wrestled with his own thoughts.

Arden had said she wanted a child as her "price" for doing him this favor. The expression on her face—part grief, part yearning, he decided—indicated more than just the ticking of her biological clock. He'd seen grieving pet owners wear that look.

Had Arden lost a child? Would she tell him if he asked?

Griff snorted to himself. Not likely.

Not yet, anyway.

They had their first lover's quarrel as they passed through Macon around four o'clock.

"I am not a short-tempered man," Griff said through set teeth. "But you're testing my limits."

Arden stared out the side window. "You know as much as you need to. My past is finished and of no interest to anyone, including me."

His fist thudded on the steering wheel. "Lovers—people who are thinking about spending their lives together—share their histories. Childhood days, teenage years and college...all of it contributes to the person you've become. Your memories matter."

Most of Arden's childhood memories involved windowless rooms containing a music stand and a violin. "We aren't spending our lives together. Just a few weeks."

"Why are you threatened by my questions? Wait—you're in the Witness Protection Program, right? If I discover who you really are, they'll find you and kill you."

She couldn't repress a chuckle. "I wish I could use that excuse, because you might actually let this rest."

"You won't say where you were born?" He sounded almost discouraged.

Perhaps if she gave him a few details, he'd be satisfied. "Okay, you win. I was born in New York City and lived there with my mother until I was nine."

He turned his head to give her a big grin. "Not so hard to say, was it? What happened when you were nine?"

"We moved around quite a bit." Because she was performing in Europe and Asia.

"Where did you graduate from high school?"

"I was homeschooled."

"Ah. And college?"

Now *she'd* reached her limit. "New York."

"Does that meant New York State University? New York University? Or a college which shall remain nameless in the city of New York?"

"Does it matter?"

"Are you trying to drive me crazy?" With a twist of his wrist, bluegrass music blared into the space between them, painfully loud.

But Arden endured it without comment, refusing to give him the satisfaction of admitting it bothered her. Griff drove for an hour without changing the volume or glancing in her direction. Though she regretted the hostility between them, she couldn't bring herself to admit more.

Because admitting that she'd attended Julliard would lead him to ask about her musical career. If she told him the truth, he'd pry into the reasons she wasn't playing now. She'd have to reveal her approaching deafness, and from there move on to her gullibility and foolishness. As hard as she'd worked to bury those memories, telling Griff about them would bring everything back to the surface.

Why put herself through that?

Finally, he turned down the radio volume. "I'm sorry I yelled," he said. "Maybe I'm not as even tempered as I claimed to be."

"I can understand your frustration." She turned slightly toward him. "Just believe me—nothing in my past matters today, and none of it affects you in the least. As far as we're concerned, history started on New Year's Eve."

"I'll try." He swallowed hard. "So what details shall we concoct for the benefit of the nosy people in Sheridan? Let's make up a really good story, so they'll be suitably impressed."

Arden hadn't even begun to think of a story when Griff snapped his fingers. "I've got it. How about we say you're a lost relative of the last Russian czar?"

Within an hour of their arrival, Arden decided that her current predicament made press conferences look like quiet time at the public library.

The Campbell family proved to be huge, comprised of not just Griff's parents and three sisters, but their husbands and children, too, all of whose names she was supposed to remember. Plus his cousins—at least five of them, with their own spouses and kids.

"I'll make you a cheat sheet," Griff whispered shortly after they arrived. "You can study in bed tonight."

Was it his breath on her ear that sent a shiver up her spine? Or just the prospect of having to know this many people by tomorrow morning?

Seated at the long table in the Campbells' dining room, Arden managed to taste, chew and swallow exactly one bite of a delicious potato casserole before the questions started.

Griff's oldest sister, Dana, sat on her right. "So, where did the two of you meet?" She resembled her brother, with the same curly blond hair, pinned into a loose knot at the back of her head, and those beautiful blue eyes. Both of them were the image of their father, whose piercing gaze had already flustered Arden more than she wanted to admit.

"We met in Miami." Arden took a sip of iced tea, trying to recall the story they'd decided to tell. "On the beach, actually."

Dana's eyes narrowed. "Most people don't talk to strangers on the beach."

"My dog had slipped his leash." They'd introduced Igor to the crowd, then put him in the laundry room with a blanket and his dinner. "Griff caught him and was walking along the shore looking for his owner."

"Sounds like him."

Arden gave a silent sigh of relief.

"But Igor still isn't too friendly with Griff, is he? I mean, he doesn't try to play with him or anything."

"I'm afraid not." Time for improvisation. "But you'll notice that Igor isn't friendly with men in general. The shelter where I found him said his previous owner was, to put it mildly, abusive, and had left Igor with a real grievance against males." She offered what she hoped was an encouraging smile. "We're working on it, though. I think Igor will come around in time."

The youngest Campbell sister, Kathy, spoke from across the table. Arden turned to watch her lips, but the competing conversations in the room muddled the beginning of her comment.

"...love Griff," Kathy said. "I've seen him coax foxes and deer to eat from his fingers."

"That's a good way to get rabies," Dr. Campbell pointed out from the end of the table. *His* forceful voice would be audible no matter how high the level of background noise.

"Which is why I've had my rabies vaccinations."

Griff turned from talking to his mother, on his other side. "Why don't y'all let Arden eat some of this delicious food? There's plenty of time ahead for answering questions."

She sent him a grateful glance.

"So take your own turn, bro." Lauren, the middle sister, resembled her mother and Kathy, with soft, curling brown hair and green eyes. She, too, sat across the table. "How long have you two been dating?"

"That was July," Griff replied promptly, "when we met on the beach. The fourth, to be exact. We were watching fireworks and Igor bolted because of the noise."

"You've been in Miami all this time?" Mrs. Campbell's question sounded loud in the sudden silence around the table. "But I thought you said—"

Griff held up a hand. "I did say. I spent most of the time I was gone traveling around the Caribbean. I hit the Bahamas, Turk and Puerto Rico, then Montserrat, Barbados, Tobago and most of the islands in between. But..." He raised his wineglass in Arden's direction. "I went back to Miami more and more often. For a little longer each time."

Arden had to admire his acting ability. He didn't betray the lie with so much as the flicker of an eyelash.

"And you live in Miami all the time, Arden?" Mrs. Campbell's reaction had so far been the most reserved in the family. "On the beach?"

Now everyone at the table had stopped talking to listen, so she could hear easily enough. "I have a condo there."

"In a high-rise," Griff added, "with an amazing view.

Watching a storm come in over the horizon is better than any Hollywood movie."

"And what kind of work do you do in Miami?"

She turned toward Dr. Campbell to answer his question. "I—"

But Griff spoke at the same moment. "I'm going to make Arden eat in the kitchen from now on," he declared. "She'll starve to death out here."

"You're right." His dad pretended to look sternly around the table, but his eyes twinkled. "No one is allowed to talk to Griff or Arden again until they've left their seats."

Arden gave another silent sigh as the focus of attention became more scattered. Even Griff addressed his food, rather than her.

But when she put her hand into her lap for her napkin, he reached over, grasped her fingers and squeezed.

As appeared to be their custom, the family sat late around the table, drinking wine and carefully avoiding asking Arden more questions. Her offer to help with clearing the dishes was met with a small smile and a shake of Mrs. Campbell's head.

"No, thank you. Just sit there and relax." Her three daughters and several cousins did get up, however, leaving Arden at the table with the men. She might have found that relaxing enough, but Griff hitched his chair close to hers and put his arm around her shoulders.

"This is what I'd do if we were authentic," he murmured, taking her hand off the table and twining his fingers with hers. "Thanks for putting up with all this. I know it's not easy."

She smiled, trying to look as if he'd said something

sweet and romantic. "It's not exactly hard. You have a very nice family."

"Too nice, sometimes." He leaned close and kissed her cheek.

"What does that mean?" Her face felt hot where his lips had touched.

"Not my dad—he's your usual gruff, grumpy, take-care-of-yourself old guy. But being the only boy with three sisters and a mom is like trying to swim in a pool filled with feathers. Soft, sweet-smelling feathers."

Arden laughed. "That sounds awful."

Griff gave her a dire look. "Exactly."

People began getting up from the table, and Griff stood to pull her chair out so that Arden could, as well. Unfortunately, the end of dinner signaled the resumption of questions. As Arden surveyed photographs of the family displayed on the bookshelves framing the fireplace in the den, she felt Mrs. Campbell's presence at her shoulder.

"Does your family live in Miami, as well?"

The subtext to that question came through loud and clear: *Did they know about Griff before we knew about you?*

"My mother lives in New York." Arden turned half-way around, so she could see her inquisitor without a direct confrontation. "My dad left when I was five, and we haven't heard from him since. I don't have any brothers or sisters, or cousins, that I know of." No matter how many times she told it, the story never sounded less pitiful.

"I'm sorry," Mrs. Campbell said. "We're so used to having lots of family around, I forget that not everyone is so lucky. Do you visit often with your mother? New York to Miami is a long way to travel."

The usual javelin of anger and pain stabbed through Arden. "We…" She cleared her throat. "We had a—a disagreement about a year ago. I haven't seen her since."

For the first time since they'd met, the reserve in Mrs. Campbell's eyes melted. "That's terrible. I hope the two of you can resolve your differences soon. I can't imagine not speaking to one of my daughters for a year—or even a day! I had a hard enough time when Griff vanished. He was out of touch for several months, and I went nearly crazy with worry."

Arden turned the rest of the way around. "He didn't tell you he was leaving?"

Griff's mother nodded. "He did, but no one anticipated that he wouldn't call or even send an email. It's not like him to cut himself off from everybody."

Arden looked across the room, where Griff was playing rock, scissors, paper with the eight children circled around him. "Being betrayed by the person you expected to marry changes you in ways you don't understand. Or even recognize, at first."

Mrs. Campbell followed her line of sight. "You sound as if you've experienced that kind of pain yourself."

Having revealed more than she intended, Arden hoped her dismay didn't show on her face. "Um… I was engaged. Then I discovered he was unfaithful, so I broke it off. But I haven't mentioned that to Griff. If you wouldn't mind—"

"No, of course I won't tell him. But I can promise you that my son wouldn't hurt a woman."

"I know." Somehow, Arden did. Part of Griff's appeal derived from his courtly behavior. He was a gentleman in every sense of that old-fashioned word. "He's different from any man I've ever known."

"We're certainly proud of him." Rosalie Campbell smiled as she watched him lose the game. "We never again want to see him suffer as he has this last six months."

"Believe me, the last thing I want is to cause trouble for Griff. Or anyone."

That meant she couldn't afford to stay too long or get too close to the family who loved him. Otherwise, there would be pain all around when she returned to her solitary existence on Chaos Key—with, perhaps, a child of her own to cherish.

And these people would hate her for taking that baby away.

So they simply couldn't find out. She would have to leave before anyone even suspected she might be pregnant, Griff included. Judging by his family, and by what she knew of him so far, he was not a man who would let go of his child.

Unfortunately for them all, Arden had remade herself into a woman who refused to share. Not her child, not her life…and definitely not her heart.

Griff gave each of the kids a high five hand slap, then looked around in time to see his sisters advancing toward Arden with more questions on their minds. After enduring a chat with his mom, the last thing his fiancée needed was another round with the Campbell interrogation team.

He arrived just in time to head them off. "Nope, no more tonight," he declared, stepping between the in-quisitors and their victim. "Arden and I are taking Igor for a walk and then she's going to get some rest. It's been a long couple of days."

"Why, Griff, whatever do you mean?" Dana fluttered her eyelashes at him in her best *Gone with the Wind* imitation.

"We just want to make Arden feel at home." Kathy usually played Melanie to Dana's Scarlett.

Lauren twirled an imaginary mustache. "And worm her life history out of her." She finished up with a wicked laugh.

"Tomorrow," he promised, and put his arm around Arden's shoulders to guide her toward his parents. "Tomorrow's another day."

As they said good-night, his dad held Arden's hand for a moment. "I didn't get much of a chance to talk to you, young lady. I'll look forward to that in the days ahead."

Arden smiled widely, as if she wasn't terrified. "I will, too, Dr. Campbell. Griff's told me how much he admires you."

Griff didn't remember saying anything like that. But it sounded good.

Then his dad looked at him. "With the holiday over, office hours are back to normal, but I'll give you tomorrow and Tuesday off. We'll expect to see you bright and early Wednesday morning."

"Yes, sir." If not for the weight of his dad's hand on his shoulder and the brief squeeze from those strong fingers, the words would have sounded like punishment. Reading between the lines, though, Griff knew Jake was glad to have him back.

"'Night, Mom." He leaned forward to kiss her cheek.

"Thanks for the terrific dinner. Best food I've had in, oh, about six months."

"Yes, well." She gave him a hug, then stepped back. "Arden, I'll be back in my classroom at seven-thirty tomorrow morning, but I'll leave some breakfast at the house for whenever you're hungry. There is a coffeepot with supplies in the cottage, and a few snacks if you should get hungry tonight."

"Thank you, Mrs. Campbell. I'm so glad to be here."

Griff expected his mother to invite Arden to call her by her first name. But as the pause lengthened, he realized she wasn't going to do that.

"Let's go rescue that dog of yours," he told Arden. "'Night, everybody," he called to the room at large.

Then, finally, they were outside in the cool, crisp night, with Igor sniffing his way through the rye grass his dad always put down to keep the lawn green through the winter.

"The fresh air smells good," Griff said. "That was a long time to be closed up inside the house. After eight hours inside the car."

Beside him, Arden nodded. "Island life is different, isn't it?"

He nodded in turn. "There's always a breeze."

"And clouds scudding across the sky, night or day."

"The splash of waves on sand and birdsongs in the trees."

"True." She drew an audible breath, then blew it out in a cloud of white. "Still, your family is happy to get you back. They'll be glad to support you through the ordeal of the wedding. I don't think you really need me here at all."

"Oh, but I do." He moved ahead of her onto the small

porch of the guest cottage, pulled the screen door back and then pushed the front door open. His mother had left a lamp on the hall table switched on, so they didn't have to step into darkness. "I couldn't face my family, let alone the rest of the town, if you weren't here."

Arden had shut the door behind her, and now leaned back against it. "But why, Griff? Your family knows how badly you were hurt when Zelda canceled the wedding. You don't have to camouflage your feelings."

As Igor disappeared down the dark hallway on a sniffing expedition, Griff walked through the front of the house, turning on lights. "Living room, dining area, kitchen. I don't want them feeling sorry for me."

She had followed him into the hallway. "Sympathy isn't pity."

"I don't want sympathy, either. This is the bedroom." The lamplight showed pink and peach where he'd been expecting green. "Mom's redecorated since I was here. That's her stress reliever—wallpaper and paint. There's a full bathroom attached." He walked over to open the door.

Arden stayed by the doorway into the hall. "She said she was very worried when you left. That you didn't call or email."

Griff thrust his hands in his pockets. "What was I going to say? 'Having a miserable time, glad you aren't here'?"

Shaking his head, he joined her in the doorway. "Tonight, because of you, I wasn't the prodigal son, coming home to be forgiven and taken care of." He set his hands on her shoulders. "Instead, I came home proud, bringing with me a lovely woman who, as far as they know, is crazy about me. We're deeply in love and planning a perfect life together. I may have left town a failure, but I came back a winner."

She wrapped her fingers around his wrists. "They're not completely convinced, you know. Your sisters, your mother and dad—they're still suspicious."

"So we'll convince them." Griff bent his head to breathe in the citrus scent of Arden's hair, then lingered to kiss her smooth forehead. "If I stay here for a while, that should help." He brushed his mouth over her temple, her cheekbone and the curve of her jaw. "How would you like to spend the time?"

Her breathing had changed. "Parcheesi? Backgammon?"

"Right." He released her and started down the hallway. "I think there's a set in the living room—"

"You're not going anywhere." She gripped his elbow to stop him, then pulled him around to face her.

Not that Griff made it hard. He'd only been teasing.

So she was smiling as her arms circled his neck. "How about spin the bottle?"

He folded his arms around her waist. "Let's skip the bottle part."

"Good idea."

Still he paused a moment, studying the flecks of green in her gray eyes and anticipating the pleasure promised by her soft, rosy mouth...until, with a desperate little sound, Arden dragged his head down and pressed her lips against his.

Relief swamped him first—he wasn't in this thing alone, thank God. Then desire surged through him and he drowned in it, pulling Arden tight against him to indulge all of his many fantasies about kissing her. Her sweet mouth surrendered and he took full advantage, tasting and stroking, groaning with pleasure as she made her own demands, satisfied her own needs.

She wore an ocean-green cashmere sweater that seemed to disappear beneath his palms…but not quite, so he slipped one hand underneath to find her skin every bit as silky as he'd anticipated. The new jeans he'd admired because they were tight meant he couldn't do the same at her waist, but he smoothed a hand over the curve of her hip and the swell of her bottom and was rewarded when she pressed her belly even closer to his. Then she lifted her knee to the outside of his thigh and he pretty much lost his mind. The sane part of it, anyway.

Strong and hard and sure…he felt like an anchor to Arden, a rock she could cling to while her head spun and her knees dissolved. His hands moved on her body, a glorious, intimate pressure she wanted to feel on every inch of her skin. Or that might be his mouth, instead, exploring the arch of her neck and the curl of her ear.

Clearly, they both had too many clothes on, because she couldn't get his shirttail out of his jeans fast enough to satisfy her craving for the feel of his flesh beneath her fingertips. She needed him closer, needed his weight on top of her to bear down against the aches he was creating there, down low, with just the press of his palm over her breast.…

"Ow!" He jerked away, staggering back against the other wall of the hallway. "Damn it, what is your problem?"

Dropped all the way to ground zero, Arden sagged against the door frame, panting and staring. "Wh-what?"

Griff paid no attention. He was shaking his leg, trying to detach the dog's jaws clamped around his calf.

"Igor!" She grabbed his bright green collar and pulled. "Bad dog, Igor. Release. Stop it."

"Ow!" Griff put out his hands. "He's got his teeth in my leg. Don't shake him anymore. Talk to him calmly. Try coaxing him away."

"Igor." Arden knelt beside the dog, stroking his sides and back. "Igor, let go. Good boy, come on, good boy. You made him stop. That's a good doggy, Igor. Let's get a treat."

Though it seemed to take forever, once Griff stood still, Igor finally backed off.

"Now follow through," Griff told Arden. "Give him a treat."

"Are you all right?"

"Sure." He straightened and took a deep breath. "But maybe I should head back up to the house."

"Um…okay."

He gave a half smile. "Maybe Igor could stay in the kitchen while I make my getaway?"

Arden took the dog to the kitchen and gave him a chew bone, then made sure both doors to the room were shut.

"I am so sorry," she said as she joined Griff at the front door. "He has had all his vaccinations." She eyed the rip in Griff's jeans. "Maybe you should see a doctor tonight, though. Dog bites—"

He straightened up from leaning against the wall. "Are an occupational hazard for veterinarians. Don't worry about me." With a knuckle under her chin, he lifted her face to his for a restrained kiss. "I'm just sorry we were interrupted. You pack a powerful punch, Ms. Arden Burke."

She felt her cheeks heat with a blush. "So do you. I

hope…" Taking a deep breath, she finished quickly. "I hope we'll pick up where we left off. Soon."

Instead of smiling, as she expected, he gave her a serious, searching look. "Me, too. G'night," he added, giving her a last caress. "Sleep as late as you want and come up to the house when you're ready."

"I will."

She closed the door behind him and leaned back against it. Those moments in Griff's arms had amazed her—outside her music, she'd never before been so lost in the pleasure of the moment. Her mind had been completely overcome by her body's reaction to Griff's touch.

That reaction, she hoped, would burn itself out once they'd made love a few times. She couldn't afford to become dependent on him for sex, or for anything else— his consideration, his gentleness, his encouragement and protection, for instance. She'd be living her life alone, fending for herself and, she hoped, a child.

Griff Campbell was simply a pleasant—well, more than pleasant—means to an end. As she released Igor from the kitchen and got ready for bed, Arden promised herself she would remember that fact.

Because if she didn't, this entire effort would become yet another exercise in despair.

Griff limped around the yard for a while, letting the frigid darkness serve as tonight's version of a cold shower. He visited the near pastures, but the horses stayed away, unsure of his identity in the dark. When the throb in his calf had overcome the unsatisfied ache in his belly, he allowed himself to head back to the house.

Wearing his shirt and boxers, he was sitting on the

side of the tub in the downstairs back bathroom, scrubbing Igor's teeth marks with soap and hot water, when his dad appeared at the doorway.

Jake leaned against the door frame. "Run into a wild coon outside?"

"Just an overprotective canine." Griff turned off the water. "Can you hand me a towel?" When his dad reached for the pale peach one hanging within his reach, Griff shook his head. "You know Mom doesn't want blood on her good linens. I need one of the everyday towels."

"Right." His dad stepped into the laundry room and came back with the appropriate cloth. "Doesn't look too deep. You might want some antibiotics, though, since it's more puncture than scrape."

"Yeah. He had a pretty good hold of me, even through the jeans. Which are now useful for painting in and not much else. Brand-new, too."

"The world well lost for love."

"Right." With his skin dry, Griff applied antibiotic ointment and gauze pads, then rolled tape around his calf to hold things in place. "I suspect I'll survive."

"Love, or the dog bite?"

His dad, Griff realized, had stayed up to investigate. Time to be careful about what he said. "The dog bite. Love is always fatal, I believe. Don't we all die still loving somebody?"

"If we're lucky. You seem to have found a replacement for Zelda pretty fast. Sure it's not just a rebound romance?"

"Oh, yeah." His dad didn't need to know exactly why he was so sure. "Arden is a fantastic person. I think you'll realize that as you get to know her."

He wasn't lying with that one, but he felt as if a huge bell had rung inside his chest, and the vibrations just kept going and going....

"I hope so. She's certainly beautiful. A little quiet, I thought. Not comfortable in a crowd."

"I'm sure Mom told you she's not from a big family. Our hordes of cousins would scare anybody."

"True. They're mostly your mother's family." They shared a grin, because that was the standard line. Anything wrong always happened on the other side of the family. "Well, I'll look forward to the quieter times when we can get to know your Arden better."

Griff picked up his ripped jeans and dirty towel and followed his dad out of the bathroom. The shadowed hallway provided good cover for anything his face might give away. "Me, too."

"So did you get to do any real work while you were down in the islands? Or did you drink the time away?"

"I volunteered for different clinics and rescue groups, when I could find them. There are some marine animal facilities scattered around, all still dealing with the aftermath of the oil spill and the last few hurricanes."

"Not a total waste of time, then." Jake headed toward the master bedroom.

Griff watched the door close behind his dad, knowing he shouldn't let that last comment go unchallenged. But why start an argument his first night home?

He climbed the stairs to his room, instead, and settled into the bed he'd slept in since he was ten, where he'd hidden magazines of various kinds under the mattress and dreamed about everything from hot cars and hot music to hot women.

Apparently, he had one of those on his hands right

now. Under Arden Burke's cool exterior burned a fierce fire. After so long alone, Griff had a pretty good inferno going, himself. Together, they could burn up the night. Many nights, he hoped.

With the dog locked away somewhere else.

As he punched his pillow into shape, though, Griff reminded himself to be careful. The lady wanted something from him—that's why she'd come along. This wasn't a friend doing him a favor. Arden wanted him to make a baby for her. Quid pro quo.

So getting too involved would leave him in the same place Zelda's defection had. But he didn't want another woman to miss, or a relationship to mourn. Good times, salvaged pride and an easy goodbye—surely that wasn't too much to ask.

And if it was, he was tired enough that even his doubts couldn't keep him awake tonight.

Over breakfast the next morning, Griff offered to take Arden into town. "I can show you off to the populace, in line with our agenda, and you can tour the booming metropolis of Sheridan, Georgia."

"Can we walk?" She took a deep breath of crisp air when they stepped outside. "It's a beautiful day, not too cold at all."

He squinted, as if measuring the distance. "Depends on how long you want to walk. We're about three miles from the middle of town."

A glance down at the knee-high boots she'd bought just yesterday dampened her enthusiasm. "Um, maybe not this time."

"So, we can drive the Jag. Or…" He lifted a questioning eyebrow.

"Or?"

"We could ride my bike."

Arden took a quick breath, hardly daring to hope. "As in motorcycle?"

"As in Harley."

She clapped her hands. "Oh, yes. Please?"

Griff pulled a ring of keys out of his pocket. "I hoped you'd say that."

In a matter of minutes, she was straddling the motorcycle at his back, arms around his waist and the wind in her face. "This is glorious," she called over his shoulder. "I've always wanted to ride a Harley."

"Glad I could be your first," he yelled back, with that mischievous, slanted grin she was beginning to look for.

Griff piloted them to the center of town and found a parking place along a tree-lined street with quaint storefronts on each side. At one end stood an impressive brick courthouse with white columns and a white steeple on top. At the other end, long stretches of lawn and huge, leafless trees surrounded the statue of a mounted soldier.

"Here we are," Griff said, removing his own helmet and holding a hand out for hers. "Beautiful, anachronistic Sheridan, Georgia. Population eight thousand, give or take a few. Home to the last remnants of the antebellum South."

"Lovely." Arden noticed the live pine garlands swagged across front porches, the wreaths made of real magnolia leaves and holly sprigs, all of them tied with red bows. "I'm sure it's wonderful at Christmas."

"Of course. The different church choirs come together on Christmas Eve to sing carols on the courthouse lawn." He motioned up and down the street.

"Folks stroll around with hot cider and cookies, greeting their neighbors. It's a scene straight out of—"

He broke off, then swore under his breath. "I don't believe this. Not first thing."

Arden looked around. "What's wrong?"

She didn't see anything dangerous, or unusual. Just a pair of women walking toward them on the sidewalk. Mother and daughter, judging from appearances, busy in conversation. Both of them were pretty blondes, well-dressed and with perfect makeup. They didn't notice Griff until they almost ran into him.

The younger woman looked up at that moment. Her face went white and her jaw dropped. "Oh, my God," she whispered.

"You know I hate it when you use that expression," her mother said, still focused on a notepad in her hand. Then she, too, looked at Griff. Arden worried for a second that she might actually faint.

Griff nodded to the older woman. "Hello, Mrs. Talbot. Happy New Year."

Then he took a deep breath and looked directly at the daughter. "I have somebody I'd like y'all to meet." Reaching out, he drew Arden close to his side. "This is my new fiancée, Arden Burke."

His arm felt like iron around her shoulders. "Arden, this is Mrs. Talbot. And my former fiancée, her daughter Zelda."

Chapter 5

"How do you do?" Arden realized that the phrase really didn't make much sense in this day and age. But at least she'd said something. "Nice to meet you" really wouldn't have worked.

Griff's ex-fiancée was having more trouble. Her gaze had not left his face, except for a brief flicker in Arden's direction. Her mouth kept opening and closing, reminding Arden of her one visit to Sea World.

Zelda cleared her throat. "Where have you been?" Her voice remained hoarse. "Your family has been worried sick."

"Thanks for your concern, but we're all doing well." Griff's half smile—in fact, his whole face—seemed frozen. "I understand you'll be walking down the aisle on Valentine's Day."

"That's right." Zelda lifted her chin. "We're mailing the invitations this week. I'll be sure you get one."

"Don't forget to write 'and guest' on the envelope. I wouldn't want Arden to sit home by herself that night."

"Of course not." Zelda flashed a brittle smile. "I'll have to tell Al you're back in town. He'll be watching out for you." She took hold of Mrs. Talbot's arm. "Now, if y'all will excuse us, we've got a dress fitting."

With a tug, she started her mother along the sidewalk at a fast march. Looking back over her shoulder, she said, "Nice to meet you," but turned away quickly before Arden could reply.

Keeping his arm around her shoulders, Griff began walking in the opposite direction. Arden had no choice but to go along, almost jogging to keep up with his long, fast strides.

As they approached an intersection, she thought he might plunge blindly into the street, so she leaned backward and planted her feet, hoping to slow him down, at least.

"Griff," she said at the same time. "Griff, stop."

To her relief, he did. After a couple of seconds, his arm fell to his side and he turned to her. "Sorry about that. Are you okay?"

"Are you?"

He wiped a hand over his face. "I could use a drink, but I'm not going to find one in this town until after noon. How about more coffee—or tea, hot chocolate, whatever—and a big dose of something sweet?"

"Lead the way."

A few steps took them to the door of the shop on the corner, which he opened. "This is Patty's Place. As a little kid, Miss Patty started baking goodies with her parents. Now she runs the shop, along with her daughters, Pam and Peg, and her husband Pete."

Arden gave him a skeptical look. He crossed his heart with a finger and then held up his hand. "I swear. Their last name is Pierson."

She followed him to an empty table, where he pulled out a white wrought-iron chair for her. "I suppose Patty and Pete couldn't help falling in love. Or that his name was Pierson."

Griff nodded as he sat down. "And once it's gone that far, why not have fun?"

"True." Glancing around, Arden noticed the curtains on the windows, printed with purple and yellow pansies on a background of purple stripes. The walls of the shop had been painted a pale lavender and hung with large flower posters in which one color predominated. The menu, clipped into a holder in the center of the glass-topped table, had been printed and bordered in that same color.

"Purple," she said, looking at Griff. "Patty, Pete, Peg and Pam like purple."

His true, relaxed grin finally appeared. "When life hands you lemons…"

"Make grape juice?"

He laughed. "Exactly."

Before the echo of his laughter had died away, a young woman scurried up to their table. "Griff Campbell—welcome home!" She leaned over to give him a hug. "When did you get back?"

"Just yesterday." He hugged her in return, mouthing *"Pam"* over her shoulder to Arden. "You're growing up too fast. What year are you in now?"

"I'm a junior." She straightened her apron, made from the same fabric as the curtains.

"Majoring in…?"

She rolled her eyes. "Chemistry, but don't remind me. I've still got pages of problems to work on before school starts back next week. It's so good to see you, though. Mom only had to bake half as many pumpkin cheesecakes as usual last fall. She didn't know what to do with herself."

"I'll try to catch up this year. Hey, Pam, let me introduce you…." He gestured toward Arden. "This is Arden Burke. Arden, Pam Pierson."

They nodded to each other. "Glad to meet you," Pam said. "What can I get for you this morning? We just pulled some pumpkin bread out of the oven and glazed it with cream cheese icing."

"That sounds terrific." Griff looked at Arden. "What would you like?"

They ordered coffee, tea and two servings of the pumpkin bread, which appeared almost as soon as Pam had left the table, carried by Patty, herself.

"Griff Campbell, stand up and give me a proper greeting." She was very tall, big-boned and full-bodied, with a braid of blond hair wrapped around her head and the signature pansy apron. "You don't take off again without saying goodbye, you hear?"

"Yes, ma'am," he mumbled from somewhere deep within her embrace.

In the next moment, Peg—also aproned—and a man as tall and big as Patty—Pete, of course—joined them at the table. Introductions and catch-up took several minutes, until Patty shooed her family back to the kitchen.

"Ten pound cakes," she said, pulling a chair over and sitting down between Griff and Arden. "For the dinner dance at the club this weekend kicking off parties for Al and…" Her voice trailed off. "Sorry, Griff."

"No problem, Miss Patty." He took a sip of coffee. "We just ran into Zelda on the street, as a matter of fact, and no tragic gestures ensued. We'll all be polite and get through this thing just fine. Besides..." He reached across and took Arden's hand. "I've got myself a winner right here. You won't hear any sour grapes from me."

Patty's plain face broke into a smile. "I'm so glad. The town was really torn apart when you left. Zelda had her supporters, of course—mostly her mother's friends and their daughters—but lots of folks were mad as anything that she'd treated a good man like you so wrong. Some folks gave her a really hard time about it."

Griff frowned down at his plate. "I'm sorry to hear that."

"The bitterness faded," Patty assured him. "Folks are back to normal, more or less." She looked at Arden. "Dr. Griff is a favorite around here. As is Doc Campbell, who has saved the life of a pet for just about everybody in town. We were all pleased to have his son come back to work with him, after watching him grow up and all. He was here most afternoons after school for twelve years, always asking for a peanut butter cookie and a glass of milk. Got so I'd just run a tab, and his dad would pay it at the end of the week. 'Course, my Queenie got sick then—heartworms, the nasty things—and Doc treated her and kept her for me for six weeks until she could come home and be herself again. After that, the Campbell kids got their cookies for free."

She slapped the pansy-covered apron across her thighs and surged to her feet. "They probably forgot about those cakes and I'm gonna have to start all over again. Good to see you, Griff." Her hand fell heavily on his shoulder. "And I'm so glad to meet you, Miss Arden. Come back as often as you can."

Patty made her way across the room, speaking to other customers as she went, before vanishing behind the tall display cases of pastries and baked goods at the back. Arden sipped her tea and enjoyed every last crumb of the delicious pumpkin bread, but Griff, she noticed, simply played with his.

"You're not eating," she said. "What are you thinking?"

"I'm not sure. This last hour was..." He shrugged without finishing the sentence.

His reaction confirmed for Arden the extent to which he still cared about Zelda.

"You handled yourself well, especially since you didn't have any warning." She could only imagine how she would react if she ran into Andre, her ex, on the street. "I would probably have run screaming in the opposite direction."

"Well, I didn't scream, anyway." A rueful smile curved his mouth briefly. "I could have been more— what's a good word?—*nonchalant*."

"She was upset, too. I doubt Zelda or her mother noticed your tension."

He sat for quite a while without speaking, turning the handle of his coffee mug from one side to the other. Finally, he stirred. "I hate to hear that folks gave her a hard time."

"You would expect your friends and family to be upset on your behalf, wouldn't you?"

"Well, Al and Zelda were my closest friends." He shrugged. "Did they need to be punished for falling in love?"

Arden sat forward. "That's the price they pay, isn't it? Should they hurt you so deeply and have no repercussions?"

His surprised look made her aware of how agitated she sounded. "You're quite fierce about it. Almost as if you've been in the same situation."

Now she was the one staring at her plate. "Well, yes, I have been. I was engaged. He was unfaithful. So I broke it off."

Four teenagers came in the door at that moment. Giggling and chattering, they arranged themselves at the table next to Arden and Griff.

"Be right back," he told her, and went to the register. He tried to argue when Peg refused to allow him to pay for their order, but gave up gracefully in the end. "Free flea spray," he promised over his shoulder as he walked back to Arden, "for that long-haired princess of yours."

He pulled her chair out as she stood up. "They have a Pekingese," he said as they walked out. "So I'll just have to pay for the pumpkin bread in kind."

"That's nice of you." She glanced back at the door as it closed, and laughed. "I didn't notice when we went in—the door is purple." A delicious, eggplant hue.

"Yep." With a hand at the small of her back, he indicated they should cross the street. As they arrived at the opposite curb, he glanced up and said, "That's new."

Arden followed his gaze, but not his train of thought. "What's new?"

"Hear that chirp? Since I left last summer, they've added sound to the crosswalk signals."

She hadn't heard anything. But she could pretend. "Oh…yes. I think that's supposed to assist people with impaired vision." The deaf, like her, would be able to see the flashing Walk and Don't Walk signs.

"Right. There's always something new to spend tax money on. Anyway, since the worst has already happened, let's get this tour started and enjoy the morning. What do you say?"

"Excellent." Especially if that meant she didn't have to reveal any more details about her past. Griff had taken her statement about Andre at face value, then moved on. He didn't pursue the issue, which was exactly what she wanted.

The less he knew about her, the better. And the less she depended on him, the easier she would find her return to Florida.

Because no matter how pretty the town of Sheridan might be, Arden didn't intend to stay one minute longer than she absolutely had to.

Griff played tour guide for the rest of the morning, recounting as much town history and as many anecdotes as he could remember about the buildings and the people. Sheridan was a pretty place in the spring, with masses of azaleas and dogwoods in bloom, or in summer with the crape myrtle trees blooming pink on Main Street and pots of flowers on every doorstep and porch. They were close enough to the mountains that autumn could be gorgeous, once the leaves began to change.

Winter seemed austere in comparison, with the grass turned brown and only the pine trees providing any green. Of course, there were many, many pine trees.

But without the decorative plants, the architecture of Sheridan came clearly into focus and, as a result, Griff preferred this time of year in his hometown.

"The first settler arrived in 1764," he told Arden. "And by the 1800s a thriving little town had been built. According to local mythology, General Sherman passed within twenty miles on his way to Atlanta, but since the town was named for another Union general, he marched by without doing any damage.

"So we've got some nice antebellum houses still standing." He halted in front of the iron gate guarding the Statler mansion. "This one dates to 1846. Tobacco brought in a lot of money, even in those days."

Arden nodded. "Beautiful. Hard to maintain, but lovely."

"Nowadays the family lives in New York most of the time. Watch out," he said, catching her around the waist as she stumbled. "This sidewalk is rough in places."

He started to move on, keeping his arm around her, but noticed that she glanced back at the big house.

With a deep breath, she turned away. "You're quite the history buff, aren't you? Is that your hobby, when you're not doctoring animals?"

"I can't help soaking it in." They crossed the street to the entrance of City Park. "I've been hearing these stories all my life. And, yeah, when I do have time to read something besides vet journals, I tend to choose history."

A bench stood beside the footpath not far from the gate and Griff steered them in that direction. "Would you like to sit down?"

Arden smiled. "Perfect timing. My new boots are still stiff." She perched on the seat at an angle, looking out over the park. "I can imagine this view in summer—the trees leafed out and the flower beds full of blooms, the fountain in the center…it must be glorious."

"Sheridan's pride and joy." He stretched both arms along the back of the bench. "This whole side of town used to be part of the Statler estate, and they donated the land for City Park."

"Does it ever snow here?" She gestured to the downhill slope before them. "That looks like a great hill for sledding."

"About once every ten years we get a snow deep enough to build snowmen and use a sled. Hasn't happened in quite a while."

"Maybe it will snow while I'm here," she said, turning in place to lean against his arm. "Living on the ocean, I do miss snow, sometimes."

Griff curved his body toward hers. "Judging by that condo of yours, you could take long vacations in Switzerland, if you wanted to."

Arden shook her head. "I'm not much into traveling these days. Certainly not that far."

He took her left hand in his. "And does that reluctance have anything to do with the cheating fiancé and the broken engagement?"

She stiffened in his arms.

"I know, you figured I would let it drop. But we've been engaged three whole days. You should know me better by now."

"I…" Her exasperated breath was a puff of steam in the cold air. "I thought you had learned to respect my privacy."

"I grew up in a small town. Nosiness is part of my genetic makeup. Are you going to tell me about this jerk?"

She hesitated a long time. "He was twelve years older, very handsome," she said eventually. "I really wanted to be careful, not risk too much in the relationship until I was certain, but…almost before I realized, we were involved…intimately. Getting engaged seemed like the right thing to do. But then I—I found him with someone else. Someone I'd trusted." She paused again. "I threw a huge tantrum, he retaliated by telling me how many other women he'd betrayed me with and asked for his ring back."

Griff couldn't resist the urge to chuckle. When she looked at him indignantly, he said, "I can't imagine you in a temper tantrum."

"Not pretty, I assure you." She drew a deep breath. "We were at a hotel in…in Italy. I threw his ring in the pool and wished him good luck finding it. Then I left and flew home."

"Good move! Your reaction to being dumped was much stronger than mine."

Her cheeks flushed bright pink. "It was childish. But, really, he deserved to lose something for treating me so badly."

"I agree. Did he find the ring?"

She shrugged. "I haven't heard."

"What about the person you caught him with—did you deal with her?"

"We had a…discussion. But we haven't spoken since."

Her voice reminded him of one of their earlier conversations. What was it…?

Then he remembered. After the dream that had caused her to cry, she'd said, "We're estranged." About her mother, in that same tone.

Griff sucked in a quick breath. "Your mother? He cheated on you with your mom?"

In the next instant, Arden was on her feet and walking away.

Catching up, Griff didn't try to stop or even slow her down. He walked along, hands in his pockets, as they traversed the entire length of the park—about a mile. And when she finally slowed, he did, too.

"I'm sorry," he said. "That's more pain and insult than one person should ever have to bear."

"Yes."

"You didn't deserve such treatment."

She jerked to a stop and stared up at him. "Why do you say that?"

He shrugged. "I blamed myself for Zelda dumping me. I'm guessing you wondered at least once if you'd done something to provoke the way he behaved."

As he watched, her gray-green eyes filled with tears. "I tried to be what he wanted…"

Griff put his arm around her shoulders and turned her so they could walk back toward town. "Lucky for you, he showed his true colors before you married him. You don't have to try anymore, because you're all any decent man could want. And you should believe what I'm saying without question."

"Why?"

He stopped under the bare branches of an oak tree, shifted to stand in front of her, and cupped her face with his palms. "Because I am your fiancé. I know what I'm talking about."

She managed a small chuckle. "I guess that's as good a reason as any." Then she clasped his wrists with her own strong fingers. "And what about you? Have you decided to believe that you didn't deserve being dumped a week before your wedding?"

"Well…"

"And that you didn't do anything to drive Zelda away?"

"No fair, turning my own advice around on me."

"Oh, yes, it is fair. Zelda could have been honest with you much sooner and made the entire issue less painful. Maybe she couldn't help falling for Al. But she didn't have to wait so long, either. Do you see that?"

Arden's fierce gaze and the determined set of her chin were pretty convincing. "I might be able to see that."

"Good." Her mouth softened into a smile.

Griff couldn't resist taking the chance to sample the curves of that smile with his own lips. He'd always thought smiling kisses offered a special kind of pleasure.

What he hadn't bargained for was the way even the lightest touch from Arden's mouth could stir the coals of desire into an open flame. One minute they were sharing light caresses, smooth and easy…but the next minute, smooth and easy got buried under a hot flow of need.

And then a runner breezed past them. "Geez—get a room, why don't ya?"

Griff loosened his arms, which had somehow gotten wrapped around Arden's body, and allowed her to back up. She spent a few seconds releasing her grip on his sweater in the process.

"We'll keep walking, instead," he said. Hearing the roughness in his voice, he cleared his throat. "Though I like his basic concept."

Arden nodded. "Walking is good."

They returned to the Harley, and Griff was just pondering the best place to have lunch when his cell phone vibrated.

The number on the screen was his dad's private cell phone.

"Excuse me," he told Arden, then answered the call. "What's up?"

His afternoon plans got shot to hell with three sentences.

He nodded, though Jake couldn't see it. "I'll be right there."

Arden gave him an inquiring look as he closed the phone.

"Dad's in surgery with an emergency and an office full of clients," Griff explained, handing her the smaller helmet. "And he just got a farm call that's also an emergency, of the life-threatening kind. I'm going to have to go out there."

"Of course."

He blew out a frustrated breath. "I don't even have time to take you back to the house. I could call Kathy—"

"Let's just go where you need to be," Arden said. "Don't worry about the extra baggage."

Grinning, he climbed onto the bike. "Yes, ma'am."

A five minute ride got them to the clinic, where Toni, one of the vet techs, was standing by the back door. "Your truck is loaded," she told him, after a curious glance at Arden. "Stacy Winfrey got the horse to the barn and she's waiting for you."

"Thanks." He took the keys she offered. "Toni, this is Arden Burke. Can you show her into my office, get her something to eat and make her—"

Arden put a hand on his arm. "Could I come with you? I'll stay out of the way."

Griff frowned. "This is not a good call. It'll be messy. We might lose the animal."

She straightened her shoulders. "I'll be okay. I won't make a fuss."

He didn't have time to dither. "Get in. I'll phone," he told Toni, and slid behind the wheel.

"Not the first case I would choose to come back on," he muttered, more to himself than her.

But Arden had heard him. "What happened?"

"This is a breeding farm with about fifty mares and a bunch of stallions, including this one—Rajah, a Thoroughbred. They paid well over a quarter of a million for him."

"Dollars?"

"Oh, yeah. The handsomest guy you'd ever want to see, but on the high-strung side. Today, he decided to go through a board fence."

She put a hand over her mouth. "Oh, no."

"Now he's got a piece of board in his chest. My job is to get it out and sew him up good as new."

"Do you think you can?"

"Maybe." He pulled in a deep breath. "If we all pray hard enough."

Chapter 6

Arden didn't know what to expect as she followed Griff into the barn. She only hoped she didn't do anything to distract him from the problem at hand.

A woman stood waiting in front of a stall, her face as white as the T-shirt she wore.

"Thank God." She grabbed Griff's arm with both hands. "I gave him the ace, like you said. But he's been pretty quiet overall. Didn't give me any trouble about walking up here."

"Good." Griff slid back the bolt on the stall door. "Let's take a look."

The stallion stood in the center of the large space, motionless except for an occasional flick of his tail. He was huge and muscled, with a glossy, dark brown coat, black mane and tail, and white on his feet and nose. Right now his head hung low and his eyes were nearly closed. His breathing sounded loud in the silence.

A large towel had been clipped around the horse's neck and chest. Griff removed it, and Arden clapped both hands over her mouth to keep from crying out. There wasn't much blood, but the exposed muscles and the ragged end of a board protruding from the stallion's chest made a gruesome sight.

Griff, however, surveyed the injury with a calm detachment, squatting in front of the animal to get a close look. He lifted the stallion's lip and pressed a finger to the gum, put a stethoscope against his side and listened to several different places for quite a long time. Then he left the stall.

"He's doing okay," he told the owner. "His vital signs are good and he hasn't lost much blood. His lungs and heart don't appear to have been touched. But I don't want to subject him to a forty-five minute trailer ride with that board in his chest. So we'll just take it out here."

The woman nodded. "I scrubbed the walls and floor of the wash stall with bleach while I was waiting for you."

"Excellent. Walk him down there slowly while I get some equipment."

Unlike his usual lazy strides, the steps Griff took back to the SUV were quick and purposeful, as were his movements when he got there, selecting the equipment he would need.

"It's better than it could have been," he told Arden as she stood to one side. "But that board's in deep. The real challenge will be to remove it without leaving any splinters behind."

"I can't believe the horse is so calm. Doesn't it hurt?"

"Horses can be amazingly stoic, especially when

their legs aren't involved. But the owner gave him a sedative while she waited. That's the 'ace' she mentioned—acepromazine."

"Ah." Arden couldn't resist asking the next stupid question. "Is there anything I can do?"

He glanced up, his blue eyes smiling. "Thanks, but I think we're okay. I'll let you know if I need something."

The stainless steel tray holding his equipment rested on a stand with wheels, allowing him to push it down the barn aisle to a large, well-lit area where Rajah now stood on black rubber mats.

"I'd like to keep his head up," Griff said. "So we'll put on this padded halter and link it through there." He nodded toward a chain suspended from the ceiling. "I don't think he'll notice, as zoned out as he is."

In another few minutes, Rajah stood nearly upright, with sheepskin lining around his nose holding his head in a more natural position.

"Ok." Griff rubbed his hands together, then picked up an oversize electric razor from the tray. "Time for a haircut." He bent and began to shave Rajah's chest.

Arden took the moment to glance along the barn aisle, which looked as clean and neat as a human dwelling. She noticed a low bench against the wall near the end, and went to bring it back.

"Perfect," he said, sitting down without pausing in his work.

"I should have thought of that," the owner said, standing with her hand on Rajah's back. "Sorry."

Arden shook her head. "You've got enough on your mind."

The drone of the shaver seemed to go on forever, as Griff cleared a wide area of hair around the puncture, coming closer and closer to the torn edges. Finally he bent in and, with small, deft strokes, clipped hair from the jagged rim.

"Whew." He sat up at last, turned off the clipper and stretched backward. Then he stayed motionless for what must have been five minutes, studying the wound.

"I need another pair of hands." He looked at the owner and then at Arden. "And what I want you to do is not nice."

They both stared at him without speaking. "The board has to come out. I want to be ready to deal with bleeding, if it happens. Can one of you handle the board?"

The owner moaned and put her face against Rajah's side. "I can't," she whispered.

Arden took a deep breath. "How?"

"Good girl." Griff got up and went to the tray to pick up a couple of paper-wrapped packets, handing the largest to her. "Surgery pack. Sterile. I'll need you to open it for me in a few minutes." Another pack contained sterile towels and the third, gloves. "I'm going to scrub up and get into the gloves. You'll open the packets for me and lay them out. Then you'll pull out the board—slowly, straight as you can without twisting or turning it."

"Do I need gloves?"

"You don't have to be sterile—the board certainly wasn't. But you can wear gloves for your own comfort, if you want."

Swallowing hard, she looked directly at the wound. The point of what looked like a wooden stake stuck out from Rajah's chest about six inches.

"How much is inside?" she asked.

"Don't know," Griff replied. "His vitals are stable, so his chest cavity is intact. I think. I hope. With luck, there's only a few inches, and it'll be an easy fix."

Arden nodded. "Okay. I'll take some gloves."

"They'll be a little big." Griff picked up a thin package, fingered the edges apart and pulled them open, revealing a pair of latex gloves. "Don't worry about keeping them sterile."

While Arden pulled on the gloves, Griff went to a sink in the corner. First, he scrubbed a stainless steel pan and rinsed it thoroughly. Then he began washing his hands, scrubbing all the way to his elbows with a foamy orange soap.

As they waited, Rajah's owner looked over at Arden. "Hi. I'm Stacy. Sorry we haven't had a chance to be introduced." She stroked the horse's neck near his mane. "I'm a little preoccupied."

"I'm Arden, and I understand. I'm sure I'd be hysterical if something happened to Igor, my dog."

"I'm just so glad Griff could come." Stacy glanced at the corner, where he was still scrubbing. "He's always so calm and reassuring. Knows exactly what to do." She drew a deep breath. "Even when a horse has been this unbelievably idiotic."

Griff joined them beside the animal, his hands held in the air, still dripping. "You'll need to get the faucet, Stacy." Then he stepped toward the tray. "Open the middle-size packet, like I did the gloves—by pulling the edges apart," he told Arden. "The towels inside are sterile, so I'll use one to dry my hands, and I'll spread another one on the tray. Then I'll need another pair of sterile gloves."

She did as he asked, easily opening the package and

holding it steady while he took out a towel. "Good job," he said. "You didn't fumble at all."

Arden hadn't expected to fumble. Her arms were strong and her fingers nimble, thanks to twenty-five years of violin work. Her ears were the problem, not her hands.

Griff pulled on the sterile gloves before opening the largest packet on the tray—a set of surgical tools, including scissors, and thread for stitching.

Then he blew out a quick, hard breath. "Okay. Raj here's still looking good, so we're gonna do this thing. Ready, Arden?"

"Yes."

"Start with one hand, thumb and two fingers holding the board. Move it slightly back and forth. Yes? Easy? Good."

Step by step, he gave her directions in a clear, quiet tone. Arden fixed her eyes on the board but kept her mind still, allowing Griff's voice and thoughts to flow through to her hands, as if they were his own.

"Okay, that's good. Yeah, pull—gentle, slow. Right. Keep pulling...yeah...yeah. Oops. Probably shifted a little when he moved afterward. Just back up a little, side to side. Okay, maybe a tiny twist, a little more twist... Right. Good, keep on, just slow, slow, slow. Good. Yes... okay, back up again, wiggle, a little twist, then pull, yes, yes, you're doing fine. Okay, okay, okay—yes!! Throw that damn board in the trash."

He grinned at her, and Arden grinned back, holding the wretched piece of lumber between her hands.

Then he shouldered her out of the way to step in front of the horse. "Stacy, get that big bottle of sterile saline on the floor and pour it into my pan. I'm gonna scrub the chest area, clean out this wound and get our boy here back to business."

By the time Griff retreated and stripped off his gloves, Rajah had started to wake up. Stacy loosened the rope to the halter, freeing his head, and he looked around, eyes still half closed, but brighter and more aware than Arden had yet seen them.

"He is gorgeous," she said.

"And he makes beautiful babies." Stacy smiled for the first time in the last three hours. "His reputation as a quality stud is getting around—we even had a couple of inquiries from Europe this year."

Then she looked at Griff, whose shirt and slacks were liberally stained with red blood and orange soap. "You, however are not beautiful."

"The near future includes a shower and change of clothes," he promised. "I just have to get the mess I made cleaned up."

Arden stepped forward. "I can help with that."

"Thanks." He sounded tired. "Just throw the instruments into the basin, then wrap everything else up in the biggest drape. We'll tape it up and throw it all out. Careful of the needles and blades—see 'em?"

"I do." She followed instructions, listening as Griff explained how Stacy should treat the wound, what kind of adverse signs to look for and when to call him.

"I'll be back out tomorrow afternoon, unless I hear from you before that." He put a hand on Stacy's shoulder. "I really do think he's going to be fine and go on to sire at least two Triple Crown winners."

Stacy actually laughed. "I hope you're right."

"Always," he told her. "Keep him in the stall but don't worry if he lies down. I'd be thrilled if he felt like rolling, so don't worry about that, either. Take his temperature every three hours or so, unless he seems punk, then take it right away. Most important of all…"

He looked at her, frowning, and Stacy's eyes widened with alarm. "What? What should I do?"

"Get yourself something to eat. Get some rest. Don't stand up all night watching the horse."

She allowed her whole body to sag in relief. "Yes, sir. I'll do that."

"Good." He glanced around the area, but Arden had checked to see that she had gathered everything they came with. "I think we'll do the same ourselves, for now."

Stacy walked them to the truck, thanking them profusely. "I'm so glad you were here to help," she told Arden. "I don't think my brain started working until that board went into the trash can."

"I'm glad to meet you and Rajah," Arden replied. "Do give yourself a chance to relax."

"I will." Stacy closed her door and backed away as Griff started the engine. She was still waving when they went down the hill and out of sight.

At the bottom of the slope, Griff braked and put the truck into Park. Then he slumped in the seat, letting his hands drop to his sides and his head fall back.

"Man," he said, with a long sigh.

"Tired?"

He put his palms to his face, pressing his fingers against his eyes. "I haven't focused that hard, that long, on anything this last six months."

"That's quite a case to come back to."

"I would have chosen a nice, easy dog spay my first day back. But you don't get to pick and choose. That's what keeps the work interesting." He paused. "More or less."

She wondered at that addition, but didn't comment. "Would you like me to drive? If you stay awake and give directions, I don't mind."

"No, I'm fine." He straightened and shifted back to Drive. "Again I have to say that you are a woman of many mysteries. I could almost believe you've taken nursing training of some kind. You were a big help, and I know Stacy appreciates that as much as I do."

"I'm glad I could contribute to the process of getting Rajah healed."

"Have you spent time with horses? Done some riding?"

She shook her head. "Not at all."

"Are you interested in trying? We could take a couple of the horses for a walk tomorrow, see the rest of the farm. We've got an older mare who can be trusted with the greenest of greenhorns."

"Does that mean me?"

"Yeah—somebody who doesn't know what they're doing."

"I'm not sure. Let me think about it." Sports had never been part of her life. She rarely exercised, other than her walks with Igor. And horses…what if she fell off? She'd never had a broken bone in her life, not even a sprained ankle.

Really, though, what did she have to lose? Her hands, once insured for a million dollars, were now worthless. She'd been sitting on an island for the last year doing absolutely nothing…except being bored.

"Let's do it," she told him. "I'm ready to try something new."

* * *

The afternoon shadows had lengthened by the time they picked up the bike and got back to his parents' house. But the house itself was empty.

"Dad's still at work, of course." Griff had called the office during their drive. to make his report. "Mom's classes end at two-thirty, but she could have had a faculty meeting. Or gone to the gym, the grocery store, or to one of my sisters' houses. Who knows?"

He looked down at himself. "I need a shower and new clothes. Come upstairs with me." When she looked dubious, he smiled. "There's a sitting area where we all kind of hang out. You can wait there while I change."

Arden followed him up the steps. "This is a very large house. Did your parents build it?"

"My grandparents did the building." He flipped switches as they climbed, bringing light into the darkened house. "They had six kids— all meant to help with the farm work, of course. But Dad went off to college, the four girls got married to business types and my uncle went into the army. So Granddad gave up farming and moved with my grandmother to a retirement community in Tampa."

"Did you visit while you were there?"

He shook his head. "I didn't know what I'd say to this crusty old guy who spent most of his life wrestling food out of the red Georgia clay." Yet another example of his overall failure this last year. But Arden didn't need to bear that burden. He gestured to the U-shaped arrangement of recliner couches. "Have a seat. I'll be back in a few minutes. Make yourself comfortable."

Once in his room, he started to unbutton his shirt and

then stuck his head back out the door. "You can peek at my room, if you want to."

She looked so shocked and appalled at the idea, he couldn't help chuckling all the way through his shower.

After taking the time to shave again, he dried off and pulled on his jeans, but was still carrying his shirt with two fingers when he returned to his bedroom and found Arden staring at him from across the room.

"You said I could look," she said, her cheeks turning bright pink. "I didn't hear the water cut off."

Grinning, he leaned against the door frame and crossed his arms. "No, the plumbing is pretty quiet. Be my guest."

She turned back to the bookshelf. "You really are a history buff. Churchill's history of World War II, *The Rise and Fall of the Roman Empire,* and all these other thick tomes full of facts. No comic books for you?"

"Are you kidding?" He went to the chest in the corner and pulled out the first drawer. "What's your pleasure? Batman? Spiderman, Fantastic Four, Daredevil… and these are only the early issues. I've got more boxes in the attic."

Standing beside him, she laughed. "I understand. Looks like you read almost anything you could get your hands on."

Griff closed the drawer. "That would be correct. I can't remember a time when I didn't read."

"I don't see much in the way of sports trophies." She leaned back against the chest. "But surely you were an athlete."

"Why would you say that?"

He watched her gaze travel down the length of his

body and up again, only then remembering he was standing there without a shirt on.

"You're in great physical shape." She spoke slowly, her voice a little deeper than usual. "You have a long stride and big hands."

His whole body tightened, belly and thighs and chest, arms and rear end, the muscles growing thick with tension. He cleared his throat. "Thanks. I, uh, played basketball, baseball. I've been on horseback since I was four or five. Swimming, running. Whatever seemed interesting at the time."

Only one physical activity, however, could possibly interest him at this very moment.

"Did you work construction on your six months off?" Arden had, incredibly, taken a step closer. "You've got a good tan."

He wasn't sure his brain retained enough blood supply to answer even simple questions. "I volunteered at some, uh, animal clinics on the islands. Most of them needed structural repairs. So, yeah, I worked construction."

Her hand alighted on his arm. "That doesn't sound like the wastrel you first implied you were." She stroked up to his shoulder. "I'm not the only one with mysteries, Dr. Campbell."

"Let's clear this one up right away. Are you by any chance seducing me?"

She watched as her other hand came to rest on his chest. "I think so." Then she looked into his face. "Yes."

"Glad to hear it." His shirt fell to the floor as he shaped the curve of her waist with his hands. "For a second there, I was afraid I'd wake up and discover you're just a dream."

"No dream." On tiptoe, she pressed her lips against his mouth. "No Igor."

"No complaints."

In the next instant, he pulled the cranberry-colored sweater she wore over her head, letting it fall somewhere behind her. Underneath, she wore a silky beige camisole and bra. He ached to get those off her, too.

But he couldn't concentrate because Arden had her hands all over him—his chest, his stomach, the bones of his ribs and the muscles of his back. Kneading, stroking, lightly scraping her nails over his skin, she had a good grasp of exactly what to do to drive him crazy.

And then she started using her mouth.

Griff bore it as long as he could, until his knees wobbled and his thighs shook and he knew he wouldn't be standing in another minute. Wrapping his arms tight around her, he walked both of them to the bed.

Sitting almost immediately became lying, and then Arden moved on top of him, with a knee on either side, to continue the torture.

"You have to know," he panted, because he couldn't resist saying it, "that this is the ultimate fantasy for most teenage guys in the universe."

Arden sat up and looked down at him. "What's that?" Her hands didn't stop their teasing.

He groaned. "Lying in your own bed in your own room, making love with a gorgeous, sexy, incredibly hot woman like you."

"You used to think about it?"

"Oh, yeah."

"And how did it end?"

"Messily."

"We can do better than that."

"Yeah?"

For an answer, she bent to kiss him again. There were no words then, because neither of them had the breath to speak. Clothes slid off, dropping to the carpet. Skin to skin, body to body, Griff investigated the beautiful shapes and textures, tastes and scents, sharing his own in return. Time and again they approached the summit, but backed away, slowed down, allowed trembling fingers to relax.

Until finally there was no backing down, no retreat, no stopping either of them. He fitted himself inside her and began to move, breathless with pleasure, until a rush of heat stunned him and a light erupted behind his closed eyelids, like fireworks and sunrise and starburst all at once, the most magnificent explosion he'd ever experienced.

And even though he didn't deserve it, because he hadn't been thinking about much of anything but how she made him feel, he heard Arden give her own strangled cry of pleasure. Her body stiffened beneath him, around him, and he knew she had reached the same glorious place.

Thankful for that gift, Griff rolled to his side, because he was bigger than she was, but kept her cradled against his body, her head pillowed on his arm.

"You're fantastic," he mumbled, smoothing hair back from her damp, flushed face. "I will never be the same."

Her sleepy smile widened. "I was inspired by the company I'm keeping."

"Thank you, ma'am." He kissed her forehead.

"Mmm. You're most welcome."

The day had ended pretty well, he concluded, after the disaster of meeting up with what's-her-name on the street. The stress of the surgery had added to his fatigue, though, and if he had his choice, he'd fall asleep right this minute. Maybe he should reach down to the bottom of the bed for a blanket first. Even with their shared warmth, Arden might get chilled—

"Griff?" His mother's voice came from the foot of the staircase. "Griff, are you up there?"

Arden gasped. They both sat straight up on the bed. Both totally naked. In flagrante delicto, indeed.

"Y-yeah, Mom. I'm here. Arden and I are both up here."

She glared at him, shaking her head.

"I'll come up," his mother said.

Griff went to the door, which was open, for heaven's sake. "Don't bother, Mom. We were just coming down. Really. We'll be right there."

A pregnant pause followed. He could practically visualize his mother as she interpreted the situation.

"Fine," she said, in a cool, reserved voice. "I'll make tea."

"Sounds good," he called. "See you in a minute."

He reached for his shorts and jeans and looked over to see Arden pulling up her own. He'd seen her embarrassed before, but never had her cheeks blazed so bright a red.

"I am not going down there," she whispered. "I refuse."

"What are you going to do? She knows you're here."

"Because you told her so!" Picking up her sweater, she fought her way in, realized it was inside out and swore as she took it off again. "How stupid could you be?"

Griff fought the urge to laugh. "It'll be okay, Arden. We're all adults. We'll get past this."

"I will not get past being caught in your bed—naked, of all things—by your mother, of all people."

"So you're going to…"

"I'm leaving by the front door." She pulled the sweater down to her waist and smoothed her hair. "Then I'm packing my suitcase and my dog and going back to Florida, where I will never have to face your mother, your father or your family ever again!"

Chapter 7

Arden did exactly as she'd threatened. Storming into the guest cottage, though, she realized Igor needed to go for a walk.

She took him out the sunroom door and tried to stay behind the building as much as possible, in case Griff's mother might be able to see her through the kitchen windows of the main house. And if Griff came after her, perhaps he wouldn't search near the forest, where Igor liked to explore.

The sun lingered just above the ridges of the mountains, and the air had chilled considerably since noon, so Arden found herself getting cold long before Igor had satisfied his curiosity. She wasn't used to temperatures in the forties, of course. And she wasn't used to leaping straight from sexual satisfaction to a state of panicked embarrassment.

"Come on, Igor. Let's go." Tugging on his leash, she

forced him to abandon an interesting fallen tree to walk back with her across the small lawn. "I'll make your dinner before we leave."

After mixing the canned and dry food she fed him, she refilled his water dish. Then she went into the bedroom to pack. But her hysteria had spent itself, and instead of pulling out her suitcase, she simply sat on the bed with her head in her hands.

Much as she wanted to, she couldn't blame anyone else for the disaster that had occurred. The entire situation had been her fault. She'd intended to stay in the sitting area upstairs, had even picked up a magazine to read. But then Griff had put his head out the door, sent her that troublemaking grin and invited her to peek into his room. His unbuttoned shirt had revealed a tanned, muscled chest and the strong column of his throat— images she couldn't get out of her mind once he disappeared again.

And she had to admit to being curious. What did a boy's room look like? She'd never seen one, never visited a family where she was encouraged to play in the children's rooms. A peek wouldn't hurt.

But she was always fascinated by the books in any room she entered. And so she'd been drawn to his collection…and then he'd walked out of the bathroom without a shirt. How was she supposed to keep her distance, seeing his chiseled shoulders, his strong forearms covered with golden hairs, and the flat plane of his stomach? When they stood close, he'd smelled of some tangy soap and fresh air. Seeing the droplets of water sprinkled across his chest, she'd simply given in to every impulse she'd managed to control over the past three days.

With a moan, Arden fell sideways and curled up

on the bed. Three days. She'd just had sex—wild, joyful and totally wonderful sex—with a man whom she hadn't known existed before New Year's Eve.

And his mother had caught them…or near enough. How could Arden face Mrs. Campbell with that knowledge in both their minds? Surely this qualified as a horrible abuse of her hosts' hospitality. Arden wouldn't be surprised if Griff's parents asked her to leave. She should really save them the trouble and take off.

But she had promised Griff she would stay until the wedding, and she hated to go back on her word. The look on his face today as he'd confronted Zelda had revealed the depth of his pain. Some people wouldn't understand how much courage such a gesture required. For them, returning to the place where you'd been exposed and mortified might not seem so hard.

Arden knew differently. In Italy, she'd walked on stage three nights in a row to play the Bach D Minor Concerto for Two Violins with the top violinist in the local orchestra—one of the women with whom Andre had betrayed her. After each performance, she had held hands with that woman as they took their bows and accepted a kiss on each cheek. The other woman had only smiled, but Arden had read the truth in her eyes.

And in her dressing room that last night, Arden had lost the baby—Andre's baby. Within weeks, she'd abandoned her career and the life she'd always known. How could she sentence Griff to a similar emotional desolation?

Leaving now would also mean abandoning her hope of having a baby. This wasn't the right time in her cycle—she needed another week, at least, to be truly fertile. If she didn't fulfill her part of the bargain, Griff couldn't be expected to complete his. Everything they'd done so far would have been for nothing.

Nothing, that is, except the pure physical ecstasy of making love with a man unlike any she'd ever known. Arden admitted her experience was limited—she'd lost her virginity to Andre and hadn't been with another man until today. But she'd slept with Andre for two years without coming close to the exquisite sensations of this afternoon. The earth had, indeed, moved. Now she wanted to experience that earthquake again. And again.

Blowing out a deep breath, she sat up on the bed and pushed her hair out of her face. Staying meant confronting Mrs. Campbell and the situation. She would have to brazen it out, she decided, leaving the explanations and reparations to Griff.

They were his family, after all. This was his home. She was just passing through.

Griff was spreading garlic butter on slices of French bread when a shy tap sounded on the kitchen door.

"Come in," he called, gesturing with the knife in his hand. "Welcome to Italian night."

Arden stepped inside, shutting the door quickly behind her.

"I'm the sous-chef," he told her, going over for a quick kiss. "She gives me the menial tasks. And lets me eat the food when it's ready, which is the important point."

"I hope you'll join us," his mother added. "I always make more pasta than any of us need to eat."

"That sounds delicious." Arden cleared her throat. "Can I help?"

Griff looked at his mother and saw that she was about to refuse…but then, in a split second, she changed her mind. "I've put vegetables by the sink." She brought a big wooden bowl and tongs out of the cabinet. "Would you toss together a salad?"

Arden smiled. "I'd love to."

His dad came in the door from the garage about seven-thirty. *"Viva la pasta!"* he shouted, after he'd kissed his wife. "Just what a working vet needs—besides a glass of wine. Anybody else?"

Griff exchanged looks with his mother and with Arden. They all said, "Me" at the same moment.

"Right." Jake nodded. "It's been that kind of day."

Talk over dinner covered the emergencies at the clinic—a Chihuahua having trouble birthing her puppies, a Labrador that had eaten a bath towel and, of course, Rajah's surgery.

"Sounds like that turned out pretty well, considering," Jake said. "I called Stacy on my way home. She said the horse is bright-eyed and eating. She also talked about how fabulous you and your assistant were. Who went with you?"

"Arden."

His dad sent a surprised glance in Arden's direction. "The surgery didn't bother you?"

She shook her head. "I thought it was fascinating. Although Griff did most of the hard work. I just wiggled the stupid board loose." She hadn't said much else during the cooking or eating process.

"I thought I'd go out there again tomorrow and check up on him." Griff took a second helping of pasta and tomato sauce. "Stacy was a little squeamish about packing the wound."

"Enough." His mother held up a hand. "No graphic details at dinner."

Griff and his dad rolled their eyes at each other.

"Besides," she continued, "I have a slight dilemma we should deal with."

"And what's that, darlin'?" His dad used his second glass of wine as an excuse to thicken his slight Georgia accent. In the family's ongoing *Gone With the Wind* drama, he took the role of Ashley Wilkes.

"Dee Patrick called me this afternoon. She wanted to assure me that the invitation we received for her cocktail party Friday night, in honor of Zelda and Al, included Griff and his fiancée."

Griff continued to twirl his linguine around his fork, watching the process closely. He could feel Arden's gaze on his face.

"I wanted to tell you two so you could decide what to do about that. There's also a dinner party next Saturday at the club, hosted by Trip and Kayli Morgan. I expect I'll hear from her tomorrow."

Carefully chewing his pasta, Griff didn't respond right away. He realized his mistake when his dad zeroed in on the important detail.

"Your fiancée?" He looked from Griff to Arden and back again. "It's official, then? You're getting married?"

Words failed him. Fortunately, Arden came to the rescue.

"We've talked about it," she said calmly. "And Griff did introduce me to Zelda as his fiancée this morning. But since we haven't known each other all that long, or spent a long period of time together, we'd like to wait before making a public announcement. Right now, it's more of a family affair."

"Including Zelda," Jake said. "And her mother. Which means the whole town." He frowned at Griff. "You let your pride get the better of you, I'm thinking."

Griff relaxed his clenched teeth. "I guess I did. No harm done. I don't mind the whole town knowing about Arden. She's not something to hide under a barrel."

"The explanations are awkward," his mother murmured.

His temper surged. "Too bad."

"You'll be polite to your mother." His dad got to his feet, looming over the table. "Or you'll answer to me."

Griff stood as well. "Yes, sir." He looked down at his mother. "I apologize, Mom. I didn't mean to snap at you. If anybody wants an explanation, just refer them to me. I will politely explain the situation to everybody in town, one by one by one, if necessary."

She nodded. "All right."

"Now, if you'll excuse us, I'm going to walk Arden to the cottage. I'll return shortly and I'll be happy to clean up the kitchen." Not that there was much to do. His mother had always been an avid proponent of "clear as you go."

"That's fine," his mom said.

But Griff, still furious, hadn't waited for permission. He had pulled Arden's chair out and was opening the back door.

"Good night," Arden said quietly, with a nod to each of his parents. "A delicious dinner, Mrs. Campbell. Thank you so much."

"You're welcome," slipped through just before he shut the door with a sharp push. Grabbing Arden's hand, he headed across the lawn.

"You walk very fast when you're angry," she commented. "I'm going to have to start wearing jogging shoes all the time."

"Sorry," he growled, slowing down. "I'm just tired of being treated like a kid—a little kid with behavior issues."

"Parents develop habits of thought, I suspect, that can be difficult to change."

"You're too generous. My dad needs to control every situation. My mother wants everything to go smoothly. Running counter to either of those expectations causes friction."

"We're all adults. We can deal with it."

He stopped dead and turned to look at her, aided by the full moon overhead. "I recognize the source. But what are you trying to say?"

The cold wind whipped around them as she hesitated. "You were so casual, when I was upset about the…the situation earlier. Why not apply the same standard to this problem?"

Griff crossed his arms. "Go on."

"Your parents can hold whatever expectations make them happy. But what you decide to do is an entirely separate issue."

"Easy enough to say."

"And very hard to do?" She shrugged. "I guess that depends on whether you're an adult or an overgrown adolescent."

"That's harsh."

"That's truth, Griff. Independence comes with a price, usually a painful one." She turned toward the cottage. "Now I'm freezing and I'm going inside."

He followed her. "You sound like you've had experience."

"Yes." When she tried to close the door, he slipped past her and shut it behind him. She glared up in exasperation. "What are you doing?"

"I want to hear about your declaration of independence."

"The details aren't important."

"To me they are. What happened?"

"I told you this morning. I broke off my engagement."

He thought for a moment. "Because you discovered him with your mother. From whom you are now estranged. So you broke up with her, as well. You kicked them both out of your life?"

"I couldn't live with either of them."

"And you went to Chaos Key. Alone."

"Yes. Until Igor."

She looked so forlorn, he couldn't resist putting his arms around her. And he breathed a sigh of relief when she didn't resist.

"You're a strong lady, Arden Burke." He stroked his fingers lightly through her hair. "And you're right. The decisions I make don't have to meet parental expectations." Lifting her chin, he kissed her delectable lips. "I demonstrated that this afternoon, I believe."

She smiled against his mouth. "Definitely a rally for independence."

The magic between them flared again and Griff could easily have surrendered to the flow. A whole night in bed with Arden, a chance to drift into sleep and then wake with her warm body against his...

"I have to clean up the kitchen." He kissed her cheeks, nose and forehead. "You can get a good night's sleep."

"Not what I wanted," she complained, with her arms locked around his neck.

"Me, neither. But I offered."

"You talk too much," she told him, opening the door to the wind.

One last kiss and he walked out into the cold. "I know."

The morning dawned wet as well as cold. Arden awakened early after another deep sleep, and had just poured herself a second cup of tea when the phone rang.

"Lousy weather for a horseback ride." Griff's voice carried an early morning growl. "So I suggested to Dad that I come to work today and take Friday off for our ride. What do you think?"

Her first thought was panic—what would she do for a whole day without him?

Sanity returned with the thought that she'd only known him four days altogether. "That sounds like a good plan. Enjoy your first day back."

"I'll do my best."

As the morning progressed, Arden couldn't deny the relief of being by herself again, not having to consider someone else's opinion on what she ate for breakfast or what to do afterward. A long bubble bath and a conditioning treatment for her hair consumed several hours, along with a romance novel by a favorite author she found in the shelf-lined room designed as a library.

Coming out of the bathroom after the last hair rinse, she heard the answering machine switch on.

"Hey, Arden, this is Kathy. Um, Kathy Burton. Griff's sister. Anyway, since he went to work today, Dana and Lauren and I thought maybe you'd like to do some shopping this afternoon. There's the cocktail party on Friday and the dinner dance on Saturday, and I don't know about you but I don't have a stitch to wear. We thought we'd meet at Pirouette for lunch at one. Call me and I'll come pick you up."

Shopping with the sisters. Of all the events she'd encountered so far in Griff's hometown, this, at least, she was prepared for.

When a vintage red Volkswagen Bug stopped in front of the cottage at twelve-thirty, Arden ran through icy rain to get inside.

"Not quite our usual winter weather." Kathy smoothly shifted gears as they chugged along the highway toward town. "I'm glad you had a chance to see Sheridan in the sunshine first."

Arden had stopped wondering how everyone knew everything about her day with Griff. "I enjoyed the tour very much, especially the park. I—" She almost said "I wish" but managed to catch herself. "I want to see it in summertime, with all the flowers blooming."

Kathy winked at her. "The way I heard it, you and Griff weren't spending your time there observing the scenery."

Everyone knew *everything*. "Do you live in town," Arden asked, "or near your parents?"

"Right now we're in a little bungalow in town. But we're looking for a larger place we can afford. We'll need more room soon." She patted her waistline. "About June eighteenth, we think."

Arden tried to breathe, but felt as if her lungs, heart and belly had shriveled inside her skin. "You're expecting a baby?" She swallowed hard and struggled to smile. "Congratulations."

Kathy's grin brightened the gray day. "Thanks. We're excited."

A black cloud of envy filled Arden's head. What else should she say? How could she hide her own despair? "Does Griff know? He hasn't mentioned it."

"I haven't had a chance to tell him since he got home."

"He'll be pleased, I'm sure." Realizing her hands had balled into fists, Arden stretched out her fingers, though relaxing any part of her body didn't seem possible at this moment.

"Yeah, he does like kids. He's the only one of the four of us who actually earned money babysitting in junior high. He'll be a great dad one day."

Assuming he knew he was a father. Could Arden change the subject now? "I love your car—not many people have the original model. Where did you find it?"

"My husband works on old cars as a hobby. This one was my wedding present."

"What does he do when he's not working on old cars?

"Didn't Griff tell you? He's a minister. Sermons every Sunday, Wednesday night services, always on call—that's my Jim."

Arden sat in silence for a few moments, grateful that the heavier traffic in town had claimed Kathy's attention. The prospect of spending the weeks until Valentine's Day with a family anticipating its first grandchild was enough to send her straight back to Chaos Key right away. She wanted her own baby. Not the vicarious pleasure of someone else's pregnancy.

And the thought of a minister as a close member of Griff's family worried her. He would have strong opinions about children conceived without benefit of marriage. His ideas would be probably be heeded by the rest of the Campbells. If he discovered she was pregnant and planning to leave, she doubted he would remain silent.

And she was beginning to wonder if keeping a secret of any kind was possible in the town of Sheridan, Georgia.

"Here we are." Kathy pulled the Bug into a parking space in front of an outdoor shopping center. "It's still raining and I didn't bring an umbrella, so we'll have to make a run for it. See the lime-green door straight ahead? That's Pirouette."

They left the car and began walking quickly across the slick, wet asphalt. Arden had worn black leather boots for just this sort of situation, but Kathy had chosen high heeled pumps in a bright red.

She laughed as she drew attention to the fact. "I won't be wearing these kind of shoes in a couple months. I have to take advantage of every chance I get."

A moment later, she cried out. Arden, a couple of steps ahead, turned just in time to see her drop to the pavement.

Rushing back, she knelt by Kathy, who was now on her knees. "Are you okay? Should we call an ambulance?"

"No. No, I'm fine. Just give me a hand to stand up."

A man joined them, and helped out with a hand under Kathy's elbow. "You watch yourself, Miss Kathy," he warned. "You don't want to be falling like that in your condition."

Griff's sister rolled her eyes as he walked away. "You can't keep anything quiet in this town."

"I believe you." Arden offered her own elbow. "Hold on to me until we're out of the rain."

Inside the restaurant, their wet shoes slipped on the marble floor tiles, so Kathy kept a grip on Arden until they reached the table. Seeing them, Dana and Lauren jumped out of their chairs.

"What's wrong?"

"What happened? Are you all right?"

Kathy shushed them as she sat down. "Yes, yes, I'm okay, except for scraped knees and a huge case of embarrassment. It wasn't that bad a fall. See?"

As they stared at her, she swept her thick, curling hair back from her face and ears. "I didn't even lose my hearing aids."

Chapter 8

By the time Kathy dropped Arden off at the cottage, the cloudy day had given way to darkness. Standing on the porch surrounded by shopping bags, Arden watched the Bug's rear lights travel up the drive and past the Campbells' house. Then she opened the door and shifted her purchases to the floor of the front hall before going to fetch Igor for a predinner walk.

Listening to him sniff among the wet leaves and grass, Arden finally had time to consider the afternoon and its implications. Lauren, Dana and Kathy could be as funny as Griff and were just as easy to talk to. After a delicious lunch, the four of them had prowled through every dress shop in Sheridan, and there were quite a few. The Campbell sisters had teased each other, but also complimented and critiqued when necessary. Arden had received what she recognized as a gentle version of the same sisterly treatment. She had enjoyed the sense of family immensely.

And therein lay the danger.

She could like them too much for her own peace of mind. Depending on Griff's sisters for opinions and advice—or just for the pleasure of their company—would be all too easy.

The revelation of Kathy's hearing problems further complicated the issue. Arden hadn't asked for specifics and no one had volunteered. The sisters might think Griff would have explained to his "fiancée." Kathy didn't seem to have the smallest difficulty understanding conversation, even in a crowded restaurant setting. On the other hand, Arden had found herself losing the clarity of voices even more frequently than she had at dinner with the Campbell clan. Perhaps the clatter of dishware had made the situation worse. Or her condition might have deteriorated.

She wasn't sure whether Kathy's pregnancy announcement or the reminder of her own impending deafness had been the low point of the day.

With Igor walked and fed, she carried her shopping bags into the smaller bedroom to sort through her purchases. Dresses for day parties and dances and the wedding, plus some clothes for horseback riding soon hung from a rack on the closet door. She'd also indulged in a new outfit simply because she loved it—dark gray leggings and a silvery cashmere sweater to wear over them would be warm and cozy on cold rainy evenings in Georgia.

The doorbell sounded just as she slipped the sweater over her head. Igor ran down the hallway ahead of her to stand guard at the door. Through one sidelight window she could see Griff on the porch.

"Back to the sunroom," she told Igor, clipping the leash to his collar and leading him away. "We're going to have to work on peace negotiations between you and Griff. But until we do…" As she shut him in, she was pleased to see the dog settle on his bed, apparently content to observe life through the windows.

Then she hurried back to the front door. "Sorry to keep you waiting," she said, pulling back the panel. "I…" She hesitated, because he held a big carton in front of him, which gave off a tantalizing aroma. "What do you have there?"

"Dinner from New Moon, the best Chinese food in Georgia." As she stepped back, he came in sideways and headed for the kitchen. "I decided the weather discouraged taking you out, so I'd bring the restaurant here." He set the box on the kitchen table.

"Also champagne, because…" He shrugged. "Because we like champagne."

"Excellent planning." Arden moved toward the cabinets. "I'll get plates—"

His arms came around her from behind, and his warm mouth pressed against the curve between her neck and shoulder, revealed by the wide cowl of the sweater. "I thought we could reheat the food later," he murmured, stringing kisses over her skin. "What I'm really craving wasn't on the New Moon menu."

Romance novels spoke of thrills—Arden now understood the sensation, like tiny streams of excitement coursing over and through her body from the places where he set his lips. She wanted so much to surrender and let desire flood through her.

But the revelations of the day tied her to sanity. Her doubts and worries about the situation refused to be shut off.

"Mmm," Griff said, bringing his hands to her shoulders. "You're tense tonight." He kneaded gently, finding all the tight spots between her elbows and the nape of her neck.

Arden almost whimpered. "That feels so good." Tears burned her eyes at the intensity of the relief.

"My dad let slip the big news today." He wrapped his hands around her head, massaging a different place with each finger.

She could barely think for the pleasure. "About...?"

"Kath's baby." His fingers shifted, resumed their magic. "I'm gonna kill her for not telling me." Annoyance edged his tone.

"She wanted to." Arden couldn't believe she was playing peacemaker between brother and sister. "You've only been home a couple of days."

"That should have been the first thing she said. 'Welcome home, bro. I'm having a baby.'"

"Perhaps she didn't want to distract attention from... um...me."

"Maybe. Stupid." His hands settled quietly on her shoulders. "Feel better?"

"Much." She was tempted to suggest they eat now and gradually recover the mood for sex with champagne.

Sex with Griff was, however, the only way to reach her goal. She'd agreed to this crazy plan in order to get pregnant. The more often they had sex, the more likely she would be to conceive.

And so she turned in Griff's arms, raising her face to his. "Now, what can we do to satisfy *your* appetite?"

After three days of rain, Friday served up sunny skies and warmer temperatures. Griff woke early, with anticipation, and puttered around the house for several hours until he could legitimately show up at the cottage at nine to take Arden riding.

She met him at the door wearing breeches, boots and a heavy sweater.

"You look great," he said, admiring the fit of those tight pants and the line of her legs in riding boots. "But I thought you said you'd never done this before."

Her smile was sheepish. "I haven't. Kathy suggested I'd feel more comfortable in the right clothes, and be safer with boots instead of sneakers. She took me to a tack shop and helped me find what I needed."

Griff shook his head. "That girl is an expert when it comes to shopping and spending money—other people's money, especially." Then he grinned. "But I love her. I'm not complaining, as far as you're concerned. You will enjoy the ride more without a pair of jeans chafing your legs. And the gloves are a good idea—you have soft hands. So, are you ready?"

"I'm ready," she declared, then swallowed hard. "I think."

"You'll do fine." He led her to the pasture behind the cottage, took a couple of halters off the rack by the gate and handed her the red one.

"This is for Dorsey. She's the quietest, gentlest mare on the planet and pretty much goes on autopilot. All you have to do is sit there and look beautiful." He winked at Arden. "So you've got this covered."

She smiled. "Flattery will get you everywhere."

"That's what I'm hoping." To prove it, he leaned in for a quick kiss.

And then lingered, because the truth was he could have kissed her all day long, could have turned both of them around to go back to the cottage and its warm, cozy bed. Every minute he spent holding her, every hour they spent making love, left him completely satisfied, and at the same time hungry for more—an unsolvable, delicious dilemma.

But he banked the fire she'd ignited and called up a grin, instead. "Let's get those horses."

The animals, of course, had decided to spend their morning in a sunny spot at the corner of the field farthest from the gate. They looked up from nosing the ground as the humans approached.

"Dorsey is the dark one," Griff told Arden, "the bay with the white moon on her forehead. Cowboy is brown and white and black—a tricolor pinto, we call him. Or paint." He demonstrated with Cowboy how to put on a halter. "Nose through here, pull up behind the jaw, then buckle behind the ears. That's all there is to it. Now you try on Dorsey."

After just a couple of false starts, Arden got the halter in place. She grinned at Griff in triumph and he nodded.

"Good job. Now we lead them to the barn." He pointed in the general direction. "Back across the field, through the gate on the other side and then to the left behind those trees."

A quick study, Arden followed his instructions about brushing and hoof cleaning without a problem, thanks in part to Dorsey's patient nature. The saddles and bridles followed quickly, then they went back to the stable yard to mount.

"There's nothing to hold on to," Arden said, staring at the English saddle on Dorsey's back. "How do I stay on? For that matter, how do I get there?"

"That horn you were expecting just gets in the way," Griff assured her. "Come around here, to the mounting block." Leading Dorsey, he positioned her beside the low set of steps. "Climb to the top," he instructed Arden. "Put your left foot in the stirrup…yep. Grab her mane with your left hand—no, you won't hurt her. Hold the saddle with your right. Now just swing that right leg up and over. Up, up…and over. Then sit. See? Not so hard."

"Whew." She looked scared and excited at the same time. "It's farther from the ground than I thought." Wiggling a little, she settled in. "And the reins?"

"Like this." He showed her how to position the leather straps through her fingers. "Just leave them loose for now. Dorsey won't go anywhere until Cowboy does. So I'll park you right here—" he led her a few steps ahead "—until I get on, and then we'll ride."

He mounted Cowboy without using the block, and found Arden staring at him when he sat down.

"How do you do that from the ground? He's so tall."

"Practice—I've been doing this since my head only came to the bottom of the stirrup." He brought Cowboy alongside Dorsey. "The hard part's done. Now we just sit and look at the scenery."

Griff couldn't have asked for a nicer morning. The horses behaved, and Arden gradually relaxed until she looked as if she belonged in the saddle. He'd missed the farm in his months away, so reacquainting himself with the nooks and crannies, the hills and dells and groves, was a pleasure all in itself.

Arden didn't talk a lot, but a woman who lived alone would not, by nature, be a gabbler. He didn't know any of her habits very well, although sometimes he felt as if she'd always been part of his life. Their minds seemed calibrated to fit together, so he wasn't always explaining his jokes or why he'd made a particular comment. She simply understood.

And though many mysteries remained hidden behind that beautiful face, they bothered him less and less. He didn't need to know everything about her. What she brought to the here and now was enough.

Not even considering the fantastic sex. If she wasn't pregnant now, it wasn't because they hadn't tried.

The thought cast a shadow over his sunny morning. Arden had come to Sheridan because they'd made a deal. He would get to show her off and she would get pregnant. Whether or not they enjoyed their time together was, in fact, irrelevant.

Griff had a hard time remembering that detail. He liked her more with each meeting, in private or in public. He craved making love to her the way an alcoholic craves liquor. She could become very necessary in his life, very fast.

Except *she* would be planning to leave town once Zelda and Al had left for their honeymoon.

"I think you've run the gauntlet this week," he said, distracting himself from the prospect of a future without Arden Burke. "First, a family dinner—though not every relative we could call on was present."

She laughed. "Oh, heavens. How many more could there be?"

"Hundreds. Then the ultimate embarrassment with my mother and a family argument."

"Let's not go there."

"You survived lunch and shopping with the sisters, even meeting the ex. Plus horse surgery and Miss Patty's reminiscences."

"There's this weekend still to come, though."

The cocktail party and the dinner. "Let's not go there today, either. As far as I'm concerned, we've crossed the first set of hurdles, and you cleared every single one."

"I'm glad you think so."

"Has anything come up that I need to fill you in on? Any questions or comments we should cover?"

She rode in silence, letting Dorsey choose her footing across the steep slope of the hill as they headed toward Cripple Creek. Once they'd crossed the stream, with Dorsey stepping carefully across the rocks, Arden stirred in the saddle.

"I was surprised to learn that Kathy wears hearing aids."

He hadn't expected that comment. "Since babyhood, as a matter of fact."

"Can I ask what happened?"

"She caught bacterial meningitis, though we never figured out how. We were just lucky we didn't lose her. When she finally did recover, our parents gradually realized she couldn't hear well. The hearing aids help, and she's a whiz at lip reading. All of us learned sign language, thinking we'd need it, but we almost never use it with her."

"I wouldn't have guessed." Arden stared straight ahead. "She seems to understand even when she's not looking at you."

"Her hearing is about forty percent, I think. So if the surroundings aren't too noisy, with too many voices, she makes out pretty well."

"I see." Arden nodded, but still didn't look at him. "So she won't pass her...problem...on to her child."

"Nope. Purely an accident. They might have a few qualms about the vaccine, but I suspect Jim will convince her to go for it. Homeschooling is all well and good, but even colleges still look at your shot record before they let you in the door." He'd expected to provoke a laugh, or at least a smile, but Arden didn't seem to hear. Or just didn't get it.

After a minute, though, she returned from wherever her mind had been wandering. "So what's the secret to going faster with Dorsey, here?"

Griff grinned. "That's the first step. I never offer to speed up until a new rider asks. Now, for the trot, what you're gonna do..."

Within a few minutes, Dorsey and Cowboy were trotting along the level stretch of road, with Arden posting as if she'd invented the practice. Cheeks pink with the wind, hair flowing and eyes bright, she was a picture of health and happiness that smote Griff in the heart.

I'd be happy to call Sheridan home, he thought, *if Arden Burke would stay here with me.*

That evening, Griff pulled the Jaguar into a line of cars snaking up to the front door of the Patrick home.

"Valet parking," he said. "Of course." Instead of his usual relaxed driving position, he sat upright with both hands gripping the steering wheel. He hadn't smiled even once since picking Arden up at the cottage.

"Tell me about the Patricks," she suggested. "What should I know to make this ordeal easier?"

"Ted Patrick practices law—personal injury and malpractice cases, mostly. Hence the huge house. His wife, Dee, is Zelda's mother's closest friend, president of the Garden Club and the Women's Club and the Junior League. She pretty much runs the town. Their son works for his dad and their daughter married more money. I think she also does room decorating."

"Interior design, I believe it's called."

"Right." He tapped the wheel with his fingers. "If we could move on, actually leave the vehicle, then we could get this thing over with."

Arden shifted in her seat, feeling slightly smothered even in her beautiful, spacious car. Her stomach hadn't been feeling good all afternoon, and now her muscles ached, no doubt from the two hours she'd spent on Dorsey's back. Griff had gone to visit Rajah after their ride, so she'd taken a nap, thinking she'd wake refreshed and ready for the party. But she still felt tired.

Perhaps the stress of the situation had made her nervous. She'd been a victim of stage fright occasionally in the past, at especially important concerts. Once she was involved with the music, her nerves and her twinges had always disappeared.

So she agreed with Griff wholeheartedly—they would be better off if they could just get into the house.

They reached the head of the line, finally—the spot in front of the steps, where the car doors were opened by a young man on each side.

"It's showtime," Griff muttered, and reached over to squeeze Arden's hand. Hard.

"Hey, Dr. Griff." The redhead on the driver's side shook his hand.

"Hey, Rusty." Upon emerging from the car, Griff assumed his usual friendly demeanor. "Good to see you."

"Thanks. Hey, remember my hound, Bo? Thought we'd lost him to distemper, but you pulled him through? You oughta see him these days—ninety pounds of muscle, fit as a fiddle."

"I'm glad to hear that. You're keeping him vaccinated now, right?" Coming around the car, Griff put his hand at the small of Arden's back as they started up the steps.

"Sure thing, Doc. I learned my lesson. And don't worry—I'll take good care of your car here."

"Thanks. There are a few advantages," he murmured into Arden's ear, "to having everybody in town know your face."

"I'm glad you think so." She was grateful she couldn't say the same.

Just inside the front door, a man and a woman greeted the guests. "Griff Campbell. Good to see you, son." From his short, stylish salt-and-pepper hair to his custom-made suit and Italian loafers, everything about Ted Patrick whispered money.

"You, too, Mr. Patrick. Let me introduce you to Arden Burke."

The attorney's hands were soft as they closed over Arden's. "I'm glad to meet you, Arden. Please enjoy yourself this evening."

Like a stage curtain, Arden's public persona fell into place without effort. "I'm sure I will. You have a lovely home, Mr. Patrick."

"All the credit belongs to my wife," he said, passing them along to the plump blonde woman on his left. "I just make the money. She spends it. Look who's here, honey. Griff and his friend."

"Griff!" Dee Patrick's squeal turned several heads in their direction. Standing on tiptoe, she threw her arms around his neck. "It's so good to see you home again."

His face reddened—from embarrassment or lack of oxygen, Arden wasn't sure which—and he stepped back as soon as she released him. "Thank you, Mrs. Patrick. This is—"

"Arden." Dee's look was coy and her hands were cold. "But I've heard there's a little more than friendship going on with you two. I expect we'll be having another nuptial party here real soon, won't we? Now, y'all go get yourselves something to drink and something to eat. I'm sure everybody here will want to talk to you, once they've seen Zelda and Al."

To Arden's dismay, she seemed to be correct in that prediction. As soon as she and Griff moved away from the reception area, two friends he knew from high school stepped up to talk to them. A married couple of about the same age joined them, but then the two men were replaced by an older man and woman whose daughter Griff had dated. As his date, Arden couldn't move from the spot, hemmed in as they both were by a constantly changing barrier of busybodies.

Across the room, however, the official stars of the evening drew an even bigger crowd. Zelda wore a fitted red dress that brought highlights to her honey-blond hair and depth to her blue eyes. The diamond on her left hand flashed under the lights, but was not remarkable for its size. Her smiles seemed genuine, and when she looked up at her groom-to-be, Arden felt her throat catch. Their locked gazes blatantly conveyed love and trust.

Al McPherson was not the brawny type Arden had

expected, but slender instead, even bony, with a long, serious face, deep-set eyes and a sheaf of straight dark hair falling over his forehead. He wore a plain charcoal suit and a nondescript tie, and though he smiled easily, he never released his grip on Zelda's hand.

The crowd around Arden and Griff shifted again, but when she focused on the new faces, she was relieved to recognize Kathy and Lauren.

"We thought you looked trapped," Lauren said in a stage whisper, as Griff remained captured by an older gentleman who would not be dislodged. "So we brought you some punch."

"Wonderful." Arden took a sip and closed her eyes in relief. "I didn't realize how thirsty I was."

"You two are a sensation," Kathy said. "Zelda's probably jealous that you've taken over her party."

The thought made Arden even queasier. "I hope not. I certainly didn't intend to." Turning away from Griff slightly, she drew the sisters closer. All the noise in the room made following the conversation difficult enough. She didn't want Kathy and Lauren to speak loud enough to be overheard—especially by their brother.

"Don't be so dramatic," Lauren told her sister. "Zelda's not the jealous type and you know it."

Arden looked at her in surprise. "She isn't?"

Kathy pouted but Lauren shook her head. "Zelda's a nice girl. We were all ready to call her sister until she dumped Griff."

Giving in to her own curiosity, Arden asked, "You didn't have a clue that she might not be committed to marrying him?"

"Nobody knew," Lauren replied.

"I did," Kathy said at the same time.

Arden and Lauren both stared at her. "You did?" her sister demanded.

"I saw her with Al once, up in Clarksville, in the mountains. They were sitting at a table, holding hands, talking. Neither of them looked happy. I knew it was serious."

"And you didn't tell Griff?"

"I'm not a snitch. And I didn't want to hurt him...or make it any easier for her."

"For who?" Griff said at that moment, pivoting to join them. "Or whom, maybe?"

Lauren and Kathy seemed to have been struck dumb, so Arden supplied an answer. "Dana. We were discussing our shopping trip the other day."

"Was everybody as successful as Arden?" he asked his sisters. "Because the dress she's wearing is a scorcher."

Arden smiled, glad to think that she'd made the right choice with her clinging, strapless black dress and finely woven stole.

Before Lauren or Kathy could respond, though, he looked over their heads in the direction of the guests of honor. "The crowd has shrunk to a manageable size. Shall we pay our respects?"

"Have a drink first." Kathy held out the punch she'd brought for him.

Griff took the glass and tossed back the pink liquid in one swallow. His face contorted. "Bleh. Pink lemonade and champagne? What a foul idea." He slipped his hand between Arden's elbow and her ribs. "Here we go."

His grip got tighter as they approached Zelda and Al, driving Arden's tension higher in response. Somehow, as they joined the receiving line, the dynamics of crowd movement brought them to the guests of honor right away.

Zelda's eyes widened when she saw them. "Hi, Griff. And…and Arden, right?"

"Yes," Arden said, extending her hand. "We didn't get to talk on Monday morning. You have my best wishes on your upcoming marriage."

"Th-thanks." Zelda's hand shook her as fingers brushed Arden's. "It was nice of you both to come tonight."

"It was nice of your mother to ask Dee to invite us," Griff said, his voice unusually deep.

All at once, they seemed to be the only people standing with the happy couple. Arden felt as if a bank of stage lights highlighted the four of them.

"Al, honey." Zelda tugged on the hand holding hers. "Look. It's Griff and—and his friend, Arden."

Al turned to face them. "I'm pleased to meet you, Arden. Welcome to Sheridan."

Then his stony brown gaze met Griff's steel blue one. Al's right hand lifted, wrist stiff and straight, at the same time as Griff extended his. The two hands, one light-skinned and the other bronzed from the sun, met and gripped until both sets of knuckles turned white. Each man spoke one word.

"Al."

"Griff."

In the next instant, as if struck by a hammer, the two hands broke apart. Al felt for Zelda's grasp. Griff's fingers clenched Arden's elbow.

He spoke into the silence. "We're out of here."

Before the collective gasp had died away, he swept her past the Patricks and out the front door.

Chapter 9

The downside of valet parking was that you couldn't make a quick getaway. You had to wait for the attendant to notice you, find your ticket and then bring the right car back. You had to scrounge in your wallet or your pockets for a tip—or borrow from the woman you came with, which was a total embarrassment. Only then was escape possible.

Griff blew out a huge breath when the doors finally shut on both sides of the Jag and he could put his foot on the gas pedal. After a few minutes of driving blindly through the Patricks' upscale neighborhood, he brought his brain back on track.

"How about a real dinner? Somewhere my suit and your dress fit in? We do have a fancy French restaurant in Sheridan, it's called—"

"I don't think so, thanks." Arden's voice sounded tight, rigidly controlled.

"What's wrong?" He moved his hand to cover hers on the seat, but she slipped her fingers away. "Arden?"

He heard her sharp breath in the darkness. "Are you going to ignore what just happened? What you did?"

Griff pulled his hand back. "Sounds like a good option."

"You investigate the behavior of others—you want to know every detail of my past, my—my motivations and my reasons, my plans for the future. But you don't stop to examine your own?"

Jaw clenched, he took whatever turns became available, heedless of direction. "I'm aware of my own faults. Believe me, I know exactly where I come up short."

"This is not about failing, Griff. This is about facing your life and making it work."

"Which you, living like a hermit on a deserted island, know so much about?"

"I made my choice deliberately and was quite…satisfied, thank you very much."

"That's not true, Arden, and you know it. You're happier after a week in Sheridan than you ever were on that pile of sand."

"And you are an expert at evading the issue. But I won't allow it this time. What you just did, in the middle of a very nice party, was rude and immature."

"I shook their hands. I said hello."

"And you stalked out as if you'd shaken hands with the devil himself."

"Well…"

"Are you still so in love with her that you can't bear to see her happy?"

He opened his mouth…and then closed it again because the automatic answer he'd started to give surprised him so much.

When was the last time he'd thought about Zelda as... well, as the woman he wanted to be with for the rest of his life? For six months, he'd been laboring under a sense of rejection and loss, but was he missing *her*—or simply the habit of being half of a pair?

Because these days, when he saw a woman in his mind's eye, when he thought about who to talk to, spend time with...make love with all day and night...the face was Arden's. The body in his dreams, the voice in his head, the laugh he wanted to hear when he encountered something funny—they all belonged to Arden Burke.

His foot had eased off the gas as he pondered, and the car had slowed almost to a stop. He braked and shifted into Park, then turned to face her. "Arden—"

But now she sat with her head against the back of the seat and her eyes closed.

"Honestly, Griff, I'm really not feeling well. I'd like to go home—" She stopped short, then continued after a pause. "That is, to the cottage. To bed. If you don't mind."

"No problem." He made the turns that would take them back toward the farm. "Are you just tired, or really sick?"

"Both, I think."

"I'm sorry to hear it." He stayed close to the speed limit as he drove, torn between avoiding trouble and making Arden comfortable as soon as possible.

"Why don't I make you some tea," he offered as they stepped into the cottage, "while you get into bed?"

She shook her head. "Igor needs a walk first."

Griff suppressed a wince. "I'll take him out."

For the first time since leaving the party, their eyes met and held. "Neither of you will like that."

"We'll manage." He gave her a gentle shove down the hallway. "Get into your gown, crawl between the sheets. I'll multitask in the kitchen."

Her shoulders lifted on a sigh, but she did as he directed. With a cup of water heating in the microwave, Griff took the dog's leash and opened the door to the sunroom.

Igor had been lying with his nose on his front paws, but when he saw Griff, he came immediately to an alert stance. Even without a voice, this canine could growl.

"Want to go outside?" Griff showed him the leash. "I'm here to do the honors."

Igor's hackles rose as he approached.

"Oh, come on, son. Your mom doesn't feel good. Let me take care of both of you without a hassle. Tonight, anyway. Tomorrow, you can resume the hostilities. I, by the way, am a totally neutral party where you're concerned."

Igor glanced toward the sunroom door and then toward the kitchen. Griff could almost see the dog considering his options.

Then the hairs standing up along Igor's back smoothed and his ears relaxed. If a dog could look resigned, this one was.

"So I clipped the leash to his collar," Griff reported to Arden a short time later, "staying as far away from his chops as I could manage. We took the prescribed constitutional and now we're in for the night. You have a cup of tea. What else can I do for you?"

Propped against the head of the bed, she looked nearly as pale as his mother's white cotton sheets. "I can't think of anything. You should go find yourself something to eat."

"I won't starve." Unsure of what she was thinking, still marveling at the discovery he'd made only a few minutes ago, he went down on one knee beside the bed.

"Maybe I should stick around, in case you need help during the night." He set his fingertips lightly on the back of her hand, thought it felt cold, a little damp. Her cheek, when he rested his knuckles there, was just as cool. "You don't seem to have a fever."

"I don't." She set the tea mug on the bedside table. "My stomach is upset, that's all. I'm sure I'll be fine tomorrow. Have dinner. See a film. Go back to the party and talk to your friends—you can blame your sudden exit on me."

"I don't think so. Remember, you're my camouflage."

She gave a slight smile. "That's right. We agreed."

The idea came from out of nowhere, but hit him hard. *She could be pregnant.* Maybe Arden's queasy stomach signaled a baby. His mother always said she knew the morning after she got pregnant.

The idea drove him to his feet. "I guess I will get some dinner. Maybe I'll check in on you later, before I hit the sack. And tomorrow morning, early." Leaning down, he kissed her forehead. "I hope you feel better. Call the house if you need me."

Her fingers fluttered against his cheek. "Of course."

Outside on the front porch, he stared at the Jaguar, trying to figure out what to do next. Not the party. He'd atone for his sins at the dinner dance next weekend, if Arden was up to going.

And not the bars. He needed to think, not drink. An idea concocted with champagne insights would have to be completed cold stone sober in order to succeed. These next few weeks might be trickier than he ever could have imagined.

A baby would mean he'd fulfilled his part of the bargain. Arden could stay until the wedding, then leave, and they'd both have gotten what they wanted.

But she would be taking his child with her. Faced with the existence of a son or daughter he would never meet—without the veil drawn across his reasoning skills by champagne—Griff's conscience cringed. His gut cramped. A man didn't abandon his own flesh and blood to be raised by a woman alone. Not if he could prevent it.

Considering flesh and blood, his family would be devastated to discover the existence of a child they knew nothing about. Jake and Rosalie Campbell had been looking forward to grandchildren since their kids left college. Was he going to deprive them of that joy?

Most important, Arden should not be allowed to resume the solitary life she'd "chosen" for herself. He couldn't begin to guess what had driven her into isolation, although a philandering fiancé who slept with her mother would be a good start. But the lady was meant for life and love and happiness as part of a family. His family.

Somehow, Griff decided over peanut butter sandwiches, he would have to change her mind about leaving. Surely, given enough time, she would come to love him. But he had only five weeks till the wedding.

Five weeks would have to be enough.

Waking up, Arden kept her eyes closed while she assessed her state of health. Curled up underneath the featherlight covers, warm and relaxed, she felt well enough. Especially if she ignored the emptiness beside her, a space Griff usually filled quite nicely.

Igor jumped onto the bed and came to lick her face, his usual signal to go outside in the morning.

"Yes, yes, I understand. Wait just a second." She turned to her side to get up.

Instead of landing on her feet, though, she found herself on her hands and knees on the floor, as the room spun around.

Folding her legs to sit against the side of the bed, she closed her eyes and tried to make the world stand still. Igor nosed at her face again.

"I know, Igor. I'm trying." Poor dog. He'd been inside all night long.

She undertook a harrowing journey, lurching from the bedpost to the door frame to the hallway wall, then the kitchen table and counter, all the while feeling as if her brain were sloshing around inside her skull.

Only when she opened the back door did she remember that this was Georgia in January, not the Florida Keys. The temperature hadn't yet reached forty degrees at 7:00 a.m. Walking outside in bare feet and her nightgown was not a good idea.

At this point, Igor started pulling at the leash, anxious to get into the grass for his morning exercise. Given the state of her equilibrium, he quickly jerked her onto the frost-coated lawn. She squealed at the contact of ice with skin, and pulled back, trying to retreat.

At the edge of the woods, something moved, something fairly big. A deer, she guessed, squinting in that direction. She'd watched them grazing behind the cottage on other mornings.

Igor, however, was not satisfied to watch. Obeying his instincts, he surged into the chase, sprinting toward the animal and yanking the leash free from Arden's grasp.

The deer whirled and vanished into the woods, with the dog at its heels.

"Igor! Igor, come! Come on, Igor. Breakfast," she called. But her dog had decided to hunt his own meal this morning. Arden stood out on the stone terrace until her feet were quite numb, but Igor did not return. She would have to dress, get shoes, go find him...

Her stomach chose that moment to revolt. Arden was sick on the grass and then, when she had stumbled drunkenly into the house, sick again in the bathroom. When the spasm passed, she was tempted to simply lie on the floor and go back to sleep. Anything else would be too hard.

But instead she got to her feet and managed to splash her face with cool water. Back in the bedroom, she dragged her nightgown off and pulled on the gray leggings and silver sweater, because they were easiest. Then, exhausted, she sat on the bed and picked up the phone.

As if he'd been waiting, Griff answered on the first ring. "Arden? How are you this morning?"

At the sound of his voice, she burst into tears. Whether or not he understood what she tried to say between sobs, he waited until she paused.

"Hold on," he said. "I'll be right there."

She'd barely hung up when the front door opened. In the next minute, he was beside her on the bed, picking her up and setting her on his lap.

All Arden could do was cry.

He pressed his mouth against her forehead and cheeks. "Still sick? You feel hot."

She nodded.

"You need to be in bed." But when he started to put her there, she shook her head.

"Igor," she managed to say, trying not to cry. "He's in the woods. After—" she hiccupped and sniffed "—a deer. I dropped the—the leash."

Griff nodded and folded her tight against his body. "It's okay, honey. Igor knows where you are, and he'll get himself back just fine."

"He's n-never been in these woods." Her teeth were starting to chatter. "There might be bears."

"Bears are hibernating this time of year. And they mostly eat plants. Plus, Igor's faster than any old bear." Griff rocked back and forth. Despite herself, Arden felt soothed.

When she had calmed down, he pulled back the bedcovers and placed her on the sheets, then tucked the blankets over her. "You stay right here. I'm going to get my mom to come down with a thermometer to take your temperature. We'll scare up some medicine to make you feel better. Then I'll go out and find Igor the man-eater. But you don't move, understand?"

Exhausted, Arden nodded. Her eyes wanted to close, and she let them, now that Griff was here. She could trust him to take care of everything.

The day passed like a soft-focus dream. Mrs. Campbell floated in and out, offering pills and water. At some point, Arden came awake to find a woman she didn't know pressing a stethoscope against her chest.

"Hello there," she said, her voice deep and mellow. "I'm Dr. Loft. I practice general medicine here in Sheridan." She moved the stethoscope to a different place. "How are you feeling?"

Arden took stock. "Cold," she whispered, with a shiver. "Dizzy. Sick."

"You have a fever." Dr. Loft put the stethoscope in the pocket of her white coat. Her fingers, warm and firm, pressed on the sides of Arden's throat and under her jaw. "We've got a nasty virus going around and I suspect you're playing host this weekend."

She pushed up the sweater to poke at Arden's belly in various places. "Does this hurt? This? Breathe in and hold it. Again. Okay, I'm done."

As Arden straightened her sweater and pulled the covers back up to her shoulders, the doctor dragged a chair over to sit by the bed. With her dark skin and long, elegant neck, she looked like an Egyptian queen.

"I don't have a medicine that will chase this virus away," she said, making notes on a clipboard in her lap. "You can take regular pain pills for the fever and muscle aches. I can give you a prescription for the dizziness and for nausea. You'll just have to ride this out, but in three or four days you should be pretty much back to normal.

"Eat what you can, and drink—we don't want you dehydrated. If you're not feeling absolutely well in a week, I want to see you in my office." She set a business card on the bedside table. "Any questions?"

"Do you…" Arden pulled in a deep breath. "Do you deliver babies?"

"For uncomplicated pregnancies, yes. I refer high-risk patients to a specialist." Her eyebrows drew together over dark brown eyes. "Are you pregnant?"

"N-no. I don't think so."

"Are you trying to become pregnant?"

Despite the chills shaking her, Arden thought she could feel herself blush. "Um...yes."

Dr. Loft got to her feet. "In that case, I definitely want to see you in a week, even if you're feeling terrific. You should be taking vitamins and eating a balanced diet. Let's make sure you're in the best possible health for this adventure."

As she picked up her medical bag, Arden cleared her throat. "I didn't know doctors made house calls anymore."

Her throaty laugh filled the room. "This is a small town. We do favors for each other. Dr. Jake came to my place when our Great Dane puppy got into a fight with a stray dog. I couldn't manage my eighteen-month-old daughter and an injured animal. So when he called, I was glad to return the favor."

"Igor." Arden sat up suddenly, then fell back with a groan as the room whirled. "Did Griff find him? Is he back?"

The doctor put a hand on her shoulder. "I'll find out. You stay in bed and keep calm."

Mrs. Campbell came in a few moments later. "Griff is out looking for Igor," she said, smoothing the pillows and blankets. "I'm sure he'll be back any minute now."

"But it's late, isn't it? What's the time?" Arden wanted to see the clock, but her head was too heavy to lift.

"Don't worry, sweetie." A soft hand brushed the hair off her forehead. "Everything will be okay. Just relax."

"I can't lose him," Arden fussed. "He's all I have...."

Griff's third trip into the woods felt like an exercise in futility. After eight hours, Igor could be anywhere in the county. And Griff would prefer to be sitting with Arden, watching her sleep.

As his mom had pointed out, though, Arden would feel better when the dog came home, virus or no virus. So here he was, fighting brambles, tramping through mud and wearing out his voice calling for the truant animal.

"Igor. Igor, come home, buddy." His dry mouth couldn't send out much of a whistle. "Damn it, Igor. Come. Now."

He heard his dad's voice, over to the south, and an echo from Kathy's husband, calling off to the north. They could cover the ground faster this way. What would happen if they didn't find the dog, though, would be his responsibility alone.

The Campbell portion of the forest ended on a ridge above a deep, brush-filled ravine. The wooden fence marking the boundary line wouldn't have kept a deer or Igor on the property.

Griff stood on the edge, staring down into the gully, as his dad came up beside him. "I haven't been down there. The sides are steep."

"That's Fletcher property," Jake said. "They do some trapping."

Jim joined them. "The little guy could have stepped in one."

"So could we," Griff pointed out. "But I guess there's no other choice."

Soil had washed down the walls of the narrow valley, leaving slippery rock and gravel exposed. The trees seemed to grow just far enough apart to avoid being used as handholds. Only a few steps down, Griff found himself on his butt, sliding sideways into a thorn bush.

"You okay?" his dad called.

"Yeah." Braced on his downhill leg, Griff wiped his scraped and bloody palms on his jeans. "Be careful, though."

At the words, he heard Jim fall in turn. Moments later, the sound of tumbling rocks came from the other side. "Dad?" There was no answer for way too long. "Dad, are you there?"

"Hell, yes," Jake growled.

"Are you hurt?"

"No. But I'm too old for this."

"We're all too old for this," Jim yelled back.

They reached the bottom without breaking any bones. Griff turned to look back the way he'd come. "And we thought getting down here was the hard part."

The afternoon sun had passed beyond the rim above, leaving the bottom of the ravine in twilight. Stepping carefully, peering at the ground in order to see a trap before he tripped it, Griff continued to call for Igor. But as the minutes passed, then an hour, his hopes began to die. If they hadn't found him by now...

He hated the image in his head of Igor, voiceless, stuck or trapped or somehow unable to travel, marooned all night in the woods. Not too many hunting animals would be out this time of year. But a hungry coyote would be glad for easy prey.

"Getting dark," his dad called. "We'd better start back."

"Agreed," Jim yelled.

"But..." Griff sighed. "Okay. Let's shift about a hundred feet to the left as we go, to cover different ground." For him, that meant more difficult traveling, including a mini-gulch or huge ditch, depending on your definition. Visibility decreased to almost zero, which he didn't realize until he walked into a tree.

"Ow." He stumbled to the side, stepped into a hole and landed flat on his face. "Aw, hell."

He lay there for a minute, glad just to be off his feet, even if that meant lying on the damp ground with bugs wriggling around underneath him.

Then something wet and slimy crawled over the nape of his neck.

He swore and sat up, swiping at the back of his head. Through the darkness, a pair of bright eyes gleamed at him. Panting breaths created puffs of smoke in the cold air.

A wet tongue slathered across his mouth.

"Well, hello again, Igor." Laughing, Griff wiped his mouth on his sleeve. "Fancy meeting you here."

Chapter 10

After spending Sunday and most of Monday in bed with a freshly bathed Igor at her side, Arden did, indeed, feel almost back to normal.

How could she be otherwise, with the amount of attention and care she'd received? Mrs. Campbell had checked in several times a day, bringing soup, tea, books and even music—a portable disk player and a variety of CDs. She hadn't, fortunately, insisted on actually turning the thing on, and Arden had ignored its presence in the bedroom.

Kathy had stopped by with more books and stayed to chat, then took Igor for a long walk. Lauren brought a loaf of homemade bread and a jar of strawberry jam—the first food Arden felt like trying once her appetite began to resurface. Dana's chicken soup made a wonderful first meal.

Though he had to go to work Monday morning, Griff had remained within her reach most of the time, once he'd brought Igor home. He and Dr. Campbell and Jim recounted for her their "safari" into the "dangerous jungle" beyond the farm's border, making her laugh even while she still felt sick.

She tried to thank them for the return of her precious Igor, but they refused to acknowledge anything out of the ordinary.

"Happens all the time," Griff's dad said, with a shrug. "He just needs to learn the boundaries, is all."

"You can walk him out there, once you're well." Jim had ventured only as far as the bedroom doorway. "Show him where to turn around and come home. He's a smart one—he'll learn in no time."

"I'm not so sure about that," Griff said later, as he sat in the armchair he'd pulled over so he could put his feet up on the end of the bed.

Arden frowned at him. "Are you saying he's not smart?"

"Just the opposite. I think he knew where he was and what he was doing. He probably enjoyed his day as a wild thing in the forest."

"Would he have come back on his own?" Her eyelids tended to droop—the medications for dizziness and nausea made her sleepy.

"I expect he would have tried, but they get distracted, you know, by this scent or that leading off in another direction. I'm just glad he found me."

"Oh, so am I." She reached out to pet Igor's head, then let her hand fall on the part of Griff she could reach   his sock-covered ankle. "Thank you so much."

He was still there when the medicines wore off in

the wee hours of Sunday morning and she ran for the bathroom.

"Here," he said, when she'd finished. "Let me wipe your face."

Sitting on the side of the tub, Arden sighed. "I am so sorry."

"Nothing to be sorry for." He patted her face with a dry cloth. "Everybody gets the flu."

"I don't." She opened her eyes to see his skeptical smile. "Honestly, I haven't been sick like this in years. Since college, at least. Except for the migraines. And even those had stopped."

"Interesting." Keeping an arm around her shoulders, he walked her back to bed. "I don't know what you did before you went to Chaos Key. But maybe coming into contact with people again has introduced you to illnesses you haven't encountered before. Pathogens are constantly mutating, you know, to avoid the immunity their hosts develop."

"I keep forgetting you're a scientist." With a gulp of lukewarm tea, she swallowed the pills he offered. "When do you see Rajah again?"

"Monday afternoon will be my last visit. He's doing great and I think Stacy can handle him from now on."

"Miracle worker," Arden murmured, snuggling in and closing her eyes as he tucked the covers around her. "Hero."

"I'd better call the doctor. You're obviously delirious."

"My hero," she insisted, then fell deeply asleep.

That word stayed with Griff all day Sunday and through the work week.

Hero. What did it say about Arden's feelings? Had she started to love him?

Or was he setting himself up to take another fall? Had he found the right woman…or made a fool out of himself once again? He couldn't just ask her outright. Not while she was sick, and once she recovered, not just any old time—with his parents listening at dinner, or when Arden brought a huge, specially ordered lunch to the office on Wednesday as a way of saying thanks to Jake for helping find Igor.

And even though he and Arden spent the evenings together, Griff—for once in his life—didn't want to push too hard. With a month to go before Valentine's Day, he would prefer not to know if she thought of their relationship in terms of room, board and terrific sex. Not while he was doing whatever he could to transform their contract into commitment.

The weekend after Igor's great escape presented them the perfect opportunity to show off their "romance" at the Morgan's dinner dance, held in the country club. Griff was determined to be on his best behavior. No veiled insults or smart comments, no stalking out. No dagger-sharp looks. Just a polite evening spent being attentive to the woman he came with. The woman he loved.

Arden made that a simple task. She opened the door at the cottage wearing a close-fitting dress the color of thunderclouds, sprinkled with crystal beads like raindrops. "You look gorgeous," he said, after swallowing hard. "I'll be the envy of every man in the room."

She inclined her head with the grace of a princess. "Thank you, kind sir. You're dressed quite nicely as well. A dinner jacket becomes you."

"Maybe we'll win a trophy for Best Couture," he joked. "Or they'll name us king and queen of the ball."

She cleared her throat. "I think that position's already taken."

Griff snapped his fingers. "Oh, right. Zelda and Al are the guests of honor. We'll have to settle for second place."

Arden gazed at him for a moment. "I guess we will." A click of toenails at the end of the hallway advertised Igor's approach. "I'll put him in the sunroom and then I'm ready to go."

"He's holding a grudge," Griff said when she returned, wearing a black wool coat over her gown. "I still can't get near him without those lips curling."

"I know, and I'm sorry." She waited on the sidewalk as he opened the door of the Jag. "I guess he's just possessive."

It occurred to Griff to wonder how Igor would react to a baby as part of their household, but that would be the wrong question to ask at the beginning of the evening. And since the doctor had diagnosed Arden with the flu, there didn't appear to be anything to worry about on that score. Yet.

He had timed their arrival at the club a little on the late side, to avoid the possibility of encountering Zelda and Al without other people around. The line for valet parking moved smoothly tonight and they pulled right up to the entrance staircase.

"Trip Morgan was only a couple of years ahead of me in high school," Griff told Arden as they climbed the steps. "He's a big wheel with insurance, has an office in Atlanta and another one in Charlotte. His wife and Zelda are best friends."

The Morgans stood at the door to the ballroom. "Hey, Griff." Trip had a strong grip, which he practiced several times a week on the golf course. "Glad to have you back in town."

"Thanks. This is my friend, Arden Burke."

Trip's sandy eyebrows rose high on his forehead. "The pleasure is all mine, Miss Arden. Thank you for coming. Kayli, it's Griff and Arden Burke."

Ice coated his wife's greeting. "Welcome, Griff." Kayli offered her fingertips, but he'd barely touched them when she jerked her hand away. "It nice to meet you, Ms. Burke." Before Arden could smile, Kayli turned to the next person in line.

"Ouch," Arden said, moving away. "I believe I've developed frostbite."

"We could leave." Griff halted just inside the door. "You don't deserve that kind of treatment."

She shook her head. "We're here to show off, remember? Let's dance."

Her reference to their arrangement left him feeling cold, but he managed a bow. "Your wish is my command."

When they stepped onto the parquet dance floor, though, Arden melted into his arms and the world became a perfect place. "We'll just keep dancing all night," Griff said, putting his mouth close to her ear and inhaling the luscious scent she wore. "Maybe I can bribe the band to forget about their break."

Her silent chuckle rippled through him. "There are union rules, you know."

He hadn't, actually. "Mandatory breaks?"

"And Broadway shows are supposed to end before 11:00 p.m. It's in the actors' contracts."

"Now, why do you just happen to have these esoteric pieces of information in your brain?" Drawing back a little, he looked down at her. "Are you a former chorus girl? A closet stripper?"

"Nothing like that." This time, she laughed out loud. "Nothing at all."

They got two dances in before the dinner bell rang. Griff saw Kathy waving wildly at them from a table in the back corner. "I think we're sitting with my family." He walked Arden in that direction, noticing more than one appreciative male glance follow them. "One big happy family, isolated in the rear to avoid trouble."

"Shush," his mother told him, overhearing. "I'm assuming you're on good behavior tonight."

"I am." He seated Arden and then took his own chair. "Are we sure there won't be hemlock in the mashed potatoes?"

They all survived the meal, despite his dire expectations, and he raised his glass with goodwill for every single toast made to Zelda and Al. They could have a great life together, as far as he was concerned.

He'd intended to resume his nightlong dance with Arden when the band returned to the stage, but he looked around to see his dad pulling her chair back.

"Wait a minute," Griff protested. "She's my date."

Jake nodded. "And I'm cutting in, son. That's the way these social things work."

"Don't pout." His mother put her hand on his arm. "Dance with me instead."

"Nothing to pout about in that," he said, meaning every word. "After all, you taught me the steps. At least I'm tall enough to lead now."

Out on the floor, they glided past Arden and Jake.

"She looks beautiful," his mother said. "So elegant and graceful."

Griff steered past Jim and Kathy with a nod. "No arguments from me."

"And I might be mistaken, but you seem quite happy."

"I can't say no to that, either."

"Because of Arden, I gather?"

Griff grinned. "Ready for a dip?"

His mom smiled up at him and he bent close, supporting her back as she arched away. When they straightened again, a few bystanders applauded.

He grinned in that direction but continued dancing.

"Quite an evasive maneuver," his mother said. "But I won't forget the question just because you sent the blood rushing to my head. Is Arden Burke the woman of your future?"

Turning his head, he found her on the other side of the room, laughing at something his dad said. Could he trust in a future with Arden Burke? Could the desire they'd discovered blossom into something more for her, as it had for him?

"That's the plan, Mom." He prayed he was hiding the uncertainty chilling his insides. "Forever is what I'm shooting for."

Dr. Jake Campbell danced like a professional.

Arden knew she did not. "I apologize for stepping on your toes," she told him. "Dance lessons never showed up on my list of classes." In fact, band and dance music had played such a small part in her life that she could hear them without emotional qualms.

"What did you study?" Dr. Campbell's blue eyes, more incisive than Griff's, seemed to probe her soul.

"The usual," she said, trying to cover her mistake. "Math, science, history…"

"And did you specialize in college? Griff mentioned you attended a New York school."

"I didn't finish—didn't earn a degree." Which was the truth; her concert commitments had prevented her from completing her last year's course work. Her Julliard diploma had been an honorary award.

They danced in silence for a minute, and she began to hope the interview had ended. Knowing Griff, however, she wasn't surprised when his father didn't give up.

"So what exactly do you do with your life?"

She drew back to look into his face, which had much the same grooves as Griff, just more pronounced. "I'm sorry?"

"You don't have to earn a living." He eased her through a turn. "You live alone, except for the dog. Why do you get up in the morning?"

The breath she drew was shaky, but she fought to keep her voice steady. "I don't owe you an answer to that question."

"I'm curious," he said, still in the calm tone he'd been using, "since my son seems to be planning a future with you. What do you see yourself doing in a year, or five or ten?"

Tonight, she might be the one who walked out on the party. "I haven't thought that far ahead, Dr. Campbell. Griff and I are still getting to know each other." Would this music never end?

"I'm not sure he's been thinking much at all, lately."

Arden had finally caught her breath. "Or perhaps you simply dislike the fact that he's not following the path you laid out for him. That he's thinking about something other than what he can do for you."

Dr. Campbell grinned. "You have claws, I see. What's wrong with wanting to work with my son, taking care of the animals belonging to our friends and neighbors?"

"Nothing…unless Griff's interests lie in a different direction."

"And do they?"

"That's a question you should ask him."

He tilted his head, acknowledging that truth. "You're beautiful and intelligent, Arden Burke. But are you good for my son? Can the two of you create a successful partnership?"

At long last, the music slowed and crescendoed into a final chord. Arden stepped backward, almost surprised and definitely relieved when Dr. Campbell released her.

"Griff thinks so," she said, in answer to the last question. "Nothing else matters. Thank you for the dance."

Then she turned and left the ballroom, seeking what little privacy the restroom could offer.

Griff saw Arden back away from his dad. She crossed the dance floor with quick steps and disappeared through the door to the restroom.

When Jake returned to the table, Griff nudged Kathy out of her chair and took her place next to their dad. "What did you say to her?"

He shrugged. "I asked the standard father-in-law questions. Where are you from? Where are you going?"

"Nothing you say in this kind of situation is nearly so harmless. I don't want you threatening her, Dad. I won't stand for it."

From Jake's other side, Rosalie Campbell made a sound of protest. "You make him seem like an inquisitioner."

"Yes." Griff nodded. "I've talked to my brothers-in-law, if you haven't. He gave all three of them a pretty hard time, simply for having the temerity to want to marry his daughters."

"I have a responsibility to keep my kids safe," Jake said.

"You have a responsibility to allow us all to grow up. Stay out of this, Dad. Arden and I are doing fine without interference. If you've upset her in any way, I'll…"

His dad gave a tolerant—and somewhat condescending—smile. "You'll do what?"

Griff stood up. "I'll start thinking seriously about where else in the country Arden and I will be spending the rest of our lives."

He heard his mother's gasp, but walked away without looking back.

Instead of privacy, Arden found Lauren and Dana sitting in the lounge area of the ladies' room.

Dana looked up as she came through the door. "Oh, no. That bad, was it?"

Lauren, on the sofa, slid to the side. "Come sit," she said, patting the cushion beside her. "Dana, pour a glass of champagne."

Arden widened her eyes as Dana went to a sideboard along the wall and took a bottle from the wine cooler sitting there.

"Zelda's smart," Lauren remarked, holding out a glass for her sister to refill. "She knows we come here to relax away from our men."

"God bless them," Dana added, just as Kathy came through the door. "They're sweet and necessary, but sometimes they drive you nuts."

"Dad's special." Kathy dropped into the armchair and put her feet on the matching ottoman. "Where Jim can be annoying, even frustrating, Dad is…"

"Brutal?" Lauren suggested.

Dana shook her head. "That's a little harsh."

Lauren sipped her champagne. "Demanding isn't quite right."

"Arrogant, impertinent and intrusive." Arden swallowed a gulp of her champagne. Then caught her breath in case she'd insulted the man's daughters.

But the three sisters nodded. "That covers it," Kathy said. "You can be comforted by the fact that you haven't suffered alone. Jim didn't call me for a week after Dad had a talk with him."

"I had to track Gary down at his mother's house in Tennessee." Dana rolled her eyes. "He wasn't sure he wanted to come back."

Lauren put a hand on Arden's arm. "My Steve was a Marine, so he stood his ground. But he did say he'd never been so scared, and that I'd better be a good wife after what I'd put him through." She winked. "I proved it to him on our wedding night."

With champagne bubbles easing her tension, Arden was able to laugh with the other women. "I'm sure your dad is concerned about Griff's happiness." She got to her feet along with them. "But the decision belongs to Griff." A thought struck her. "Did your father interrogate Zelda, too?"

The Campbell sisters didn't know the answer to that question. As she prepared to return to the ballroom,

Arden had to wonder if Jake Campbell's interview with Zelda had anything to do with the broken engagement.

Stepping through the door into the hallway, she found Griff waiting just outside. "Are you all right?" He looked her over, took her hands in his, then released them and cupped her cheeks with his palms. "Did he give you a bad time? Tell me the truth."

She could tell him only some of the truth—as usual. "He was…inquisitive. And intimidating. But I'm fine, and we're wasting the music." Clasping his hand, she walked toward the ballroom. "Come on."

Before they could reach the dance floor, however, they encountered Zelda and Al, sharing what must have been a rare moment alone. Their romantic pose—she was straightening his tie as he brushed wisps of hair back from her face—daunted Arden.

But she and Griff couldn't turn back, couldn't change direction. She didn't even get the chance to glance at him to see his reaction.

"Hello again," Zelda said warily. Tonight's dress was pink. "Thanks for coming."

"It's a lovely event," Arden told her. "The champagne in the ladies' room is a brilliant idea."

Zelda's laugh sounded like treble bells ringing. "I think so. I've always wished someone would do that— so I did."

Al frowned at his fiancée. "What's the point of champagne in the restroom?"

"I don't get it, either," Griff said.

"It's a girl thing." Zelda patted Al's arm. "Don't worry about it. Let's go dance." She gave a little wave and led him toward the front of the room.

Arden looked at Griff, just behind her.

"Lead on," he said. "At least till we get the rhythm."

He wasn't as good a dancer as his father, but his arm fitted exactly right around her waist, and their hands clasped like two halves of a whole. Their steps blended and their bodies swayed with the same timing, the same *feel*.

Arden sighed and rested her head on Griff's shoulder. If she could trust, without reservation, only one person in the world, it had to be Griff Campbell. Honorable, conscientious, considerate and kind…what more could she ask of a man?

Great sex, she supposed. And Griff managed that feat, too.

As the evening wore on, they stopped occasionally to drink champagne or to chat with someone he knew, but never for more than one song. Older guests started to leave, but the younger crowd stayed on to dance. Fast numbers and slow ones, waltz, swing or rumba, Griff and Arden tried them all.

Until, around midnight, she had to admit her feet were giving out, and he confessed his bow tie was choking him. Leaving the dance floor, they found Trip Morgan and thanked him for his hospitality.

"One of the kids got sick," he told them, finishing off the last of what looked like a glass of bourbon on the rocks. "Kayli went home to take care of him. The story of my life." He poked a finger into Griff's chest. "Beware, my friend. The good days only last for a little while."

"That was either very profound," Griff said, once they were in the car, "or totally absurd."

"I vote for absurd." Arden wound his tie between

her fingers. "Your days are what you make them, good or bad."

An echo of Dr. Campbell's question came back to her. *What do you do with your life? Why do you get up in the morning?*

The man had a point. What had she accomplished in the last year? What would she accomplish in the years ahead?

Parking on the gravel drive in front of the cottage, Griff said, "Stay right there. Don't move."

Then he came around the back of the Jaguar, opened Arden's door and bent down. "Put your arms around my neck."

"You don't have to carry me in," she protested, laughing. "I can slip my shoes back on."

"Just wrap your arms around me." He scooped her up and lifted her out of the car. To save them both a fall, Arden did as he asked.

She also turned the doorknob so he could push through into the house. He shut the door behind them with one foot, but didn't set her down.

"I'm heavy," she murmured as he stood there. "You can't hold me forever."

"I think I could," he said quietly. "I want to." He kissed the top of her head, her temple, her cheekbone. Then Arden turned her face up so their lips could touch.

His arms tightened around her as he walked steadily down the hallway. She clung to his shoulders and gave herself up to the mouth plundering hers.

In the bedroom, he eased her bare feet to the floor. His hands moved over her body and her dress disappeared. Jacket, shirt, shoes, socks and pants followed, every layer between them stripped away.

"You are so much more than I imagined when we met," Griff said, stretching her arms above her head as she lay beneath him. "I never dreamed this would happen to me."

"Ah, Griff." She wanted to say the words, to share the feelings that seemed likely to tear her apart.

But the wildness took over then, and she could only gasp. Fireworks couldn't begin to describe the magic shooting through her. Exploding suns came closer to the mark.

When she could finally think again, when her body had relaxed and her brain reassembled, she turned her head to tell Griff what she felt.

Eyes closed, mouth open, he snored into her face.

But, thinking of champagne in the ladies' room, Arden simply smiled.

Chapter 11

As ordered, Arden visited Dr. Loft on Tuesday. She'd never thought about the need for vitamins *before* she got pregnant. Like most women, she wanted to do the best for her baby.

Whether that included keeping the child a secret from its father and other family members was a question she had begun to ask herself more often than was comfortable.

Dr. Loft's receptionist required her to fill out information forms, including past medical issues and current health. Arden found some of the questions painful to answer, but she told the truth. Doctors couldn't be lied to.

The exam was as careful and complete as Arden had expected. After giving her time to dress, Dr. Loft returned to the room and sat down on the rolling stool, then thumbed through the papers in her hand.

"You seem to be in good shape," she said. "No more dizziness or nausea?"

"Not at all."

"Good." Again, she referred to one of the forms Arden had filled out. "According to your history, you had a miscarriage a little over a year ago."

"Yes."

"That's too bad." The doctor followed up with other clinical questions. "And now you're trying to get pregnant again?"

"Yes."

"Well, then, I'd like to make a recommendation. Not a requirement, you understand. A precaution, at most. I'd like to refer you for an ultrasound exam of your abdomen."

"Why?"

"Since you've had one miscarriage, I'd like to be sure there are no problems with your reproductive system as you try to conceive again."

After scheduling the appointment for Friday, Arden left the office, but then sat in the car for a long time, trying to think.

Dr. Loft had been reassuring as she explained her reasoning. The fact remained that she believed there might be something wrong.

And the possibilities for Arden's future—dreams she'd just begun to believe in—had suddenly been called into doubt.

Saturday's brunch for the bride and groom took place at the Sheridan Fine Art Museum.

"Remarkable," Griff commented as they arrived, "for its total lack of any fine artwork."

Arden gave him a reproving glance. "Kathy brought me here earlier in the week. I thought there were some nice paintings and a couple of good sculptures."

"Exactly. 'Very nice' and 'good.' But not 'fine.'"

"This isn't New York, after all."

"You would know." He opened the door for her. "I'm still wondering about your mysterious past, by the way. Don't think I've forgotten."

"I wouldn't be so naive." Arden smiled at him, but he thought he saw shadows in her eyes. She'd been a little tense this week, distracted. He wondered what she could be thinking about. And he felt a little hurt that she still wouldn't confide in him. What did he have to do to prove she could trust him?

Standing in yet another receiving line, Griff congratulated himself on the plan to bring Arden to Sheridan as his fiancée. Once word got around, thanks to Zelda, and once his family had appeared to accept her, he hadn't had to deal with questions or sympathy. The plan they'd concocted together, on that beach four weeks ago, was working perfectly.

After waiting ten minutes, they finally stood near their hostess, Mrs. Hilary Crumpler.

"Zelda's great-aunt," Griff whispered. "Sheridan's social arbiter."

Arden frowned at him. "Thanks for the advance warning."

"I am simply devastated," Mrs. Crumpler was saying to the older lady in a pink dress in front of Arden. "Thirty minutes before my guests are due to arrive, the pianist calls to say he cannot perform—he has smashed his fingers in the car door. Can you imagine?"

"Oh, my dear." The woman pressed Mrs. Crumpler's

hand with both her own. "Such a tragedy. What will you do?"

"My husband is trying to set up some sort of recorded music, but…" She gave a disdainful shrug. "Not at all what I wanted." Then she turned toward Arden. "And how are you— Oh, my stars!"

Her gasp echoed off the marble floors of the museum entry hall. "I can't believe this." Somehow, she had grabbed Arden's hand and now held it tightly. "Arden Burke? *The* Arden Burke?"

"Yes." Arden stood as if paralyzed.

Griff stepped closer. "This is my fiancée—"

Their hostess brushed him away with a wave of her fingers. "I know who she is. I just never imagined, when I issued you an invitation—much against my inclinations, I must tell you, because I don't believe an ex-fiancé has any place at a bride's celebration of her wedding—as I say, I never could have imagined that your guest would be such a renowned young lady. I am so honored to meet you, my dear. I've attended many of your concerts, in New York and Washington and San Francisco."

Griff's stomach dropped into the soles of his feet. Concerts? San Francisco?

Mrs. Crumpler made a show of releasing Arden's hand. "I shouldn't hold your fingers so tightly, should I? We wouldn't want to damage these priceless instruments."

Arden took a long step back. Griff had never seen her so pale, even when she was sick. "Thank you for inviting me—"

"Oh, my dear, thank you for coming." A flirtatious look came over Mrs. Crumpler's face. "Can we dare ask you to play for us? What a delight, what an honor that would be, to hear an Arden Burke performance right here in Sheridan."

Arden shook her head. "I'm afraid I can't."

"Oh, please, Miss Burke, it would be the highlight of my entire year." The old bat actually had tears in her eyes.

"I'm sorry. I don't have my—my violin with me, Mrs. Crumpler."

Griff's memory flashed on the violin case he'd seen in the corner of the beach cottage. Then he heard an echo of Arden's denial that she was a musician.

Mrs. Crumpler sighed deeply. "Ah, such a tragedy. However, I have also heard you play the piano, and we do have one of those. Would you favor us with a few pieces?"

A resigned smile settled on Arden's face. "Of course."

The next hour tested Griff's patience and his temper. He called upon every ounce of good manners he possessed to refrain from biting people's heads off. He did not want to talk or eat or drink champagne punch. He certainly did not want to answer questions, accept compliments or, God forbid, make explanations.

He wanted to listen.

Seated at the piano, Arden paused for a few moments with her hands resting on her thighs, staring at the keys. When she lifted her head, she met Griff's gaze with an expression he couldn't read.

Then the music began. He didn't recognize the flood of notes pouring from the piano, but he knew a master composer when he heard one. Knew, as well, that Arden's performance was close to flawless. She didn't have a piano at the beach, in the Miami condo or here in Sheridan, so she couldn't have practiced for weeks. The woman had to be a musical genius.

He could only imagine what kind of artistry she would demonstrate with a violin.

Each time she came to the end of a selection, the audience applauded wildly. Cries of "More, please," came from every direction. Arden consented—first with a slow, dreamy piece followed by something fiery and brilliant—but then turned around and held up her hand.

"I'll play awhile longer," she announced, in a voice that carried throughout the museum, "but this is not a concert. Please feel free to enjoy the lovely brunch Mrs. Crumpler has provided and your chance to chat with the guests of honor, Zelda Talbot and Al McPherson, the bride and groom-to-be."

No one moved or spoke for a couple of seconds. Arden stared at them, frowning, and finally made a shooing motion. "Go talk among yourselves," she ordered.

With a general laugh, the guests broke into groups and conversation resumed, with a piano accompaniment. Now Griff recognized the tunes as popular ballads and show pieces—"easy listening music" played by a virtuoso.

"I can't believe it." Lauren came up on one side of him.

On the other side, Dana pinched his arm. "You never said a word."

Griff didn't look at either of them.

"Oh, my gosh," Dana whispered.

Lauren gripped his arm. "You didn't know?"

He didn't confirm or deny, and eventually they abandoned him to talk to the rest of his family.

But that left him prey to everyone else, and he couldn't refuse to talk, though he said as little as possible.

"Yes, she's terrifically talented."

"I'm very proud of her, of course."

"She, uh, wanted to remain incognito, since this is really the time we should be thinking about Zelda and Al. Have you talked to them today? They make a good couple. No, no hard feelings at all. Things work out for the best, don't they?"

When Al and Zelda came over, the conversation got stickier.

"She's quite a star," Zelda said, her eyes a little bright, her voice a little harsh. "Aunt Hilary's been filling me in."

Griff stayed silent, to avoid fueling the fire.

Al put his arm around his fiancée. "It's not that big a deal, Zel."

"Yes, it is." She clasped her hands together. "International concerts when she was nine years old. Julliard. Multiple recordings in the stores. Quite a phenomenon, Griff. You should have said something."

Hearing details he'd never known felt like getting slapped across the face. "I—"

But Zelda had more to say. "I was happy for you, knowing you'd found somebody to love after I canceled the wedding. You could have made me truly jealous, though, with this kind of news. Why wouldn't you want a…a superstar like Arden Burke? You must be so relieved I didn't hold you to *our* wedding."

This time it was Zelda leaving the room, brushing through the crowd without a word as she escaped.

Griff looked at Al. "Sorry."

"Yeah, sure." The groom took off after his runaway bride.

Arden stopped playing soon after that, and was immediately surrounded by the nosy and the purely complimentary. Griff retreated to the food table, consoling himself with smoked salmon sandwiches and lemon bar cookies.

"This is quite a surprise," his mother said, joining him. "Why do you suppose Arden didn't tell you any of this?"

"That," Griff said between gritted teeth, "is what I intend to find out."

Griff seemed his usual smiling self as they said goodbye to Mrs. Crumpler and suffered through her fulsome gratitude for the music.

As soon as the museum door shut behind them, however, his clasp on Arden's elbow turned to stone. A glance at his face showed her a steely glint in his eyes. She defined the way he closed her car door as a slam.

Well, she'd known for the last two hours this wouldn't be easy. "Griff—"

He held up a hand. "I'd rather not talk while I'm driving."

"Too bad," she told him. "I'm not a child who will be seen and not heard."

"That's pretty obvious."

"Why don't you just say what you're thinking?"

"Because I don't like to use that kind of language in front of females."

"Don't hesitate on my account."

"I'm not. I like to think of myself as a gentleman, that's all."

Arden decided then that she didn't want to talk to him, anyway.

But when she faced him on the cottage porch, planning to suggest they talk later, he shook his head.

"We're not putting this off any longer. It's time for the truth."

They confronted each other again across the living room, both standing behind a chair, both holding onto the back.

"So you're a violinist," Griff started. "A major talent, doing concerts all over the world when you were a child. Recording artist. Famous. You've eaten dinner and performed at the White House."

"Once. Ten years ago." She smiled, but he didn't.

"Why the big secret? Did you think I was too stupid to appreciate the facts?"

"No!" She pressed her fingers against her lips for a moment. "All of that is in the past, Griff. I retired at Christmas, a year ago. I don't perform, record or even practice anymore."

"Why?"

"Can we sit down?"

After a long moment, he dropped into the chair in front of him.

With a sigh, Arden eased into the armchair. Her back muscles had stiffened as she played. By now the stiffness had given birth to cramps. "About two years ago, reviewers of my performances started saying I was off pitch in the upper register. I wasn't hitting the highest notes exactly in tune."

He didn't comment, so she took a deep breath and continued. "I practiced more, tried different violins, took lessons, without results…until the day my teacher said, 'Hear that? It's terribly flat.' I realized I didn't hear the note at all. Except in my imagination.

"To make a long story short, I went to a specialist who determined I was…am…" She still hated the word. "I'm going deaf."

Leaning forward, Griff propped his elbows on his knees. "There's no solution?"

"Not in terms of the music. Hearing aids or cochlear implants can't restore the kind of acuity I need." Arden braided her fingers together. "The broken engagement occurred at the same time. I found myself a place to hide—Chaos Key—and I've been there ever since."

She couldn't tell him the rest. Not until she'd seen the doctor on Monday. She might have miscarried because she was defective. If babies were never going to be possible for her, that was something Griff should know.

"How long will you be able to hear?"

"I've lost most bird sounds in this last year, like that traffic chirp you noticed. I can't hear it at all. Crowds confuse me more than I remembered." She shrugged. "I probably have a few years of hearing left, perhaps not that long. Or perhaps I'll only lose a percentage, then stabilize. The doctors don't know and can't predict."

He fell back into the chair. "But why hide who you are? I don't understand that part."

She opened her hands in a helpless gesture. "I really didn't think it mattered. I'm not that person anymore—I don't perform or record or have anything to do with music. So why bring it up? Besides…" She owed him this much, at least. "Talking about the music would require explaining why I don't play. I didn't want to reveal that part."

"Why would it make a difference? Especially after

you found out about Kathy, I would think you'd see it's not a problem."

"Kathy's hearing loss had a cause. Mine could be… genetic. They don't really know."

"But what…" Griff frowned at her for a minute. Then his puzzlement cleared. "A baby. You thought…" He pressed the heels of his hands against his eyes. "You thought I wouldn't want you to have my child if I knew you were…were going deaf."

Arden couldn't look at him any longer. She nodded, staring at her hands twisting in her lap.

"I guess that makes sense. We did have an agreement. You wouldn't want to jeopardize your payout." He dropped his own hands to the arms of the chair. "This has all been about making a baby for you. I should've remembered." Shaking his head, he gave a harsh chuckle. "Instead, I've made a fool of myself. Again."

Three weeks before Zelda's wedding, the Campbell clan gathered for dinner on Sunday night—just the immediate family—to celebrate the first ultrasound of Kathy's baby. Seated around the big dining room table, they passed the print of the scan from hand to hand, making comments that ranged from the ribald to the ridiculous. Rosalie wiped tears from her eyes with her napkin. Jake brought out champagne to toast the new Campbell son. Kathy's baby was, very definitely, a boy.

Griff had escorted Arden from the cottage, of course. They were, in the eyes of his family, an engaged couple with a shared future ahead of them. And they'd become very good at keeping up the pretense. In public.

In private, their relationship had taken a long step backward. Those rules they'd talked about in the beginning—no prying, no confessions—were back in full force.

Tonight, Arden seemed even quieter than usual. She held the ultrasound print for about five seconds before passing it on to Dana, on her other side, without comment. Then she looked down at her plate again.

Following her gaze, Griff saw that she only toyed with her roast chicken. He put an arm along the back of her chair and leaned close to speak into her ear. "Feeling okay?"

She nodded without looking at him. "Fine."

He couldn't confront her about that lie in front of the family. Later, when they walked out to the cottage, he tried.

"What were you thinking," he asked, as they lingered on the porch, "when you were looking at the ultrasound?"

"I don't know." She glanced away from him. "Cute, sweet…the usual."

Griff turned her around with a hand on her shoulder. "I don't think so. More like, 'How will I survive the next hour until I can be alone?'"

"Not at all."

"You wore that exact same look when we left the little girl with her mother at the mall. The one you found under the rack of coats. It was as if something terribly precious had been taken from you."

She walked to the end of the porch. "I want a child, you know that. Seeing other people's babies, I—I have to work hard not to be jealous."

Griff went to stand behind her, and couldn't resist closing his arms around her. "You'll have a baby of your own soon enough." His laugh sounded harsher than he intended. "We're working on it. That was part of the deal, remember?"

She moved, turning to face him. Her expression was a portrait of despair. "Yes. I remember."

Then her hands linked behind his neck and pulled his head down. Their mouths met, fused, consumed.

Once they made it inside the house, the sex was hotter than ever.

Arden arrived at Dr. Loft's office with time to spare, but then had to wait for an hour, due to the doctor's attendance at an emergency. Between trying not to think about the reason she was there in the first place and worrying about what the doctor might have to say, she had reached a high state of tension by the time her name was called.

Waiting another thirty minutes in the small examining room didn't help, even though she didn't have to take off any of her clothes this time. Arden couldn't read, couldn't concentrate, couldn't relax. She could only sit and fret.

Finally, a knock on the door preceded the doctor's entrance. "Hi, Arden." Dr. Loft smiled widely. "I'm glad to see you because I have good news."

Arden sat up straighter. "Really?"

"The ultrasound looks great," she said. "No adhesions or blockages, no inflammation, nothing that should prevent a normal pregnancy from coming to term."

"What...what about the other baby?" Arden asked in a low voice.

"We often don't know why a baby is lost. Stress, or a defect in the fetus itself...there's no easy way to tell.

But what I can say is that you're in good shape, and I see no reason you shouldn't have a healthy baby soon. It's just a matter of time."

Arden lifted her shoulders, making room for the deep breath she pulled in. "I'm glad to hear it."

"I'm sure you are." The doctor rose from her stool. "I'll get you a prescription for prenatal vitamins, and you can call to set up a test when you think you might be pregnant."

"One more thing." Arden clenched her hands into fists.

Dr. Loft turned with her hand on the doorknob. "What's that?"

"I'd like to get fitted with a diaphragm. For birth control."

Chapter 12

It had been one hell of a week.

Now that Griff had returned, his dad increased the surgery load at the clinic and okayed a heavier appointment schedule on Mondays, Wednesdays and Fridays, with farm visits set up for Tuesdays and Thursdays. Emergencies, as always, got fitted in immediately.

As a result, the workday stretched until seven-thirty or eight, or even later if a patient needed supervision or a farm emergency required more time. Griff spent all Tuesday night at the clinic, treating a collicking pony. If the pony hadn't cleared his intestinal blockage by noon on Wednesday, the owners would have had to take him to the state university for surgery. Wednesday included two spays and three castrations, plus six regular appointments every hour.

Griff called Arden on the drive home, explaining

that he'd sleep in his own room at his parents' house rather than disturb her. But he hadn't made it past the couch in the den before collapsing, asleep before he hit the cushions.

Tonight, Friday, his sisters had abducted Arden for the evening, citing "girl stuff." Griff hated to think what that might mean, other than he wouldn't be able to spend the evening making love to his "fiancée." Sex was the only way they could really communicate anymore.

And he hated to waste the whole night at home alone. He wasn't in the mood for a bar or a restaurant filled with strangers, so he decided to check in at the country club. Not his usual hangout, but he would probably see somebody he knew to talk to.

Wearing the required jacket, though not the optional tie, he strolled into the club as if he spent every Friday night there.

"Good evening, Dr. Campbell." The manager, who'd been there as long as Griff could remember, stepped out of his office to shake hands. "We're glad you stopped by. Can I get you a table in the dining room?"

"Thanks, Harris. I thought I'd just eat in the lounge, if that's okay."

"Of course. I'll send Thomas in to take your order."

The General's Den, as the lounge was called, had once been the bastion of the male members of the club, a center of social intercourse on evenings and weekends. There wasn't much of a crowd these days, but Griff said hello to the three patrons present, all of them his dad's age, then settled into a secluded corner seat with a view of the basketball game on TV, and a tall, cold beer.

As he ate, he gradually picked up on the unmistakable sounds of a party coming from down the hallway.

"Hey, Vince, what's going on?" he asked, when the bartender brought a refill for his beer. "Sounds like a frat mixer."

Vince rolled his eyes. "More or less the same thing. It's a bachelor party for Al McPherson, in the club room. Open bar plus kegs of beer. We'll be hauling them out in wheelbarrows."

Griff didn't comment. To himself—and to Arden, if the subject arose—he would admit that he missed his best friend and hated knowing that he couldn't be Al's best man. Not that they'd ever thought in those terms... until Griff and Zelda had gotten engaged.

But maybe Al was already in love with Zelda at that point, and hated the assumption that he would be the best man. When had things changed among the three of them? How, Griff wondered, had he missed the signs?

As he indulged in the club's signature dessert—banana bread pudding—he watched a giant cardboard mock-up of a wedding cake roll past the door of the lounge, complete with lacy "icing" on the sides, plus a pair of dolls in wedding dress on top.

"The strippers," Thomas said, taking away Griff's empty plate. He was only about seventeen, still young enough to grin when he added, "Wish I could be in there when they jump out."

"You'll get your chance." Griff made a mental note not to attend his own bachelor party, should there be one. There was only one woman in the world he wanted to see naked, and she didn't jump out of cardboard cakes. Thank God.

Inevitably, Al's party spilled out of the club room. Inebriated revelers, most of them friends or acquaintances of Griff's, wandered into the lounge to watch the ball game and harass the bartender. The older patrons soon abandoned the scene, but Griff couldn't resist remaining as an observer. None of the drunks had noticed him. As long as he kept his mouth shut, he wouldn't get into trouble.

Then Al wove his way into the room. He patted a few backs, called for a double whiskey, neat, then turned around and fixed his bleary gaze on Griff's face.

"You," he said loudly. "What're you doin' here?"

Griff got slowly to his feet. He kept his voice down, as he did when he talked to Igor. "Leaving."

But his old friend stepped in front of him. "Runnin' away again?"

"My specialty."

"No, your specialty is screwing up my life."

"Don't do this," Griff begged. "Let it go."

That wasn't going to happen. Al had always brooded over his hurts, then exploded to release the pressure. "Do you know how long it took her to get over you leaving? Huh? It was six weeks before she'd talk to me on the phone."

Leaning against the wall, Griff folded his arms. Maybe the solution was to let him talk it out.

"Then I finally got her to say yes, plan a wedding, get started on our life together and what happens? You show up again. Only this time…" He wiped a hand over his face. "This time, you bring another woman with you…one who has every guy in town panting over her."

Behind Al, the lounge had gone quiet, except for the TV. So they all heard Griff when he said, "Shut up, McPherson. Not another word."

But Al wasn't listening. "And Zelda goes crazy. Absolutely insane. 'He wants me to be sorry,' she says.

'He's trying to make me jealous.' And damn if it didn't work. I couldn't—"

"That's enough." Griff grabbed him by the shoulders, turned him around and pushed him toward the door. "The party's over for you, buddy. You're going home."

They got as far as the entry hall before Al recovered his balance and his instinct for self-defense.

"Oh, no, you don't. I'm not lettin' you order me around." He pivoted, then started swinging.

Griff ducked, but didn't hit back. "Give it up, Al. You never could beat me in a—"

He saw the last punch coming, but reacted a second too late. Knuckles slapped into flesh. Pain bloomed on the side of his head from ear to nose.

What he hadn't counted on was the shove in the chest that followed, and the crack of his skull against the floor.

Or the black hole he fell into after that.

Arden had accepted Kathy's invitation to join the Campbell sisters' "girls night out" for only one reason—by going, she could avoid an entire Friday evening alone with Griff.

His hectic week at the office had worked to her advantage, because he'd been too tired in the evenings to do much more than eat dinner and go to bed. He certainly hadn't been his usual eagle-eyed, perceptive self.

She believed she could hide the truth from his sisters, too. Especially since Kathy had promised champagne as the drink of choice for the evening. A glass or two would keep Dana and Lauren from noticing anything off in Arden's mood. And she figured she'd get a boost of her own from the bubbly, at least enough to evade Kathy, who would be staying sober because of her baby.

Then she walked into Kathy's charming bungalow and found that girl's night included Griff's mother, which created a much more dangerous situation. She might not be as insightful as her husband, but any hint of a threat to Griff's welfare would put her on alert.

"I'm sorry I'm late," Arden said as she gave Kathy her coat. "I missed a couple of turns." Because she'd been musing over her deception with Griff rather than watching where she was going.

"Arden." Rosalie Campbell caught her hands and squeezed. "I just got here myself. I'm so glad you decided to come."

"Champagne," Kathy said, offering a glass to each of them. "Dana and Lauren are already ahead of you. Drink up."

Once they were all seated in the living room, the conversation developed in a predictable direction.

"I haven't had a chance to talk to you this week," Rosalie began. "Semester exams are as onerous for the teachers as they are for students. And I haven't seen Griff at all. But I'm still fielding questions about you from everybody in town. You're a concert violinist, and you never said a word? I'm just so amazed. And delighted, of course."

Arden took a gulp of champagne. "Mrs. Campbell, I know you must feel I've been deceptive—"

Dana nodded. "Dad stomped around all day Sunday, muttering, 'I knew she was hiding something. I knew it.'"

Rosalie gave her daughter a disapproving glance.

"That's overstating the case. But…why, Arden? Did you have a reason for keeping your career a secret?"

She explained about her retirement. "You saw what happens when people learn that I play," she said. "And, really, it's pretty painful to have given up what was once my entire life."

The four women nodded in sympathy.

"I avoid most music," she told them honestly. "I'd rather not have to think about what I can no longer do. It's not a good coping mechanism, I admit. Perhaps I can improve with time."

Lauren, sitting beside Arden on the couch, put a hand over hers. "I do understand. I used to play basketball— I had a college scholarship and just knew I could lead a championship team. Then I blew out my knee in a skiing accident. I haven't watched a basketball game since. It would hurt too much."

"Exactly." Arden breathed a sigh of relief. Her story had been accepted. "Keeping the secret avoids situations like last weekend, where I can't get out of performing."

Then Kathy spoke up. "But why did you stop playing? What caused you to retire?"

After drawing a deep breath, she explained about her hearing loss.

"Now I understand." Griff's mother nodded. "And I'm sure Jake will, as well. There have been times when he asked me not to mention his profession at a party or in a crowd. People try to get him to deliver a diagnosis in the middle of dinner."

"You play the piano beautifully, of course." Rosalie brought up the subject again as they gathered around the dining room table to fill their plates from a buffet of Kathy's favorite appetizers. "Couldn't you have continued your career with that instrument?"

The question required more creative truth telling. "I don't have a professional repertoire on the piano." Pretending a calm she didn't feel, Arden spooned artichoke dip onto her plate and added crackers. "I couldn't compete at the same level as before."

"But you would still have your music."

"Perhaps I can move in that direction. But my retirement occurred at the same time as my broken engagement. There was just too much to deal with."

"How awful." Griff's mother folded her into a hug. "You went through a terrible time, didn't you? And call me Rosalie," she whispered. "It's past time I said that."

Blinking back tears, Arden set her plate on the table and rested her hands on Rosalie's shoulders, gingerly returning the embrace. She couldn't remember the last hug she'd received from her own mother.

While they ate chicken Kiev and wild rice for dinner, the conversation became more general, and Arden found herself diverted for minutes at a time from her preoccupation with a barren future. The champagne did seem to help, and she allowed herself to drink more freely than usual. After all, she didn't have to worry about harming a baby anymore.

Once they'd each had a substantial helping of Kathy's "better than sex" cake, they relaxed again in the living room with refilled glasses of wine.

"I had an ulterior motive for asking y'all over tonight," Kathy announced.

Dana groaned. "I am not scrubbing your kitchen floor."

"And don't put me down for the bathrooms, either," Lauren said.

"Of course not." Kathy frowned at her sisters. "You two wouldn't get anything clean enough to suit me."

A sisterly pillow fight ensued, as the girls threw couch cushions back and forth, while Arden and Rosalie ducked, laughing.

Kathy stockpiled the pillows thrown at her behind her chair, where no one could reach them. "Mom, could you bring out the books?"

Rosalie went to a closet, returning with large, flat volumes of wallpaper samples, plus thick piles of fabric swatches.

Kathy looked at Arden. "My Jimmy is totally color-blind. Ask him how a room looks, and he says 'Fine, darlin'. Do these socks match?' And of course they don't, because one is blue and one is green. So when I decorate, I have to solicit other opinions. And now that I'm getting into the fourth month with Junior here—" she placed a hand on the slight mound at her waist "—I thought I'd start getting ideas on the nursery. So tonight we're havin' a decor orgy, so to speak. Dig in, girls, and show me what works for you."

With cries of delight, Lauren and Dana slid from their chairs to the floor and began leafing through wallpaper pages. Rosalie started with fabrics. The samples, mostly from children's collections, featured animals of every description, toys, clouds, clowns, castles and farms, cities and parks, fields and mountains, printed in colors from pastel to bold and bright, in every imaginable style and design.

Arden reached for a wallpaper book, then drew back her hand and finished her glass of champagne instead.

She tried looking over Rosalie's shoulder, but her heart twisted at visions of fluffy lambs printed on pale aqua cotton, bunnies on pink, bears on yellow.

The cover of the book at her feet caught her attention—a fully decorated nursery, all white furniture with red, yellow and blue striped fabrics on the bed and at the windows. Above a white chair rail, the wallpaper featured balloons in those same colors floating merrily through the sky. Below the rail, a wallpaper mural depicted a little town with shopping district and offices, neighborhoods and churches, a big park and outlying farms and fields with horses and cows—a child's world on the walls.

And in the center of this perfect room sat a happy, dark-haired mother holding a little boy with blond curls and blue eyes.

Arden stared at the picture, losing awareness of anything happening around her as she drowned in what-might-have-been.

"Honey, are you okay?" Rosalie set a hand over the fists Arden had clenched in her lap.

Looking up, Arden found the three sisters staring at her, too.

"What's wrong?" Kathy crouched in front of her. "Are you sick?"

In the next moment, the phone rang, and Arden was saved by the bell.

Once his dad arrived at the hospital, Griff wasn't surprised to see his mother show up.

But he was somewhat startled when, one after the other, his sisters, their husbands *and* Arden entered the emergency room cubicle.

"You all didn't have to come down here," he protested. "I told Dad he shouldn't have called. I was out for only a few seconds."

"More like ten minutes," Jake growled. "The folks at the club called the ambulance."

Lauren, Dana and Kathy took up one side of the bed, with their men and his parents on the other. Arden stood at the end, looking pale and frightened.

He ached to get his arms around her and chase the shadows from her eyes.

First, he had to answer all the questions, including what happened? Who did this? Why? What did you say? What did he say? Why didn't somebody else stop him? Why did you try?

And he had to deal with his dad's anger. "I'm going to tan that boy's backside when I get hold of him."

"You're going to stay away from Al if Mom has to tie you in a chair," Griff told him. "Leave him alone, all of you. Zelda, too. We need to stay out of their way until the wedding."

His mother nodded in approval, but the girls took more convincing.

Kathy propped her hands on her hips. "She dumped you, and I think a little suffering is good for her."

"She's suffered," Griff said. "At least as much as I have. And Al's had the worst of it."

"They could have let you know sooner," Dana said. "They embarrassed all of us, waiting till the last minute."

"Not to mention how hard you worked on the house, only to sell it." Lauren shook her head. "I painted and wallpapered. I put a lot of work into those walls."

"I know you did." Griff grabbed her hand. "But it's

over and done, and we need to forget. Let's think about the future." He looked at Arden as he said that, but she avoided his eyes.

"So, can you leave now?" Kathy asked. "You don't have to spend the night, do you?"

"Waiting on test results," his dad said. "Then they'll let us know."

The doctor did a double take when he came in a few minutes later. "Did I miss the reunion announcement?"

"Just the standard family conference," Griff announced. "So, can I leave?"

"The CT scan looks good. Do you have someone who can keep an eye on you overnight?"

Nine people in the room nodded.

The doctor surveyed the group of them, then turned back to Griff. "I guess you're covered. I'll sign your release papers."

"Thanks," he said, offering a handshake as his sisters hugged each other and everyone else. "I told you I was fine."

"Better safe than sorry." The doctor waved as he left. "Enjoy the reunion."

The argument over where he would spend the night might have lasted until dawn if his mother hadn't spoken up.

"Griff has a very capable woman to look after him tonight. He doesn't need his sisters—"

"Though he loves them," Griff interjected.

"—or his parents. Arden will make sure he's alive and kicking tomorrow morning."

Jake was still protesting as Rosalie pushed him out of the room. "You're the one who sent him to the woods at age fifteen to live off the land for two days. Don't try to coddle him now."

She came back to the bed and bent over to kiss Griff's cheek. "I'm glad to see you've learned so much in these last six months," she said quietly. "I'm proud of you."

And she stopped by Arden as she left. Griff couldn't hear what she whispered, but saw Arden nod.

Then, finally, they were alone. "Come here," he said, sitting up on the side of the bed and holding out his arms.

After hesitating a moment, she walked over to wrap her arms around his waist.

Griff sighed. A truce, of sorts.

"I'm glad you're okay." She rubbed her forehead against his shoulder. "I can't believe Al pushed you like that. Isn't that dirty fighting?"

"I think it's mostly called drunk and disorderly." Griff took a deep breath, drawing in crisp, floral perfume, creamy shampoo, almond lotion and lavender sachets, plus the unique essence of the woman herself. "Let's go home."

At the cottage, he insisted on taking Igor for a walk while Arden got ready for bed. "Fresh air cures everything," he said, when she argued with him.

"Except frostbite," she retorted.

Griff found himself grinning at her. "I won't be gone that long."

When he returned to the bedroom, the lights were already off—not Arden's usual style. The bed was empty, but a crack of light showed under the bathroom door. Not sure what message he was supposed to be getting, he donned his sweatpants and a T-shirt before climbing between the sheets.

She turned the bathroom light off before opening the door, and crossed the room in darkness. When he reached for her, she didn't turn away.

"Arden," he whispered, tracing the contours of her waist, her hips and thighs with his palms. "We don't have to be so angry."

"No." Her lips played with his earlobe. "We don't."

Saying "I love you," though, was simply too hard. Using the words, even in a pitch-dark room, required more pride than he could risk.

And so they spent another wordless night together, connected in every way…except the one that mattered most.

Chapter 13

Arden spent the two weeks before Zelda and Al's wedding playing her part as Griff's devoted fiancée—it was, she knew, all she would ever have of him.

They went to church together, to the movies and to the local flea market on Saturday morning. They rode Dorsey and Cowboy on Sunday afternoons. Frequent invitations for dinner with some of his friends and their wives filled their evenings, until they could return to the cottage and spend the dark hours making love. Those nights might have been why Griff was so tired most days at work. Neither of them would have traded sex for sleep.

They were getting along better, on the surface, at least. They could laugh together, and share jokes. Of course, Arden was all too aware of the secrets she continued to keep from him. And despite his efforts, Griff obviously couldn't forget the secrets she'd revealed. With such distrust between them, Arden sensed she wouldn't be staying in Georgia much longer.

Her last lunch with the Campbell sisters took place on the Wednesday, before Zelda's wedding, again at Pirouette. No slippery asphalt marred the occasion— the sun shone and a temperature above sixty degrees allowed them to sit at a table on the terrace.

Arden did her best not to think of this as a farewell luncheon, though she didn't expect to see any of them in private again. The four of them laughed throughout the meal, and she thought she'd been keeping up appearances quite well.

Once Lauren and Dana had left to return to work, however, Kathy leaned her elbows on the table and propped her chin on her fists. "I've been dying to talk to you for days. I'm so glad I finally got the chance."

Arden had wondered if she would have to account for the way she'd broken down at Kathy's "decor orgy." She was surprised when none of the Campbell women had brought up the subject.

And Kathy had evidently moved on. "Since you told us about your hearing loss, I've wanted to share some thoughts with you. There are programs that provide assistance for partially or completely deaf kids so they can go to regular public schools. You would make a terrific volunteer—an example of what can be accomplished despite this disability."

Arden tried to be polite. "Thanks, but—"

"Another idea I had was music appreciation classes for children with partial deafness—you could help them experience the sounds to the extent of their ability, help them physically sense the vibrations, that sort of thing. What do you think?"

Arden thought she might faint, because she couldn't get a decent breath. As Kathy spoke, some kind of weight seemed to have settled in Arden's chest, compressing her lungs.

In all the months since she'd first heard the word *deaf* applied to herself, Arden had tried to distance herself from that fact. She'd arranged her life so she didn't really need to hear to get along. No one spoke to her, the dog didn't bark—the world could become totally soundless without affecting her in the least.

Then Griff had arrived, bringing with him relationships and conversation and music, damn him. She'd learned to talk to people, to enjoy them, to actually forget the defect that had so diminished her existence.

And now Kathy wanted her to *use* that flaw? To *celebrate* her disability as a model of how to cope? To pretend she didn't wake every morning in despair because she couldn't hear the birds sing?

"I—I'll think about it," she managed to say without screaming. "It's an…an interesting idea." She grabbed the check off the table. "I'll take care of this, but I have to be…somewhere in just a few minutes." Leaning in, she kissed the air beside Kathy's cheek. "Take care."

That was one lesson Griff hadn't needed to teach her, Arden decided, driving out of Sheridan at a speed considerably over the legal limit.

How to run away.

On Thursday afternoon, Griff found himself returning to the office from a farm call on the same side of town where the house he'd once owned was located.

Out of curiosity, he took the still-familiar turns leading to his former address. He intended just to see the place and how it was being taken care of, and then drive on.

The first change he noted was color—he'd painted the siding a soft yellow and the shutters bright blue, but the new owner had wanted a mellow green with white. Even in winter, he could tell the landscaping had been improved, with trees and shrubs enhancing what had once been a plain grass lawn. But then, he'd planned for Zelda, with her green thumb, to design the plantings after their wedding.

A car sat in the driveway, a silver compact similar to the make Zelda drove. As Griff approached, he realized it wasn't just similar—it was the exact car Zelda drove. Then he glanced at the mailbox—a bigger and prettier style than the one he'd put up. Lettered on the side was the last name of the residents: McPherson.

Griff slammed on the brakes and stopped the SUV beside the driveway, shut off the engine and stalked to the front door. Pushing the bell with one finger, he didn't release the pressure.

As the door opened, an irritated woman's voice said, "I hear you, I hear you. My goodness, what is your—" Zelda stood on the other side of the screen, staring at him. "What do you want?"

At that moment, he saw honest fear in her eyes. Zelda, the girl he'd known since grade school, could actually believe he might hurt her.

His anger leached away. Shoulders slumped, he blew out a breath. "I drove by to see the place, then realized you were living here. I only want to talk, Zelda. Can I come in?"

Because she knew him, she could recognize the change in his feelings. "Sure, Griff. Come on in."

The living room contained furniture—some of which he recognized from Zelda's old apartment—and boxes. "We're still moving stuff in," she explained, gathering wrapping tissue off a chair so he could sit down.

"You haven't been living here since... June?"

She sat down on the coffee table, the paper clutched in her lap. "No. I—I couldn't."

"I see." No wonder Al had been so worked up. "I didn't know the name of the buyer. I just got a check from the lawyer. So I was surprised when I saw the mailbox."

"Your family didn't tell you?"

Griff shook his head. "Maybe they thought I knew. Maybe I should have—I wasn't paying too much attention back then."

Zelda nodded. "I didn't tell people around here for a long time."

"But why would you and Al want to live here? Why not get a house I had nothing to do with?"

She hugged the paper in her arms a little tighter. "We missed you, Griff. Both of us, all the time. We betrayed you, and yet we still loved you and wanted you in our lives."

Hard stuff to hear. Griff gripped his hands together between his knees, staring at the floor.

"Al found the house first, saw it was for sale and told me about it. I came by myself and I just about died, seeing all the work you'd done for me. So Al and I decided we owed it to you to live here."

Griff looked up. "You do know that's weird, right? I mean, you came here to tell me you wouldn't marry me, and now you'll be living here with the guy you dumped me for. It doesn't really make a lot of sense."

"Probably not." Zelda's smile was sad. "I always loved you, Griff. I always loved Al, too. You asked me out first, he stepped aside, and everything just kind of flowed from there. I flowed with it."

"So what went wrong?"

She sighed. "Being with you, Griff, takes so much energy. Mental, emotional, physical—I always felt like I was falling behind. Always running to catch up. It's nothing you do or say—just the way you are. Al and I move at the same pace. We're not so brilliant, not as dynamic or exciting as you are. But we fit." Her smile was a little bit wicked. "Boy, do we fit."

"I'm glad," Griff said, from his heart. "I want you to be happy."

"I know you do." She let the paper fall to the floor and came to stand in front of him, holding out her hands. "I am sorry we hurt you so badly. I should have known my own mind a long time before I did. But weddings take on a life of their own—you get so wrapped up in the process you don't look ahead to the final result. I didn't, anyway, until almost too late."

Grasping her hands, Griff stood up. "What happened?"

"Your dad came to see me one afternoon."

"My dad?" Griff released her and started to pace. "My dad is the reason you broke up with me?"

"No. Well…" Zelda flushed when he stopped to stare at her. "He just talked, Griff, about marriage being a big challenge, needing all that two people can give to each other. And when I thought about it, I knew I wasn't enough for you."

"That's not what I thought."

"But I did, and so it would have mattered one way or the other. Then Al caught me speeding one day, out on Old Orchard Road. He actually gave me a ticket!" She laughed, still obviously delighted. "On the ticket form, he wrote, 'It's not too late. Marry me, instead.'"

Griff laughed, too. "Good for Al. He knew what he wanted and he went for it." Then Griff looked down at her. "You have my best wishes for a happy life, Zelda. God bless you both."

"Thank you." She pulled his head down. "Here's your kiss from the bride."

Her lips touched his briefly, with absolutely no sparks. He hugged her, recognizing the rebirth of friendship from the ashes of a romance.

The front door slammed open. "Get your hands off my wife," Al declared. "You can't have her."

Griff did as ordered. "I don't want her." He glanced at Zelda. "With apologies, you understand."

She stood with her hands on her hips, facing her fiancé. "I understand someone's being a jerk. Stop it, Al."

Al wasn't listening. He headed for Griff, hands up and ready to grapple.

"Not this time, buddy." Griff sidestepped. "The back of my head still hurts."

A couple of quick moves he'd learned in the islands swept Al's feet out from under him and dropped him hard onto his back, knocking the breath out of him.

"I owed you that," Griff said. "Be grateful for the carpet. You can apologize in the receiving line at the reception." He stepped over Al on his way to the door. "Congratulations, by the way. You've got a beautiful bride." He pulled the door closed behind him on the way out.

"I wish I could say the same," he muttered to himself. And then sighed.

Arden awoke smiling on Valentine's Day, thinking of the sensuous night just past and inhaling the delicious aroma of coffee.

"Happy Valentine's Day." Griff sat down on the bed beside her and leaned over to give her a coffee-flavored kiss. "Don't get up. I'm ready to leave."

"Too bad. We could have breakfast in bed. Again." They'd spent all of the rainy Sunday just past exactly that way. "Is the weather better?"

"Still raining, and spitting snow. Not quite what you hope for on your wedding day." He kissed her again and stood up. "I'll see you this afternoon. Dad kept the surgery schedule light and there are no appointments after three, so I have a good chance of actually making it to the wedding by six."

His well-laid plans fell apart when a prize mare on the far side of the county had trouble giving birth. Griff called Arden on his way out, predicting he would return in plenty of time to dress and drive her to the wedding.

He called again with twenty minutes to spare, telling her to go on without him.

Finally back at the cottage, he hurried into his dress pants, then went to the bathroom to shave. Arden must have waited until the very last moment before getting ready, and she'd left more of a clutter than usual—her makeup bag, cosmetics and hair tools littered the counter.

Griff pulled out the electric razor to give his jaw a

smooth finish, surveying the feminine disarray as he worked. A rolled up tube—obviously not toothpaste—caught his eye.

The label stopped his heart for several seconds.

Spermicidal lubricant.

He flipped off the razor and looked at himself in the mirror. "Now why would you be trying to kill the little buggers if you wanted to make a baby?"

After waiting as long as she dared, Arden reached the church just before the grandmothers of the bride and groom were to be seated. The Campbells filled up an entire pew, so she sat alone, farther back, leaving space for Griff on the aisle.

When she'd confessed that she'd never attended a wedding, Griff had enacted for her, in hilarious detail, the traditional Southern marriage service. She now felt quite prepared to enjoy every aspect of Zelda and Al's ceremony.

Especially since she would not be having one of her own.

The church, dating from before the Civil War, was lit by candles and filled with large arrangements of white lilies and gladiolas accented with red roses. The customary tune of Wagner's "Wedding Chorus" played quietly as Zelda's attendants came down the center aisle, each dress a slightly deeper shade of pink than the last, until Kayli Morgan appeared as the matron of honor, wearing a true, deep red. The five of them made a lovely gradient effect at the front of the sanctuary, balanced on the other side by Al's friends, all wearing black tuxedos with red and pink roses in their lapels.

Zelda's entrance was heralded by trumpets from the

organ and a sudden crescendo. She wore a lovely, full-skirted dress, with a long veil over her face, and carried a trailing white bouquet.

Griff slipped into the pew beside Arden a moment before the minister started to speak. He gave her a tired grin, then took her hand and directed his attention to the bride and groom.

So here they were. They'd accomplished what he'd set out to do six weeks ago—project the image of a successful and satisfied man as he returned to his hometown. She'd fulfilled her side of the agreement and given him an adoring girlfriend to show off. No one had expressed the least doubt about their relationship. She could go back to Chaos Key with pride in a job well done.

And if her heart was broken, that wasn't Griff's fault. He'd done absolutely everything a man could to make her happy. The flaw was hers. And she would bear the cost alone.

The marriage ceremony took only minutes, which seemed odd given the amount of time spent planning and anticipating it. Al and Zelda faced each other, holding hands, as the minister asked the standard questions. "Do you take this man…for better or worse, richer or poorer…as long as you both shall live?" After the vows, Al and Zelda lit a candle together, then knelt while the minister prayed. And then came the official pronouncement: "Ladies and gentlemen, I am pleased to present to you Alexander and Zelda McPherson."

Mendelssohn's triumphant recessional rang through the church. Audience members rose to their feet as Al and Zelda returned along the aisle, smiling widely and greeting people on either side. The bridesmaids and groomsmen followed, creating a brushstroke effect of red against black, which would produce a lovely image to treasure through the years.

Griff turned to Arden. "Are you okay?"

"Are you?" He'd told her about talking to Zelda and Al at their new house, with a humorous slant that seemed to prove he'd recovered from the betrayal.

"I'm great." They made their way outside through the press of people, sharing the standard "Wasn't it a lovely wedding?" comments as they went.

On the front steps of the church, however, the conversations changed abruptly. "Look at that," Griff said. "There's your snow, Arden."

After a cloudy day of cold rain mixed with ice and a few snowflakes, nightfall had brought about a change in the precipitation. In the short time they'd been inside the church, a thin layer of white had coated the grass and shrubs. Like a heavy fall of powdered sugar, snow coated the bare tree branches and the individual needles of the pine trees.

She clapped her hands in appreciation. "Beautiful. What a breathtaking scene—everything draped in white for the wedding."

"Except the roads," Griff pointed out. "Safe driving and a winter wonderland. That's the advantage of a Southern snowfall. No shoveling."

They were the only people still standing on the steps; the rest had hurried through the falling snow to their cars, heading toward the wedding reception at the country club. A limousine pulled up at the curb to collect the bridesmaids and groomsmen, and in the general confusion, Arden and Griff headed for the Jaguar.

"We'll party for a little while," he promised as they

drove. "But I want a few minutes alone with you during the evening. We need to talk."

"Yes," Arden said quietly. "We do."

Chapter 14

"One thing you can always count on at the club," Jake Campbell announced at dinner. "Decent food."

Arden smiled, and the rest of the family signaled their agreement. They had all been seated together again, but not at a table tucked into a corner this time.

"A ringside seat," Griff had commented as they sat down. "Right on the dance floor and with a direct line of sight to the head table. I guess it pays to be nice to the bride and groom."

The wedding reception was everything Zelda could have hoped for, Arden thought—beautiful, delicious and crowded. Red and white flowers emerged from tall vases on the tables and a red rose lay across each dinner plate. Confetti made up of tiny red and white foil hearts had been sprinkled across the white table-cloths. The new Mr. and Mrs. McPherson had given all their guests a memorable Valentine's Day evening at no charge. Their wedding would, Arden suspected, be remembered for years.

She knew she would remember laughing with the Campbell family all during the meal, dancing with Griff and pretending—just for a couple of hours—that she could share the rest of his life.

Her final dance with his father would not be easily forgotten. He had asked and she had hesitated.

"Afraid of me?" he said, with a challenge in his eyes.

"Of course not." But she was, and he probably knew it when she put her cold fingers into his warm hand.

He didn't say anything for a few minutes, leading her with his expert grace through some fairly complicated steps. Then he drew back so they could see each other. "You've improved."

"There have been several dances since that first one," she reminded him. "Griff and I have practiced."

"And, of course, you have a natural sense of rhythm. You would have to, in order to play so well."

"Yes." *Here we go,* she thought.

"I'm sorry to hear you're losing your hearing," he said. "That's a tragedy for your fans, as well as a personal loss."

"Thank you." She looked over his shoulder, trying to hide her surprise.

But he could read her as easily as Griff did, it seemed. "Didn't think I could be human, did you?"

"I wasn't sure. But Rosalie married you, so I knew you must have a soft spot somewhere."

"Touché." He sent her into a spin and brought her back again. "You've been good for Griff."

"I'm glad."

"I know he's been restless. Small town veterinary practice isn't the most exciting life path, being composed of hard work and never enough time off."

"But there are rewards in helping the animals and their owners." She had driven with Griff out to check on Rajah one afternoon. Though the stallion's wound was still healing, he was back to his energetic, magnificent self.

"I like it. Griff thought he might want something different, I think. Or somewhere different. That was one of the issues between him and Zelda. But since you've been here, I'm getting the feeling he sees himself settling down."

Arden blinked hard. "I think he's seen his hometown in a new light. Less of a burden, more of a blessing."

"His mother and I would like that." The song came to a close and Jake slowed their steps to a halt. Then, to Arden's surprise, he bent low over her hand, pressing a kiss on her knuckles. "And we thank you," he said.

Speechless with astonishment and emotion, Arden returned to their table with her dance partner this time, instead of running off to the restroom. Jake made sure she had champagne, then solicited his wife's hand for the next dance, and they left her alone at the table for a moment. As she scanned the crowd, she couldn't find Griff. But his sisters were mingling at different places around the ballroom. Dana, in her bright orange gown, was talking to friends whose sons played soccer with her own. Lauren, wearing bright blue, was deep in discussion with her best friend, probably about a new cooking venture they hoped to launch on the internet. Kathy seemed to be showing off her elegant maternity evening dress in green silk to a circle of mothers-to-be. Not that she had much of a bump to accommodate.

The sight of women with round bellies foretold of the babies to come drove a knife through Arden's heart. She had known this evening would be hard—and the worst was yet to come. But maybe she could go to the restroom for a few minutes, while the rest of them were occupied, and regain some measure of strength and self-control.

She met with a number of delays on her way to the ballroom doorway, as people she'd come to know stopped her to comment about the wedding, the gowns, the food…. Arden felt more desperate with each encounter, but forced herself to stay calm. Finally, she did cross the threshold and, with a last glance over her shoulder, turned toward the restrooms.

Only to run straight into Griff. "I was just coming to get you," he said. He wasn't smiling. "Would you like to sit down for a while in relative peace?"

Calm poured over her like cool water. "That sounds nice. I'm hoarse from talking."

With his hand at her waist, he walked down the hallway—past the lounge and the restrooms, all the way to the end, where he opened a door. "I think we'll be safe in here. Most folks aren't interested in the sunroom after dark."

Arden stepped in and gasped. "They don't know what they're missing." Furnished with wicker chairs and ceiling fans, the room had been constructed with huge windows taking the place of walls. The sills were low enough to be stepped over, leading guests out to the garden beyond.

Of course, tonight that garden was covered with

snow. An inch more had fallen since they'd left the church, and the landscape illumined by the tall outdoor lights resembled New England more than the sunny South.

"Add a sleigh and some reindeer and we could make our own Christmas card." Griff spoke from somewhere off to the side. "I've never seen it quite so pretty."

She looked at him and he came toward her and took one of her hands in his, holding it lightly.

"I've never known such a beautiful woman." He kissed the back of it and then, to her surprise, released her and turned away.

"Griff?"

He stood staring out one of the windows. "Most of all, I have never allowed myself to be duped by anyone the way I have with you."

She realized all at once that the room was ice-cold. "What do you mean?"

"You've been a woman of mystery from the beginning. That was part of your charm, I guess, especially after I'd been dumped by a girl I'd known since grade school."

He looked over his shoulder. "Is this a game you play with every man who wanders into your life? Or am I just really stupid?"

"Don't say that. I've never been with another man like…like this."

"I should be grateful for that, I suppose. If it's true." He turned to her, grim-faced, his spine straight and stiff. "You have kept so many secrets, I don't know if I can trust even one piece of information you've given me."

"Everything you know about me is true."

"Ah, there's the justification. I get it—you simply lie by omission. That's a fine line you walk, Ms. Burke."

"What are you talking about?"

"Were you ever planning to have a baby? I can't figure out what you had to gain from this little charade, otherwise. Whatever, you're clearly not expecting to have one now." He sent her a humorless grin. "Spermicidal jelly doesn't make good babies."

Arden put her hand to her mouth. She'd been rushing...it must have fallen out of her bag.

At this point, she could only end the entire episode with dignity. "No, it doesn't. I decided that...that I wouldn't have a baby. We obviously weren't staying together."

"We were never staying together, remember? Why would you think otherwise?"

"Because I—" She caught herself before she could make the one irretrievable mistake. "I decided it wasn't fair to take a child from its father and grandparents, to deprive your family of the baby they would have l-loved."

"You didn't think I might want a part in this decision?"

She squeezed her eyes shut, but felt tears escape, nonetheless. They slid down her face and dropped off her chin, no doubt making spots on the raw silk of her dress.

With his hands in the pockets of his slacks, Griff shrugged. "I guess you'll find some other fool to give you a baby. A guy with fewer family obligations to consider."

"No. I've decided I won't have a child by myself. A baby needs a family."

A long silence stretched between them. Griff stood motionless, as if he'd turned to ice.

Arden took a deep breath. "I lost a baby last year. Andre's baby. I learned I was pregnant only a few days before I…found him with my mother. Then I—I miscarried. When you wanted me to come here, I thought I could replace that baby. Fill the empty place inside me with another child. But I wasn't thinking about that little person, about what he or she would need. Now I am."

She cleared her throat. "That's my last secret, Griff. If there's anything else you want to know, send me a letter. I'll answer any question you ask."

Turning on her toe, she forced her stiff legs to move, ignoring the pins and needles in her feet as she walked over the stone floor. She thought he might say something, might try to stop her at the last moment.

But even though she hesitated, holding the door open for endless seconds, Griff's pride made the final choice.

Letting the door close behind her, Arden fetched her coat from the checkroom and waited for the valet to bring the Jag around. At the cottage, she made sure her note for Mrs. Campbell could be seen on the kitchen counter.

Then she and Igor headed south.

"It's a little chilly in here for a nap."

Griff hadn't heard his dad open the sunroom door. But he didn't reply, or move from his slouch in one of the wicker armchairs, even as Jake approached across the stone floor.

Tall and slim in his tux, the elder Dr. Campbell crossed his arms and propped his shoulder against a window frame. "Where is Arden? Your mother and the girls have searched the ladies' room. This was the last place in the club we hadn't checked."

"Gone." Griff cleared his throat. "Home."

"Alone?"

He managed a jerk of his head. "Florida."

Jake pulled up a bench and sat down. "What happened?"

His quiet, concerned tone broke through Griff's defenses. "It was all a sham," he confessed, keeping his gaze on the icy world outside. "I brought a beautiful woman home with me to avoid looking like a loser. We agreed she would stay through Zelda's wedding, then we'd have a fight and go our separate ways." A chuckle escaped him. "Mission accomplished. In record time."

"You lied, in other words. To your mother and your sisters."

"Yes. And to you. Hell, to the whole town."

"When did you cook up this scheme?"

"I met Arden on New Year's Eve. On the beach."

His dad gave a long, low whistle. "She's quite an opportunist."

Griff erupted from the chair to stand over his dad, hands fisted at his sides. "That's complete bullshit. The plan was mine alone. I had to convince her to come with me."

"And what does she get out of this collusion?" Jake didn't appear to feel threatened. "Not cash, I gather."

As fast as his anger had surged, it drained away. Griff let his shoulders slump. "A baby," he said roughly. "She wanted a baby."

"Dear God." The wicker bench fell over as Jake straightened to his full height. "You let her leave when she was carrying your child?"

A jangle of pain in his dad's voice connected Griff to that moment, six weeks ago, when he'd glimpsed a vital repercussion of his plan but failed to follow through. Now he could see the detail he'd ignored all too clearly.

He'd brought Arden to his family, thinking she might take away a baby they would love. That careless intent was bad enough. But he'd also given them the woman herself, asked them to accept her as a member of the family. To love her, worry about her, plan a future with her. And then just let her go.

He had fallen in love with Arden Burke. Why wouldn't his family do the same?

"I'm sorry," he said, for the first time looking his dad in the face. "I was drunk that night and scared to come home. Arden seemed like the answer to a prayer— I wanted her the moment I saw her." He shrugged. "Maybe I fell in love with her at first sight. Maybe I thought I deserved some payback for what Zelda put me through.

"But she's not pregnant." He answered his dad's skeptical glare with a nod. "She changed her mind and started using birth control. I guess she didn't want any ties to me at all."

"Well, that's something to be grateful for." Jake's shoulders relaxed. "Now all you have to do is face your mother."

Rosalie cried, once the whole family was back at home and sitting in the den, but not for the reason Griff expected.

"Poor Arden," his mother said, wiping tears and her makeup onto the tissues her husband offered. "No wonder she's been so unhappy these last few weeks."

When Jake snorted, she fixed him with a fiery stare.

"Don't be so harsh. Arden has never had a family or people to love her. I can only imagine how hard it must be for her to give that up."

"She didn't have to go," Griff pointed out. "All she had to do was tell the truth. I would have accepted anything she'd done to keep her."

"Evidently not," Kathy said. "You couldn't accept that she hadn't told you everything." When he frowned, she only shrugged. "That's just logic."

"She hasn't had much experience with forgiveness," Jim pointed out. "Maybe she didn't know how to ask."

"And you didn't offer." Dana's icy stare rivaled Jake's for its paralyzing effect. "Did you?"

The discussion proceeded with a thorough dissection of Arden's emotions, motivations and needs, a comparable analysis of Griff's psyche and enough tears to drown a dinghy.

But he removed himself mentally and emotionally from the process. They were his family, and they'd forgive him eventually. Whatever punishment they inflicted in the meantime would be no less than he deserved.

Finally, with various gestures of sympathy or displays of disappointment, his sisters and their husbands went to their own homes. His parents went to bed without saying much at all, which meant more deliberation to come.

Griff sat on alone, staring at the fire. His thoughts had dwindled to a mix of sadness, longing and, yes, some anger.

Mostly, though, he simply missed her. She couldn't be more than a hundred miles away, but it might as well be a thousand. What could he do to bridge the distance?

Arden's last words came back to him. "If there's anything else you want to know, send me a letter. I'll answer whatever you ask."

He was at the secretary desk before he realized he'd moved, with a sheet of thick note paper in front of him and a black pen poised and ready.

"Dear Arden…"

A March visit with her audiologist documented the continued decline in Arden's hearing.

At the front desk, a woman who reminded her of Rosalie Campbell wanted to set up the next appointment.

"I'll call," Arden told her. "When I'm ready."

"But—but…" Distress wrinkled the secretary's forehead and widened her eyes. "You should maintain a regular schedule of examinations. The doctor says so."

Arden smiled. "I don't need the numbers to know my deafness is getting worse. I'll come back if I have doubts. Thank you." Waving away the continued protests, she left the office and stepped out into bright Miami sunshine.

Her mother waited nearby on a bench under a palm tree. She looked up from her newspaper crossword puzzle as Arden sat down. "How did it go?"

"As expected." Arden shrugged, hardly bothered by the news. Compared to losing Griff, losing her hearing didn't matter much. "My acuity is down to about fifty percent. I've lost most of the high frequency tones." She paused as a thought struck her. "Maybe I should play the cello."

"Or the tuba." With the puzzle folded into her purse, Lorraine Burke lifted her pale face to the breeze. Her bright blond hair, barely an inch long, didn't stir. "Contrabassoon? I always enjoyed the bassoon."

"Bass drum." Arden pantomimed the sideways strokes. "Boom, boom, boom." As her arms dropped, she caught sight of her watch. "We have fifteen minutes to reach the clinic."

Lorraine sighed. "My favorite part of the day."

"At least you get to sit in a comfortable chair."

Arden's mother laughed. "Now, there's a bright side. Five hours in a recliner."

Rosalie Campbell would probably have offered a hug with the laugh, but Arden's reconciliation with her mother hadn't progressed quite so far. Still, they were living in the condo together until this round of treatments ended, and managed to communicate without arguing most of the time. If Arden had taken the first step—a phone call made one stormy night in late February, when she thought the loneliness might kill her—Lorraine had responded with grace and gratitude.

The daily visits to the chemotherapy clinic, where Arden occupied a folding chair while her mother mostly dozed in the big recliner, had allowed them time together without confronting the past. Knitting had become a new pastime for them both, inspired by posters at the hospital requesting blankets for children and newborns. Arden had already donated the box items from her now-empty closet. So far, she'd knitted and unraveled at least two blankets' worth of faulty rows. Today, she would start once again.

First, though, she took Griff's letters out of her bag. She carried them all with her, all the time. His voice came through so strongly, she could almost believe he stood beside her. And she needed him there.

She had kept her promise and answered every question he asked, which meant revealing her childhood, the years spent traveling, the isolated college days. He hadn't responded with pity, however, which made each confession a bit easier. She'd asked a few questions in return, and the envelopes they sent back and forth were becoming increasingly heavier as their letters stretched to five and six pages. He always made her laugh. Sometimes, she thought they could spend their lives together in correspondence and be content.

Then there were the nights she woke up aching from a frustrated dream, only to lie for hours longing for Griff's arms around her. His letters became torture, at that point—she could hear him and see him in her mind's eye. But what she craved was his touch—warm, assured, erotic.

"You're wearing that expression again," her mother said in a sleepy voice.

Arden kept her eyes on her hands as she folded the letter and composed her face. Then she looked up. "What expression would that be?"

Lorraine shook her head. "Why don't you just ask him to come? Haven't both of you been punished enough?"

"Punished?" The word struck her as completely wrong…and then, in the next moment, completely right.

Of course she deserved to suffer, after the way she'd treated Griff. And maybe she'd wanted to punish him for his anger. For sending her away.

But surely punishment didn't have to last forever. She and her mother were working to forgive. Was there a chance that Griff could offer forgiveness, too?

Griff tied the rented speedboat to the dock on Chaos Key and headed across the beach to the path through the trees he had followed with Arden four months ago.

At least, he hoped he'd found the same path. He wouldn't appreciate the irony if he showed up without warning, only to get lost in the jungle and die of snake-bite or starvation or alligator attack. Jaguars, maybe. Who knew what wild animals lurked in the underbrush? Besides Igor.

Then he remembered the security system and felt better. She would see him on the monitors at some point and come to rescue him.

He hoped.

Once the old mansion appeared on his right, his sense of direction improved. Or maybe some kind of mystic connection was leading him straight to Arden. At least he was going the right way.

Her little cottage came into sight just a few minutes later, shaded by live oak trees from the late afternoon sun. His gut clenched with nerves and anticipation. With sixty days of desolation behind him, he hated to take anything for granted.

But she wouldn't have asked him to come just to tell him to leave her alone, right?

Lifting his hand to knock on the porch door, he hesitated. Would Igor come tearing out to rip him up? They never had managed to make friends, even after the rescue. Griff still had scars on his leg from the last bite.

"Aw, hell," he muttered, knocking anyway. Igor would need a minute or so to chew through the screen. Griff could be up in a tree before he got out.

The woman who stepped onto the porch was a stranger. She didn't have a dog with her.

"Hello," she said. "Looking for someone?" Her blond hair was cut pixie short; her pale skin flushed with pink. A tall woman, she wore a bright turquoise muu-

muu that ended above her ankles, but not because she was heavy. Her collarbones showed plainly above the neck of the dress and her arms below the short sleeves were bone thin.

He recognized her eyes, though—the shape and set of them, the stormy green color. Arden might have inherited her dad's dark hair and ivory skin, but she had her mother's eyes.

"I'm Griff Campbell," he told her. "Are you Lorraine?"

She held the door open for him to step inside the porch. "That's right. Lorraine Burke."

He shook the hand she offered, noticing the sharp bones. "Glad to meet you. Arden says you're feeling better."

Her smile was Arden's, too. "I am, thanks. But that's not what you want to talk about right now, is it? She's down at the beach with the dog."

"Thanks."

Back at the main path, he took the turn leading to the western side of the island, where they'd met. Though the walk sloped downhill, the minutes seemed to stretch into hours. He thought he'd never get there, until a sudden turn brought him straight out onto the white sand beach.

The empty beach.

Griff groaned out loud and dropped onto his knees. She'd written, asking him to come. Now he couldn't find her. How much longer could the universe torture him?

A distant shout, off to the right, gave him the answer. He scanned the horizon and saw a dark spot running back and forth. Igor. And maybe, just maybe, the pale shape following would not be an illusion?

He waited on his knees, watching, as the pair drew closer. Whatever Arden wanted to say, he'd be glad to beg, if that would convince her to come back.

She was throwing a stick for the dog as they approached, giving Igor ample opportunity to run. Finally, the stick landed about a hundred yards up the beach from Griff.

Igor raced to pick it up, but dropped the stick as soon as he recognized the man nearby. Then he charged.

Griff tried to scramble to his feet, but the dog was too fast. Igor's front paws slammed into Griff's shoulders, pushing him back into the sand. Covering his face with his arms, Griff waited for the first chomp.

But Igor seemed more likely to lick him to death. Snuffling and panting, he acted as if he'd just found his best friend in the whole world.

Arden arrived and laughed as she watched. "Absence makes the heart grow fonder," she said finally. "I think he's missed you."

"Yeah, yeah, Igor. I missed you, too." Griff pushed and tugged and played with the dog as he struggled to stand in the slippery sand. "Right. Got it. Down, there's a good boy. Now stay."

To his surprise, Igor did stay for a moment, before dashing off to snap at an incoming wave.

"Whew." Griff tried to brush himself off, to restore some order to his hair and clothes. "He's, um, energetic. A good thing," he added, talking at random. Finally, he gave up and just stared at the woman he'd come to see. "How are you?"

"Wonderful." And she did, indeed, look great, with cheeks rosy from the sun and eyes as bright as sunlight on the ocean. She wore loose linen shorts and a flowered shirt that reminded him of the ones he'd worn during his exile. "You came."

"Of course." He wasn't going to burden her with the hell he'd lived in these last weeks. "You asked me to." After a pause, he asked, "Why?"

"Only a fool throws away the chance to bring love and laughter into their life."

Griff threw back his head and laughed. "That's *my* life lesson you're talking about. The one I had to learn."

"And I decided," Arden said, "that I don't want to be a fool anymore."

"That makes two of us. Thank God." He closed his arms around her.

She looked up at him. "Will you take me back, Griff? And will you take me home?"

"If you'll take me back and forgive my foolish, stupid pride."

"Oh, yes, I will."

Then he kissed her over and over, and she kissed him, until they dropped to their knees in the warm sand. And still he held and kissed her, stretched out beside her with their bodies pressed tightly together, celebrating the return of joy.

At last they could relax a little, and breathe. With perfect timing, Igor ran up to be petted, to sniff and nose and lick both their faces, before running off again to chase a seagull.

Arden said, "And in the interest of divulging secrets, I got some news this morning."

Griff brushed her hair back from her face. "What news was that?"

Instead of answering, she reached into the breast pocket of the shirt she wore and pulled out a stick.

A wand, his mind corrected. A small wand with a plus sign at one end.

"You're pregnant?" he whispered.

She nodded, her face as bright and beautiful as he'd ever seen it. "I guess I was too late with the diaphragm."

He grinned. "That's a good omen…for a big family."

Arden nodded. "It is. And I only found out this morning. I wrote because I wanted to be with you, Griff, baby or no baby."

"I believe you."

Her smile dimmed as she gazed into his face. "I'm still losing my hearing. I may very well become completely deaf."

Griff took a step backward. Using his arms, hands and fingers, he gave her his response in American Sign Language. "It's not a problem," he signed, "I love you. Forever."

Arden's smile returned, more brilliant than ever. "I love you, too," she signed. "I've been studying," she said, "Thinking about working wtih deaf children."

He put his arms around her once again. "So who needs words, anyway?"

The kisses they shared said it all.

* * * * *

Cathy Gillen Thacker is married and a mother of three. She and her husband spent eighteen years in Texas and now reside in North Carolina. Her mysteries, romantic comedies and heartwarming family stories have made numerous appearances on bestseller lists, but her best reward, she says, is knowing one of her books made someone's day a little brighter. A popular Harlequin author for many years, she loves telling passionate stories with happy endings and thinks nothing beats a good romance and a hot cup of tea! You can visit Cathy's website, cathygillenthacker.com, for more information on her upcoming and previously published books, recipes and a list of her favorite things.

Books by Cathy Gillen Thacker

Harlequin Western Romance

Texas Legends: The McCabes

The Texas Cowboy's Baby Rescue

Texas Legacies: The Lockharts

A Texas Soldier's Family
A Texas Cowboy's Christmas
The Texas Valentine Twins
Wanted: Texas Daddy
A Texas Soldier's Christmas

Visit the Author Profile page
at Harlequin.com for more titles.

THE SECRET SEDUCTION

Cathy Gillen Thacker

Chapter 1

Honestly, Lily Madsen thought as she watched the disheveled "cowboy" climb down from the truck, that man in the snug-fitting jeans, chambray shirt and boots was enough to take your breath away. Or he would have been, she amended, if he hadn't been Fletcher Hart. The most reckless and restless of Helen Hart's five sons, the thirty-year-old Fletcher had a reputation for loving and leaving women and never committing to much of anything—save his thriving Holly Springs, North Carolina, vet practice—for long.

"Why are you being so all-fired difficult?" Lily glared at him and continued the conversation the two of them had started before Fletcher had cut it short and headed off on an emergency call to a nearby farm. "All I am asking for is a simple introduction to Carson McRue. I'll take it the rest of the way."

"I'm sure you will." Fletcher slanted her a deeply cynical look, followed it with a way too knowing half smile, then strode toward the back door of the clinic, all confident indomitable male. "The answer is still no, Lily."

Simmering with a mixture of resentment, anger and another emotion she couldn't quite identify, Lily followed Fletcher into the building, aware that unlike the building, which smelled quite antiseptic, he smelled as if he had been rolling around in the back of a barn. And perhaps he had been, she thought, noting the sweat stains on his shirt, the mud clinging to his backside, knees, shoulders and chest.

Oblivious to her scrutiny of him, he strode purposefully into a glass-walled room. On the other side of the partition was an assortment of cats and dogs in metal cages. All appeared to be recovering from operations or illness and were sleeping or resting drowsily. On their side of the glass wall, there was another large crate with a dog inside who did not appear to have had surgery.

Lily watched as Fletcher hunkered down beside the crate and peered in. To her frustration, he seemed a lot more interested in his canine patient, than what she had to say to him. "Just what is your objection to my meeting the man anyway?" she demanded with all the authority she could muster, given the five years' difference in their ages.

Fletcher paused to give a comforting pat to the ailing yellow lab, who looked up at him with big sad eyes, before straightening once again. "Besides the fact that he's an egotistical TV star who doesn't care about anyone but himself, you mean?" Fletcher challenged.

Lily huffed her exasperation and folded her arms in

front of her, trying all the while not to notice how soft and touchable Fletcher's shaggy honey-brown hair was, how sexy his golden-brown eyes. You would think the way Fletcher acted that he was the star of a hit TV show, instead of a local vet who was—as always—in need of a haircut. Just because he had a masculine chiseled face, with the don't-mess-with-me Hart jaw, expressive, kissable lips, a strong nose and well-defined cheekbones, did not mean that she had to swoon at his feet. And the same went for his powerful, six-foot-one frame, with those broad shoulders, impossibly solid chest, lean waist and long, muscular legs.

"You don't know that for sure," she retorted defensively, privately hoping it wasn't true. "Just because Carson McRue is rich and famous—"

Fletcher headed up the stairs that led to his apartment on the second floor, unbuttoning his filthy shirt as he went. Lily was right behind him. "Let's just cut the bull, shall we?"

"I don't—"

He stopped at the top of the stairs and stripped off his shirt, leaving Lily with a bird's-eye view of lots of satiny smooth male skin, a T-shaped mat of golden-brown hair, six-pack abs and a belly button so sexy it was to die for. With effort, she dragged her glance away from his hip-hugging jeans and American Veterinary Medical Association belt buckle, before she could really give in to temptation and slide her glance lower to see what was behind that tightly shut zipper.

Oblivious to the licentious direction of her thoughts, Fletcher continued mocking her with thinly veiled contempt. "I know about the bet you made with all your friends. Okay, Lily? Everyone in town does."

While Fletcher watched, embarrassed color crept to her cheeks. Lily gulped her dismay. She never should have indulged in such bold talk at her birthday party last week. But then she never should have let her friends talk her into having two margaritas with her enchiladas, either. Everyone knew she couldn't hold her liquor. The closest she had ever gotten to drinking was the smid-gen of crème de menthe her grandmother had let them have in their milk every Christmas Eve.

Alcohol had been one of many things her beloved grandmother Rose had not approved. And knowing how badly her own parents had disappointed Grandmother Rose, Lily had grown up never wanting to similarly let her down.

Forcing herself to meet Fletcher's boldly assessing gaze head-on, Lily demanded archly, "Who told you—?" And more to the point, how much exactly did he know about what she had sworn she would do to win her wager?

"—That you've promised when Carson McRue's private jet leaves Carolina, you're going to be on it?" Fletcher picked up where Lily left off. "Well, let's see. There's my sister, Janey. My brother Joe's wife, Emma. Hannah Reid, over at Classic Car Auto Repair. My cousin Susan Hart. And everyone else who heard you swear that you could get a hot date with the dim bulb in just one week."

Fletcher Hart knew everything, all right. Except of course what had prompted Lily to make such an un-likely, hedonistic boast in the first place. She pushed her rebuttal through gritted teeth. "Carson McRue is not a dim bulb. Or an egotistical star."

That cynical smile again. "And how would you know

this?" Fletcher challenged as he unlocked the door and strode into his apartment, past the messy living room, kitchen and bedroom, to the bathroom at the rear.

Lily had the choice of following, or cooling her heels. She knew what he would have preferred, and—feeling stubbornly contrary—did the exact opposite. Pulse racing, she leaned against the hallway wall with her back to the open bathroom door and continued their conversation as nonchalantly as if every single day she did things this intimate with men she barely knew. "I know because I've watched his TV show every week for the last five years." The action-adventure show about an easygoing Hollywood private eye had been the one bright spot in many a stressful week. Lily had watched the highly entertaining program in hospital rooms and waiting rooms, as well as at home. And it had never failed to make her forget her problems, at least temporarily. Right now she needed to forget her problems. Besides, if she won her bet with the girls, they all owed her a day at the spa. If she lost and they won, well, Lily didn't want to think about what she would have to do then. Especially since Fletcher didn't seem to know about the price she would have to pay, either. Otherwise she was sure he would have already rudely brought it up.

Fletcher kicked off one boot, then the other. "Carson McRue plays a character, Lily. What you see on TV is all an act, albeit a highly polished one."

"I know that," Lily retorted drolly as she heard a zip and a whoosh of fabric…and *was that the shower starting?* Telling herself she was not going to see Fletcher naked, no matter how brazenly he was behaving, she closed her eyes and rubbed at the tense spot just above her nose.

"But no one who isn't that nice could actually pretend to be that caring and compassionate." At least Lily hoped that was the case. Otherwise, her goose was cooked. She would never be able to live down this drunken boast. Never be able to get up the nerve to do what she had to do to make good on her lost wager...

"Don't count on it," Fletcher argued right back. "And anyway, it doesn't matter." The shower curtain opened and closed. Water pelted in an entirely different rhythm and the aroma of soap and shampoo and... man...wafted out on the steamy air as Fletcher scrubbed himself clean. "I'm still not introducing you to him." He spoke above the din of running water.

At Fletcher's stubbornness, it was all Lily could do not to stomp her foot. "But he and the rest of the show's cast and crew will be here tomorrow," she protested hotly as he shut the water off, pulled open the shower curtain with a telltale whoosh and ripped a towel off the rack with equal carelessness. "And you're the only one in town who has met him."

Six heavy male footsteps later, Fletcher was standing in the hall. Knowing she would be a coward if she didn't look, Lily opened her eyes. Fletcher was standing there, regarding her curiously and unabashedly. He had a towel slung low around his waist. He was using another on his hair. And, she noticed disconcertingly, he looked every bit as deliciously sexy wet as he did dry.

"I found the guy a horse to ride while he's here. That's it. And all that required was a phone call and video-conference," Fletcher told Lily in disdain.

That was far more contact than anyone else in town had had, Lily thought enviously. Why didn't anything that exciting ever happen to her? And if it didn't, how was she ever going to leave her Ice Princess of Holly Springs reputation far behind?

"You're also going to be working at the set, as the animal-rights consultant." She diligently made her case for him to help her.

Fletcher shrugged his broad shoulders, and Lily's pulse picked up as she saw the loosely knotted towel around his waist slip a little bit.

Fletcher frowned, unimpressed. "It's a glorified title. I only took the position because of the hefty paycheck attached to it. It doesn't mean I really have any say in what goes on there. Unless of course they try to do some stunt that would actually harm any of the animals on the set. And right now, the only animal I know about is the horse Carson McRue will be riding when he takes off after the bad guys."

"Fine. Whatever." Lily did not care if Fletcher ended up being bored out of his mind. "The point is, the film crew is only going to be here for one week and you've got entrée. And I do have a bet going…"

Fletcher met her eyes, this time in all seriousness. "One that is bound to guarantee you getting hurt."

Lily's spine stiffened. She wished like heck that he would behave more modestly or put some clothes on. Not that she could actually see anything she shouldn't be seeing…or wouldn't see if he were, say, swimming.

"You don't know that," she retorted defensively in an attempt to get her mind off of what was under that towel. Was that as gloriously male and wonderfully attractive as the rest of him? And how would she—the woman of literally no worldly experience—know anyway, even if she were to see? She'd never encountered a naked man! Except on the big screen and in the movies she'd seen. And it was always a rear view, never ever the front.

"Don't I?" Fletcher let go of the towel he had looped around his neck. He flattened a hand on the wall next to her and leaned in close, deliberately invading her space. "Let's recap for a moment here, shall we?" he said softly. "Small-town girl—that would be you—who has never been out of Holly Springs, except for that one half semester she went to college in Winston-Salem before returning to finish up her studies at nearby N.C. State, tries to hook up with a Hollywood hunk who has a reputation for breaking hearts all over the world."

Lily did not need reminding how stifling her life to date had been. "First of all, Fletcher," she retorted, lifting her chin, "it was never my decision to live my whole life in North Carolina or live at home while I finished my business degree. But I had no choice. My grandmother was ill—and someone had to be there to drive her to medical appointments and see her through the surgeries, radiation and chemotherapy treatments." Lily gulped around the sudden tightness in her throat. "So I did it, and furthermore—" her voice quavered even more as she thought about the heartbreak of that awful time "—I was glad to do it."

Fletcher's eyes softened and he touched a gentle hand to her quivering chin. "I know that," he told her compassionately. "I'm sorry you lost her. You know how much I cared about Grandmother Rose. And the pets she had over the years."

Lily did know. An animal lover from birth, Fletcher knew everyone in town, and their pets. His future as a veterinarian had seemed as predetermined as Lily's, who had been tapped to continue the florist business that had been in the Madsen family for generations. The difference being Fletcher had gone into his career by choice. Lily had been forced into hers by duty. And at twenty-five, after years of sacrifice, she was getting pretty darned tired of doing what *everyone else* felt she should.

"Which is why, Lily, I and everyone else in this town who care about you do not want to see you make a fool out of yourself over an arrogant thespian."

"Don't you think that should be my choice?" Lily tapped him on the chest before she could think—then withdrew her index finger from that warm, hard chest and leaned back as far as she could into the wall.

Fletcher's eyes grew dark, as he stayed right where he was. "Not if you're going to make the wrong decision, no," he said flatly. "I don't."

"What in the tarnation did you do to that little filly?" Fletcher's brother Dylan asked, tongue in cheek, an hour later. A TV sportscaster by profession, Dylan couldn't seem to stop observing and commenting on everything around him, even when he wasn't working. But then, Fletcher noted, that was all Dylan had always been—a "watcher" rather than a "doer." Whereas Fletcher could have cared less what anyone else—save the delectable Lily Madsen—was up to as long as it didn't directly impact him.

"I don't know what you're talking about," Fletcher said, happy that his sister Janey was getting married to a man who deserved her, but wishing Janey and Thad Lantz had selected any other night for their wedding week kickoff pig pickin' in his mother's backyard.

Fletcher's oldest brother Mac, looking as much a

lawman out of uniform as in, edged closer, a plate of pork barbecue in his hand. "Lily Madsen hasn't stopped glaring at you since the two of you walked in together."

Fletcher forked up some of his own shredded pork and tangy barbecue sauce, irked because they were treating his coming in with the stubborn minx as if it were some sort of date, and it darn well wasn't. "I didn't ask her to the party," Fletcher said, exasperated. "So don't go making anything out of us coming in together." That was just the way it had happened, thanks to Lily's refusal to give up on her pitch right until the minute they walked in here side by side.

"Yeah, we know." The twenty-eight-year-old Dylan winked.

Cal continued with a salacious grin. "At least *she* was on time."

Fletcher shrugged his shoulders helplessly. Cal might have been the first of them to get married, but his wife Ashley's current OB/GYN fellowship in Honolulu had him living the everyday life of a single man again. And though Cal kept insisting it wasn't a marital separation, it looked to everyone else in the family as if it were. Particularly since it had been going on for two years now.

Not that Cal had ever looked at another woman. Ashley was—and always would be—the love of Cal's life. For all the good it did him, Fletcher noted cynically.

"I couldn't help being late." Fletcher finally answered the charge against him. "A sick cow needed my attention."

"No problem. Lily Madsen was only too happy to volunteer to go and find you and drag you over here." Cal continued teasing, even as the beeper on his belt went off, signaling a message regarding one of his orthopedic patients.

Fletcher guzzled his icy cold beer as Cal stepped away to use his cell to phone the hospital. "Can I help it if I'm not much for parties these days?" Fletcher asked.

"Who are you kidding?" Joe razzed, looking fit as a fiddle, even in the Carolina Storm hockey team's off-season as he chowed down on liberal amounts of coleslaw, beans and shredded pork. "You've never been much for parties. Always too busy tending to some sick or wounded animal."

Fletcher wasn't going to apologize for his devotion to his work. He plucked a golden brown hush puppy off his plate. "That's my job."

Thad Lantz, Janey's fiancé, joined the group. "Not twenty-four hours a day, seven days a week," Thad said with the same frank authority he used as coach of the Carolina Storm hockey team. "You've got a partner. She takes calls from time to time. Or so I've heard."

"And your point is?" Fletcher asked Thad.

"It's best to play as hard as you work."

And all he needed, Fletcher thought sardonically, was a playmate who didn't want hearts and flowers and marriage—or anything else he was ill equipped to give.

Even as he thought it a single woman came to mind. Beautiful, blond and all of twenty-five...

"I think we're getting off subject here," Dylan said, guiding the conversation back to where it began. He looked at Fletcher curiously. "We want to know what you did or said to Lily Madsen to get her so ticked off at you."

Fletcher turned and looked at Lily. She was deep in conversation with his mother and sister, and the other bridesmaids. And she looked absolutely gorgeous. Like the cherubic angel he remembered her being as a kid, and yet…all grown up. Definitely grown up. Her five-foot-five frame was slender but curvy in all the right places, her legs stunning enough to make even the most jaded guy stop and take a second and third look. Her baby-blond curls had been cut to chin-length, but these days she wore them in a tousled, unconsciously sexy, finger-combed style that drove him wild. Her soft pink bow-shaped lips had a sensual slant and the rest of her features—the straight slender nose, high cheekbones, wide-set Carolina blue eyes—were elegance defined.

She was incredibly feminine, and it didn't matter whether she was wearing the khaki pants and pastel T-shirts he sometimes spotted her in, or the kind of floaty, flirty tea-length floral sundress and high-heeled sandals she had on now. She always exuded a sort of purity and innocence that was amazing for someone her age, especially in this day and age. Which was why, Fletcher thought as Lily turned and sent a brief, dagger-filled look his way, he had to stay away from her. Which probably wouldn't be hard, given all the reasons he had just given her to absolutely loathe and detest him.

Reluctantly, he broke off their staring match and turned back to Thad and his brothers. Aware they were still waiting for an explanation, he said, "She wants me to fix her up with Carson McRue when he hits town tomorrow to start filming *Hollywood P.I.*"

"And you refused?" Mac guessed dryly.

Hell, yes, he had refused, Fletcher thought as he took another swig of his beer. "Lily is much too innocent to be hooked up with a narcissist like McRue," Fletcher said in the most disaffected tone he could manage.

"Let me guess. You gave her a hard time about wanting to go out with him at all," Cal said.

"No," Fletcher replied, beginning to feel exasperated again as Lily shot him another withering look over her shoulder, which was followed by a whole slew of withering looks from his mother and the other bridesmaids. "I simply told her the way it was," Fletcher continued matter-of-factly, defending his actions. "And I wouldn't have done that if she had just taken my hint and not asked for my assistance in garnering an introduction."

The male members of the wedding party turned to look at the female participants. Especially Lily, who still looked awfully ticked off, like her temper was sky-high. "What'd you say to her?" Dylan asked curiously.

That was just it. Fletcher could hardly recall—he had been so focused on Lily and that sexy lilac perfume she was wearing.

Fletcher swallowed around the sudden dryness in his throat as he pushed away memories of just how kissable her pink and pouty lips had been, how silken her peaches and cream skin. "I just wasn't very helpful."

Joe smirked. "Not being helpful usually doesn't earn you razor-sharp looks like that." Since getting hooked up with his wife, Emma, earlier in the summer, the pro athlete in the family suddenly considered himself an expert on all things female. "So what'd you do?" Joe prodded.

I got into a shower in front of her, in hopes of scaring her away. Unfortunately, Fletcher admitted remorsefully to himself, it hadn't worked. And now, all Fletcher could remember was Lily's eyes roving over him as her face flushed and her breathing grew shallow. And he wondered what it would be like to see her in—and just out—of the shower.

"Have we been missing something here?" Mac leaned in closer. His work as sheriff had trained him to notice absolutely everything. "Have you two got something going on?"

"Nope." Fletcher said honestly as Lily sent him yet another heated look. And just as suddenly, inspiration hit. Fletcher caught and held Lily's eyes until she finally blushed and turned away with a haughty snap of her head. "But we just might," he drawled.

Dylan scoffed. "Fat chance, considering she's got her eyes on another prize."

Fletcher had never taken well to disrespect. He wasn't going to start now. He finished the last of the barbecue on his plate. "You think I can't do it?"

"Win her attentions?" Mac sopped up the last of his barbecue sauce with a piece of sourdough bread. "You bet."

Fletcher set his plate and bottle of beer aside. "You're on."

Cal blinked, sure he had missed something. "What?"

Fletcher stepped closer and dropped his voice to a husky whisper. "Hundred dollars says I can make Lily Madsen forget all about going out with Carson McRue."

Joe shook his head, predicting, "She'll never give up on a date with the hunk, if only because it'll mean losing the bet she made at her twenty-fifth birthday party last week."

It didn't matter to Fletcher. Not in the least. Or it wouldn't, when he was through waylaying Lily Madsen at every conceivable opportunity. "She'll do it," he boasted, to one and all, aiming his thumb at his chest. "In order to go out with me."

"What were you and your brothers and future brother-in-law talking about for so long over there?" Lily demanded at the end of the party as Fletcher prepared to drive her home. The palatial, three-story white brick Wedding Inn that Fletcher's mother ran loomed across the manicured lawns.

"Nothing that concerns you," Fletcher fibbed.

All four of his brothers and Thad had wanted in on the action. With five hundred dollars riding on his wager—and his secret deathbed promise to Lily's grandmother spurring him on—Fletcher had powerful incentive to keep Lily from being hurt by Carson McRue.

She looked him up and down, color flooding her face. Feeling an answering heat well up deep inside him, he yearned to throw convention aside and simply take her in his arms and kiss her, if only to stop whatever it was she was going to say to him next. "I don't believe you," she said quietly.

Fletcher shrugged and folded his arms in front of his broad chest. "If you must know," he continued lazily, standing with his shoulders back, legs braced apart, "they were razzing me about the dirty looks you gave me all during the pig-picking."

Just as he had expected, the attitude he was exuding only served to infuriate her all the more. "Did you tell them what a cad you were?" she demanded with a haughty toss of her head, looking all Southern belle, born and bred.

Didn't have to. They had guessed as much, and of

course, he already knew. Which was another reason, Fletcher figured, it would be best if Lily continued to detest him, both before and after he won his bet, of course. He needed to convince her once and for all she needed to hold out for someone far better than either him or Carson McRue to come along and sweep her off her feet and give her the kind of life she deserved.

"Well, then," Fletcher said, taking an astonished Lily into his arms and bringing her shockingly close as he prepared to give her something to really loathe him for, "I guess it's high time I lived up to my 'reputation.' Don't you?"

Chapter 2

Lily couldn't believe it. Fletcher Hart was actually going to kiss her. Right here as the party was breaking up, in front of everyone getting into their cars. "I don't—" she said, splaying her hands across his warm, hard chest. Before she could protest further, his lips were on hers, and in one sizzling instant, all reasonable thought left her brain and she was only aware of the sensations rippling through her. The smooth lips. Seductive pressure. The incredibly good taste of his lips and mouth and tongue as he erotically deepened and took full command of the kiss. She'd heard about embraces like this, read about them, even seen them when a few of her friends fell head over heels in love with the men of their dreams, but never had she experienced anything like the tumultuous whirlwind of emotion and pleasure.

And even though she knew, in some distant part of

her brain, that Fletcher was only doing this to provoke her, the fun-and-pleasure-starved part of it never wanted it to end. Because fiery hot kisses like this, men who could kiss like this, so masterfully and evocatively, did not come along every day. As his arms wrapped all the tighter around her, and he brought her even closer to his hard, demanding length, Lily moaned, surprising herself with the sensuality of her response, and melted deeper into the embrace. And that was when she heard it—the low male laughter surrounding them.

The sound was like a bucket of ice water being dumped on her head. She broke off the impetuous kiss and looked around to see Fletcher's brothers chuckling and shaking their heads with a mixture of amusement and chastisement.

"Getting a head start there?" Dylan remarked sarcastically.

"You better watch yourself," Mac warned as he strolled to the SUV he drove whenever he wasn't on duty as the Holly Springs sheriff.

Joe sauntered past, his wife Emma's hand tucked in his. "You could find yourself married before you know it."

Joe sure had, Lily remembered, thinking of the whirlwind romance earlier in the summer that now had Joe and Emma living as man and wife.

Despite the odds against a happily-ever-after in the situation Joe and Emma had initially found themselves in, Lily had to admit the two looked very happy now.

"Ah, leave him alone," Cal said, waving off the interference of their other brothers. "It was only a kiss. Kisses don't mean anything." Cal turned his attention to her, looking every bit the compassionate doctor he was known to be. "Right, Lily?"

"In this case, definitely right," Lily confirmed stormily, trying to look as casual as if she did things like this every day when everyone knew she did not.

"From where I was standing it looked like Lily was kissing him back. And that does mean something," Thad said, as he leaned over to buss his bride-to-be's cheek. "Right, Janey?"

"That's where all my troubles started." Janey sighed, looking as happy as any engaged woman should be as she laced her arm around Thad's waist and leaned her cheek against his chest.

"It's all disgusting to me," her 12-year-old son, Christopher, said, as he tagged along behind his mother and Thad.

"Not to worry," Lily said, glaring at Fletcher. "It's not going to happen again." She hurried to catch up with his older brother Mac. "Care to see me to my car?" she asked as she fell into his protective shadow.

"Be happy to, Lily," Mac flashed her a reassuring smile before turning to send his third oldest brother a censuring look. "And not to worry, Lily. You're safe with me."

Unfortunately, Fletcher noticed right away, Lily was *not* going to be safe with the TV actor who rolled into town the following morning in a custom-outfitted silver trailer.

"Who's the beauty?" Carson McRue asked as he and Fletcher met to discuss a horse.

Fletcher followed Carson's glance. It led straight to Lily, who was loitering on the other side of the wooden barricades erected to keep the cast and crew of *Holly-wood P.I.* away from the spectators gathering to watch the action in the town square.

Damned if Lily didn't look particularly gorgeous this morning, with her tousled blond hair and her sunglasses propped on top of her head. That pale pink sundress she was wearing not only hugged her slender curves to sexy advantage, it made her look like a peach blossom, ripe for the picking. Fletcher did his best to contain his mounting frustration. Protecting the headstrong and way-too-naive-for-her-own-good Lily from heartbreak was going to be no easy task. Especially with her constantly trying to win the bet she'd made with the girls. Fletcher's only comfort was that the bet he had made was—unlike hers—strictly under wraps to those who had made it with him.

He turned back to Carson, irked by the man's crassness in everything they discussed. His true personality seemed directly at odds with the great guy he played on TV. "She's off-limits," Fletcher stated casually.

Carson lifted a well-plucked brow. "Married?"

"Just off-limits," Fletcher repeated, doing his best to appeal to the actor's sensitive side. Assuming he had one. "Her grandmother, who was her only family, died last year. And she lost the cat she'd had since she was five years old, too. She had a very rough time."

Carson eyed Lily rapaciously, his glance lingering on her hourglass of curves. He licked his lips. "She looks ready to kick up her heels to me."

Punching out the competition would get him nowhere, Fletcher reminded himself firmly. At least right now. Later, if Carson continued in his current vein, all bets were off. "If you're looking for…companionship,"

Fletcher said meaningfully, "I can direct you to some likely places in Raleigh, Durham or Chapel Hill." There were dozens of bars in all three college towns. Lots of willing young women who would give anything to spend an evening in the handsome celebrity's company.

"No thanks. I like small-town girls." Carson continued studying Lily as if she were an item he'd like to purchase. "There's a sweetness and a purity about 'em. Besides, you never know...you could be giving one of them the thrill of a lifetime."

"And then what?" Fletcher asked.

Carson looked at Fletcher as if he were an infant, and not a particularly bright one at that. "We both move on." Carson spoke slowly and directly.

Only Fletcher knew Lily wouldn't be able to move on. Were she to be seduced and abandoned by someone like Carson McRue, it would crush her vulnerable heart.

"About the horse," Fletcher said impatiently, eager to have this business finished so he could go waylay Lily again and keep her from winning the wager.

Carson frowned his displeasure. "It's the wrong color."

It was Fletcher's turn to scowl. "You asked for a roan stallion—"

"I wanted a lighter brown," Carson interrupted, running a hand through his dark brown hair. "Something with a lot more copper in its coat. This one is too close to the color of my hair."

Fletcher would have thought the actor was kidding if not for the earnestness on Carson's face.

"I'll see what I can do," Fletcher allowed, with as much professionalism as he could muster, "but stunt horses are in short supply in this area of the country.

And since you didn't want to pay to have one shipped in from the West Coast—"

"Just find what we need," Carson cut him off. "I'm expert enough to ride even an untrained horse. And while you're at it—" he pointed to a shady area, half a block away "—do something about those two dogs over there."

Fletcher turned and looked at the beagle mix and black Lab, sitting side by side in the shade, watching all the activity along with everyone else. "They don't seem to be bothering anyone."

"I'm allergic," Carson announced tightly.

Good to know, Fletcher thought.

"I don't want them barking and ruining a shot. We're going to be *filming* here later." Carson glared at Fletcher.

"Right." He nodded as if this were part of his job description.

"So call whomever you have to call and get rid of them," Carson continued.

"I'll try their owners," Fletcher said dryly.

Carson dismissed Fletcher and without a backward glance at any of the fans waving autograph books and calling his name, stepped inside his silver trailer.

Unbeknownst to him, Lily had somehow sweet-talked her way past the security guards standing watch over the barricades and was already heading toward them. She looked disappointed to have missed her chance to wangle an introduction out of Fletcher while Fletcher was talking to Carson. "Hoping to say hello?" he razzed her as she approached, wishing she didn't look quite so much like a Southern beauty queen this morning.

"Something like that." Lily looked past him, toward the door of Carson's trailer.

Fletcher moved to bar her path to the door and stood, legs braced apart, arms crossed in front of him. "Carson McRue specifically requested he not be disturbed," Fletcher informed Lily with a stern look.

Lily sighed, disappointed. "Maybe later," she hoped out loud.

Not if Fletcher had anything to do with it. Figuring, however, that Lily would not believe him even if he told her what Carson had just said about her, Fletcher let the opportunity to set her straight about the actor's true character pass. He gestured toward the two dogs chasing each other on the green. "Want to help me round those two up?" he asked her casually.

Lily's full lower lip slid out into a delectable pout. "I'm not a dog person. You know that."

Fletcher could imagine she didn't want to get her pale pink sundress dirty, and he couldn't really blame her. It looked expensive. Too expensive to be wasted on a guy like Carson McRue. "How do you know?" he challenged her playfully. "You've never owned a dog."

"So what are you hinting here, Fletcher? That dogs are superior to cats?" She looked down her nose at him. Clearly, she didn't think so.

"For a young single woman in need of protection—" *from men like Carson McRue,* Fletcher added silently "—yes. They are."

Lily lifted a delicate brow. "Maybe from know-it-alls like you," she acknowledged silkily.

Fletcher looked deep into her eyes, wishing he could haul her into his arms and kiss her senseless again. Just for the hell of it. But knowing that timing was everything, he forced himself to bide his time. He'd not only protect her when all was said and done, he'd win his bet, too. "Just come by the clinic later," Fletcher told Lily lazily and smiled as her cheeks pinkened all the more. "I'll introduce you to your new best friend," he promised.

"Don't hold your breath."

Fletcher merely kept smiling and didn't elaborate. If there was one thing he knew about Lily, she loved a good mystery, just like her grandmother Rose.

It was just curiosity, Lily told herself. That and the fact she had an order for a sumptuous bouquet to be delivered to the Holly Springs Animal Clinic reception desk at 6:00 p.m. The flowers were for the "staff" but none of the staff was there. Only the founding veterinarian, Fletcher Hart, who was looking mighty fine in a sage-green work shirt that nicely outlined his shoulders and powerful chest, and faded boot-cut jeans that did the same thing for his legs.

Fletcher came around the reception desk and took the bouquet from her with a smile of thanks. "They've all gone home."

Aware her pulse had picked up at the thought of spending time alone with Fletcher—again—Lily leaned against the counter and adapted the same lazy insouciance he demonstrated. She watched him make a big show of setting the flowers in a prominent place on the large U-shaped desktop that fronted the reception area. "You placed this order, not Mr. N. L. Spartacus."

"Well, he wanted to, but for obvious reasons he couldn't contact the shop himself so I arranged it for him."

ing her from pursuing her bet about Carson McRue. Not that she had been able to get anywhere near the actor that day, even when she wasn't working. Production company security had the area well blocked off. And Carson McRue, it seemed, was not acknowledging anyone but show personnel. At least for now....

"Hey!" Fletcher palmed his chest, caveman-style. "How was I to know you'd show up in person?"

"Because it's a well-known fact around town that all my part-time help goes home at 5:00 p.m. to cook dinner for their families. I always close."

"Okay. I admit N. L. Spartacus and I had an ulterior motive, getting you over here. And I'll show you what it is."

She looked at him blankly. He took her by the hand and led her into the room adjacent to the reception area. At the end in a big wire cage was the yellow Labrador retriever she had seen the previous day. He was lying down when they entered, but thumped his tail in greeting and looked up at them with hopeful eyes. It would have been enough to break Lily's heart, had she been a dog person. But she wasn't, she reassured herself firmly. And furthermore, didn't intend to be.

"Shouldn't you be talking to his owner?" she demanded crisply. She desperately did not want this to be her problem and she was afraid if she stayed here any longer it might very well be.

Fletcher reported in a flat, matter-of-fact voice, "His owner died four weeks ago. Spartacus—we've dubbed him N.L. because he Needs Love—was with the old guy when it happened. His owner was in his nineties and Spartacus stayed with him from the time he had the heart attack until he was found by a neighbor, three days later."

Lily caught her breath at the horror of the circumstances. "Oh, no." The poor thing....

"Anyway," Fletcher continued, his voice a little more gravelly, "Spartacus just went nuts when they tried to take the old guy away. He just wasn't going to let it happen. So the animal control people were summoned. Spartacus got one whiff of the truck that was going to take him to the pound and knew it wasn't for him, so he broke loose and ran off."

Lily pressed a hand to her heart. Her eyes were brimming with tears. "Then what happened?" she asked, the tragedy of the situation almost overwhelming her.

Fletcher shook his head, a brooding look coming into his eyes. "No one really knows. Three days ago, Spartacus showed up again at the house where he used to live, vomiting and so weak he could barely stand. This time the neighbors called my clinic, asked me to treat him. So I got in my pickup and went out to get him."

Lily looked back at Spartacus. "Needs Love" was certainly appropriate. She had never seen a dog with such a sad and lonely expression. If only he weren't so big. And strong looking. If only he were a cat. Cats, she knew. And yet he had his own appeal in that handsome big-dog way. His thick short fur was a pale, almost white-gold, and there was a stripe of darker gold down the center of his back that matched the color of his ears. On impulse, Lily hunkered down and reached out to touch him through the wires on the cage. She could feel his ribs sticking out prominently as she stroked his belly. She wondered how he had survived on his own for four weeks. She looked up at Fletcher as Spartacus

leaned over to nuzzle the back of her palm affectionately with his black nose. "What was wrong with him?"
she asked, still trying like heck not to get emotionally
involved here, as his whiskers tickled her skin.

Fletcher shrugged, his emotions as tightly under
wraps as hers were on the surface. "My guess is the
canine equivalent of severe food poisoning. I think he'd
been eating out of garbage cans while he was on the lam
and got something particularly nasty, which isn't surprising in the summer heat. Bacteria grows like wild-
fire. Anyway, he's on the mend now, and I've got to
find a new home for him." The playful grin was back
on Fletcher's face as their eyes meshed again. "I spoke
to him about it this morning and he told me he kind of
fancied the pretty blonde who had been in here has-
sling me yesterday, so I promised N.L. I'd propose pet
adoption to you."

Very funny. And designed to pull on my heartstrings.
"He can't talk," Lily pointed out.

"Come on." Fletcher assumed the boldly enthusias-
tic tone of an aggressive salesperson. "Look at those
big brown eyes and tell me you don't know what he's
thinking."

That was the problem—Lily did. And it was breaking her heart to admit she was not the person for the job.
A dog like Spartacus needed someone knowledgeable
in canine care. Telling herself it was for the best, Lily
turned away. "Have you talked to his previous neighbors?" she asked.

Frustration tightened the corners of Fletcher's mouth.
"They're all in their golden years. None of them can
handle a three-year-old Labrador retriever who is going

to have plenty of energy as soon as he recovers all the way."

Lily nodded in understanding, even as she forced herself to harden her heart. "I'm sorry about his owner," she said sincerely.

"So is N.L." Fletcher knelt down and opened the cage. The Lab struggled to his feet, and clamored out on wobbly legs. Spartacus's tail wagged, then stopped as he caught the wary expression on Lily's face.

"But I can't help you with this, Fletcher," Lily continued firmly as the Lab sat down in front of them and looked up. "But maybe you could take him," Lily suggested as Spartacus continued to gaze at them woefully.

"Can't," Fletcher said, his attitude every bit as stubbornly resistant as her own. "I live in an apartment. This dog needs a house and a yard."

Lily crossed her arms in front of her. Spartacus's well-being aside, she resented the way Fletcher was trying to make this her problem. "Like the one I live in, I suppose," she said dryly.

Fletcher's golden-brown eyes gleamed. "It is big."

"It's huge." And way too much for one person, Lily thought. But the property, which had been in her family for generations, had been entrusted to her, so she couldn't sell it any more than she could get rid of Madsen's Flower Shoppe. But none of that had anything whatsoever to do with what was going on here. "And I still don't buy your excuse for not taking him since there are walking trails that lead to the park that start right across the square." Fletcher could manage if he wanted.

"Only one problem with that," Fletcher shot back while Spartacus sat patiently at their feet, his head moving back and forth like that of a person watching a tennis game. "When I'm not here at the clinic working, I'm out on ranches and farms, taking care of large animals."

"So get Spartacus obedience trained to the highest level by your cousin Susan Hart—" who was famous for her work with search-and-rescue dogs "—and take him literally everywhere you go. You're certainly in a business conducive to it."

Fletcher rejected her suggestion with the same fervor he attached to her desire to date Carson McRue. "A good vet knows better than to get emotionally attached to his patients."

"So, adopt Spartacus and get another vet to take care of him," Lily said.

"N.L. is relying on me to get him well." Fletcher reached down to pet his head, and was rewarded with a single but heartfelt thump of tail. Fletcher straightened and stepped forward slightly, further invading her space. "Besides, there is no room in my life for a dog," he told her, looking deep into her eyes, his smile widening once again. "You, on the other hand, could use the company and protection a big handsome dog like Spartacus offers. He's been through a lot, losing his owner and all. So he's going to need a lot of TLC, especially for the first few weeks."

Lily stepped back a pace, putting a necessary distance between them. "Thereby putting the kibosh on my pursuit of Carson McRue?" she volleyed right back.

Fletcher nodded solemnly. "You know what they say. For all worthwhile endeavors, sacrifices must be made."

Lily rolled her eyes. "You're shameless. You know that?"

Fletcher grinned but didn't deny it as the phone rang in the other room. Abruptly sobering, he said, "Look, just stay with him for a few minutes, will you?" Fletcher rushed off to answer it.

Spartacus scooted closer. He looked up at Lily with those big sad eyes, silently beseeching her, and wreaking havoc on her tender heart.

"I really have to go," Lily called after him. She was not going to do this. She was not....

Hadn't she promised herself she wouldn't let anyone or anything else tie her down, or distract her from having fun, fun, fun? She did not need to be sitting home baby-sitting a traumatized dog, no matter how lovable.... She needed to be out, fancy-free, kicking up her heels, recovering her lost youth....

"I mean it, Fletcher Hart!" Lily continued.

Fletcher stuck his head back in the room, the still ringing cordless clutched in his hand, his expression reproving. "Really, Lily. What's two minutes petting Spartacus going to cost you?"

"I know what he's doing," Lily told Spartacus as the door shut behind Fletcher, and she heard him start talking on the phone. Unable to help herself, she bent down and gently petted the silky soft back of Spartacus's blond head. "He's trying to get me to bond with you so I'll want to adopt you and take you home with me. That might be a good idea in theory because the old mausoleum I live in could use a little livening up. But the truth is that I'm not sure I still have any love left to give."

Lily swallowed hard around the ache that rose in her throat. "Losing Grandmother Rose was so hard. I kept thinking I'd feel better." But instead she had remained so numb inside. So depressed and alone and hopeless, all at once. Lily stroked him behind the ears, and heard him give a little moan in the back of his throat, not so very different from a cat's purr. But unlike a cat, a species known for its aloofness, Spartacus seemed to want desperately to attach himself to her. And Lily understood that, too. She desperately missed having a family to call her own; the party at Helen Hart's the night before had reminded her of that. "But then I guess you know a lot about that, too, don't you?" Lily continued softly, still petting the extremely gentle-natured dog. "Having lost the only family in your own life."

"Okay—" Fletcher burst back in, abruptly all business "—you can go now."

The only problem, Lily thought, was that she didn't want to go, since she and Spartacus were just starting to get acquainted.

"I mean it." Fletcher shooed her toward the door. "*Hasta la vista,* baby. Vamoose. See you around."

Lily straightened with as much dignity as she could manage, wishing she were a lot taller than five foot five inches. She propped both her hands on her hips and demanded indignantly, "Where did you learn your manners?"

"Didn't," Fletcher retorted briskly. "Can't you tell?"

Lily blew out an exasperated breath, unsure whether she wanted to kiss him again or kick him in the shin. "Some things are glaringly apparent." To her frustration, he looked pleased—instead of annoyed—by her insult, as if there was nothing he would rather do than work her into a temper and stand there trading insults with her. Spartacus, however, just looked upset to see her leaving. Her heart clenching, despite her efforts to stay emotionally uninvolved, Lily paused at the door.

She swallowed hard around the ache in her throat. "Seriously, Fletcher, what is going to happen to N. L. Spartacus?"

The mirth left Fletcher's expression. "I can keep him here another day or so."

Lily's heartbeat sped up another notch. "And then what?" she demanded.

He regarded her steadily. "Like you said, it's really not your problem, Lily."

Silence fell between them, more poignant than ever.

"I'm hoping to find a family for him," Fletcher continued seriously.

"And if you don't?"

He regarded her brusquely. "That's not something you need to worry about."

"Then why did you introduce me to him, bring me over here, have me pet him?" Lily demanded.

Abruptly, the artifice, the teasing fell away. Lily thought she got a glimpse of the real, unguarded man behind his customary mask of cynicism and what-the-hell playfulness. "Because I thought —" A shadow passed over Fletcher's eyes. His expression tightened as he swept a hand through his hair. "It doesn't matter what I thought," he told her in a gruff voice, as Spartacus went back to sit on Fletcher's foot. "I was wrong."

An hour and a half later, Lily discussed the situation with the other bridesmaids as they congregated at a department store in Crabtree Mall in Raleigh, trying on shoes for Janey's wedding. "He's trying to get me to fall in love with N. L. Spartacus."

Janey eyed her. "Seems to be working."

"He thinks if I have a dog I can't continue to try and

win my bet with you-all." Lily turned to Susan Hart, Janey's cousin. "Which is why I was thinking...maybe you could take him?" Susan not only operated her own kennels on her farm outside Holly Springs, she headed up the North Carolina Labrador Retriever Rescue Association.

Susan, a voluptuous thirtysomething with champagne blond hair, shook her head wistfully. "I wish I could. But I'm at capacity and then some right now, with dogs that are coming into Labrador Retriever Rescue. You know how it is. Everyone wants their kid to have a puppy at Christmas. Six to nine months later they realize maybe this is too much work after all, and they just take the dog to the pound."

Emma sucked in a breath. "That's terrible."

"I know," Susan agreed. "But a lot of the dogs I get are able to be either adopted out to good homes, or trained to work with police and fire departments around the state. But it takes time to make a placement. Dogs that have been abandoned—like Spartacus—have issues, and require an awful lot of tender loving care, to feel secure again. That's why Fletcher won't take him—he doesn't have the time to give Spartacus the TLC he needs."

"Or so he says," Lily grumbled, wishing Fletcher hadn't made it seem to her like she was N. L. Spartacus's only hope. He had to know—from the way she had let her own needs and desires go unmet when she was taking care of her grandmother—what a soft touch she was. And how very hard it was for her to say no to someone who asked for her help, even when it was for the best. She also wished Spartacus hadn't looked at her with such sad, lonely eyes.

Misunderstanding the depth of her dilemma, Janey murmured, "You know, you don't have to go through with the bet you made with us on your birthday, Lily. If you didn't we would all understand."

Lily saw the pity in their eyes. She'd had enough of that, too.

"You really didn't know what you were saying that night," Emma continued, gently giving Lily the out they all seemed to feel she needed.

What none of them understood was that the night of her birthday was the first time in years she had felt really and truly vibrantly alive. The only other time was when she'd been arguing with—or kissing—Fletcher, and that was just because he was so darn difficult and made her so hot under the collar.

Lily looked at the young women gathered around her as she tried on a pair of strappy black-and-white sandals. "So I wasn't just foolish, I was stupid, too? Is that it?"

They all frowned in a way that let her know she was overreacting. "Reckless, maybe," Hannah conceded, as she put the correct-size shoes back in the box for purchase. "That was quite a loser's penalty you cooked up for yourself."

"One none of us would ever expect you to follow through with," Emma—who had made her own share of life's mistakes—said seriously.

Lily sighed again. They thought she didn't have it in her to be wild and crazy and fear-free. Because of the circumstances she had found herself in back in college, she'd never had the opportunity to embrace her youth the way other coeds did.

But Lily wasn't responsible for anyone else now. It wasn't too late. She could go back, recapture those years, that sense of heady freedom she had always yearned to experience.

"We could even substitute it with something else," Susan Hart suggested brightly. "Like another bar or an event where you buy us all nachos and margaritas."

And didn't that sound dull, Lily thought, even as she absolutely dreaded what lay ahead if she didn't win her bet. "I'm not going to welsh on my wager," Lily said stubbornly, refusing to back down on the audacious claims she had made. As the looks of sympathy around her deepened, she continued with a devil-may-care-air she couldn't begin to really feel. "Besides, it's not as if I'm going to have to do what I swore I would do if I lost. Because I am going to get a date with Carson McRue before this week is up." She just knew it.

Hannah Reid looked worried again. "Has he even spoken to you?"

"No," Lily admitted reluctantly. "But he was eyeing me this morning. And I know that look."

It was the same look that guys always gave her before they worked up the courage to ask her out on a date. It was only later, when they found out how dull, how prim-and-proper she really was at heart, that they lost interest in her. Just as Carson eventually would. But that wasn't the point. The point was to do something daring and unexpected that would expand her horizons, herald a new much more interesting way of life. It was an effort to break completely with the heartache of five years that had been filled with illness and grief, as well as the boredom and depression of the last year. It was a way to recast her as sexy and exciting, instead of sweet and hopelessly angelic.

"What's it to Fletcher anyway who you want to date?" Hannah asked curiously.

Lily shook her head, glad to talk about something other than reconfiguring the bet. Lord only knew. She had been trying to figure out that one herself.

"Could he be jealous?" Janey frowned.

Lily shook her head, protesting, "There's nothing between Fletcher and me."

Susan grinned as she slipped off one pair of sandals and tried on another. "The kiss last night says other-wise."

The heat of embarrassment climbed from Lily's cheeks. "Nothing besides that," Lily amended hastily. "And that kiss didn't mean anything." Even if it felt like it had, at the time....

"Maybe he wishes the kiss did mean something," Emma said sagely.

Lily stiffened her shoulders, trying hard not to re-member how movie-star handsome Fletcher had looked standing shoulder to shoulder with Carson McRue in the town square that morning. As if Fletcher were the to-die-for sexy celebrity, and Carson McRue, merely average in comparison. It wasn't as if she had to make a choice between the two of them, anyway. "Don't be ridiculous." She scowled at Emma and the others.

Just because Fletcher looked at her as if he wanted to bed her did not mean he ever would. "Fletcher is just being contrary." Lily continued her argument that nothing was going on between them. "Proving all over again that he is no Sir Galahad. And that romance, or even the hope of it, is for fools."

Silence fell between them. Fletcher had such a reputation as a mischief-loving cynic, no one could dispute that.

Lily looked at Janey. "Why is your brother like that, anyway?"

Janey's lips took on a troubled curve. "I don't know. At some point after our dad died, he just became really cynical and kind of only out for himself, his own ambitions and goals." She paused, shaking her head in bewil-derment and regret. "None of us have been able to get close to him emotionally. I mean, I know Fletcher loves us and would—when it came right down to it—do anything for us. But on a day-to-day basis? He's definitely got his own agenda and not a one of us is privy to what that might be."

The next morning, Lily picked up an assortment of fresh doughnuts, four cups of hot coffee and headed over to the barricades. Very little filming had been done the previous day and, judging by the amount of activity going on in front of one of the buildings being used as a backdrop, the cast and crew seemed anxious to make it up.

She had her cover story all prepared—that she was bringing this order by for Carson. But as it turned out, it wasn't necessary to use hijinks for an introduction. The moment Carson McRue laid eyes on Lily, he headed her way, telling the guard standing watch over the barricades to let Lily on through. As she closed the distance between them, he flashed her the cocky grin he used on TV, gallantly took the breakfast she offered and led her toward his trailer.

"I was hoping I'd get the chance to meet you," he

told her warmly as someone rushed to open the door for them. "I noticed you yesterday."

He led her inside the incredibly outfitted trailer. It had a living room, a well-equipped kitchen and a bedroom with a king-size bed.

"I wanted to meet you, too, but I couldn't get close to you," Lily said shyly. Although she was momentarily mesmerized by Carson's drop-dead handsomeness, it surprised her that he was just five inches taller than she was and rather slight in build when compared to, say, the six-foot-one, two-hundred-pound, Fletcher Hart.

"I apologize." Ignoring the breakfast she had brought, Carson went to the fridge and got out bottles of imported spring water. "Our producers are a little nuts about the possibility of anyone getting hurt, and with all the cords, power sources and booms—"

"I understand," Lily said with a smile, sitting down on the butter-soft leather sofa. She moved over slightly when he sat down a little too close to her. "It's very responsible of you."

Okay, she was here. This was her dream come true. So why wasn't she more excited? Why didn't she feel the butterflies in her tummy that she felt when she was around Fletcher Hart?

Carson looked her over from head to toe, before returning to laser in on her eyes once again. "So what are you doing tonight?" he asked, drinking deeply.

Cut straight to the chase, why don't you? Lily thought. *But why are you complaining? This will help you win your bet. And you won't have to...* Aware Carson was waiting for her answer, while she was sitting there arguing with herself, Lily said, "I've got a fitting for a bridesmaid dress."

"What about tomorrow night?" he asked, gulping down some more of that designer bottled water.

Lily knew what she would like to be doing—kissing Fletcher Hart again. But since that wasn't about to happen... She shrugged. "I don't have anything planned."

"Perfect, then. It's a date." Carson pursed his lips together thoughtfully. "I'd take you out on the town," he said after a moment, "but we'd be mobbed with my fans."

Lily didn't mind. As long as she accomplished what she had set out to do....

"Tell you what. Why don't you come to my hotel tomorrow evening—the Regency, in Raleigh—and have dinner with me there? Say around nine-thirty?"

Lily was surprised to find she really didn't want to go, at least not as much as she had initially thought she would if she were ever to get herself in this situation. But a bet was a bet and it would serve Fletcher Hart right if she were to win after all he had done to waylay her. "Sounds great," Lily fibbed, still coming to terms with the fact she was about to have dinner with a TV star.

A rap sounded on the trailer door. Carson's young and pretty female assistant stepped in. "Carson? There's a Dr. Fletcher Hart—"

She didn't have a chance to finish as Fletcher shouldered his way in. Fletcher looked at Lily and saw her sitting next to Carson on the leather sofa. He was not pleased.

"How are you doing in finding me a horse to use?" Carson demanded.

"No luck—yet. At least not in the hue you want. But that's not why I'm here. I'm here to collect my woman," Fletcher announced with all the audacity of a big-screen hero.

Lily blinked. And just as audaciously tossed a glance behind, to the left and right of her. Nope. No one else standing there.

Hands braced on his hips, Fletcher regarded Lily with exaggerated patience. "What have I told you about chasing other guys?" he demanded, as unamused by her antics as she was by his.

"Nothing," Lily said, enunciating slowly, as if he were a dunce. And truly Fletcher was behaving like one.

Fletcher gave Carson a man-to-man glance. "What can I say? This is all a game to her. She likes the chase—" Fletcher reached out, grabbed Lily's hand and tugged her off the sofa "—and I like giving her one." Behaving as if he had some right to be going all possessive on her, Fletcher tucked one muscular arm behind her knees, the other behind her back.

"You can't be serious," Lily groaned, not sure when she had ever felt so shocked and embarrassed, as Carson McRue and his assistant exchanged astonished looks.

Heart racing, she pushed her hands against Fletcher's chest—for all the good it did her. Fletcher swept her off her feet and cradled against his chest. The assistant held the door for him and Fletcher carried Lily down the steps. While everyone looked on with unbridled interest—including the townspeople gathered to watch the action, cast, and crew, directors and producers—Fletcher paused in the middle of the roped-off area. Still holding her cradled in his arms, he slowly, ardently lowered his head to hers.

"Don't. You. Dare," Lily warned.

Chapter 3

But of course Fletcher did, and when the kiss came, it was just as masterful, just as dangerously uninhibited and exciting as before. Lily moaned in a combination of fury and dismay, luxuriating in the feel of his lips on hers. For the first time in her life, she was with a man who wasn't afraid to give her the unrestrained passion she craved, and she reveled in the hard, insistent demand of his mouth on hers, the erotic sweep of his tongue, the way he brought his hands up and tunneled his fingers through her hair.

Lily told herself to resist him. She couldn't let him think he could do this to her again, kiss her just to put on a show, but there was just something about the way he held her and kissed her that totally destroyed her will. He was just so warm and strong and male, so demanding and yet so giving, too. Despite herself, Lily felt herself melt against him. She had never felt so much a woman nor been as aware of any man.

Her nipples were tightening almost painfully beneath her dress. Lower still, there was a definite pressure building, a weakness in her knees. The need, the desire, to take this somewhere quiet, somewhere private, spiraled through her body. But that was crazy, she reminded herself firmly. It wasn't as if she and Fletcher were in love, or could ever be that attached to each other—not with him as deeply cynical and domineering as he was. And she wasn't the kind of woman who would ever react this passionately out of pure physical need, never mind in front of a crowd of onlookers. But with Fletcher Hart holding her against him and kissing her as if she was already his, that was exactly what she was doing.

With effort, Lily pulled herself together and put on the brakes. And it was only then when she had come treacherously close to surrendering to him completely that Fletcher let the tempestuous kiss come to a halt.

Lily told herself she should be furious. But as he released her, heat suffused her and excitement—unlike anything she had ever felt—roared through her. Dimly, she became aware of two things. One, the larger-than-life romance she had been looking for had somehow found her when she least expected it. Not in Beverly Hills or on a private Learjet, but in her hometown of Holly Springs. And two, people were clapping! Hooting and hollering, encouraging Fletcher to take her in his arms and kiss her again. And darned if the son-of-a-gun didn't look tempted.

"You are unbelievable," Lily fumed.

"Yeah, I know." Fletcher tipped the brim of his straw cowboy hat in her direction and grinned at her unrepentantly. "You can thank me later," he promised.

"Thank you?" Lily echoed, all the more incensed.

He leaned close enough to whisper in her ear. "For helping you win your bet."

Lily blinked, and leaned back, fearful that if their bodies touched they would end up kissing again. "What?" Mirroring him, she pretended an insouciance she couldn't begin to feel.

Fletcher acted as if he were imparting top secret information, of the men-only variety. "Men like competition, Lily. I figured if Mr. Magoo—"

"McRue," Lily corrected, noting thankfully that if Carson had witnessed any of what had just gone on, he had since disappeared.

"Whatever," Fletcher continued with a disinterested wave of his hand. "Just that if he saw you kissing me right out in the open like that it might spur him on to try and stake his claim."

Lily glared at Fletcher, wishing she weren't still tingling everywhere he'd touched her…and even more tellingly, everywhere he hadn't. "Is that what you were doing?" she demanded in raging disbelief.

"Yup. Thought it would inspire him to start trying to woo you into accepting a date with him."

Lily blew out an exasperated breath and raked her hands through her hair, trying to restore order to the curls Fletcher had mussed with his fingertips. "Carson McRue does not have to woo me."

Fletcher looked incensed. "Well, he should," he counseled her sternly. "Lily. For heaven's sake! You can't just give it away."

She was going to slug him. She really was. She didn't care who was looking on. Holding on to her temper by a thread, she pushed the words through her teeth. "I am not giving anything away."

Fletcher nodded with mocking approval. "That's good. Play hard to get," he encouraged her baldly. "It works with me."

"And just so you know," Lily continued with a regal toss of her head, "Carson did not need your help getting motivated where I'm concerned. He's already asked me for a date."

For once, Fletcher didn't have a ready comeback. In fact he was silent for so long Lily almost convinced herself he cared whom she went out with.

"When?" Fletcher asked finally in a low, too casual tone.

"Tomorrow evening." Lily smiled at him smugly, glad to see that she at last had the upper hand.

Fletcher seemed to consider that. "Where?"

Lily felt her nerves tighten at the ornery look in his eyes. "None of your business."

Fletcher nodded, looking grim and almost brooding again. "You're right," he said. "It isn't."

That couldn't be disappointment she felt, could it? Lily wondered as silence fell between them once again.

"If you don't care what I do," she reasoned slowly, searching his face for some clue, "then why did you come over here and cut short my conversation with Carson like that?" Why had he carried her off and kissed her like there was no tomorrow. Lily was sure it hadn't been just to create a scene.

Fletcher shrugged his broad shoulders, stuck his hands in the front pockets of his jeans. "Because I thought you might like to say goodbye to N. L. Spartacus," he said.

"And sent that teenager in with a sealed envelope of cash and instructions."

"What can I say?" Fletcher lifted his hands in a mock gesture of helplessness. "The kid owed me a favor."

"You are shameless," Lily accused sternly. And sexy as could be, standing there, smelling of aftershave, his shaggy honey-brown hair all rumpled, and the hint of evening beard on his masculine face. If she didn't know better, she would think he was getting ready to go on a weeknight date, instead of merely ending a workday.

His expressive lips tilted up in a playful half smile. "I prefer to think of myself as a facilitator," he told her wryly.

"I'll bet." Lily sighed, wishing she didn't recall quite so acutely just how much fun it had been to kiss him, even when the proud part of her said she should have been slugging him a good one. She tilted her head, wishing he didn't have a good eight inches on her in height. The disparity in their bodies made him seem all the more overwhelming. And she did not want to be taken over by Fletcher Hart, D.V.M. Setting her jaw, she forced herself to focus on the reason for her being there. "Why did Mr. N. L. Spartacus want to send the staff flowers, anyway?"

Fletcher appeared just as distracted as she was as he let his gaze rove over her hair, face and lips, before returning with laser accuracy to her eyes. "The usual," he said seriously. "N. L. Spartacus was grateful for the care he received here and wanted to show it."

"Mmm-hmm." Lily wasn't sure whether she was buying any of this or not. She narrowed her eyes at Fletcher. "And then you set it up so I had no choice but to bring the arrangement over myself." Thereby keep-

Once again, they were in completely unexpected territory. "Goodbye?" Lily echoed, nonplussed.

Fletcher lifted his left wrist and glanced at his watch. "The guy from the shelter's going to be by anytime now to pick him up." That said, Fletcher turned on his heel and began walking in the direction of the clinic.

"You're kidding." Lily rushed to catch up with Fletcher.

Fletcher said nothing and continued walking, all the way into his clinic. Since office hours weren't set to begin yet, the only person there was his receptionist office manager. She flashed a wan smile, seeming to think the same Lily did about Fletcher's actions.

"I can't believe you are really doing this," Lily said.

Fletcher looked all the more determined as he went through a stack of phone messages the receptionist handed him. "Spartacus needs a home and a family who'll love him. The shelter is his best shot for getting adopted."

"And if he doesn't, then what?" Lily demanded, nearly in tears as she rushed into the room where Spartacus was being kept.

The big yellow lab was lying on his side in the cage, but when he saw them he lifted his head.

His expression turning almost tender it was so compassionate, Fletcher opened the door and motioned the dog out.

Spartacus lumbered slowly to his feet, stretched, then—as if sensing this to-do was all about him— sat abruptly back on his haunches and stared at them stoically, refusing to come out of the cage. And Lily couldn't blame the poor sweet dog, given what Fletcher had in store for him.

"Look—" Fletcher gestured toward Spartacus like a particularly disinterested salesperson "—he's a beautiful animal. Sad but gentle natured."

That, Lily knew, might not save Spartacus from an unwarranted end. "He could get put to sleep!"

Fletcher turned his glance away and didn't respond, reminding Lily that was all part of his job. "Do you want to say goodbye or not?" he demanded harshly, the distant brooding look back in his eyes.

Like clockwork, the shelter guy strode into the reception area, leash in hand. Lily's heart slammed against her ribs and her breath caught in her throat. Numb no longer, she stepped between Spartacus and the two men, stated fiercely, "I am not going to let you do this!"

As if sensing he finally had a savior worth his attentions, Spartacus finally lumbered out of his cage and stood looking up at Lily with his big sad eyes, his tail down between his legs.

Fletcher frowned and folded his arms in front of his chest. He looked ready to square off, too. "You don't have anything to say about it."

"Yes, I do," Lily shot right back, unable to believe how cruel Fletcher was being. Her heart going out to the poor, grieving animal, Lily knelt beside the far-too-skinny yellow lab and wrapped her arms around Spartacus's neck. She regarded Fletcher stubbornly. "I'm taking him home with me."

Fletcher's brows drew together in accusatory fashion. Unwilling to admit she had offered up a solution, he said, "I thought you didn't want a dog."

"I don't," Lily insisted as Spartacus trembled in her arms, his short, dense coat surprisingly soft and silky beneath her hands. He'd had a bath recently, and he smelled of fragrant dog shampoo. "But a lot of people who come into Madsen's Flower Shoppe do. I'll put up a sign. Heck—" she rose gracefully, tilting her head back determinedly, prepared to go toe to toe with Fletcher once again "—I'll take him to work with me and I'll find him a good home with no help at all from you!"

Lily had plenty of time to regret her actions as she walked the still-somewhat-wobbly-legged N. L. Spartacus across the town square. Her reservations were echoed by her three very talented part-time florists. Mothers all, they juggled family, home and work responsibilities and were grateful for the flexible hours Lily allowed them. "What are you doing with a dog?" Maryellen asked.

"Finding him a home." Briefly, Lily explained, as she got out the digital camera she used for taking photographs of floral arrangements and took a close-up of his handsome face. "The problem is I don't know anything about taking care of a dog."

"Well, don't look at me," the bespectacled Maryellen said as Lily hooked her camera into her computer and printed out the photo while her staff continued to gather round her.

Belinda held up hands made plump by her latest pregnancy. "I've only let the kids get hamsters."

Sheila ran a hand across her perpetually sunburned cheeks. "My expertise is limited to our parakeets."

"Does he even know how to 'stay'?" Maryellen asked as she bent to tentatively pet Spartacus's white-blond head.

Lily had no idea. "I guess I'll find out," she said,

getting out what she needed to make up the poster that would find the orphaned pet a new home.

As it happened, she needn't have worried. Spartacus never let her leave his sight. In fact, he was so hyper-vigilant about where she was and what she was doing, Lily was starting to get a little worried, as she taped a sign in the window of Madsen's Flower Shoppe. It said Wanted—Loving Home For 3-Year-Old Yellow Lab. She had taped a digital photograph of Spartacus beneath it and wrote Ask Inside....

As Lily had hoped, it wasn't long before she had drummed up some interest. A young mother with two elementary-school-age children walked in. They spotted Spartacus sitting tensely beside Lily and headed for him eagerly.

The woman bent down to inspect him. "Is this him?"

Lily smiled. "It sure is."

"What's her name?"

"It's a he. And it's Spartacus." N. L. Spartacus...

The little boy pulled on his mommy's arm. "How come he's not wagging his tail?"

The woman frowned. "He doesn't look very happy. We had in mind something a little more...exuberant."

Lily nodded, understanding the woman's feelings, even as her feelings of protectiveness toward the dog increased tenfold. "He's had a rough time," she stated quietly.

As if on cue, Spartacus moved closer to Lily.

"Well, I wish you luck in finding him a home," the woman said, gathering her kids close and backing toward the door.

The same scenario was repeated throughout the morning. People came in. Spartacus pretty much ignored them all. Even going so far a few times as to turn his head completely away.

"I wonder how hard it is to teach a dog social skills," Maryellen murmured as she put a finished arrangement awaiting pickup into the refrigerator, and then stepped to the front of the shop to check on the progress of the filming on the other side of the square.

"I thought it was kind of automatic for canines to wag their tails and look happy," Belinda said, joining Maryellen at the picture window, her attention also fixated on the TV show scene unfolding before them.

"Me, too," Sheila murmured as the four of them gathered to watch Carson McRue step before the cameras. Someone called "Action!" on a bullhorn and he began conversing with the actor in front of him. The exchange wasn't long. The director nodded his approval. Seconds later, Carson disappeared into his trailer once again.

"Somehow I thought it would be more exciting," Maryellen murmured.

No kidding, Lily thought. She had expected to be riveted when Carson McRue hit town. After all, the handsome, charismatic actor had been a favorite of hers for years. She had watched him turn from a teen heartthrob and player of bit parts into an occasional film actor and the star of his own TV show. But she found he couldn't hold a candle to the other man currently figuring prominently in her life—Fletcher Hart.

And speak of the devil…

Lily turned away from the picture window, hoping he hadn't seen her. "I'll be in the back," she said, beating a hasty retreat to her private office. She had end-of-August bills to be paid, biweekly paychecks to issue.

Spartacus was right beside her.

Seconds later, the bell over the front door rang, and Lily felt as well as heard Fletcher stride in, the atmosphere in her century-old shop changing that much.

"Afternoon, ladies," he said, his deep, low voice supercharging the flower-and-greenery-scented air with his palpable masculinity.

Lily slid sideways in her swivel-based task chair. Able to catch a glimpse of him tipping the brim of his hat toward the three ladies gathered around him, Lily scooted back out of sight and buried her head even deeper in her paperwork.

"Where is she?" Fletcher asked.

One of them must have pointed, because she heard him say, "Thanks." Seconds later, his powerful presence was filling her door frame. As their glances meshed, Lily's heart took a leap, although she couldn't imagine why. It wasn't as if she were letting him or his antics get to her....

Fletcher glanced down at Spartacus, who was sitting beside her. As Fletcher studied Spartacus, the canine surveyed him right back. No words were spoken, no contact made, and yet they seemed to be communicating—rather seriously—with each other just the same. Finally, Fletcher nodded in something akin to grudging approval. "He seems to be doing all right."

For some reason, Fletcher's presumption of incompetence on her part rankled—a lot more than it should have under the circumstances. "Didn't think I could handle him?" Lily challenged sweetly as she tipped back in her chair.

The way he looked at her then, as if he was remembering how it felt to kiss her and wanted to do it again ASAP had her pulse racing. "As you said," he reminded her with a smug male confidence that upped her emotions even more, "you're not a dog person. And that being the case, I figured you might not know what to feed him."

"Dog food?" Lily took a wild guess.

"Actually," Fletcher said seriously, leaning against the edge of her desk to face her, "canned chicken and rice puppy food would be best because it's particularly gentle on the stomach. He really needs to eat small amounts frequently, for the next week or so, while we continue to get his digestive system back in shape."

The concern in his eyes lessened her annoyance with him. Lily nodded her understanding. "I'll have to get some."

"Which is exactly why I'm here," Fletcher said. "It being lunch hour, I figured the three of us could walk down to the pet store and get what you're going to need for him."

Lily did need a dog-size water dish. The one she was using now was a three-inch plastic flower pot, with a hole in the bottom and a saucer underneath. The one time Spartacus had tried to drink from it, he had knocked it over, gotten startled and hadn't gone near it since.

"Maybe stop in the park on the way back?" Fletcher continued helpfully.

Lily wasn't very experienced in getting a dog to do what it needed to do in that regard, either. In fact, she hadn't the faintest idea how to go about it. Although she would die before admitting that to Fletcher. "All right."

She rose with as much dignity as possible and looked at him sternly. "But just so we're clear—no more kisses."

Fletcher grinned and laid a hand across his heart. "I promise. I'll be every inch the gentlemen where N. L. Spartacus is concerned."

Lily sighed and rolled her eyes as she got Spartacus's leash and clumsily attached it to his collar. "You know what I mean, Dr. Hart."

Fletcher's eyes sparkled all the more. "Indeed I do."

"I hear you and Fletcher had lunch in the park today," Janey said when Lily arrived at the bridal shop for the final fitting of her bridesmaid dress.

"Word gets around," Lily surmised happily.

Janey shot her a knowing glance. "What do you expect when you're seen kissing him in the town square at eight in the morning, in front of a crowd of oh, say, a couple hundred of the most talkative citizens in town?"

Lily tried—and failed—to erase that romantic interlude from memory. Pretending it had meant nothing to her, she waved a hand disparagingly. "Fletcher was just fooling around."

"Knowing my brother the way I do, that's obvious." Janey paused, her concern deepening as she handed Lily the dress she was to try on for the seamstress. "What's your excuse?"

Lily swallowed as she slipped out of the sundress she had worn to work. That was the problem. She had no excuse for her increasingly potent reaction to Janey's brother. All she had to do was be near Fletcher or see him and her heart speeded up, her knees went weak and every resistance seemed to fade. "He caught me off guard. And he was just doing it to help me win my bet."

Janey helped Lily slip into the sophisticated black-and-white bridesmaid dress. "You're kidding."

Lily shrugged. "That's what Fletcher claims."

"Hmm." Janey looked unconvinced as Lily stepped up onto the dressmaker's stool to look at herself in the three-way mirror. "Well, that's a new one, anyway."

Lily turned this way and that and found the alterations had been flawless. The long column dress fit her like a second skin. "Why? Has Fletcher done this before? Gotten between a woman and her potential beau just for sport?"

"No. Actually, he hasn't." Janey looked seriously worried once again. "Usually it's women pursuing him."

Satisfied, Lily stepped off the stool and turned so Janey could unzip her. "Do they ever catch him?" Fletcher more often dated women outside of Holly Springs. Probably to avoid the local gossips knowing more than he wanted them to know.

Janey sighed dispiritedly as she helped Lily out of the satin gown. "If they do, it's not for long. Which is why I want you to be careful. He's my brother and I love him dearly, but I wouldn't wish a gotta-have-my-space guy like him on my worst enemy. So be careful."

"Believe me," Lily fibbed, as she changed back into her sundress, "I am in no danger of losing my heart to him. The only reason I was with Fletcher at noon was because I needed help getting some basic supplies for Spartacus."

Janey studied her contemplatively. "And Fletcher helped you pick them out?"

"As well as paid for them," Lily said, feeling both pleased and puzzled about that. For a guy who had been trying to send the homeless dog to the pound only hours earlier, Fletcher had been very generous, purchasing all the dog necessities as well as several toys and a book on dog basics. Then he arranged the pet store to deliver all the supplies to her home that evening at five, so she could put them all away. "The only reason he bought me lunch was that we were both in the park with Spartacus, and we had corn dogs and sodas. It was no big deal. Believe me."

Janey looked even more skeptical but wisely changed the subject. "So what have you got on your agenda this evening?" she asked as the seamstress zipped up Lily's now perfectly fitting dress and got it ready to go.

"I'm going into Raleigh to do some shopping," Lily declared, pushing the lingering image of Dr. Fletcher Hart from her mind. She had a date with Carson McRue the following evening. And she was determined it would not only help her win the first part of her bet with her friends, but also mark a turning point for her. Somehow, some way, she wanted it to be a stepping stone out of her previously humdrum, sheltered existence, and change her life forever.

FLETCHER HAD HOPED to see Lily when he went to pick up his tuxedo at the formalwear shop that evening—since the fitting for the bridesmaid dresses was going on at the same time—but found out she had already left.

Doing his best to quell his disappointment, he tried everything on and headed out with formal clothes in tow. Returning home, he tried to eat some dinner and settle in with the endless paperwork that came with running the vet clinic, but again and again his thoughts turned to the blond-haired, blue-eyed angel who had very quickly come to dominate his life in recent days.

And that presence had to do with a lot more than the promise he had made to her grandmother Rose. It had to do with Lily.

He had started out just trying to divert her. All he'd wanted was to keep her from making a fool of herself over Carson McRue and to prevent Lily from getting permanently hurt in the bargain. And somehow in the midst of all that, he had ended up kissing her—twice— and wanting to make her his own.

Which in a sense made him just as bad as the Hollywood actor, because Fletcher had no intention of ever getting married or spending his life trying to make any one woman happy for the rest of their days. And that was exactly what a woman like Lily Madsen deserved— a man who could and would give her all that and more.

Which meant he had to go back to trying to waylay Lily from hooking up with Carson, while at the same time maintaining a more gentlemanly demeanor himself. Not an easy task, especially for someone who was as prone to screw-ups as he was when it came to those he cared about.

He was still figuring out how to achieve such an impossible feat when the phone rang at ten o'clock. He saw on the caller ID that it was Lily and picked up immediately.

"Hey, Lily, what's up?" he said as casually as if he hadn't been sitting around thinking about her all evening, wishing he were a better man so he could pursue her all-out—not just for now, but for keeps. Wishing he hadn't made that promise to her grandmother Rose to protect her and keep her from harm's way and any and all undeserving males. Just like him.

"Oh, Fletcher." Lily's voice caught on a heartfelt sob that went straight to Fletcher's gut.

Heart pounding, Fletcher vaulted out of his chair.

"I don't know what happened! I just left Spartacus for a short while. But he can't even stand up now and he's—he's b-bleeding!"

"Hang on, Lily," Fletcher said, reaching for his vet bag. "I'll be right there."

Chapter 4

Lily met Fletcher at the front door of the stately white Victorian, with pine-green trim, that she had inherited after her grandmother Rose's death. Although she was trying desperately to pull herself together, it was clear she had been crying. "Where is he?" Fletcher asked, all business.

Lily's lower lip trembled as she replied, "In the laundry room, where I had him while I was gone."

Together, they hurried through huge, high-ceilinged rooms filled with expensive antiques and dark heavy velvet draperies Fletcher guessed were nearly as old as the house. Lily had turned on lamps here and there, but none was enough to illuminate the majestic hallway that ran the length of the house.

She dashed through an equally out-of-date kitchen, where take-out bags from a popular Italian eatery still sat on the heavy oak table, past an open-shelf pantry into a room that had been converted to handle a modern washer and dryer. A drying rack, filled with all sorts of sheer and lacey unmentionables stood in one corner. Spartacus was curled up against the opposite wall, his back to the cushioned bed Lily had laid out for him. Blotches of dried blood dotted the white and black linoleum floor. Spartacus had been licking his front paws rapidly when they entered, but stopped and regarded them anxiously.

Fletcher got down on his haunches. "Where is he bleeding?" he asked, already starting to examine him.

Lily teared up again as she knelt down in front of Spartacus. "Right here. On the bottom of his paws."

She tried to show Fletcher, but Spartacus pulled his legs back and hid his paws beneath his torso so they couldn't get at them.

Fletcher moved in closer—his leg inadvertently touching hers in the process—and gently but firmly guided Spartacus over onto his side. Spartacus looked up at him with big sad eyes, but didn't struggle as Fletcher carefully examined the wet, saliva-stained paws. The skin between the digits was swollen and inflamed, painful to the slightest touch, and bleeding in spots. "I don't see anything stuck in here, like a piece of glass or a thorn or anything," Fletcher said, stroking Spartacus with one hand while continuing to examine him with the other.

"Then why was he chewing on them like that?" Lily demanded, petting Spartacus, too.

Fletcher looked into Spartacus's handsome face, continuing to reassure the big lab, even as he spoke. "Fear. Anxiety. He was probably scared, being left alone, and attempted to comfort himself—the same way a baby sucks on his or her thumb. And got a little carried away."

Lily sat back on her haunches, the skirt of her sundress riding up over her thighs. "Well, what can we do?" she asked, looking eager to help.

Ignoring the pressure building in his groin, the way it always did when he was near her like this, Fletcher rummaged through his brown leather vet bag. "I've got some Gentamicin sulfate spray that will help. We can put it on three times a day until his paws are better."

Lily raked her teeth across the softness of her lower lip as she turned troubled eyes to him. "Won't he lick it off?"

"Yes, he will," Fletcher replied, aware this was the first time he had ever seen Lily with her guard completely down. Even at her grandmother Rose's funeral, she had kept some of those prim-and-proper barriers around her heart, allowing people to only get so close, never reaching out to anyone. It had almost been as if she'd felt she would have been breaking some code of proper Southern womanhood by letting herself be vulnerable to anyone. At the time he had understood—he, too, liked keeping his guard up, never more so than when he was hurting. It was somehow easier that way. Now, he wondered if they both hadn't made a mistake....

Aware Lily was waiting for him to continue instructing her on the application of the medicine, Fletcher said, "Which is why it's a good idea to distract him with a walk or something right after you apply the spray."

Lily nodded, understanding, yet still looking a little apprehensive. She swallowed. "When he got up before, he was limping. That's how he got blood all over the floor."

Fletcher nodded thoughtfully. He smiled at Lily, noting the redness around her eyes was subsiding. "Got any old cotton socks you don't need anymore that you wouldn't mind donating to Spartacus here?"

"Sure." Lily was already scrambling to her feet, with another tempting flash of silken thigh. "I'll go get them."

While Lily ran off, Fletcher turned his attention to the rack of unmentionables flying like a sexy flag over his head. He knew he shouldn't be looking, but what the hell, it was probably the only chance he would ever have to discover what kind of lingerie Lily Madsen favored. From the looks of it—skimpy. Those were thongs, not grandma panties. And sheer low-cut bras of a size that looked…exactly right. Not too big, not too small.

Lily bustled back in. Catching the direction of his glance, she blushed all the harder. "A gentleman wouldn't have looked," she scolded him primly.

Fletcher grinned. He didn't know why but he sure enjoyed getting under her skin. "I think we've already established I'm no gentleman."

Her lips formed a skeptical pout. "You won't get an argument there."

She knelt beside him in a drift of lilac perfume, offering up a dozen or so socks in a rainbow of colors. "These okay?" she asked.

"Perfect," Fletcher said, thinking Spartacus was going to be the best-dressed Lab around. Now for the hard part. Frowning, he predicted, "Spartacus is probably not going to like this. So I want you to get around behind him, so you can cradle his head in your lap and

comfort him while I work." Fletcher got a roll of surgical tape and scissors from his bag and set them down
beside the antiseptic wash and aforementioned antibi-
otic-analgesic-anti-inflammatory spray.

"Just talk to him, sweetheart," Fletcher instructed
Lily, as she scooted around to comply with Fletcher's
instructions.

"Did you hear that?" Lily asked as she cuddled and
petted Spartacus as if she'd had the sad-eyed yellow Lab
since birth instead of for just one day. "He just called
me sweetheart." She frowned at Fletcher, the prettiest
picture of reproof he had ever seen. "No one calls me
sweetheart," Lily continued sternly.

Fletcher did his best to stifle a grin. "Maybe they
should," he murmured right back.

Lily drew an indignant breath. "I beg your pardon!"

"Well—" Fletcher shrugged, relishing the fact he
was getting under her skin once again "—it never hurts
to loosen up."

Leave it to Fletcher Hart, Lily thought, to get straight
to the heart of the matter. Loosen up was exactly what
she had been trying to do the night of her twenty-fifth
birthday party, and every day before and since. Loosening up was what had gotten her in such trouble. Because of that, she was either about to be embarrassed
by losing a bet she never should have made—or in a
situation with an actor who, in reality, might be a whole
lot different than the fun and affable character he por-
trayed on TV.

"Just keep petting and stroking," Fletcher instructed
as he shook the bottle, gently separated the digits on
Spartacus's paw, applied a topical cleanser and then
sprayed it liberally with the medication. "Yeah, I know,

buddy," Fletcher soothed when Spartacus yelped and struggled to be free. He held him down flat with the palms of his hands. "That last stuff stings. But the medicine is going to help, you'll see."

Fletcher continued soothing Spartacus as he worked on his paws, first cleaning, then medicating them with spray and finally pulling on socks and securing them in place with white surgical tape. By the time Fletcher had finished, Spartacus was looking up at Fletcher with a mixture of trust and affection.

"You're really good with him," Lily noted.

Fletcher shrugged. "It's my job." He dropped the scissors back in his veterinary bag and handed the roll of tape and spray to her. "Keep these. You'll need 'em when it comes time to apply the medicine again."

Lily blinked. "You don't expect me to do this by myself!"

"That's usually the procedure."

Lily looked doubtfully at Spartacus. He really had not liked that spray, but had also been smart enough to realize he was outnumbered. If she were to attempt it solo, there was no guaranteeing he would be anywhere near as cooperative. And she didn't want to screw up by accidentally spraying Spartacus in the eye or something. "Well, couldn't you come by to help me with this tomorrow before you go to work?"

"Lily Madsen!" Fletcher scolded her playfully before giving her a heated once-over. "Are you inviting me for breakfast?"

Lily continued petting Spartacus and tried not to think how debonairly sexy Fletcher looked whenever he was teasing her. "Is it required?"

He favored her with a flirtatious smile that did funny

things to her insides as he got lithely to his feet. "For a free house call that time of day?" He nodded with mock solemnity. "I should think so."

Lily wrinkled her nose at him, trying not to think how intimate it would feel to start her day off with him by her side. "I hope you're not expecting a four-course meal," she said.

Fletcher looked at her gently. "A cup of coffee and bagel would be fine."

Lily tried not to think how much she enjoyed having Fletcher around. "All right. What time?"

Fletcher shrugged his broad shoulders, then held out a hand and assisted her to her feet, his fingers lingering warmly over hers. "Seven?"

Lily groaned as she gently disengaged their hands. Not sure where this would lead, or where she wanted it to lead. "I'm not that much of a morning person," she said.

He picked up his vet bag, all lazy swaggering male. "Seven-thirty?"

"Fine," she nodded. "In the meantime, what am I going to do with him?" Lily pointed at Spartacus, who was already investigating the tape holding up his socks, nosing and licking it.

"Where were you planning to have him sleep to-night?"

"Right here, in the laundry room."

"Obviously, that is not going to work."

Recalling what had happened the last time Spartacus had been closeted up there alone, Lily sighed. "No foolin', Dr. Fletcher Hart. Where would you suggest?"

"In your bedroom. At least for now. Just put the cushion up there and then he can curl up where he can see you. Dogs are pack animals. They want to be part of the pack. And right now, like it or not, you're his pack."

"So are you."

Fletcher's eyes lit up. "If that's an invitation—"

Lily blushed and replied hastily, "No!"

Fletcher grinned again, as if thinking about all the ways he might get her to change her mind on that, then sobered, and returned—with surprising seriousness—to the subject at hand. "I assume you weren't planning to go up to bed right away?"

Only, Lily thought, if I were going up there with you.

Then wondering where that thought had come from, she pushed the idea of making hot, wild, wonderful love to Fletcher as far from her mind as possible. Clearing her throat, she attempted to be as serious as he was being. "I thought I might eat my dinner first, before I turn in. And Spartacus needs to be fed one more time, too," she said, having taken Fletcher's advice to feed Spartacus small meals frequently until his stomach was back to normal again. A fact that seemed to please Spartacus no end.

Ignoring the sexual tension simmering between them, Lily got out a can of dog food and tossed it his way. Fletcher made a one-handed catch, then caught the can opener, too. "You want to stay and eat?" Lily asked.

"Dog food?" Fletcher furrowed his brow in comical fashion. "I don't think so."

"I meant takeout," Lily explained. "I'll even share with you, if you want. As payment for this house call."

His eyes glimmered. She knew what he was thinking, even if he didn't come out and say it. "It's the only payment you're going to get, Fletcher," she warned with simpering Southern belle sweetness, "unless you'd like some flowers."

He looked over her shoulder as she opened up the take-out bags from a popular Italian restaurant. "What is it?"

Lily opened her oven and slid the foil container in to reheat. "Chicken cannelloni, salad and bread sticks."

His brow lifted enthusiastically. "And dessert?"

Lily nodded deeply in acknowledgment. "Tiramisu, of course."

His grin broadened. "You've just made an offer I can't refuse."

He knelt and spooned food into a bowl for Spartacus. Unhappy with the socks on his legs, Spartacus tried to stand, then decided against it. He made do by scooting forward to the bowl and eating while lying on his stomach. Watching, Lily predicted, "He's going to get a crick in his neck."

"Probably."

More silence. Lily was suddenly a little nervous. First-date nervous. Not that this was a date…

Gulping, she fought the anxiety starting up inside her. The feeling that said she wasn't nearly woman enough for a man like Fletcher Hart—never mind as experienced as he was probably used to.…

She turned away from the mixture of pleasure and expectation radiating in his golden-brown eyes. "I'd offer you a glass of wine but the only liquor we have in the house is a bottle of crème de menthe that is about oh…six years old. So…?" She left the question hanging.

He shook his head. "Thanks, anyway. I'll pass."

As their glances meshed and held all Lily could think about was kissing him again. Not that she had any business doing that, either. She might be looking for adventure, she wasn't looking for a broken heart. Fletcher was a man who could definitely stomp her romantic soul to pieces. All it would take was a little lovemaking, followed by a lot of his trademark aloofness and cynicism.

"You really should have a dog, you know," Lily said as she got out a couple of plates and glasses.

Fletcher lounged against the counter, arms folded in front of him, ankles crossed. He knit his brows together and teased in a soft, low voice that sent thrills coursing over her body, "Isn't that what I said to you?"

Being careful not to get too close to him, lest she lose her focus, Lily continued setting the table. "I mean it. You're so gentle with animals."

He shrugged, continuing to make himself at home. "My job to be."

"He'd make a great companion." Lily continued her sales pitch enthusiastically.

The brooding look was back in Fletcher's eyes. "What?" she said.

He studied her, as if trying to decide how much he wanted to tell her about what he was thinking and feeling. Finally, he released a short unhappy breath and said casually, "It's not something I usually discuss, but... I—we—had a dog once. When I was a kid."

"Really? What kind?"

This was a surprise. Lily couldn't recall the Harts having any pets when they moved back to Holly Springs, after Fletcher's dad died. Helen Hart had been too busy caring for her brood of six kids and turning the family home she had inherited into the premiere wedding facility in the Carolinas, the Wedding Inn.

"A beagle. Lucky didn't mind very well and I wasn't very good at taking care of him."

Lily tensed, able to see his dog had come to a bad end. "How old were you?" she asked softly, edging nearer.

The deeply cynical look was back in Fletcher's eyes. "Eight when I got him, ten when he got hit by a car and died."

"Oh, Fletcher." Lily reached out and touched his arm.

"It was my fault." Lips pressed together grimly, he continued in a low, self-deprecating voice. "I was taking him on a walk and he was pulling every which way. I got tired of being dragged around. So I just unsnapped the leash and let him go where he wanted. Which was basically everywhere," Fletcher admitted, shaking his head, his guilt over that apparent. "Into neighbors' flower gardens and on their porches, and eventually right out into the street where he got hit by a car driving by."

Her heart went out to him as she saw the sadness radiated in his eyes. She had lost her own cat to old age, having known the end was coming. She could only imagine how a senseless death like this must have hurt—especially for a child.

"I remember the screech of the brakes as the driver tried to stop, that awful thud, when you knew, even before you saw.... Then just standing there, frozen, unable to believe it had really happened. Then Lucky let out another high-pitched yelp and I rushed over to help him."

Looking angry and upset with himself, Fletcher continued telling her what had happened to his pet. "He was bleeding pretty bad and in a lot of pain. I comforted him as best I could but he died in my arms before the car's driver and I could even get him in the car to take him to the animal hospital up the street." Moisture glistened in his eyes.

Lily studied the tortured expression on Fletcher's face. It was clear he had never gotten over the loss or forgiven himself for his part in the accident. "Is that what prompted you to become a vet?" Lily asked gently.

He nodded. "I wanted to know what to do. I wanted to be able to save him." He paused and ran a hand over his face. "Of course, now I know that even a vet couldn't have done anything for Lucky. His injuries were just too severe."

"And you never had another dog."

"Nope. Losing one was enough."

Lily understood that, too. After Penelope had died she hadn't wanted another cat, either, although there were a lot of people who felt she should have run right out and adopted another Persian, just like the cat she had lost. At the time it had been unthinkable. Now that she had another pet in her life, albeit temporarily, she was beginning to wonder if her friends hadn't been right.

Fletcher turned his glance away from her. It landed on the shelf with the dark green liqueur bottle. "You know, on second thought, I think I'll take you up on that crème de menthe," he said as he pulled it off the decorative shelf to the right of the kitchen sink. He handed it to her, his fingers brushing hers in the process. "Put a little milk in it, would you?"

Lily knew what he was doing—distracting them. Willing to give him the emotional room he needed, she made a face before blowing the dust off the bottle and pouring a fingerful into a juice glass. "Somehow,

I never imagined you drinking this," she murmured as she added milk and ice and gave it a stir.

Fletcher put the glass to his lips and took a sip of the minty pale green liquid, grimacing only slightly as it went down. "Oh, there's lots you don't know about me," he teased.

Their eyes met again. "I'm beginning to realize that, too," Lily said, realizing she hadn't felt this much in ages. Maybe...ever.

"Well, that was pretty darn good for warmed-up takeout," Fletcher said half an hour later as he pushed his plate away.

"I thought so, too." Lily smiled. Between the two of them, they had eaten every bite while they talked about the upcoming wedding they were both participating in, as well as other wedding parties they had been in.

"So now what?" Fletcher asked as he got up to help her clear the table.

Finished with his own meal, Spartacus curled up beside his food dish and began working diligently on the tape that secured the sock-bandages in place.

Lily glanced up at the clock on the kitchen wall. It was almost midnight. Where had the time gone? "I've got to get him upstairs. You think he'll walk?"

"Um—" Fletcher ran his fingers through the shaggy layers of his honey-brown hair "—just a suggestion, but I think you might want to take Spartacus out back to do whatever he needs to do before he turns in for the night. Unless of course you want to be awakened by urgent whining at 3:00 a.m.?"

Something about the roguishness of his expression brought out the mischievous side of her. "His or yours?"

Lily asked with a straight face and was rewarded with a full-bellied laugh from Fletcher.

"Why, Miss Madsen." He looked her up and down in a comical parody of shock. "I do believe you just made an off-color remark."

A shock, Lily knew, since she had the reputation for being one of the primmest and most proper young women in all of Holly Springs. "Must be the company I'm in," she quipped. "As I never talk that way." Grandmother Rose would not have allowed it.

"A pity." He teased her with a look as he clasped her elbow and chivalrously led her in the direction he wanted her to go. "I rather like the newfound devilish side of you."

It took some coaxing but they finally got Spartacus to stand up. He didn't seem convinced he could walk at first, but with a little more coaxing and some nuggets of dog treat that Fletcher just happened to have in his pants pocket, Spartacus discovered he could walk with socks on his paws. He didn't have much traction on the polished wood floors, but once he hit the grass outside, he was doing just fine.

Lily and Fletcher stood in the darkness of the backyard. Once again, all she could think about was kissing him—and not for show or some other cockeyed purpose this time, but because she just wanted to feel his lips on hers once again, so sure and warm and male.

But he didn't make a move.

And soon Spartacus had done what was necessary.

"Want some help taking that dog bed and Spartacus upstairs?" Fletcher asked casually as they headed back inside.

Why not delay his inevitable departure, Lily thought.

She had never had so much fun with a man—not even on a real date—as she had with Fletcher in the past two days. "Sure," Lily said. Although it would mean having Fletcher in her bedroom...a dangerous proposition indeed, if not for their trusty canine chaperone.

Lily led the way upstairs. Fletcher followed, the dog cushion in his arms. Spartacus was right behind him.

They walked down the long dimly lit hall, past her grandmother's room with its big four-poster canopy bed, to the pink-and-white room Lily'd had since she was a child. There was a canopy bed in there, too, but it was a single, sized for a child. She had never thought about it much. Never thought about switching bed-rooms. Until she saw the look on Fletcher's face.

No wonder she was having trouble growing up, Lily realized with sudden shock. She might run a business in her professional life, but at home and in her private time, she hadn't made any strides at all. She was stuck in a holding pattern she wanted very much to break out of.

"Where should I put this?" Fletcher said, kind enough not to mention the juvenile decor.

Aware of the embarrassed color moving from her throat into her face, Lily tried hard to concentrate on the problem at hand, instead of what an experienced man like Fletcher must think of her. "Where do you think it should go?" she asked a little stiffly.

"Probably in the corner," Fletcher set the dog bed down next to the window seat that overlooked the front yard. "So he'll feel protected, but can still see you."

"Thank you." Lily smiled the brisk professional smile she reserved for customers at the shop, then, still feeling self-conscious as all-get-out, led the way back downstairs. Fletcher followed her, but Spartacus, obviously deciding it was too much trouble to go all the way down again, remained at the head of the stairs with his chin resting on the hall floor and his paws hanging over the edge.

Again, Fletcher lingered, as if he didn't want to go any more than she wanted him to leave. "Maybe I should write down all my numbers for you," he said finally, his tone as crisp and businesslike as hers had become. "So if you have any more problems, you'll be able to reach me."

Lily nodded. Did he want to kiss her as much as she wanted to kiss him? "Good idea," she said.

Fletcher looked casually at home once again. "Got a paper and pen?"

Lily nodded. "In the study, by the phone." Again, she led the way, switching on lamps as she went. Like everything else in the big old house, the furnishings were covered with old-fashioned lace doilies and slip-covered in faded floral prints.

Without really looking at the notepad she picked up, Lily handed it to him, as well as a pen.

Fletcher started to turn the page, then stopped and flipped it back.

He stared at the writing, a bemused expression on his face. "What in the name of all that's sweet and innocent is this?" he asked.

Chapter 5

Lily flushed, looking—in Fletcher's estimation—even prettier and more delectably sexy than she had when he arrived to help her with Spartacus. "Just never you mind," she said heatedly, reaching for the notepad.

Fletcher knew he should just give her "list" back, but having already seen as much as he had, the temptation was too great to ignore. "'Things I Want Before I'm Twenty-Six,'" he read out loud, surprised but pleased to have this unexpected window into Lily's soul. "'One. Stay up all night with a guy, having the best time of my life.'"

He paused and looked over at her, trying not to fantasize about what it would be like to personally help her fulfill that dream. "That doesn't sound so hard," Fletcher drawled lazily, to cover the fast growing ache inside him. "Provided, of course, you're with the right man."

Lily squared her shoulders and aimed a killer look at him. "I'm so glad you approve."

Grinning, Fletcher returned his attention to the list. "'Two,'" he read. "'Receive flowers.'" Then he quirked a brow at her, wondering what that meant.

"No one ever sends a florist flowers," Lily explained, not bothering to hide her disappointment about that.

He moved closer, liking the way her pale blond curls shimmered in the light of the study. "What do you usually get?"

She shrugged and perched on the arm of a faded, floral-upholstered club chair. Swinging one trim ankle back and forth, she tossed her head and announced, "I don't usually get presents from men."

"Well, now, that's a shame," Fletcher said. He liked the droll humor in her voice and the exasperated color flowing into her cheeks.

"You can stop reading now." She stretched across him to get her list, the softness of her breasts brushing his forearm.

"I don't think so." He whisked the paper out of her reach, stepped back and read, "'Three. Not be afraid to speak up for myself or do what I want to do, regardless of what anyone else thinks.'" He frowned, wondering what kind of questionable activity she had in mind. And if that activity concerned one Hollywood actor.

Lily glared at him from beneath her thick blond lashes. "It's not up to you to approve or disapprove of my goals, Fletcher Hart," she said.

Maybe not. But given that promise he had secretly made to her grandmother Rose, Fletcher decided he was doing so just the same. To that end, he was going to have to keep a closer eye on Lily, at least while Carson McRue was in town.

Fletcher continued going over the items on the list. "'Four. Choose my own career.'"

Huh? He lifted his eyes to hers.

Lily lifted her delicate hands, palm up. "Madsen's Flower Shoppe was just handed to me. I never said I wanted to be a florist. Ditto this house. I never said I wanted it, either. It was just given to me."

"So sell the business," Fletcher advised, a tad impatiently.

Lily blinked. "And not the house?"

Fletcher cast a look around, taking in the sturdy-built and spacious, high-ceilinged rooms. Lily could rear half a dozen kids here and not feel the least bit crowded. "It's a great place. Or it would be," Fletcher allowed, meeting her eyes again, "if you made it your own. I think you might want to hang on to it and try that before you ditch it altogether."

"Hmm. I guess I really hadn't thought about that," Lily murmured, looking perplexed.

"'Five.'" Fletcher continued down her list of things she wanted to achieve before the next birthday rolled around. "'Be swept off my feet.'" He looked at her and, unable to resist, teased, "Didn't I just do that today at the town square?"

"So cross it off my list," Lily said dryly.

"Love to," Fletcher quipped right back as his gaze focused on the next important item on her To Do list, the one that had caught his attention in the first place. "'Six—be loved in that special man-woman way.'"

Lily was blushing fire-engine red now.

Fletcher put the paper back down momentarily, feeling more like her grandmother-appointed chaperone than he preferred. "You want to explain that?" he demanded sternly.

"No. As a matter of fact, I do not," Lily replied just as stonily.

Good, Fletcher thought, because that meant she wasn't quite as ready to accomplish that particular feat as she wanted to be. He picked up the list again. "And last but not least, 'Number seven. Access my inner bad girl or be as sexy as I know I can be.'" He blinked, and read it again just to be sure. That was what it said, all right. "Whoa! Miss Lily!" he chided.

Lily wrinkled her nose at him. "Don't pretend to be shocked." She gave him a pouty look that dared him to haul her into his arms and kiss her again. With even less reserve than before... Fortunately, for both of them his conscience intervened. "But I am shocked," he told her. More to the point, he was worried. Given the nature of Lily's To Do list, Carson McRue was definitely the wrong man for Lily to be hanging around, even for a short time.

Lily reached for her "list" again. This time, he let her take it from him.

Fletcher thought about Lily's naiveté and the promise he had made, and knew he couldn't just forget what he had just learned. Or what it was she was about to do.

"You can go now," Lily said, taking his elbow.

Like hell, Fletcher thought, as he resisted her attempt to push him toward the door. Instead, he took the notepad from her, and turned the page and wrote down all his numbers for her. "If it's during the day," he told her seriously, "try the office first—they always know where I am. If it's after hours, and I don't answer my office or home phones, call my cell. But I don't answer my cell unless I'm out and about. Otherwise I keep it off. Okay?"

Lily ran her fingers through her hair impatiently. "I'm not going to need you," she stated stubbornly.

Like heck she didn't, Fletcher thought, as he left the notepad on her desk. Lily Madsen needed him more than she could say.

"Well, just in case," Fletcher reiterated firmly, "you'll know how to find me." It was high time he got out of there, before he gave in to impulse, took her in his arms and did something terribly reckless to fulfill at least a few of the items on her "list." Something they'd both likely regret.

"Are you sure you want to do this?" Hannah Reid asked Lily the following evening, when she came over to "pet-sit" Spartacus and hopefully prevent another canine-anxiety attack.

No, as a matter of fact, Lily was no longer sure she wanted to go on a date with Carson McRue. Part of it was nerves, of course—she had never been on a date with anyone famous and worried about hopelessly embarrassing herself. And the other part was her reluctance to have her idealistic image of the handsome TV star crushed. She had admired Carson McRue, Hollywood P.I., from afar for so long. She'd let him dominate her wishful thinking when it came to romance, never dreaming she would ever get to see him in person, never mind go on a date with him. And there had been comfort in that, in a weird way. Maybe because her romantic notions of the perfect moment with the perfect man were within her control in a way real life was not.

In her daydreams, people didn't get cancer or die—or say or do the wrong things. It her daydreams, everything could be perfect and scripted and happily ever after without risk. Real life, on the other hand, carried the threat of the heartache Dr. Fletcher Hart was certain she was going to endure. But she wouldn't think about that now. Wouldn't let Fletcher ruin her daydream come true.

"It's half the bet," Lily said, to her friend. If she dined with Carson tonight, then all she would have left to do was somehow wangle a ride on his private jet when he left North Carolina at the end of the week. And the residents of Holly Springs would see her in a whole new way. No longer someone to be piticd, for the familial losses and tragedies she had endured. But as a gusty and hopefully sexy woman who wasn't afraid to pursue what she wanted in this life, someone who had actually been on a date—and a private jet—with a dashing TV star.

Hannah looked at the outfit Lily had selected for the date. She didn't have to say anything. Lily knew it was quite unlike her. Which was, of course, the point. "You've got nothing to prove," Hannah said.

"Yes, I do," Lily said soberly. "I've been in a rut, Hannah." My entire life, it seems. Especially, lately.

Hannah waved off further explanation. "You don't have to tell me. I inherited a family business and a house, too."

"But—?" Lily prodded, realizing that Hannah Reid was dissatisfied with her life, too. And that surprised her. Lily had always imagined the perennial tomboy, who even now was clad in baggy engineer-stripe overalls, a form-fitting black T-shirt and scuffed running shoes, was content just hanging out and being "one of the guys."

Hannah released her long, wavy auburn hair from its ponytail. "People around here see me as a grease monkey, who only cares about fixing up or maintaining classic cars. As a result, life gets pretty darn dull. I've been thinking about ways to break free of all that, and become someone else entirely, too. At least for part of the time. But I'm not sure I want the whole town watching when I do."

Lily tried to make sense of that but couldn't. "What are you talking about?"

"Well—" Hannah took a brush out of her canvas carryall and ran it through her hair "—you've heard about people who go on vacation and sort of become someone or something else while they live it up, and then go back to their normal lives…and reality."

"And my date tonight with Carson is not…reality." Lily guessed where this was going.

"The fact you and Carson McRue are from two different worlds is probably what you find so attractive," Hannah continued thoughtfully.

No, Lily thought. *Attractive* was Fletcher Hart. It was just too bad, due to his cynical, never-stay-with-any-one-woman-for-long attitude that nothing of substance would ever develop there.

Lily's nerves had calmed marginally when she arrived at the five-star Raleigh hotel where Carson McRue was staying. She handed her car over to valet parking and walked into the lobby, heading straight for the concierge desk as directed and identified herself to the elegantly dressed man. "Hi. I'm Lily Madsen."

"Oh, Miss Madsen! We've been expecting you!"

So this was the star treatment.

The concierge handed her a small parchment envelope containing an electronic hotel key.

"I need a key to get into a private dining room?" Lily asked.

The man looked at her strangely. "That's a suite," he explained, giving her a reassuring, professional smile.

Lily paused, not sure what to do. She had signed on for a meal in a hotel dining room, not an evening in a hotel suite.

"Would you like someone to accompany you upstairs?" the concierge asked.

"No." Lily shook her head. *Because she wasn't going to be staying. Not if it appeared an assignation was all Carson McRue wanted from her.*

Refusing however to jump to conclusions—this could all be perfectly innocent—Lily took the key and headed across the marble-floored lobby to the elevators.

Scant minutes later, she was striding down the hall to Suite 531.

Strangely enough, the door was slightly ajar. Soft music was playing inside. Lily could see vases of flowers, and a room service table set up in the middle of the room. And... Fletcher Hart lounging about on the suite's sofa. He was clad in the usual jeans and solid-colored blue work shirt, but had also thrown on a burgundy tie—whose knot had already been pulled loose—and a navy sport coat. His hair was as clean and touchably soft as always, his eyes sparkling with a mischievous light.

Lily blinked and then blinked again. This had to be a mistake. 'Cause if it wasn't, she swore to heaven above, she was really going to kill him.

Seeing her, he got to his feet and crossed lazily to the portal. "Right on time," he remarked.

Lily's pulse, already racing, upped another notch. She walked in, her handbag held like a weapon at her side. "What are you doing here?" The words were smooth as silk—her feelings were not.

"Exactly what it looks like I'm doing." Fletcher kept going until they stood toe-to-toe. "I'm filling in for your date out of the goodness of my heart."

Trying hard not to notice how much she liked the tantalizing fragrance of his aftershave, Lily held on to her temper with effort. "Where's Carson?" she asked sweetly.

Fletcher cast a completely unnecessary look over his shoulder, then turned and hooked his thumbs through the belt loops on either side of his fly. "Obviously, not here. But if you'd like to confirm that for yourself, he's staying in the penthouse on the top floor. I think they're expecting you up there, too."

Not sure whether to believe him or not, although Fletcher's expression was certainly innocent enough, Lily pivoted on her heel and stomped off, steam practically rolling out of her ears. Back to the elevators. Up to the top floor, where a hotel security officer was standing guard. She gave her name. "Oh, right. Mr. McRue's assistant is expecting you, Miss Madsen. You can go on in."

Lily headed for the double doors.

Inside, the suite was a wreck, with clothes and scripts everywhere.

Carson's raspberry-haired assistant was smoking a cigarette and talking on the phone, but she motioned Lily on in. She continued talking for another five minutes, then ended the conversation and turned to Lily. "I guess you've heard your date with Carson is off."

So Fletcher had said. "I don't understand," Lily said as calmly as she could.

"Carson had to drive out to Lexington, North Carolina, to check out some horses for the show. He's obsessed with getting one that's the right color. You know what a perfectionist he is when it comes to cinematography. Anyway, he asked me to be sure and tell you not to worry, that he would work you in at some point, before he left town."

Lily ignored the relief—that she no longer had to go through with a date she wasn't particularly interested in, and concentrated instead on her anger. "Just out of curiosity, what did Fletcher Hart have to do with all this?" she asked sweetly.

The assistant looked up from the notes she was scrawling on her clipboard. "That hunky local vet?"

"That would be the one," Lily confirmed dryly.

"He arranged it."

Fletcher had figured it would take Lily ten minutes to get back to him. It took her seven and a half, and when she barreled through the open doorway of the suite he had rented for the night, she looked loaded for bear. Good. 'Cause if she was angry with him, it might keep her from pursuing any of those items on that list of hers with him and he could send her home early to the safety of that big old house she lived in. Instead of where he wanted her—in his arms. He was beginning to realize this grand romantic setting he'd concocted to fulfill her dreams was a *big* mistake.

Lily tossed her evening purse down in a great show of temper. "Just where do you get off—?" she hissed.

Deciding this had the potential to get interesting—fast—Fletcher inclined his head at the portal. "You might want to close the door behind you so you don't disturb the other people on this floor."

She marched back, the hem of her dress swirling sexily around her showgirl-fine legs. "You sent him to Lexington?"

With effort, Fletcher tore his glance from her knees and pushed aside his thoughts about what it would be like to settle down between them. "He wanted to look at a lot of horses before making his decision about which stallion he was going to use for the show. It was cheaper to send him to Lexington than trailer them up and truck them all here." Not that Fletcher couldn't have arranged that, had he wanted to. Most owners he knew would have jumped at the chance to have one of their mounts appear in a prime-time TV show.

"It had to be tonight?"

Fletcher shrugged. "Carson told me he wanted this taken care of right away, and since that's what he hired me to do…" Fletcher noticed the care she had taken with her hair. Instead of leaving it down the way she usually did, she had twisted it up on the back of her head with some sort of clip. Tendrils escaped along the back of her neck and brushed at her forehead and cheeks in a very sexy way. It was the kind of hairdo that a man just itched to take down. And she looked good with her hair that way. Too good for his comfort, considering where she had been headed.

"In any case," Fletcher continued lazily, watching as

her cheeks turned an even brighter pink, "sorry about your date."

Lily looked at him, a mixture of temper and resentment simmering in her pretty Carolina-blue eyes. "I bet."

"Nice dress, though." Fletcher continued his attempts to annoy the heck out of her as he moved to uncork the champagne. And he was glad Carson McRue had missed seeing Lily in it, because she was a knockout even at the end of a very long workday. All gussied up and clad in a drop-dead-sexy dress, she took his breath away. And with good reason. "It practically screams, 'Make love to me,' Fletcher concluded as the cork shot off in a spray of champagne.

The color staining her cheeks went from pink to rose in a flash.

"I don't know what you mean, Fletcher Hart."

"Then I'll explain it to you." Fletcher set the bottle back on the table and stepped toward her, determined to see out his responsibility and protect her. "For starters, you can see right through it to your slip." He indicated the black satin spaghetti-strapped sheath that hugged her surprisingly lush and womanly curves. Curves that until now had been hidden beneath sweetly sexy sundresses or pastel T-shirts and tailored khakis.

"It's not a slip." Lily swept a hand down the length of her body, her hand ghosting over the sheer floral-printed black fabric that clung to her breasts and waist before slipping over her slender hips and swirling out just above her knees. "It's part of the dress. And you're supposed to see it."

Fletcher didn't find that a help as he tilted his head to survey it. "Yeah, well all it makes a guy want to do is take off both pieces. Which I suppose was the point of your evening tonight?"

He saw it coming. Could have ducked. But didn't. 'Cause the more gallant part of him knew he deserved it, even as he continued to see red over the way she was unknowingly setting herself up to be seduced by the egotistical TV star. Or would have, had he not intervened, just in time. The slap was surprisingly powerful from such a genteel-looking woman, Fletcher noted, even as the left side of his face stung and heated.

"Finished?" he drawled. "Or do you want to do it again?"

Lily's mouth opened in a round "Oh!" Her hand dropped back to her side. "I can't believe I just did that." Her full lower lip shot out petulantly. "Even if you did have it coming."

Fletcher rubbed his still-stinging cheek. "Well, if you were me, you'd be able to believe it." Damn, that hurt.

She glared at him. "Why do you insist on interfering with my bet?" Her eyes narrowed as the next thought occurred to her. "Or, did you perchance put some money down on it, too? Money declaring I wouldn't succeed?"

Here was his chance to let her know about the bet he had made. Phrase it in such a good way that they'd both have a good laugh and figure a face-saving way out of this mess. One that would allow her to retain her considerable pride, and him to avoid earning her undying loathing, while simultaneously keeping secret the deathbed promise he had made to her grandmother Rose.

Only, he had the feeling she wouldn't forgive him. And he didn't want her angry at him forever any more than he wanted her to remain just an acquaintance or friend....

Aware she was looking at him, waiting for some disclaimer, he looked her right in the eye and said flatly, "I didn't lay money on the wager you made with the other bridesmaids."

He'd made his own bet.

And as he got more and more emotionally involved with Lily, was beginning to regret it.

"Then why?" Lily demanded, throwing up her hands and advancing on him. Not in anger this time, but with the urgent need to understand. "Why do you keep interfering in what I'm trying to do here?"

Easy, Fletcher thought, reining in his out of control emotions. "Because I don't want to see you hurt," he told her kindly.

"And you think Carson McRue will hurt me," Lily asserted sarcastically.

"Given the chance, yes." Which was why Fletcher was determined not to give Carson McRue the opportunity to cross off the items on Lily's list. Even if it meant Lily resented him forever.

Lily shook her head at him in mounting exasperation and sighed. "You are one misguided idiot, you know that?"

Fletcher grinned, glad to see her anger fading. "Does that mean you'll stay and have dinner here with me tonight?"

"No." Lily gave him a sexy, stubborn look that spoke volumes about her intent. "But I will stay long enough to make love with you."

Chapter 6

Fletcher's look of absolute shock and astonishment was everything Lily had hoped for—and more. She sashayed closer and grabbed him by the front of his shirt, knowing it was way past time he had the tables turned on him. "You don't believe me, do you?"

Fletcher's lips curved into an amused smile. "No, actually, I don't," he returned, looking as determined and devil-may-care as Lily had hoped to feel earlier.

Great. One more person who felt she didn't have it in her to be anything but prim and proper, a hopelessly naive romantic perennially on the sidelines of life. Lily admitted had it been TV star Carson McRue in the room with her now instead of the impossibly exasperating Fletcher Hart, that still would have been true. She would have been backing out—faster than a winning filly leaving the starting gate—on her promise to at least flirt with the idea of a wild, impetuous fling.

But it wasn't the questionably motivated Carson she was alone with in an elegant hotel room. It was the way too cynical Fletcher Hart. And Lily knew as much as he teased her that he wouldn't take advantage of her— he was much too gallant for that. Which was why she had to put him to the test right now.

"Sure about that?" she queried, saucily slipping past him to the open bottle of ridiculously expensive champagne on the table. Aware he was watching her—a lot more grimly now—she topped off a crystal flute and lifted it to her lips. Holding his eyes over the rim of her glass, she drank deeply of the exquisitely effervescent white wine, finishing half the glass in one gulp, the rest in the second.

"Okay, that's enough," Fletcher said, coming over to take the glass and the bottle away from her before she could pour herself a second drink. "You've proved your point now, Lily," he said as he set both aside then clasped her elbow. "I'll take you home."

Lily leaned into his easy grasp. Ignoring the quelling nature of his touch, she ran her hands over the solid warmth of his chest. "But I don't want to go home, Fletcher," she purred in the sexiest voice she could manage. She leaned forward, pressing her lips to the exposed column of his throat, in the open vee of his shirt. She felt his pulse skitter and jump, even as his body hardened all the more.

"Lily." He adapted a no-nonsense stance—legs braced, shoulders squared, head tilted down to hers— that would have been very intimidating if she allowed it.

Which, of course, Lily didn't. "Oh, shut up and just kiss me," she murmured, standing on tiptoe to better align their bodies.

And then, to her complete surprise, he did.

* * *

Fletcher expected Lily to stop bluffing and cry uncle the moment his lips touched hers. But instead of trying to fight him off, she wreathed her arms around his neck, opened her mouth to the plundering pressure of his and let her body melt recklessly against his. He'd thought the first couple of times he had kissed her had been amazing. Sweet. Hot. Tempting beyond all reason. But those times were nothing compared to this, he thought, as he tangled his hands in the softness of her upswept hair and she dug her fingers into his shoulders and kissed him back with a wildness beyond his most erotic dreams. Her lips were soft and warm and sweet and she kissed him with absolutely nothing held back, as if he were the gallant prince of a guy she had been waiting her whole life for…as if she wanted him to make love to her then and there. Despite the way she had taunted and provoked him, despite the promises he had made to protect her at all costs, he wanted her, he realized, as his whole body tightened and flamed. And that was why this had to stop.

Reluctantly, he broke off the kiss. Stood there, searching for some inner nobility to make everything turn out right. And found it lacking as always. "Don't you have enough to regret for one night?" he asked her quietly, wishing all the while she didn't feel quite so good in his arms. That he didn't know firsthand from her wish list just how eager she was for life experience. Especially in the sexual arena…

"That's just it," she murmured in frustration. Light blue eyes shimmering wistfully, she was up on tiptoe again, innocently offering her lips up to his. "All I've got are regrets. And I'm tired of being alone, Fletcher."

Hurt from years past laced her low voice. "I'm tired of watching everyone else have fun," she confessed as she ran her palm beneath his blazer, over his chest. "Tired of seeing life pass me by."

Had she said anything else and looked at him any other way... Fletcher could easily have refused her another kiss. But the yearning in her soft eyes and even softer voice had him ignoring his better judgment and capitulating once again.

Lily was right, Fletcher rationalized. Through no fault of her own, the freedom Lily should have had in her late teens and early twenties had been taken from her, and for far too long she had been closeted up in a life chosen for her.

She wanted adventure. Passion. Excitement. Right now she was looking for him to give it to her. What was the harm in a little kissing, he wondered, particularly if it didn't lead to anything else...?

Lily hadn't expected Fletcher to kiss her at all, never mind like this. He made her feel as if she were the only woman on earth for him, and vice versa. How could she possibly go back to the loneliness of her life now? For so long she'd had walls around her heart, and she wanted Fletcher Hart to be the man to tear them down once and for all.

Needing, wanting, to be closer still, she wove her fingers through his honey-brown hair and opened her mouth to the demanding pressure of his. He tasted so good, Lily thought, as his tongue plundered deep and their kiss took on an even more urgent quality. Her breasts pressed against the solid wall of his chest, and, lower still, she felt the hot urgency of his arousal. Desire welled up inside her, a river of unbridled passion, and her knees went weak. She had never experienced such deliciously wanton kisses, such intense aching need, and that alone was enough to make her want to see where this clinch would lead. Besides marking an end to her innocence, would making love with Fletcher change things between them in other ways, too?

Or would Fletcher remain as cynical—and aloof— as ever? And it was the thought that he might not acknowledge that something very special was happening between them that had her coming to her senses. She was in the market for a satisfying, life-changing love affair, not a broken heart.

As she broke the kiss and pulled away, Fletcher looked stunned by the abrupt change in her mood. And not the least bit happy about it. "Now what?" he demanded gruffly.

"Now," Lily said, "it's time for me to say goodnight to you and go home."

"WHERE ARE JANEY and Thad registered again?" Fletcher asked his mother the next morning when he stopped by the Wedding Inn on his way to work.

Helen Hart turned away from the outdoor wedding being set up for later in the day. It was her busy season. The inn was still booked every day in August with at least one wedding, sometimes two. At fifty-six, she was a little more curvaceous than she had been in his youth, but with her short red hair, fair skin and amber eyes, she was still one of the prettiest women around. As well as resolutely single. Although she'd had plenty of invitations, Helen hadn't dated anyone since his dad's death twenty years ago.

Helen motioned for the wedding arbor in the gardens to be placed a little farther to the left—given the semicircular arrangement of the three hundred fifty white folding chairs—then turned back to him. "We went over this the other night, Fletcher, at the barbecue."

Fletcher shrugged. "I've had a lot on my mind."

Helen wrote the name of several stores down on a piece of paper, removed it from her clipboard and handed it to him. "So I've heard," she said dryly.

Fletcher stuck it in the pocket of his sage-green shirt. "What does that mean?"

His mother turned to him, giving him the full benefit of her knowing amber gaze, before she sighed. "What's this I hear about you trying to saddle Lily Madsen with a dog she doesn't want?"

Guilt rose up inside him. It wasn't like him to be so manipulative. But then, it wasn't like him to be so interested in any one woman, either. He palmed his chest in self-defense. "Hey, she volunteered to take Spartacus."

Helen scoffed. "Only after you arranged to send the poor mutt to the pound. Why didn't you ask your nephew Christopher to care for him? Or didn't an arrangement like that suit your purposes?"

Leave it to his mother to hit the nail right on the head. "I don't know what you mean."

"I think you do. I think you've been using that poor dog to keep Lily occupied so she won't pursue that TV star who is in town filming location shots. What's his name? Carson McNally?"

"McRue, Mom. And I don't know where you got such a silly idea."

"Mmm-hmm." Helen regarded him skeptically as she gave the thumbs-up sign to the new location of the arbor. "What's going on with you and Lily?"

Fletcher tried to look as innocent as Lily. "Nothing."

Except a few kisses, he amended silently. *And the burning desire, on my part anyway, to make hot passionate love that lasts all night and well into the next day.*

Helen sighed and walked over to check on the bandstand being erected in the grass, leaving Fletcher to follow at will. "I didn't buy that excuse when you were ten. I'm not buying it now. She's a sweet girl, Fletcher."

Tell me something I don't know.

"She's been through a lot. Growing up without her parents, sacrificing her teenage years to nurse her grandmother Rose through that long illness and then grieving the loss of her only family."

Fletcher set his mouth grimly. "You don't have to tell me Lily needs protection from a guy like Carson McRue."

Nodding her approval, Helen headed back toward the white brick inn. "Is that what you're doing? Protecting her?"

Fletcher paused, knowing he had to tell someone or he was going to implode. "I don't have a choice, Mom. And if you mention any of what I'm about to tell you to anyone…"

Helen escorted Fletcher into her office and shut the door firmly behind her so they could speak in private. She dropped her clipboard and perched on the edge of her desk. "I won't tell a soul. You know that. Now, what is going on, Fletcher?"

Fletcher dropped into a chair and stretched his long legs out in front of him. "I promised Rose before she died that I would look out for Lily."

Helen mulled that over. "Why did she ask *you?*"

"I don't know." Fletcher shook his head in silent regret. "I told her I wasn't the one to fulfill her request. I mean, I'm just not a trustworthy kind of guy when it comes to something like that."

"Heavens, Fletcher! Tell me you haven't taken advantage of Lily Madsen!"

Not yet...

"I know you're cynical and not prone to any sort of responsibility not connected with your vet practice, but—"

Fletcher held up both hands in a gesture of surrender, before his mother made him feel any worse. "It's not as easy as it sounds, Mom. Lily really wants to go out with this guy."

Understanding lit Helen's eyes. "Because of the bet she made?"

Fletcher swore silently to himself. "You heard about that, too?"

"As well as the one you made."

Fletcher clenched his hands on the arms of the chair. His bet was supposed to be secret. "Who told you?" he demanded gruffly.

"No one. I just happened to overhear two of your brothers talking yesterday. They didn't know I was there, and I didn't let on that I'd heard what they were saying."

"But obviously you disapprove," Fletcher summarized.

Helen reproached him seriously. "You cannot play with someone's heart like this."

Figuring he'd heard enough, Fletcher stood. "No hearts involved," Fletcher said lightly. Not yet, anyway.

His mother scoffed, the knowing look back in her eyes. "You're kidding yourself if you think that."

* * *

Lily and Spartacus were almost ready to leave for work that morning when the sleek black limousine pulled up in front of her home. She watched in disbelief as Carson McRue got out of the car, a big bouquet of yellow roses in hand. They weren't the best quality, Lily noted but the presentation was elaborate.

As Carson mounted the steps to the covered portico, Spartacus went wild, barking and jumping. "Okay, okay." Lily patted Spartacus on the back of the head. "You can stop protecting me. I want this guy here." If only to tell him she had sort of changed her mind about going out with him, bet or no bet. She'd made enough of a fool of herself lately, throwing herself at Fletcher Hart. She didn't need to add any more romantic nonsense to the mix.

Holding on to Spartacus's collar with one hand, she opened the door.

Carson stopped, his hand on the bell. Spartacus began to growl.

Carson tensed and stepped back. "What's with Fido?" he asked, but the jovial note in his voice did not match the annoyance in his pale green eyes.

"He's just feeling protective," Lily explained while Spartacus strained against her hold. Continuing to struggle, the dog's feet moved rapidly across the wood floor. But he was going nowhere fast, thanks to Lily's tight grip on him. It looked like a parody of a Fred Flintstone cartoon.

"I meant the socks on his paws. What's that about?"

"Uh—long story," Lily said as a low, fierce growl came out of Spartacus's throat. She couldn't believe how fierce he sounded.

"Why don't you put the dog up?" Carson asked genially.

"Good idea." Lily took Spartacus by the collar and guided him over to the study at the front of the house. She pushed him inside, gave the stay command and shut the door.

The growls continued behind the portal.

Expression tense, Carson handed her the flowers. "Listen, I just came over to apologize for last night."

"Did you get the horse you wanted for the filming?"

"None of the ones that vet arranged to have me look at were right. They were all way too docile. But I did find this stallion that was something. Just exactly the look I had in mind. So we're going to use him."

Alarm bells sounded in Lily's head. An unruly stallion could be a danger under the best of circumstances. "Did Fletcher okay that?"

Carson pressed his lips together grimly. "Fletcher Hart has nothing to say about what we do or don't do on the set."

"I thought he was advising the production in a professional capacity."

He made a disrespectful sound. "That's just to satisfy the animal rights people, keep them off our back. It has nothing to do with the reality of filming. But enough about that." The hundred-watt smile was back on his face. "I want to make up to you for our canceled date last night. So how about it? Can you go out with me tonight? The jet is at the Raleigh airport. We can have dinner in any city you want. Go out dancing all night, or just sit up talking, if you want."

If Lily didn't know better, she would think Carson had read her list and was ready to provide her with all the romantic adventure and excitement she needed. "Don't you have to film tomorrow?" she asked, not sure why she was suddenly so reluctant to be alone with him.

"Yeah. And the next couple of days after that. Then we're out of here. So what do you say?"

"Oh, I wish I could," Lily fibbed. Because thanks to Fletcher Hart, and the very genuine way he had kissed her and held her in his arms, she now had zero interest in going out with anyone as superficial as Carson McRue. "But I've got a bachelorette party to attend tonight."

Carson looked unimpressed. "Skip it."

"I can't. I'm a bridesmaid in the wedding."

"So? Tell 'em you're going to be with me. They'll get over it."

"I can't do that. Janey Hart is one of my very best friends."

Carson undressed Lily with his eyes. "She'd understand," he said softly.

A shiver of distaste rippled down Lily's spine. "And I have to work tomorrow."

"No problem. You can sleep on the jet, both to and from dinner." Carson gave her a lascivious wink. "I have a *very* comfortable bed on the jet."

Lily just bet he did. "Thanks," she said, "but I really can't."

Fletcher didn't hear from Lily at all that day. A half-dozen times he picked up the phone to call her, to apologize for waylaying her date and allowing things to get out of hand the night before, and then put it right back down again. There was no point in telling her anything that wasn't absolutely true. He didn't want her going out with Carson, and the only thing he regretted about their encounter was that he had let it end with only kisses when all he really wanted to do was take her to bed. Make her his. Not just for the moment, the day, the week, but for always. And how crazy was that? He wasn't the marrying kind. Not at all. But Lily had him thinking about rings on their fingers and vows that would last forever and shared spaces. And Fletcher sensed, as he headed into the private sports bar where Thad Lantz's bachelor party was being held, it was only going to get worse in the days ahead.

"Don't you look like you need a drink," Dylan Hart observed.

"He probably heard about what the gals are doing tonight and is upset," Mac said.

The look on his law-and-order brother's face gave Fletcher pause.

"The bachelorette party is tonight, too," Cal Hart explained.

"So?" Fletcher shrugged. "What are they going to do? Make a wedding veil out of toilet paper and stick it on the bride's head?"

"We wish," Joe said, scowling. Since becoming Emma Donovan's husband, he had really settled down.

Fletcher helped himself to some peanuts from the bucket on the table. "What are they doing?"

More looks that told Fletcher he was the only one there in the dark. "Rite of passage," Joe said finally. "They're going to a bar near the State campus."

Fletcher started to have a very bad feeling about all this as Dylan continued filling him in. "Lily has a bet to pay off. You know, the one about dating Carson McRue?"

Hope flared in Fletcher's heart. "She's given up on that?"

Thad nodded. "Apparently he came by and asked her out again for tonight and she turned him down flat," Thad said.

So why were all the men in the wedding party looking so grim? "That's good, isn't it?" Fletcher asked. Lord knew he was relieved.

"Not unless she actually agrees to go out with you, which I must point out she hasn't done yet." Cal studied him with a physician's trained eye. "Has she?"

"She will," Fletcher predicted.

All the men in the wedding party buried their heads in their drinks. "What?" Fletcher demanded. Clearly, they all knew something he didn't.

Mac turned back to him. His expression was grim. "You don't know what Lily Madsen wagered she would do if she lost. Do you?"

LILY AND THE OTHER female participants of Janey Hart's wedding party got out of the white stretch limo in front of the nightclub. Just nine o'clock, but the place was already packed with college kids. Music roared from the inside. Above the front door a big hot pink banner rippled in the wind, advertising the nightly contest that drew the wildest, most uninhibited women around. And tonight, thanks to the bet she had just lost, Lily was going to become one of them.

"Gonna enter the contest?" the bouncer asked with a cheerful wink as Lily walked through the door.

Feeling as if she were on her death march, she nodded. She had purposefully timed this so she wouldn't have time to reconsider and back out. Blessedly, the events were about to begin. As the evening's host—a popular deejay from a local radio station—got up on stage, Lily looked at some of the pitchers on the tables. "I'm really going to need a margarita. A pitcher of margaritas."

"Margaritas are what got you into this situation in the first place," Susan said.

Janey grabbed Lily's arm, suddenly as much a mother to Lily as she was to her twelve-year-old son, Christopher. "You know you really don't have to do this, Lily. We'll all put our heads together and think of something else."

Lily thought of the boasts she had made and shook her head stubbornly. "I'm not chickening out. A bet's a bet. I said I'd do it. I will."

Hannah rolled her eyes. "You were three sheets to the wind at the time!"

"Doesn't matter," Lily said grimly. Maybe this would teach her not to *ever* behave like such a fool again, lost teen years or not.

The microphone came on as the music cranked up even louder. "Okay, ladies. Let's go," the announcer said. "Everyone who's gonna participate up on stage."

Lily flushed, already feeling hideously embarrassed.

"And remember the rules. No bras. If you're wearing any kind of undie, you're disqualified. Okay?"

Lily swallowed and reached under her plain white T-shirt to unfasten the clasp. She was already beet-red and she hadn't even done anything yet.

"Uh-oh," Hannah said, looking toward the door.

Susan Hart scowled as she turned her gaze in the same direction. "What are *they* doing here?" she demanded, looking no happier than Lily to see they had a hometown audience.

Lily gulped as she saw all five of the Hart brothers and Janey's fiancé, Thad, coming toward them, Fletcher in the lead. Clad in the usual snug jeans, custom-fitted boots and solid-colored cotton shirt, Fletcher looked so ruggedly handsome and sexy, she felt herself go weak in the knees.

As he crossed to her side and took her by the arm, the air left her lungs in one big whoosh. "I don't care what bet you made—" he pushed the words through clenched teeth "—you're out of here."

Lily resented his taking charge of and imposing restrictions on *her* life. Wasn't that what she had been trying to get away from? Ignoring the flare of his nostrils and the take-no-guff-set of his broad shoulders, she folded her arms in front of her, and glared up at him. "You don't have any say about what I do or don't do, Fletcher Hart!" she shot back furiously, digging in her heels.

"The hell I don't." Still holding her tightly, he leaned down until they were nose to nose. "The only one ever going to see you in a wet T-shirt is me."

Chapter 7

"Now what?" Lily demanded, as they exited the Wild Girls Only nightclub.

Fletcher tightened his grip on her elbow as they rounded the corner to the parking lot where he had left his pickup truck. "I'm taking you for a frozen custard."

Pretending she wasn't relieved to have been hustled out of a seedy place she had never wanted to venture into in the first place, Lily propped her fists on her hips and squared off with him contentiously. "Why?" she demanded as her newfound recklessness took over once again and urged her to explore life to its limits.

Fletcher took one of her wrists in his hand and forced her to continue walking away from the raucous activity of the college bars. "Because every time I got in trouble and my dad needed to talk to me, he took me out for ice cream."

Lily scowled, as they rounded a corner at the end of the block and the noise abruptly died down. She hated the fact Fletcher looked so at ease when she was still tied up in knots. "You're not my father." *And I'm not in trouble. Not yet anyway. Although if he kept looking at her that way, as if he wanted to keep everyone else at bay, all bets about that were off, as well....*

"Well, right now I'm the closest thing you've got to a male protector in your life," Fletcher countered dryly. He continued to look at her in his very sexy, very determined way. "What were you thinking anyway?" He sighed his exasperation loudly. "Going into a place like that?"

The college bar had been more raucous than Lily had expected, but she'd be darned if she admitted that to him. She shrugged as if she did wild and crazy things like that all the time. "It was part of the bet."

Fletcher shook his head in silent reproach. The set of his lips was grim again as they reached his pickup truck. "So I heard."

Lily leaned against the passenger door. Fletcher adapted a no-nonsense stance—legs braced apart, one arm stretched out beside her and braced on the roof of the cab, the other resting on his waist—that would have been very intimidating had she allowed it. She didn't.

Lily lifted her chin another notch, daring him to try and chastise her for living her life to the fullest in whatever cockeyed way she chose. "How did you find out the terms?" she demanded.

Fletcher narrowed his eyes, his glance reminding her she had almost done something she would surely have regretted, newfound freedom or not. "Joe knew. And so did Thad."

So Emma spilled the beans to her husband, and Janey had told her fiancé. Knowing how close the two women were to the men they loved, Lily wasn't surprised. Nor did she mind. Especially when she herself longed to have someone she could confide everything to. Someone like Fletcher Hart? If only he were the marrying kind...instead of someone who had long maintained he only had the inclination and energy for one lifetime commitment—to his work.

"They were clearly worried," Fletcher continued pragmatically.

Somehow, Lily wasn't surprised to find the whole Hart clan was now looking out for her. It seemed if she had the support of one, she had the backing of the entire family. "And disapproving, as well, I guess?" Lily said lightly as she moved away from the lock.

Fletcher opened the door and helped her inside. "That, too." He looked at her again as he slid behind the wheel. "Now what?" he asked, eluding to her deepening scowl.

"I still have to pay off my bet."

"Not that way you're not," he said firmly. And the look on his face told her he meant it. If he even caught wind of her going near that place again, he'd be right there to stop her. The thought was as comforting as it was annoying.

Not that she really wanted to take off her bra, get hosed down and then have the quality of her breasts voted on, for heaven's sake.

Honestly, Lily thought, as she buried her face in her hands. What had she been thinking? Was being exuberantly youthful worth that kind of humiliation, just so you could someday look back and remember when you had been wild and uninhibited? Or was there a better way? A way she had yet to discover?

Fletcher drove a couple miles away from campus, then pulled into the parking lot of the frozen custard shop. At almost ten there was still a line at all the customer windows of the outdoor stand. The picnic tables scattered about were full of customers, too.

Lily watched him get out of the truck but made no move to follow him. Maybe it was time they called a halt to this evening. She really didn't think she wanted a lecture from him on the error of her ways, anyway. No point in him telling her what she already knew.

He came around to her side anyway and held the passenger door. "What kind of custard do you want?" he said.

"I want to go home," Lily said quietly.

His golden-brown eyes filled with compassion and he flashed her one of his sexiest smiles. "Just take a look at the menu." He clasped her hand. Together they walked over to the glass windows that served as the order area for the frozen-custard stand. Lily didn't mind the lineup. It gave her time to study the extensive menu painted on the boards above the windows, and consider how hungry she really was. And since Fletcher was paying…

As they moved away from the window with their delectable sundaes he guided her to a low brick wall that edged the grassy area surrounding the custard stand. Making sure they were out of earshot of everyone else, he sat down and stretched his long legs out in front of him. Lily sat down, too, making sure there was a good distance between them. Which, of course, he promptly closed simply by sliding toward her. "So, back to what we were talking about," he stated casually.

As if he didn't know. Lily cast her glance at the stars gleaming in the sky overhead. "Your youthful travails."

"No." He edged closer so their sides were touching in one long electrified line. "Yours."

Lily shifted back a little and then turned so her bent knee was touching the rock-hard muscle in his blue-jean clad thigh. She sent him a level look, aware her heart was racing again. "I lost the bet, Fletcher. I had to pay up."

He left the spoon in his mouth and paused to consider that. "You've still got time to get a date with Carson McRue."

Lily scoffed and met his too-innocent gaze head-on. "Ha! Not if you have anything to do about it."

He grinned wickedly.

"I notice you're not denying it," Lily observed, feeling the heat of excitement climb to her face.

Fletcher lifted his broad shoulders in an unapologetically lazy shrug. "I never pretended to *want* you to go out with him."

Lily refused to let herself think what that might mean. Save the fact Fletcher Hart was the most exasperating, ornery man she had ever met in her life. "Then why didn't you let me go through with the contest tonight?" she asked, aware the heat welling up inside her was nothing compared to the heat in his gaze.

"Like I said…" All the humor left his face, replaced by something much more dangerous. His voice dropped another seductive notch. "I don't want anyone seeing you in a wet T-shirt but me."

Lily swallowed at the rough note of possession and protectiveness in his voice. "And what does that mean?"

He shifted toward her and nudged her knee playfully with his. "What do you think it means?"

Lily felt a melting sensation in her middle, completely at odds with the emotional territory she was attempting to stake out. "That just because we've kissed a few times and verbally sparred even more that you're suddenly interested in me?" she asked lightly, pretending she wasn't playing with fire here.

His expression turned serious. "Not suddenly," he said quietly, offering her a bite of his custard.

As the creamy chocolate melted on her tongue, Lily lifted a curious brow.

He favored her with a sexy half smile, his eyes roving her face. "I've always had a thing for you," he told her softly. "From way back."

This was news. Lily caught her breath.

Trying to act normal, she spooned up some mint-chocolate chip for him. "You never acted like it."

He acknowledged this with a dip of his head, his eyes never leaving hers. "You were too young," he said quietly. "Five years is a big difference in your teens and early twenties. Then by the time the playing ground was more level, and you were old enough that I could consider asking you out, you were going through too much with your grandmother and her illness to get serious about anyone."

Lily's heart took a triple leap. With effort, she tried to keep herself from making too much of his unexpected confession. She swallowed the knot of emotion in her throat. "Did you want me to get serious about you?"

"Well, I didn't want to be one of the legions of guys

you dated once or twice and then never saw again, if that's what you're asking."

Her Ice Princess of Holly Springs rep reared its ugly head again, gained from years of being too polite to turn anyone down—no matter how ill suited they were to her—when she was asked out. Grandmother Rose had told her to go out at least once with anyone who asked her...because you never knew... The love of your life could be right there in front of your eyes. So Lily had done that, working her way through many of the single guys in Holly Springs. But there had never been any sparks, and after one date, sometimes two, they both always knew that.

Hence her reputation...

Well deserved, Lily supposed. Until now.

Now, there were sparks.... With the man she had never dreamed she would be kissing, or talking to on a regular basis, or sitting here sharing sweethearts and secrets...

She knew what this meant to her. Everything. But what did it mean to him? As she looked deep into his eyes, she couldn't honestly say. So she looked away. "I never meant to hurt anyone's feelings," she confessed softly, wanting Fletcher to understand this much about her. "In fact, I tried really hard not to do so." That was why she'd said yes to dates maybe she shouldn't have said yes to and ended things as soon as it was clear there wasn't any real chemistry.

"I know that," he said softly. "I've done the same thing and ended up with the same kind of pretty much undeserved love-'em-and-leave-'em reputation."

They were quiet again, but it was a companionable silence now. "Is that why you've been kissing me?" Lily asked finally, putting her empty paper cup and spoon aside. "And chasing me? Because you've decided it's time to make your move?"

Briefly, emotion flashed in his eyes, but it was gone before Lily could decipher it. He released a lengthy sigh. Looked serious and adult and responsible again. "I'm worried about you, Lily," he said finally, all traces of the ardent suitor disappearing as quickly and inevitably as they had appeared. His lips thinned. "And I'm not the only one. You haven't been yourself since your grandmother Rose died last year. First you were so withdrawn you barely cracked a smile. You just seemed to be going through the motions of your everyday life."

Lily really didn't want to talk about this. She rolled her eyes. "So I was like a Stepford florist, is that it?"

Ignoring her sarcasm, he continued searching her face. "Then the past few weeks you've been…kind of… I don't know. Unusually adventurous, I guess."

Lily felt the heat creeping back into her cheeks. She told herself it was the unduly warm temperature of the August evening. "That's a nice way to put it."

His glance scanned her, taking in the white T-shirt and the tight jeans she had bought as a twenty-fifth birthday present to herself. "You have to admit you haven't been acting like yourself," he said softly.

Lily rubbed the toe of her sandal across the grass and felt the soft blades tickle her bare toes. Another first. Grandmother Rose had always insisted Lily wear stockings or silk socks of some sort beneath her trousers because true ladies didn't show their bare feet off in public. It just wasn't proper.

Wanting—needing—Fletcher to see where she was coming from, Lily confessed emotionally, "That's just the point, Fletcher. I don't know who I am. I've never had the chance to find out. I've just been so focused on everyone and everything else." Eyes burning, Lily shook her head. "I missed that time during my college years where I should have been exploring all the different facets of my personality. I was forced to grow up and be the person Grandmother Rose needed me to be. I never went to the beach with my friends and just hung out. Never drank too many margaritas or dated anyone I really shouldn't, or had wild and crazy se—"

"Sex?" Fletcher guessed where she was going.

Lily clapped a hand over her mouth. She couldn't believe she had almost said that. She ducked her head, blushing furiously, unable to meet his eyes. She rubbed her foot across the velvety grass again. "You know what I mean."

"Yeah," he said slowly, leaning forward to rest a companionable hand on her knee. "I think I do." He squeezed her thigh. "And I think it's something we can fix readily enough, without you partaking in a wet-T-shirt competition."

"What are you planning?" Lily demanded, looking every bit as excited as Fletcher wanted her to be.

"Exactly what you'd think." Fletcher flashed her a mischievous smile, glad he finally knew what the problem was because now he knew how to fix it, too. "A way for you to get in touch with your inner bad girl." He lifted his brows in taunting fashion, leaned closer still and settled his hand on her thigh in unmistakable sexual intent. "Unless, of course, you're chicken."

Lily quivered beneath his touch, looking as if she wanted him to lead her astray, even as she wanted to keep guarding her heart from any damage he might inflict.

But Fletcher knew he wasn't going to hurt Lily. Rather, he was determined to keep her from getting hurt.

"Am I going to like this?" she asked, even as he took charge of their trash with one hand and helped her to her feet with the other.

Already guiding her toward the parking lot, Fletcher leaned down to teasingly whisper in her ear, "There's only one way to find out. Isn't there?"

He opened her door for her, then climbed behind the wheel. Moments later he dialed the cell phone mounted on the dash, leaving it on speakerphone so Lily would see he planned no secrets between them. Two rings later, a male voice answered. "Cal Hart here."

"Hey, Cal." Fletcher smiled over at Lily. "It's Fletcher. The party going okay?" They could hear chatter and laughter and country-and-western music in the background.

"We've sort of combined operations," Cal said above the din of clinking glasses and more laughter. "Where are you?"

"With Lily." Fletcher took her hand and pressed the back of it to his lips. "Say, mind if I...uh, borrow your orchard tonight?"

Cal's chuckle rumbled over the cell phone connection. "I'm not even going to inquire," he promised dryly.

"Thanks." Fletcher released Lily's hand and cut the connection before his brother could ask him anything more.

Lily raked the edge of her teeth across the plumpness of her lower lip. "Why did you ask him that?"

Pausing only momentarily to note how pretty she looked in the glow of the street lamps overhead, Fletcher backed out of the space. He drove out of the lot, anticipating the evening ahead. "So Cal wouldn't pull in to his driveway, see someone parked out there and think he needed to call the sheriff's department on the trespassers out there. Unless, of course, you'd like someone to call the sheriff on us, just to make it more exciting." He waggled his eyebrows at her playfully. "In which case I can pick a few places where we'd be likely to get picked up pretty darn quick."

Lily's eyes widened as she clapped a hand across her heart, unknowingly drawing his attention to the soft round breasts enticingly encased in snug white cotton. Which in turn made him wonder what she had on beneath, since he had seen the transparent wisps of lace drying in the laundry room. "You're taking me parking?" she gasped, amazed.

"Sure." Fletcher shrugged as if it were no big deal, when to him it *was* a very big deal. "Why not?" As they stopped at the next traffic light, he looked at her playfully. "You ever been?"

She shrank in her seat even as her eyes glowed with excitement. "Well, no."

Fletcher reached over and patted her knee again. "Trust me," he reassured her, "it's a lot more fun than a wet-T-shirt competition."

Lily bit her lip again, her cheeks growing ever pinker. "You're awfully sure of yourself, aren't you?" she asked.

Fletcher just smiled.

"I didn't think you were going to do it," Lily said a short while later as Fletcher turned his pickup into the country home owned by Cal Hart and his away-on-a-fellowship physician wife.

Fletcher drove right past the home Cal was renovating in what little spare time he had and continued on down the gravel lane that went past the barn to the sprawling orchard beyond. Lily guessed it encompassed about ten acres. There were more apple, pear, peach and cherry trees on the property than she'd ever imagined possible.

"Why? Would you rather go cow-tipping?" he asked her in mock seriousness. "'Cause we could do that. I even know a trick or two...."

Lily held up a hand, feeling a sort of perverse amusement as well as ever-escalating excitement at what they were about to do. "I bet you do. And no, I don't want to go cow-tipping, Fletcher." As far as she was concerned, there were some teenage adventures better left unexplored. That was one of them.

"Then parking it is." His lip took on a sensual slant as he drove slowly down the gravel lane that wound around through the rows and rows of trees. He took his hand off her knee to gesture expansively. "Pick your spot."

Lily wondered just how far he was planning to take this. "You pick since this was your idea."

He flashed her a crooked smile as he stopped the truck abruptly and cut the motor with a decisive flip of the ignition switch. "I don't hear you protesting all that much."

Lily swallowed hard as he reached behind the seat to pull out a lantern-style flashlight. He switched it on, and the beam illuminated the moonlit sky to the romantic aura of a dimly lit restaurant. "That's 'cause I'm curious," she said, watching as he pulled out a bucket and a plastic trash bag.

He got out of the truck. She joined him at the front of the truck. "Mind if we pick some fruit first?"

She watched him set the battery-powered lantern on the hood of the pickup. "You're kidding."

"No." He paused to line the farm bucket with the plastic bag, then looked up at her in all earnestness. "Unless you'd rather get down and dirty right away...."

Lily leaned against the front of the pickup, the bumper hitting her just above the knees. "You're making this oh-so-romantic." Which maybe was his purpose? To discourage her? But as he looked down at her in the soft glow of the lantern and the moonlight filtering down through the trees, it appeared discouragement was the last thing on his mind.

"Ah, so it's romance you want," he theorized softly, dropping the bucket on the ground and sifting both hands through her hair. "Not just hot, wild, sex."

Actually, she wanted that, too. So much. But not as part of some experiment to quell her lust for passion and adventure. Ignoring the heat emanating from his body, she murmured in a low tone rife with exasperation, "Fletcher."

"Hmm?" Looking as confused as she was about what was going on between them, he reached out and ever so gently, tentatively, touched her cheek.

"What are you doing?" *Besides making me want you as never before, even if this isn't about love, or is ever going to be....*

Brought abruptly back to his senses by her tone, Fletcher emitted a long, lust-filled sigh as he picked up the bucket again and stepped away from her. "Exactly what it looks like," Fletcher replied. "I'm trying to keep me and you out of trouble against all my baser instincts."

Lily caught him by the shirtfront and hauled him against her. "Maybe I like those baser instincts," she said, her heart pounding as she took charge of the situation once again.

Fletcher ran his hands down the length of her sides, eliciting tingles wherever he touched. "Baby, you haven't seen those baser instincts."

But she would like to see them. So much, now that they were alone again and doing something that felt so deliciously...forbidden. She took his hand and kissed the back of it, loving the warm, masculine texture of his skin. "So why did you bring me out here?"

He turned their entwined fingers around and kissed the underside of her wrist with his open mouth and the butterfly touch of his tongue. "To give you the chance to be bad even though I think you'd rather be good."

He knew her so well. Trying to do some of the things she had done tonight was like trying to wear a pair of shoes that just didn't fit. No matter what you did, what pose you took on, you were never going to be comfortable.

"And I don't want to see you do anything else you're going to have to regret," he said quietly, serious now, letting their joined hands fall back to their sides before disengaging them altogether.

"Like my birthday bet," Lily guessed around the sudden tightness of her throat, the disappointment in her heart. Once again, the noble side of Fletcher had taken charge, the side that wanted to protect and shelter her. Just as Grandmother Rose had done.

Painfully honest, his eyes touched hers. "That's right."

Her emotions in turmoil, Lily pushed away from the front of the truck and began walking through the orchard. "What would you know about having things to regret?" She flung the words over her shoulders.

As far as she could see, Fletcher might be cynical as could be, when it came to his personal relationships, but he'd never done anything he'd regretted. Except maybe go on a date with someone he should never have said yes to in the first place.

"Oh, you'd be surprised," he drawled, catching up, wrapping an arm around her waist and tugging her near.

"Tell me," Lily said, adjusting her steps to mesh with his.

For a long moment, she thought he wasn't going to answer, then he tightened his fingers on hers and let the lantern fall on a nice patch of grass. He sank down on the grass and watched as she did the same. "There was the last time I ever saw my dad."

Lily stretched out beside Fletcher, so they were lying face to face in the moonlight. "What happened?"

Fletcher ran his hand over the grass between them. "He had taken me out for ice cream and I basically wasn't speaking to him." Fletcher looked into her eyes and this time it wasn't hard for her to read his thoughts. "He wanted to talk to me alone about my grief over our dog's death. He knew I felt responsible, and he wanted to make it better. But I didn't give him the chance. I just turned away, demanded he take me home, and he did." As he paused, Lily felt a bond growing between them that she never could have envisioned, and her heart swelled at their growing closeness. "The next day he left on a business trip." Fletcher's lips tightened sadly. "His plane crashed and I never saw him again."

Lily touched his arm compassionately. "Oh, Fletcher."

He tensed at her touch and rolled over onto his back. Throwing an arm across his eyes, he continued in a rusty-sounding voice. "So you see, I've had a lifetime of regrets since I was ten." He paused, shook his head, let his arm fall. "It's no way to live. Believe me."

Lily continued stroking his arm. "Your mother must've told you that your dad understood your reluctance to talk about what had happened, that you were just a kid, acting on your unhappiness."

Fletcher turned his glance away, but not before Lily caught a glimpse of his pain.

"My mother doesn't know. I never told her."

Lily blinked, stunned. The Harts seemed so close. She couldn't imagine any secrets between them. "But surely—"

Fletcher cut her off with a shake of his head and continued wearily. "I don't think she and my dad had a chance to talk that night because when Dad and I got back from the ice cream place there was some plumbing crisis going on. One of the bathrooms was flooding, and by the time they got it cleaned up, it was late."

"So you never told anyone what happened between you and your dad that night?"

Rolling to face her once again, Fletcher shook his head. "Why make anyone else in the family feel worse than they already did over losing him?" he asked in a low, brooding voice. "Besides, my mother was a wreck. She had six kids, limited life insurance, no job. She didn't know how she was going to get by. She had to sell the house up north and move back here to be near family. Then her parents died shortly thereafter and left her the Wedding Inn."

"Only, it wasn't a business back then," Lily recalled.

"Just an overly large home with flagging upkeep and impossible taxes. But she saw the potential and began working her heart out. We all helped and…"

"The more time passed…" Lily guessed where Fletcher was going with this.

"The more pointless it was to talk about what had happened between me and my dad," Fletcher concluded, looking at her as if he wanted—needed—her to understand. "Anyway, since then I've tried really hard not to give people the impression I'm anything more than exactly what I am," he concluded cynically, the devil-may-care note back in his voice.

Lily lay on her stomach in the soft grass, her chin propped on her upraised palm. "Which is what, Fletcher? A wonderful vet and even more wonderful human being?"

He shook his head, not apologizing. Making no excuses. Just telling it like it was—in his opinion, anyway. "The kind of guy who—at least in his personal life—has a talent for doing and or saying the wrong thing. *Every time.*"

And she was part of his personal life, Lily knew. Which might not bode well for them as a couple, unless she could change his mind about this. "You're selling yourself short," she told him gruffly.

He tugged on a lock of her hair. "What would you know about it?"

Lily brushed off his hand and scrambled to a sitting position. Determined to be serious about this. "I know that when it comes to me and my problems you say and do the right thing every time, Fletcher Hart."

He caught her by the waist and the next thing Lily knew she was on her back again, Fletcher sprawled over her. "You consider the right thing bringing you out here to get hot and heavy with me?" he murmured as he pushed her knees apart with one of his and slid between them, settling more deeply between her spread thighs.

Oh, my. This was turning very sensual, very fast. Lily braced both her forearms against the hardness of his chest, loving the warmth and strength and danger of him. "You haven't made out with me," she taunted back just as lightly. *Yet.*

The wicked grin was back, more devastating than ever. "Oh, I think we can remedy that." He kissed one corner of her mouth, then the other.

Lily's plan to make him work for it was already disintegrating. Her lips parted slightly and she let her head fall back. "Do you?"

"Oh, yeah." He took her forearms, put them around his shoulders and dropped his head. Then he took her mouth in a long, hot, searing kiss. Lily had never been wanted quite this way, never wanted this way. She arched up against him, needing, yearning, until there was only the fierce reckless pressure of his lips on hers, the strong warm cage of his arms, the demanding pressure of his body draped over hers. She felt like his woman and he kissed her until she felt like swooning, then kissed her some more until she clung to him and whimpered low in her throat. Until she kissed him back the way he was kissing her, with every fiber of his being. With a low groan of pleasure she tangled her fingers in his hair and brought him closer yet, straining toward him until it was clear that if they kept this up they would have a decision to make.

His breaths coming as raggedly as hers, Fletcher broke the kiss and lifted his head. Arm anchored around her waist, he rolled so he was beneath her, the proof of his desire as unmistakable as her own. He stroked his thumb across her lower lip, the arch of her brow, the line of her cheek. "Lily," he murmured with all the tenderness she had ever dreamed, "I want to make love to you."

Her body was throbbing everywhere. His was, too. "I want to make love to you, too," Lily whispered, reaching for the hem of her T-shirt.

His expression determined, Fletcher caught her wrist before she could go any further. "No way is our first time together going to be here."

Chapter 8

"So much for being out with a bad boy," Lily drawled as they left the orchard and headed back to Holly Springs. She tried not to feel disappointed she hadn't already lost her virginity.

"Believe me." Fletcher reached over and squeezed her hand. "You'll thank me later when you're ensconced in a nice comfortable bed." Keeping one hand on the wheel, he lifted her wrist to his lips, traced the inside of it with his lips and tongue. "Your place or mine?"

She thought of the twin canopy bed she had slept in since she had been a little girl. And for a lot of reasons never bothered to change. "I think you have the more comfortable bed," Lily allowed, aware, but not surprised at the way her heart was still pounding. After all, a big turning point in her life lay ahead...

"Good point." His mouth kicked up at the corner. He

steered the truck over into a gravel turnaround alongside the road, shifted it into park and leaned across to kiss her again, hard. She leaned toward him and kissed him back. He reached down and released his safety belt, then hers. The next thing she knew she was being shifted across the bench-style seat and onto his lap. He brought her down across his hard-muscled thigh and the proof of his desire for her. The fiery intimacy of the contact robbed her of breath and left her shaken as the demanding feel of him scorched through her jeans. If this was what it was like now, she thought, as his mouth continued to mate with hers, his tongue stroking, tempting, tasting, heaven help her when they got to the really good stuff. She was about to melt from the inside out as it was...

And he was just as hot and bothered as she was, his skin burning through the fabric of his shirt and jeans with fiery intensity as he took full, masculine possession of her lips, then moved to her ear. One hand came up to cup her breast through the fabric of her T-shirt, while the other was unsnapping then unzipping her jeans. Lily moaned as his fingers slipped beneath the lacey edge of her thong panties to find her...there. The contact shot a jolt of exquisite pleasure through her, making her moan. She heard him chuckle as he began to kiss her again, and then she was being shifted off his lap again onto the cool leather seat of the cab. She stared over at him, aware her nipples had hardened into aching points, and lower still, there was a telltale dampness...and pulsing need.

The windows of the truck were fogged up. Her head felt the same way. She looked at him from a misty, pleasure-filled place. "Did I...?"

"No, no." He regarded her gently, looking struck by her innocence once again. "But you will several times before night's end, I promise." After reaching over to zip and snap her jeans, he refastened her seat belt then his. "Right now—" he looked determined as he checked to make sure the road was clear, then drove back out onto the country highway "—we've got to concentrate on getting all the way home."

"Good idea," Lily said, studying his handsome profile in the soft light of the dash. Because if they stopped one more time she sensed there would be no more holding back on either of their parts, no matter where they were....

"So." Fletcher's voice was gravelly with need as he searched for something nonarousing for them to talk about. "What about Spartacus—?"

Somehow it seemed safer to close her eyes and let her head fall back against the padded headrest, than continue looking at the lips that had already given her so much pleasure. Lily drew in a shaky breath, aware she could barely think coherently. "We don't have to walk him or anything. He's with your nephew, Christopher, for the evening." She licked her lips and tasted... Fletcher. "I don't have to pick him up until tomorrow morning."

"So we've got the whole night?"

Lily swallowed around the sudden, parched feeling in her throat. "If you want it," she said shyly, knowing he was more than man enough for her. Was she woman enough for him?

"Oh, I want it," he said softly, reaching over to tangle his fingers in her hair. He teased her gently. "Now if we could just hurry up and get there...."

Lily chuckled as he continued to drive safely nevertheless. "You really are in a hurry, aren't you?" The look on his face said he couldn't wait to start making love to her, really making love to her....

"To get started." He sent her a gentle, protective look as smug male confidence exuded from him in mesmerizing waves. "As for the rest, I plan to take my time."

And take his time he did. It was Lily who was in a hurry, who kept trying to speed things up. No sooner were they in the door to his apartment, than she was in his arms again, kissing him passionately, her desire for him fast outstripping everything else. Her fear about it being her first time...her wondering if it was going to hurt...seemed irrelevant. Lily cared only about the comforting feel of his arms around her, the enticing hardness of his body pressed up against hers and the blossoming love in her heart. She knew this was supposed to be just a casual fling—and maybe for him it was, she thought, as they continued to kiss each other hotly and possessively. But for her it was another step to a brand-new life filled with excitement and passion and the freedom to be and do whatever she wanted and needed. It was a life without restriction, and her body ignited as did her soul. This felt so right. Fletcher felt so right as he gave in to her urgency, swept her up into his powerful arms and carried her toward his bedroom, not setting her down until they had reached the side of the bed.

The covers were rumpled, as if he had just gotten out of them. He looked down at her, a pulse working in his throat, as Lily drank in the tantalizing fragrance of soap and man and the deliciously masculine cologne he favored. "If you want to opt out of this," he said, "now's the time."

Lily grinned. How like Fletcher to be the antithesis of the cynic he was publicly thought to be, and try and protect her, even now. "Not on your life," she said as she went up on tiptoe and kissed him yet again. Being here with Fletcher like this was her every fantasy come true. "And to show you," she murmured, taking the hem of her T-shirt and lifting it above her breasts, over her head. She flung it off and stood before him in a transparent wisp of a shell-pink demi-bra.

His chest rose and fell with each ragged breath. "Damn, Lily," he said as she reached around behind her, undid the clasp and let the bra slip off her arms.

His eyes darkened as he took in the silky curves of her breasts and jutting nipples. As their eyes met and the air between them reverberated with excitement and escalating desire, Lily felt more womanly than she had in her entire life.

"You are so beautiful."

"It's no wet T-shirt."

"Doesn't have to be." He took her hand and held it against the front of his jeans. "Can't you feel what you do to me?"

Lily smiled. So this was what it was like to be desired, to be wanted so very much you could hardly stand it.

"Your turn," she whispered playfully. He undid a button and then pulled the shirt over his head, flung it off and away from him.

For a moment, Lily could only stare. He was beautiful, too. More than beautiful. His shoulders were even broader than she had realized, his chest nicely muscled and satiny smooth. A mat of honey-brown hair spread across his chest and flat male nipples, before arrowing down to the waistband of his jeans. "Keep going," Lily said as she lounged against the bureau.

Holding her eyes, he reached for the buckle on his belt. "I thought it was ladies first," he teased, all too willing to strip for her if that was what she wanted. And it was...

"Not tonight." Lily smiled as he pulled off his boots, then dropped "trou," and without her even asking, divested himself of his dark gray boxer-briefs. His arousal was so pronounced, so velvety smooth, she couldn't tear her eyes away from it. "Damn, Fletcher," she murmured a little bashfully as he strode near.

"What are you thinking?" he asked as she continued to stare down at the visibly throbbing length.

"That there is no way that is ever going to fit inside of me."

He grinned. "Yes, it will. You'll see."

Lily brushed a hand across the taut skin of his abdomen. Paused. Licked her lips. "I don't know about that," she said shakily.

"Trust me. I do," Fletcher murmured back. He trailed his mouth over the tops of her breasts. Lily felt the hot moistness of his breath on her skin and a hot rush of desire swept through her. Her eyes drifted shut, even as she wondered how someone so big and strong and male could have such a tender touch. And then his lips were moving lower still, caressing the sensitive undersides of her breasts, the valley between, before settling on the sensitive tip. Her knees went weak as his mouth closed over her, drawing deep, and her body thrilled and burned with everything that had been missing for her. She moaned, arching up against him, tunneling her hands through his hair, holding him close even as she wanted more and more and more.

"You like that," he whispered as he replaced his lips with the pads of his thumbs and straightened to kiss her again, deeply, erotically, as if she were his and always would be....

"Oh yes," Lily whispered back. Making love with Fletcher was so much better than she had ever imagined it could be.

"Then let's keep going, shall we? 'Cause it's still your turn."

He stepped back. Lily had only to look into his eyes to know what he wanted her to do.

Mouth dry, she stepped out of her sandals. Unsnapped, then unzipped her jeans. She was trembling as she shoved them down her legs, stepped out of them. And stood before him clad only in the wispy pale pink thong. This time she didn't even have to ask. He liked what he saw. Very much.

She started to take it off, but he caught her hand and drew her down onto the bed. "Let me."

The next thing Lily knew she was lying on her back. Fletcher was once again parting her knees and lying between the cradle of her thighs. Her thong was still on. It didn't seem to bother him one bit as he kissed his way across the top edge of the fabric. Then he drifted lower, suckling gently. The friction of his lips and tongue through the barrier of lace was almost more than Lily could bear. She arched up off the bed. Her thighs fell even farther apart. Fletcher's free hand slid between them, stroking the tender insides from knee to pelvis and back down again. She was teetering on the edge of something wonderful…hot and melting inside…

"Fletcher," she moaned again, catching his head between her hands. He chuckled softly again, and this time her thong came off. And then his mouth was there, with nothing in between them, his fingers were parting the tender folds, sliding inside her. Making lazy circles, moving in, up, out again. Driving her crazy as more moisture flowed. And then something else was happening. She was trembling, aching, exploding inside until she quivered with pleasure and nearly shot all the way off the bed.

And Lily knew…finally…finally…

When she could, she lifted her head and found him stretched out beside her, smiling at her with a pleasure every bit as potent as her own. Lily caught her breath at the desire still etched on his handsome face. "That was it?"

His smile widened as he savored the way she continued to tremble and stroked her body playfully. "Let's call it a good start." He eased between her legs again, with a masculine resolve that had her surrendering to him all over again. "We've still got a ways to go."

Lily could see how much he cared, by the gentle restraint in his gaze. He was determined to make this as good for her as it was for him, first time or no. "How did I get so lucky?" she whispered around the sudden lump of emotion in her throat.

He draped a leg over hers and, still holding her as if he never wanted to let her go, still watching her face, let his fingers do their magic once again. "Beats me," Fletcher whispered back, his golden-brown eyes dark with a longing that seemed to go way beyond the sexual. "I've been asking myself the same question for days now," he whispered back meaningfully, his arousal pressing against her hip.

And then he was kissing her again, bringing her to the brink again, surprisingly quickly this time. Sheathing himself. Protecting them both. Shifting his strong hard body overtop of her. Kissing her full on the mouth until their bodies took up a primitive rhythm all their own, until their was no doubt how much they wanted their bodies to mesh. And then she was lifting her hips, pleading wordlessly for a more intimate union, and he was easing her knees apart, lifting her and parting her, pushing past that first fragile barrier to the welcoming warmth inside.

For a moment, Lily didn't think it was going to be possible. He was so big and so hard and so hot, and she was so tight. But as he rocked against her with gentle, patient insistence, she discovered their bodies were made for each other after all. And then they truly were one and the possessive look in his eyes made her catch her breath. Awash in sensation, Lily let her head fall all the way back, let the abandon overtake her. And then she was moaning again, whispering his name, urging him on as the remaining boundaries between them dissolved into a wild, sensual pleasure unlike anything she had ever known. And he, too, was soaring, pressing into her as deeply as he could go, and they were lost, free-falling into an ecstasy that warmed her body and filled her soul.

"I guess you were right," Lily said as they cuddled together afterward. She pressed her lips against his chest. "You did fit."

His laughter rumbled up inside his chest, a warm and

welcoming sound. As he turned to face her, he looked proud to have been the one to claim her. "Who said dreams don't come true?" he murmured with a playful wink as he shifted her so she was beneath him, and began to make love to her all over again.

Indeed, Lily thought. Hers certainly had.

Fletcher fell asleep with Lily snuggled against him, only to be rudely awakened by the phone ringing at 4:00 a.m. He groaned, reluctantly unwrapping his arms from around Lily's soft, incredibly warm and feminine body, and knocked the alarm clock off his nightstand while trying to get to the phone. "Fletcher Hart," he growled into the receiver as the metal clock continued to clatter against the hardwood floor before coming to a noisy halt that did little to stir the beautiful woman sleeping beside him. "And this damn well better be an emergency," he warned bad-temperedly.

"It's Dylan. And it is. I need a ride to the Raleigh-Durham airport."

Damn. Fletcher rubbed the sleep from his eyes. Wasn't it just his luck that the best night of his entire life would have to be so rudely interrupted? "When?" he growled in a way that let his younger brother know this better not become a habit. Now that Lily was his, Fletcher had plans for his nights.

"Now," Dylan said even more urgently. "My flight to Chicago departs at 6:05 a.m. and I'm supposed to be there two hours prior to departure to check-in. Obviously, I'm not going to make that," Dylan continued in his smooth TV sportscaster's voice. "But if we leave in the next ten, fifteen minutes I could probably make my flight."

Fletcher scowled as Lily finally began to stir. It felt as if he just went to sleep five minutes ago and yet all he wanted to do was make love to Lily all over again. Which might be possible if she woke all the way up... and wanted him, the way he now wanted her. "Any particular reason you called me?" he asked dryly. Instead of one of his other four brothers. All of whom lived in Holly Springs, too.

"We were all out until 2:00 a.m. and you went home early and I didn't think you'd be doing anything in particular right about now." Dylan paused meaningfully. "Are you?"

Just the most important thing in my entire life. "Besides sleeping?" Fletcher affected the most bored tone he could manage. "No. And what are you doing hopping on a plane to Chicago? Aren't you supposed to be here through the weekend given the fact our sister is getting married on Sunday?"

"Yeah, I know, I'm supposed to be on vacation until after the ceremony. But there's some kind of emergency at the TV station where I work and there's an all-hands-on deck meeting at the studio at noon today." Dylan's voice tensed even more. "You know how volatile things can be."

Fletcher did. The anchors and broadcasters were hired and fired all the time in that industry, often for very little reason save the station manager's whim. It wasn't an arena he would want to work in. But his sports-minded and hopelessly telegenic younger brother loved it.

"I figure I better be there," Dylan told Fletcher soberly.

"Gotcha," Fletcher said, knowing now why Dylan

had called him. He was trying to save face and manage his fears, and Dylan figured Fletcher would be the least likely to pass judgment or advise him to get another career.

"But I'll be back in time for the wedding," Dylan promised matter-of-factly.

"Rehearsal?"

"That I can't say, but…"

"I understand," Fletcher said, knowing his brother was in an impossible situation. If he did go and ended up missing the wedding, the family would be ticked off at him. If he didn't go and lost his job as a result, he'd be screwed, as well. "I'll be over to get you in a minute," Fletcher reassured him.

"Thanks. I'll be on the front steps at the Wedding Inn."

Another problem. "You didn't tell Mom you're leaving yet, did you?" Fletcher guessed and could practically see his brother's grimace in return.

"She'll find out soon enough when she reads the note I left for her on the kitchen table," Dylan said.

Shaking his head at his younger brother's cowardice—this kind of exit would *not* bode well with their mother—Fletcher hung up. Lily was propped on one elbow, watching him. She looked deliciously ravished. In need of proper loving again. And he had to leave. Damn.

"What's happening?" Lily asked as Fletcher stood and pulled on his jeans.

Briefly, Fletcher explained Dylan's predicament.

Lily got up and began to dress hurriedly, too. "Well, of course he has to go back to Chicago," she said.

Fletcher hoped his sister, Janey, felt that way. She

might not. Brides were known to be irrational about their weddings, even women as normally cool, calm and collected as Janey. He had learned that growing up around the Wedding Inn. When it came to love, common sense often went right out the window.

"Besides," Lily continued as she bent over to slip on her sandals, "I need to get home soon, anyway. Lest our friends and neighbors see me departing at the crack of dawn and deduce I spent the night with you."

Fletcher didn't want Lily's reputation damaged any more than she did. He regretted having put her in this position and knew he should have thought about that before coaxing her to spend the entire night with him. Not that he was surprised by the lack of foresight on his part, he chided himself unhappily. If there was a mistake to be made, he usually made it. And larger than even this one was the bet he had made with Thad Lantz and his brothers, regarding Lily.

Lily looked at him curiously. "It'll be okay, Fletcher," she promised. "Really."

Would it? Fletcher wondered. Particularly if Lily ever found out what he had done....

Fletcher was still thinking about a way out of the mess he had created for himself when he dropped Lily at her home, pulled her to him and kissed her soundly. He might have inadvertently won his bet, but he could also lose everything that mattered to him. Particularly if word were to get out among the residents of Holly Springs. "We're going to have to talk about how to handle this. We can't have your reputation impugned."

Lily rolled her eyes at his concern. "After my too many margaritas incident and the bet I made—and lost—I don't think that's a consideration anymore," she drawled, before continuing even more recklessly. "And besides, wasn't that my purpose anyway? To reinvent myself in a wilder manner? So I would no longer be the prim-and-proper Lily or the Ice Princess of Holly Springs?"

She hadn't just slept with him for that reason. Had she? He asked himself.

"You helped me find my inner bad girl, Fletcher Hart." Lily smiled and kissed him soundly once again as she slipped from the cab of his truck. "And for that I thank you."

When Lily went over to Janey's to pick up Spartacus on her way to work later that morning, Spartacus leaped up from his spot near the front door and wagged his tail so hard he nearly fell over.

"He sure looks happy to see you!" Janey's son, Christopher, noted, moving a little stiffly as he ushered Lily inside the house. He was still recovering from an athletic injury, incurred over the summer, but otherwise looked good. His freckled cheeks glowed with healthy color, his blue eyes lively, his smile as friendly as could be.

Glad to see the gangly athlete doing so well, Lily knelt down to pet Spartacus and rub him behind his ears while he nuzzled her like a long-lost friend. "I'm happy to see Spartacus, too," Lily said and realized it was true.

"Are you going to adopt him?" Christopher asked, watching her expression carefully.

For the first time, the denials Lily had at the ready did not roll readily off her tongue. A dog, and the care he required, sort of conflicted with her new wild-and-free lifestyle. On the other hand, she was emotionally attached to the handsome yellow Lab.

"I don't know. I've never thought of myself as a dog person," Lily said finally as Spartacus stopped wagging and turned his soulful eyes up to hers. He seemed to know intuitively that Lily was thinking about finding him a home elsewhere.

"Well, if you decide you don't want him or can't keep him or whatever, let me know because I think I want him," Christopher said urgently.

"Christopher," Janey said as she walked in, "we talked about this. If you get a dog of your own, you need to have plenty of time to spend with him, especially at the beginning. And right now you still have physical therapy for your athletic injury last month, and school and homework and your part-time job at the arena. Honey, it's just not practical. And it wouldn't be fair to a dog like Spartacus who has already been through so much and needs so much tender loving care, just to feel safe and loved again."

Christopher nodded, understanding, but no less disappointed.

"Hey," Lily said, "tell you what. As long as I've got him, you can come over and see him and walk him anytime you want. He wasn't so good at first but he's getting pretty decent on a leash now. And you can even pet-sit him now as your schedule—and your mom—allow."

Christopher turned to Janey for permission.

Janey smiled. "Of course you can pet-sit Spartacus. In fact, I think it's a great idea for all concerned."

"Thanks, Mom." Christopher beamed. "And thank you, Ms. Madsen. You're awesome."

Lily grinned back. Maybe it was Fletcher, maybe it was just the fact she was finally getting over the loss of her grandmother, but she was beginning to feel really happy.

"Let me walk you out," Janey said. She and Lily headed out onto Janey's front porch, Spartacus on a leash beside Lily. As they stood there together, Lily realized Janey and her son wouldn't be living there much longer. After the wedding, Janey and Christopher were set to move into Thad's much larger home. Being the practical woman she was, Janey had already put her home on the market. The Realtor's For Sale sign whipped around in the mounting wind as Janey cast a worried glance toward the darkening sky.

She looked back at Lily. "You're thinking what I'm thinking, aren't you?"

Lily nodded unhappily, guessing at the nature of her best friend's thoughts. "That this storm front heading into the area is going to put a damper on your outdoor wedding plans?"

Janey nodded. "If it rains for three days, there's no way we'll be able to have the ceremony in the formal gardens at the Wedding Inn. Even if we use tents, the ground will be a squishy mess. There'd be no walking on it, especially in heels."

"Thinking of moving it inside?" Lily asked, glad to see Janey was taking this in stride.

Janey nodded. "The chapel at Unity Church where we attend services is available for the ceremony, and we can use the Oak Room at the Wedding Inn for the reception. Although, if we do that, it's really going to mess up what we had planned in terms of flowers."

Lily knew what Janey meant. They had been planning to use the inn's lush garden hedges as an intricate part of many of the arrangements, draping garlands of flowers around the perimeter of the outdoor "chapel" where the ceremony and reception had been slated to take place.

"A wedding trellis woven with wildflowers just isn't going to look right inside the church," Janey worried. "Not with the stained-glass window overlooking the sanctuary."

"I agree. Tall sterling-silver candelabra would be better."

"And the Oak Room is so formal. But it's the room where we can seat two hundred for a wedding supper."

"I agree. Changing the site of the reception and the ceremony will require a complete redesign of all the flowers. You're probably going to want to go with something more in keeping with a traditional indoor wedding if you move it inside."

"But the flowers have already been ordered, haven't they?" Janey guessed, looking all the more worried.

Lily nodded. Janey had wanted to create a "sun-kissed meadow" effect for her Sunday-afternoon ceremony. She put a reassuring arm around Janey's waist. "I think we can still use all the flowers we ordered. We're just going to have to get more creative with how we arrange them."

"Oh, this is such a mess." Janey cast another look at the sky as big fat raindrops began to fall. "I so wanted my wedding to Thad to be perfect."

"And it will be," Lily promised with a smile, giving her friend's waist another squeeze. She didn't know if it was having Fletcher in her life, or the fact that she just felt so free to do what she pleased now, but suddenly she felt invincible. Like she could and would meet every challenge that came her way. "You just leave everything to me," she said.

"Thanks. I will. And speaking of you…"

"Yes?"

Janey cast a look over her shoulder to make sure her son was nowhere in sight. He was still inside, stuffing papers and books into a backpack. "What's going on between you and my brother?" Janey whispered.

"Fletcher?"

Janey rolled her eyes and quipped drolly, "That would be the one, all right."

Lily shrugged. The passion she felt for Fletcher was so new, she did not want to share it. "Nothing."

"Nothing, as in nothing really is going on?" Janey persisted in a voice barely above a whisper. "Or nothing, as in I'm really in love with him?"

Lily hesitated. She hadn't been aware she was wearing her heart on her sleeve. But since she was, maybe it was best she confide in someone. "It's that obvious?" she whispered back.

Janey nodded, her amber eyes serious.

"I've known him forever," Lily said. And she had always been attracted to him, even when he drove her crazy. "But we've never interacted the way we have lately," she finished shyly.

Janey reached over and squeezed Lily's hand. "Sometimes that's the way it happens. You just have to be in the right place at the right time with the right person."

It certainly felt as if that was the case all right, Lily thought, as Spartacus sat beside Lily patiently on the porch. Lily looked at Janey as the rain began to come down in earnest. Since they were talking, she could use some "sisterly" words of wisdom. "You got involved with Thad Lantz awfully fast." They'd begun seeing each other in July. Here it was August, and the two were getting married. "Do you have any qualms?"

"No," Janey said, and she looked so serene Lily knew it was true. "I feel like I've finally come home. It's funny, you know. For so many years, I felt I had to leave Holly Springs and live away from here to find my bliss. But it doesn't work that way. Your bliss isn't out there, somewhere else. It's right here—" Janey pointed to her heart "—inside. It was just up to me to find it. And now I know that true happiness is having a home and a child and a husband and being surrounded by family and friends. Doing work I care about, in a place I really adore is the icing on the cake. But I could do work I still loved a lot less and be happy, as long as I had Christopher and Thad and my mom and my brothers. And maybe, one day, even a dog. Although probably not until next summer," she finished wryly.

"You really do have it all," Lily said.

Janey leaned forward to give her a hug. "And someday you will, too," she promised.

Lily hoped that was the case. Finally, it seemed, she had found a man she loved. A man who had the potential to make her really, truly happy, not just for the immediate present, but for the rest of her life. The question was, how did Fletcher Hart feel about her?

"You'll never guess what I just heard!" Sheila told Lily and Maryellen breathlessly as she returned from her lunch break.

"Action?" Maryellen teased.

Lily smiled. Like almost everyone else in Holly

Springs, her three part-time employees couldn't seem to resist going over to gawk at the TV production being filmed in the historic downtown area. Not that there was much to hear. They were kept well back from any dialogue being spoken and had to content themselves with watching—from a distance—the individual scenes being filmed.

"No. Custom Florists from Raleigh just got fired from their set-decorating job."

Belinda settled on a stool and rested a hand on the baby growing inside her. "You're kidding. Their work is spectacular."

"I know, but that burgundy-haired girl—you know, the one that wears all the eyeliner…"

"Carson McRue's assistant."

"Right." Sheila nodded vigorously as she slipped off her rain jacket and hung it on a hook by the door. "She came over and told them they had to leave. They weren't going to be decorating the church for the wedding scene."

"Maybe they're just delaying the filming because of the rain."

Lily knew not much had been going on that day thus far because of the heavy downpours.

"That's what Custom Florists hoped," Sheila continued as she put her umbrella out to dry. "But it's not the case. Carson's assistant told them not to come back tomorrow, either. Carson McRue Productions would send them a check for any time spent thus far, but they weren't going to be needed after all."

Lily shrugged, refusing to get excited. "It's possible the set decorators are going to do it themselves. This weather delay has to have cost them a pretty penny. So maybe they're just trying to make it up that way."

"Carson McRue doesn't come across like a man who pinches pennies," Belinda said.

"Don't look now, but here comes the assistant," Maryellen murmured.

And right behind her was Fletcher Hart. He held the door for the assistant, waiting while she closed her umbrella, then marched toward Lily purposefully. The assistant spoke first. "Ms. Madsen? Carson wants to see you over in his trailer."

"About…?" Lily asked while her staff glanced at her hopefully. Lily was trying to keep her mind on business, but it was difficult—to say the least—with Fletcher standing there in a long yellow rain slicker and hat looking as sexy and indomitable as any cowboy who had ever come in out of a storm.

While Fletcher took off his hat and ran his fingers through his rain-dampened hair, his amber eyes giving off a welcoming glint, the assistant popped her gum and ran her index finger across one heavily made-up eye. "Um, officially, I think he wants you to decorate the church or something," she said.

Lily paused as Fletcher leaned a shoulder against the wall and regarded her with the same intensity he had used when making love to her over and over again.

Feeling herself go weak in the knees, just contemplating what had happened the previous night and what she hoped would happen again very soon, Lily turned her attention back to the conversation at hand. She wasn't averse to new business, celebrity or otherwise, but she had previous obligations that had to be met first. "When?" she asked, wishing Fletcher would stop looking at her as if he were thinking about kissing her again. It was making it impossible for her to concentrate.

"Whenever the rain stops and they can continue with the filming," the assistant said.

It wasn't supposed to cease for at least another day. Lily noted Fletcher was not looking happy about the request. "And unofficially?" Lily asked Carson's assistant.

She popped her gum again. "Carson's bored, waiting out this rain, and he'd like someone to while away the time with, as per usual."

Not good, Lily thought as Fletcher lifted a coolly discerning brow. "Why me?" Lily asked as Fletcher's scowl deepened. *He was behaving as protectively as her grandmother had when she was alive.* Lily didn't like it. His coming to her rescue last night had been one thing. His obvious skepticism of her ability to make a proper judgment about a business decision was another.

Doing her best to conceal her hurt that Fletcher had as little faith in her as her grandmother ultimately had, Lily turned her glance back to Carson's messenger.

The assistant shrugged. "You're young, blond, pretty, got that whole innocent angel thing going for you. It's exactly his type, when he's on location anyway."

And what was Fletcher's type? Lily wondered as she briefly sought his glance once again. At the moment it did not seem to be anyone as independent-minded as she was. Under normal circumstances, anyway.

Across the square, the door to Carson's trailer opened. His costar for that episode stormed out, moving hurriedly across the blocked off area. She did not look happy.

It wasn't too hard to figure out what was going on. Able to feel her employees hovering around her like concerned mother hens, Lily smiled at the assistant. Two days ago she would have jumped at the chance to spend time alone with Carson McRue, even if she spent that time fending off amorous advances. Not now. She had all the passion and excitement she needed in her life with one Fletcher Hart.

"I don't think so," Lily replied without an ounce of regret. "Thanks for asking, but we're all working pretty hard on the flowers for the Hart-Lantz wedding."

The assistant muttered something indecipherable. "Carson isn't going to like this," she warned.

Lily kept working on the arrangement in front of her, one of dozens of summer bouquets that were going to be placed around the church and in the Oak Room at the Wedding Inn. Ignoring the masculine possessiveness radiating from Fletcher, she said, "Not my problem."

The assistant sighed as she exited the shop, re-opening her umbrella as soon as she cleared the door. "Don't we wish we could both say that," she said over her shoulder.

As soon as she left, Fletcher came toward Lily. He looked relieved she had turned down both the work and the chance to spend time alone with the TV star. "I'm meeting my brother Joe at Crabtree Mall in Raleigh to do a wedding errand. We're going to have lunch while we're there. You want to go?"

Lily was tempted, despite her unexpressed pique with Fletcher. "I wish I could," she said wistfully, feeling suddenly unbearably restless. Unable to help but note how handsome he looked standing there, hat in hand, with the rain dotting his thick hair, she continued softly. "But we've got way too much to do here to get ready for Janey's wedding." And she needed time to think. To figure out how to handle this relationship if that was indeed what it was going to be, and not just the brief, passion-and-fun-filled fling she had initially signed on for.

"A rain check then," Fletcher answered oblivious to the interested looks emanating from Lily's employees.

Lily nodded her assent. And when they did talk alone again, she was going to have to counsel him on what rights—if any—being her lover entailed. Because there was no way she was going back to a life of being told what and what not to do, in business or her private life. Even if she was head over heels in love with him.

"Dylan seems to think we all owe you a hundred bucks," Joe told Fletcher lazily as they walked into Crabtree Mall to pick up the wedding rings for Thad and Janey.

"Yeah?" Fletcher pretended he had nothing to hide. "Where did Dylan get that idea?"

"The smile on your face when you picked him up this morning."

Fletcher shoved aside his guilt about a promise that was surely broken. "I smile all the time," he told his hockey-playing younger brother.

"Not when you're hauled out of bed at 4:00 a.m., you don't." Joe regarded Fletcher closely. "Seriously, what's up with you and Lily Madsen? Are you just chasing her to win this bet you made with all of us?"

To Fletcher's irritation Joe seemed to think that could indeed be the case. "The bet has nothing to do with my getting her out of that club last night," Fletcher bit out.

Joe remained unconvinced as they strolled past a popular clothing chain. "Then what does?"

"I was just looking out for her."

"Does Lily know that's all it was?"

"Lily knows the score." That she's my woman now and will be from this point forward.

Joe swore roundly, shook his head. "From where I was standing it looked like Lily was reading a lot more into it than that."

Good, Fletcher thought. Because he was, too.

"If she ever finds out about the bet—" Joe continued, prophesizing grimly.

Fletcher cut Joe off. "She'd never understand. Which is why I'm not going to tell her. And none of you is, either." Maybe in time, when he and Lily were close enough, when she trusted him enough to understand he had never—would never—hurt her, Fletcher would be able to tell Lily everything. About the promise to her grandmother, as well as the bet. Right now that was hardly a foregone conclusion on Lily's part. Particularly since she seemed to be treating their relationship like an exciting fling—nothing more, nothing less.

"Well, I hope you know what you're doing," Joe said worriedly as the beeper at Fletcher's waist buzzed.

Fletcher frowned as he unclipped the electronic device from his belt and saw who was calling.

"Clinic?" Joe asked.

Fletcher shook his head. "Carson McRue Productions."

Chapter 9

Fletcher surveyed the beautiful young stallion being unloaded from the horse trailer in the middle of the town square. There had been a break in the rain that had inundated them for two days, but the streets were wet, the gutters full of pooling water, and it looked as if it could start up again at any moment. The gray weather perfectly matched his unpleasant mood.

"There's no way I'm signing off on this," Fletcher told Carson McRue as the stallion Carson had personally selected to be in his show snorted and pranced about nervously.

"I think you misunderstand your role," Carson McRue said as out of his peripheral vision Fletcher saw Lily step out of Carson McRue's trailer, multicolored papers in hand. She was followed by Carson's burgundy-haired assistant. What the hell…?

"You don't call the shots here," Carson continued haughtily. "We do. You, Dr. Hart, are a figurehead or paper-pusher at best."

Trying not to think what Lily had been doing in the arrogant actor's trailer, Fletcher turned his attention back to the important argument at hand. The temperamental horse was tossing his head and straining against the lead as his trainer attempted unsuccessfully to get the animal saddled up. "Yeah? Well, I'm not too ineffective to misunderstand the basic safety issues involved in using that horse. I know that animal. I've worked on him. He's far from trained. There's no way you can put him in a crowd situation, never mind expect there's a chance he'll do what is expected of him while you are filming."

"Why don't you leave that to me?"

"I would," Fletcher shot back angrily, "if I hadn't been hired to oversee the treatment of animals on this set."

"Well, fortunately that's something that can be easily fixed. You're fired."

Fletcher blinked. "What?"

"You heard me." Carson McRue signaled to one of the uniformed production security men who was standing guard around the perimeter of the barricaded area.

"Dr. Hart is no longer to be given access to the set."

The burly guard reached for Fletcher. Fletcher held him off with an upraised palm. "I'm leaving," he told the guard. To Carson, he said, "You're making a mistake."

"Mine to make," Carson retorted, smooth as silk. Turning away from Fletcher, he lifted his hand expansively. "Lily. Get all the papers signed?"

What papers? Fletcher wondered as Lily neared

them. Her cheeks were flushed, whether with guilt or awareness of Carson's TV star status, Fletcher couldn't tell. "Yes, I did," Lily told Carson in a crisp professional tone.

"I'll see you first thing in the morning then— 6:00 a.m. Unity Church?"

"I'll be there," Lily promised. Refusing to make eye contact with Fletcher, she gave Carson a brief smile and hurried away.

Carson gave Fletcher a look of triumph, then headed off to the still-bucking and snorting horse.

Fletcher strode after Lily and followed her down Main Street and into Madsen's Flower Shoppe. "What was that about?" he asked. Outside it began to rain in torrents once again.

Lily set the papers on the counter and didn't answer right away.

"Tell me," Fletcher said, his heart sinking like a stone, "you have not just agreed to work for Carson McRue."

Lily's moment of feeling good for her unasked-for coup d'état faded as quickly as it had come. Aware that Sheila, Belinda, Maryellen and even Spartacus—who was curled up on his cushion behind the counter chewing a rawhide—were all watching her with wide-eyed amazement, Lily motioned Fletcher into her private office. "Let's take this in there," she said.

Chin high, she led the way. Fletcher followed.

Lily shut the door behind them, noting his whole body was taut with tension. "I'm sorry you got fired."

"Not as sorry as Carson McRue and his production are going to be when that horse wrecks everything— and possibly everyone—in sight."

Lily paused, her stomach fluttering nervously. "You really think someone will get hurt?" she asked quietly.

Fletcher nodded grimly. Worry darkened his eyes. "Yes, I do. He needs a stunt horse that is used to following directions and working around cameras."

Her own problems forgotten, Lily searched for a solution. "Can't you appeal to someone?"

"Who? McRue owns the production company. It's the production company that's liable."

"Maybe it will be okay," Lily said, sitting down on the edge of her desk.

For a long moment, Fletcher remained motionless. He looked unconvinced. Then he abruptly gave it up and sauntered closer.

"You haven't explained what you were doing in Carson's trailer."

She tilted her head at him, wondering what kind of rights he thought their intimacy of the night before gave him. "Do I owe you an explanation?"

Fletcher paused. He seemed to think so, but stubbornly refused to admit as much. "It's a job, Fletcher," Lily told him, her exasperation mounting as she moved away from the desk, and away from him.

"Right." He sent her a glance that told her he didn't intend to jump through any hoops for her. "And I'm the tooth fairy."

Lily whirled to face him and planted her hands on her hips. "Exactly what are you accusing me of here?"

His glance drifted over her pastel T-shirt and trim khakis before returning ever so slowly to her eyes. He lounged back against the opposite wall, one booted foot across the other, his body at an angle. His eyes glinted with a mixture of doubt and cynicism that stung. "You wanted to date him," he reminded her softly. "That date was circumvented."

"By you," Lily reminded, not about to let Fletcher get the upper hand or begin to think he had the right to tell her what she could and could not do. She was no longer in a place where she would allow herself to be reined in.

"Do you still want to date him?" Fletcher asked.

Lily stared at Fletcher in confusion. *I thought I was dating you. I thought that was what us making love meant.* Had she been wrong? Had it been just a one-night stand and she was too naive, too inexperienced, to know that? All Lily knew was that she couldn't discuss it here. Couldn't bear to find out here and now she had been wrong about Fletcher's intentions toward her. She didn't want to know she had been just a pleasant albeit different diversion for him.

He shoved a hand through his hair. "Listen, Lily, I know you don't want to hear it, but you can't handle him."

And she'd thought her days of being coddled and treated like an infant were over. "What I can't handle is you!" Lily said, starting for the door.

Fletcher moved to block her way. He gave her a self-assured, faintly baiting look. "The guy wants to go to bed with you."

Lily tossed her head. "You are so cynical!"

He closed in on her deliberately, not stopping until there was a scant two inches between them. He looked very grim. Disapproving, almost. "I'm right!"

Lily threw up her hands in frustration, refusing to back away, even though being this close to him made her heart pound and her body tingle all over. "You always think things are going to turn out badly and expect the worst of everyone."

"At least I'm realistic," Fletcher countered just as determinedly. A hint of the old cynicism flashed in his eyes. "Not going through life in a protective bubble. Blaming everyone else for your innocence, when really it's your inability to wise up and see the world as it really is instead of the way you wish it was!"

"Okay. That's it!" Lily grabbed him by the shoulders and shoved him toward the door.

On the other side, Spartacus let out a short, warning bark, then a low, fierce growl.

"Out of here!" Lily commanded Fletcher.

Fletcher went, albeit not willingly, through the storeroom where the worktables and big refrigerators were kept toward the back door. As she opened the alley door, he started to say something else. Probably another warning. Lily's temper kicked into full gear and she cut him off with a look.

"You're right—I don't want to hear it!" Lily snapped and slammed the door after him.

"And so the miserable rain continues," Lily told Spartacus hours later as she tore down yet another heavy velvet drapery and added it to the heap on the wide plank pine floors. It was dark outside, but she had left one plantation shutter open so Spartacus could see the street outside. And it was as she turned her glance that way that Spartacus let out a low warning growl. Lily saw the shadow of a man with familiar kick-butt posture moving across the porch. Then the doorbell rang.

Her heart racing in anticipation, she went to get it

with Spartacus trotting at her side. Fletcher was standing on the other side of the threshold. Raindrops glistened in his hair and dotted his starched long-sleeved navy blue shirt, jeans and the toes of his custom boots. He had a bouquet of flowers in one hand and a box of candy, a CD and a DVD in the other. He held them out. Her eyes locked with his, she accepted them wordlessly and felt her heartbeat kick up yet another notch as their fingers brushed. Damn him, she thought, for making her want him all over again.

Knowing if she didn't stop looking into his beautiful amber eyes she would end up in his arms, kissing him again as if there was no tomorrow, she dropped her gaze to the gifts he had brought. Closer inspection showed the DVD to be an old Disney favorite Lily recalled watching with her grandmother when she was a kid. *"Pollyanna?"* she remarked dryly.

A smile tugged at the corner of his lips. "I thought we could watch it together and you could help me learn how not to be so cynical."

"And the music?" Ignoring the butterflies jumping around in her stomach, she pointed to the soundtrack for *Love Affair*.

He shrugged his broad shoulders affably and leaned his shoulder against the portal. "Figured it sort of fit the mood since that was what we were in. The flowers were on your list of things you wanted to experience. And Janey may have mentioned to me you have a fondness for gourmet chocolates."

Despite her earlier decision to stay angry with him just this side of forever, she was impressed. And she wondered what it all meant. "You went all out here," Lily noted cautiously.

Their gazes meshed, held. "I wasn't taking any chances," Fletcher told her softly, all the love she had ever wanted to see in his eyes. "I wanted you to let me in the door so I could tell you just how sorry I was for behaving like a jealous fool today."

Just that swiftly, her anger with him evaporated and the last of her pride disappeared. "Come in." She motioned him across the threshold and went to put her gifts down. She still didn't know where their relationship was headed or if they even had a relationship. All she was certain of was that she was very glad to see him.

Spartacus, however, was not so quick to forgive. He was still on his cushion in front of the window, but he had stopped chewing on his rawhide and was watching Fletcher with dark cautious eyes.

Fletcher seemed to know an apology was called for there, too. He hunkered down beside Spartacus and offered his hand, palm up. "Sorry I scared you this afternoon, buddy," he said. "I was just going all protective on my woman here."

My woman. Lily thrilled at the words.

Fletcher rubbed Spartacus behind his ears. "One of these days you're going to fall for some good-looking female and all you're going to want to do is keep her safe, too. But what you've got to realize is that the really strong and feisty ones like Lily here can protect themselves." Fletcher paused and looked at Lily meaningfully. "They don't need us to step in and do it for them."

"Amen to that," Lily said quietly as her world righted once again.

Fletcher stood, took Lily into his arms. "I know you felt smothered sometimes, growing up," he told her as he smoothed a hand through her hair. "I'm sorry if I did the same thing to you."

Lily accepted his apology as their eyes meshed. "Just don't do it again," she cautioned softly.

"Yes, ma'am." Fletcher tipped an imaginary hat at her.

Lily broke into a grin while Spartacus regarded Fletcher for another long, assessing moment. Deciding he could trust Fletcher again, Spartacus wagged his tail once tentatively, then more eagerly. Fletcher patted the Lab on the head, then gestured at the sketch pads strewn across the coffee table, and the draperies heaped in piles on the floor. "What's going on here?" Fletcher asked Lily.

Lily shrugged, a little embarrassed by the mess. "I was working on the plans for Janey's wedding. You know we're moving the ceremony indoors?"

Fletcher nodded. "Mom said something about it when I talked to her earlier."

"So we're having to reconfigure all the floral arrangements, some of which we went ahead and did today and put in the refrigerators at the shop. I think I've finally got it all worked out although I want to go over the revised plans with Janey tomorrow just to be sure." It was important Janey be happy with the finished product.

Fletcher's gaze went back to the velvet heaped on the floor. "You're taking down the drapes for cleaning?"

Lily shook her head. "I'm getting rid of them," she said firmly. "If I'm going to stay here, it's time I made this place my own."

Fletcher had to admit it opened the place up, getting rid of all the heavy velvet drapery. She'd also removed the doilies from the tables, rolled up the ancient rug with the cabbage patch roses and taken a couple of not particularly interesting paintings from the wall. It had left white marks on the yellowed floral wallpaper of the front parlor.

"What are you going to do in here?" Fletcher asked, pleased to see Lily taking charge of her life.

"Strip the walls, paint them creamy white and put two comfortable sofas in here in a neutral hue. Probably put down a gorgeous fire-engine-red Persian rug and use accessories to tie it all together. I want to bring this place into the twenty-first century."

Fletcher envisioned the new décor. "I think Rose would approve."

Lily met his smile shyly. "I think she would, too."

The companionable feeling between them deepened. Fletcher edged nearer. "What are you going to do with the rest of the stuff?"

"I've contacted several antiques dealers. They're coming in to appraise the belongings of the house. I'm going to sell all but the most basic pieces and use the proceeds to finance the refurbishing."

He sent her an admiring glance, pleased at the strides she was making. "You really are moving on."

Already, she didn't seem to need him the way she had just a few days ago. And although he was relieved to see it, the change worried him, too. He had started to like the way she turned to him for comfort and advice. Not to mention the distinctly male satisfaction he derived whenever he charged to her rescue. For the first time, he saw himself as half of a couple. And although that was alarming—it was a lot easier not to get emotionally or romantically involved—it was also a sign that he was growing up, too.

Lily raked her teeth across her soft lower lip and turned her gaze up to his. "You started me thinking the other night. I realized a couple of things. I love Madsen's Flower Shoppe. I love being a florist. It's what I would have done regardless." An affectionate glimmer crept into her eyes. "And I love this house. The reason I felt trapped was that I never took either over and made it my own. I never tried to create a life for myself different from the one Grandmother Rose envisioned for me."

"But you're ready to do that now," Fletcher ascertained, not sure why the possibility of that should worry him so.

"Oh, yes," Lily said. She closed the distance between them and wreathed both slender arms about his neck. "And I know *exactly* how I want to start."

Chapter 10

Lily had never been the aggressor. But if she wanted to leave her reputation behind, she knew she had to start going after what she wanted, and she couldn't think of a better place to do that than right here, right now. She rose on tiptoe, tangled her fingers in his hair and kissed him deeply. Responding passionately, he plundered her mouth, wrapped his arms around her and brought her close. She trembled in his arms and then his lips were on her throat, the lobe of her ear, the soft hollow beneath.

"Much more of this," Fletcher whispered, his warm breath teasing her ear, "and I'm going to want to take you upstairs."

Lily smiled and drew back so he could see the hunger on her face. "Then that makes two of us," she told him softly, tucking her hand in his, "because I want to go upstairs, too."

Leaving Spartacus curled contentedly up by the front windows, still chewing on a rawhide and watching the occasional car go by, Lily and Fletcher walked up the massive walnut staircase that dominated the foyer. Not content to let her call all the shots, he stopped to kiss her on the landing and then again at the top of the stairs. Shivers danced along her skin, from every point of contact, every tender caress. Emotions soaring, Lily kissed him back, enjoying the feel of him against her—and the knowledge that soon they would be together again in the most intimate way a man and woman could be. Blood rushing hot and needy through their veins, they continued kissing their way down the hall. But instead of going all the way to Lily's bedroom, Lily stopped him at the master bedroom suite.

Fletcher's eyes widened. Lily knew what he was thinking. It looked like a tornado had hit in there, too. She had rolled up the rugs, torn down the heavy brocade draperies that had hung on the bed and covered the row of windows that fronted the street and taken down all the ancient knickknacks and doilies and heaped them into boxes. She'd had new linens delivered to the store that day, which she had promptly brought home and put on the bed. They went well with the white plantation shutters still on the windows. Two scented candles stood sentry on the twin nightstands. There was a fresh bouquet of lilacs on the bureau, another on her old-fashioned mirrored dressing table.

"Wow," Fletcher said, still looking around.

Lily brought their clasped hands together and rested her cheek against the back of his wrist. "About time I abandoned my childhood bed and moved into the grown-ups' quarters, wouldn't you say?" She turned his hand over and pressed a kiss into the callused warmth of his palm.

Fletcher nodded, even as a hint of some unidentified emotion—guilt maybe—flashed across his handsome face. And just as suddenly, Lily felt Fletcher pull away from her emotionally once again.

Lily sat down on the edge of the bed. She toed off her sandals and ran her toes across the bare wood floor. Fletcher was still standing there, looking as if he'd just had a major attack of conscience. Which again made her wonder: What was this relationship of theirs? Where was it really going? He'd just now said they were lovers, that he wanted to see things her way.

Maybe it was time she saw things from his perspective, too. "Are you sorry for deflowering the florist?" she quipped. Was it her previous virginity that was suddenly at issue here? Was that making him feel beholden to her in some way he didn't really want?

He locked gazes with her and sauntered closer, abruptly looking as relaxed about what was happening between them as she was. "No. Oddly enough, I'm not," he told her tenderly. "Although—" the corners of the mouth that had given her such unbelievable pleasure quirked up in a self-deprecating smile "—the gentlemanly part of me—the part of me that was reared by Helen Hart—thinks I probably should be full of remorse."

"But you're not," Lily ascertained happily.

He sat beside her on the bed. "No. I'm not. I'm happy that I was your first—your only—lover. The question is," Fletcher said, his eyes darkening ardently, "how do you feel about being robbed of your innocence by me?"

Lily knew a lot was riding on her answer. "Truthfully?"

He nodded soberly, looking deep into her eyes.

"Happy." Lily swallowed around the sudden parched feeling in her throat. "And content in a way I've never been before." She couldn't explain it. She just knew whenever she was with Fletcher like this, she felt safe. Cherished. Protected. In a way she never had before, and never would again....

"Good. Me, too," Fletcher said then he took his time kissing her again. "Now all we have to do," he teased her lightly, already unbuttoning his shirt, "is figure out how we're going to go about making everything else on that wish list of yours come true."

Lily blushed hotly. There was no doubt at all in her mind what he was referring to now.

"I thought you wanted to speak up for yourself, access that inner bad girl and be the sexy woman you know you could be," he teased.

It was all Lily could do not to groan out loud. Pretending a great deal more insouciance than she felt, she stretched out sideways on the bed and propped her head on her upraised hand. "So here's my chance?" she replied playfully. "Is that what you're telling me?"

His eyes held the keys to thousands of erotic fantasies. He waggled his brows at her suggestively.

As the silence drew out between them, she realized he really expected her to confess her secret sexual fantasies to him. A self-conscious heat filling her from head to toe, she turned away from that knowing gaze. Moaning and falling back on the bed, she threw her arm across her face to further shade her feelings.

Smelling nicely of aftershave, mint-flavored toothpaste and soap, he sprawled next to her, looking ready to wait her out until dawn if necessary. He leaned over to kiss her shoulder. "It's not really that hard, Lily."

Lily moaned again, even more loudly. "Says the experienced one."

He plucked the forearm from her eyes and placed it above her head. He traced the uppermost curve of her breasts with his fingertip. "I'm not as experienced as you might think. Except in my fantasies." The wicked gleam was back in his amber eyes as he confessed huskily, "*There* I think I've probably earned a few awards."

She perked up a little at the thought she wasn't the only one capable of daydreaming. A lot. "Yeah? Really?"

He nodded.

Lily thought about that. "What are your fantasies?" she asked curiously.

Fletcher slid a hand beneath her T-shirt and lightly caressed her abdomen, before sliding up over her ribs to her breasts. Making an L of his index finger and thumb, he brought his hand up over her lace-covered breasts, down again, then up, rubbing her nipples into aching points. "I thought we were doing yours." He leaned over to first reveal and then kiss her navel.

Telling herself there would be plenty of time to reach fulfillment later, Lily lifted his hand and set it beside her. "We're getting to that." She sat up and faced him, cross-legged, on the bed. "You first."

He lay back lazily, arms folded behind him. The cynical smile that had always been so much a part of him was back. "You really want to hear this," he said.

Lily nodded earnestly. Maybe this didn't have to

be such a one-way street. Maybe she could make his dreams come true, too.

"Well, since you brought it up, I always wanted my lover to do a striptease just for me."

Lily felt as if she had just won the lottery. She slapped her knee. "You're kidding. That's one of mine!" she said excitedly.

Fletcher lifted a disbelieving brow. "You wanted your lover to strip for you?"

"Well, sure. After I stripped for him, of course."

He sat up slowly and eyed her cautiously, the hint of a very naughty smile tugging at the corners of his lips. "Well? What do you say? Are you up for it?"

Lily bit her lip. He was really going to do this. "We don't have any stripper music," she said.

His grin widened to a voltage that melted her insides. "I bet you've got something that's sort of sexy," he encouraged her. "You being a person with an inner bad girl and all."

Lily paused. Part of her wanted to run and hide. The other part of her wanted to see this through to the exciting end. Just as she knew the chance to be this playful, this adventurous might not ever come again. And hadn't she waited a lifetime to break free of the many constraints around her?

"Ahhh. You're weakening. I can see it," Fletcher teased.

No way was he going to be able to call her chicken. "You wait here," Lily directed with a toss of her head. "I'll be right back."

Fletcher lay back on the bed and closed his eyes while Lily sashayed on out of the bedroom and down the hall to the childhood bedroom where most of her belongings were still stored.

A few seconds later, he heard the music floating down the hall. Interesting choice, he thought, as he lay there listening to the defiantly sultry voice of a popular rock star. And even more interesting attire.

Lily had shed the khakis and pastel T-shirt she'd been wearing when he arrived and was standing there in a getup that could only have come from one of the more risqué lingerie places at the mall. Curves that were almost too sinful to be borne were spilling out of a red lace bustier, matching garter and thong. Thigh-high stockings and high heels that made the most of her spectacular legs completed the drop-dead sexy look. She had a silk scarf in her hands and was dancing to the song "Fever." Proving, Fletcher noted as his lower half suffused with heat, she had all the moves required to stop a man's heart.

Mouth dry, he watched as she sashayed closer, never losing the beat. She grinned at the look on his face. Gripping the ends of the scarf with both hands, she pirouetted closer, giving him maximum view of the curves spilling out of her décolleté.

Deciding to enjoy the show, he stayed right where he was. Let out a low wolf whistle. "Wow," he said again in thoroughly male appreciation, urging her on.

Eyes gleaming seductively, she climbed up beside him on the high four-poster bed, and careful of the heels she was still wearing, moved to straddle his torso. Taking one arm from behind his head, she brought it toward her, then got the other. Wrapped both wrists in silk, binding them together.

Fletcher lifted a brow, wondering what she was up to

now. "You said it was my choice," she reminded playfully.

"And a fascinating choice it is," he agreed as she lifted his wrists, and still straddling him, secured his wrists to the post on that side of the headboard. Finished, she stayed right where she was. Expression intent, she reached down and began unbuttoning his shirt, starting at the top and working her way down.

"I thought you were the one going to be doing the disrobing," he murmured.

She leaned over to reveal the surprisingly ample swells of her breasts. "Don't you like the view?"

"Oh, I like." He caught his breath as she smoothed her hands over his chest, eliciting sparks of fire every place she touched, and wondered where his trademark cynicism had gone. Because now it was Fletcher who felt as if he'd never experienced such sexual intimacy before. "It's just—" he groaned as she found his belt and worked her magic on that, too "—I don't want to get ahead of you." And at the rate they were going, he was going to hit the finish line before she even entered the race.

She sent him a wickedly provocative look as his heart hammered in his chest, all angel and innocence again. "Why don't you let me worry about that?" she whispered seductively. Looking intent on what she was doing, she unzipped his fly, slid her hands inside. By the time she actually cupped him in her palm, he was throbbing with the need to possess her.

Grimacing with the effort to control his building desire, he reached up to try and free himself.

She caught his fingers before he could reach the knot. "You'll have your turn later."

"Promise?"

She whispered a sigh of pure pleasure. "Oh, yeah."

Their eyes locked. Agreement made, she moved back down his body, stripping off his boots, socks and pants as she went. The shirt was obviously going to have to stay on, they realized at once. She couldn't get it off unless she untied him, and the decidedly mischievous look on her face said she obviously had no intention of untying him. Who would have thought that she'd be such a vixen…?

She smoothed her hands over the muscles of his thighs, slipped them beneath him to trace the small of his back and the curve of his buttocks, before moving forward again to the most sensitive part of him. "Kiss me," he murmured, promising himself that when it was his turn, he was going to repeat the sweet torture, and then some.

"All right." She slid lower and put her mouth on him.

That hadn't been what Fletcher had meant. But it felt so damn good all he could do was close his eyes and groan. Lost in the feel of her moving so sweetly and patiently across him, taking possession, claiming him as her own. Just as he wanted to claim her. "Lily—" He caught his breath again.

"Right." He was pretty sure she deliberately misunderstood as she moved away from him and got back off the bed. "Time for the floor show, hmm, Fletch?"

Proving all over again how adept she was at moving to the beat, she moved her body sinuously, capturing his complete attention before slowly reaching behind her to unclasp her bustier. It took forever before her breasts spilled free, but seeing that creamy flesh and apricot nipples as the lace fell away from her silky skin brought forth a pleasure of another kind. Ditto each individual high-heeled shoe and stocking, the garter belt and finally the tiny triangle of string and lace. By the time she had bared herself to him and climbed back on the bed, Fletcher felt he had been wanting her his entire life. And maybe he had been, he thought as she climbed astride him, slipped a condom on him, because she looked like she had been waiting for him, too. "Untie me," he rasped, eager to take her the way she was meant to be taken—utterly and completely.

Lily grinned, all bad girl now. "No." With another wickedly playful grin, she bent over him, her breasts teasing his chest, her thighs cupping the outside of his. Holding his face between her hands, she kissed him. It was…magic.

"Stubborn," Fletcher murmured against her mouth, and then all rational thought was lost as she fused their mouths deeply and completely and opened her body to his. Hot, wet silk. Fevered kisses. Soft, warm breasts. She was everything he had ever wanted in a woman, and more. As she flattened her torso over his, he lost himself in the ecstasy of making love to her, putting everything he had into the joining. He waited until she soared to shattering erotic heights before he finally let go, too.

For long moments afterward they lay together, breathing hard, her face buried in his neck. Enjoying the pleasure of feeling her close, he kept his eyes shut, letting the aftershocks flow through them. Until aching desire surged through him once again. Damned if he didn't want to hold her close. "Lily." The word came out half warning, half-frustrated moan.

"I know." She laughed softly and reached up to undo the knot. As soon as he was free, he caught her with both hands and brought her back down on the sheets beside him. "You're a very bad girl," he told her as he stretched out over her, his body already hardening once again.

"I know." She reached out to stroke him.

"And you enjoyed every minute of it," he said as he claimed her, with hands and lips and tongue.

She arched her back as he made his way to the sweet ripeness of her breasts. "Oh, yes."

"And now," he said, taking the tantalizingly aroused peak into his mouth, "it's my turn to be bad."

Lily hadn't imagined Fletcher would be ready to make love to her again quite that soon. She gripped his shoulders, hard, trembling at the way he was pleasuring her. "Want me to put my outfit back on?"

"Later," he promised, pausing only long enough to shrug out of his shirt and toss it onto the floor with the rest of his discarded clothing. He ran his palms over her shoulders and down her forearms. "Right now I want to learn every inch of your body all over again. Do unto others, you know…."

She laughed softly as he tickled her ribs, brushed his lips across hers and took her earlobe between his teeth. "I never imagined making love could be so much fun."

He kissed his way back down her body, suffusing her with heat. He grazed her nipples with his thumbs, then slid his thigh along hers, easing them apart. "I had no idea, either."

He stroked along the inside of her thighs. "I mean, I knew it would be passionate," Lily rasped as he continued his sensual exploration of her body. She shuddered as he slipped two fingers inside her. "And I hoped it would be exciting, but—"

He rubbed and stroked in a way that was too outrageous and erotic for words until her insides clenched, asking for more, and sweet, hot liquid flowed. "No slam-bam-thank-you-ma'ams in your future?"

She took another breath and opened her eyes to look into his. She knew he was taunting her, the way she had taunted him, and she was enjoying every second of it. Not that she planned to let him know that. Yet. "I should say not," she informed with exaggerated hauteur, daring him to try and arouse her any more. "I want a man who knows how to take his time."

He grinned, as if he knew just the way. "I guess I should work on that." He slid both hands beneath her and lightly squeezed her buttocks in his palms. "You know what they say."

Lily gasped again as he touched her. "What?"

"Practice makes perfect." Gathering her close, he rolled so she was on top of him and kissed her again, deeply, passionately.

"That's—pretty darn close." She felt his manhood pulsing against her, poised to enter.

"Mmmm. I don't know, Lily." Parting her knees with his, he settled more deeply between her, his hands on her hips, lifting and positioning her. "I think I could do better."

As his mouth found her again, she practically shot off the bed. And this time it was she who was holding on to the headboard, shuddering, as her emotions skyrocketed and the climax she'd felt minutes before came roaring back. She moaned and bucked and he brought her back down to just below his waist.

"Now see?" he said playfully, as he stroked her again

with his hand. "That's the kind of response I was looking for."

Lily trembled all the harder, all playfulness forgotten, her desire for him as intense as the feelings swelling in her heart. "Fletcher?"

"Hmmm?"

She cupped his shoulders and settled more intimately over him, beginning to wonder how she had ever managed without him. "I want you inside me."

He looked at her tenderly. "I want to be inside you, too." He reached for the condoms on the bedside table and quickly sheathed himself.

The next thing she knew they were changing places once again and he was moving over her. His skin was hot as fire, his body quivering with the effort of his restraint, as he possessed her all over again with a passion and determination that took her breath away and sent her soaring once again into sweet hot pleasure.

As they lay together, trying to recover for the second time that night, Lily buried her head in the warmth and strength of Fletcher's chest. He felt so good against her, so right. She realized she had never been happier in her life, and Fletcher seemed to feel that way, too.

Not wanting the moment to get too serious, however, lest she scare him away and ruin the best time she'd ever had with the best man she had ever known, Lily filled the silence with a joke she had been waiting her whole life to make.

"Well, I think I've found her." Lily sighed contentedly against Fletcher's shoulder as she stroked imaginary patterns on his chest.

Fletcher lifted his head, his eyes still dark with wanting her. "Who?"

"My inner bad girl."

Fletcher rolled, so Lily was on her back. His eyes were gentler than she had ever seen them, his look more protective. "I'm glad," he told her warmly. "I want all your wishes to come true."

There was just one more....

And it was an important one.

I love you, Fletcher, Lily thought. And I *think* you love me. But unsure how such a wildly passionate and deeply honest revelation like that would be received, unsure of what his intentions truly were, she once again kept silent and merely cuddled closer, enjoying the feel of his warm strong arms wrapped around her.

Chapter 11

"You're sure you want to do this?" Fletcher asked at 5:45 a.m. as Lily was getting ready to go to work.

Lily had wondered when the subject of Carson McRue Productions would come up. She didn't want anything to come between them after the wonderful night they'd had. But she also knew this was a precedent-setting situation with Fletcher and she was prepared to stand her ground. Even under fire.

"It's a 'piece of cake' job, Fletcher," she told him softly. "They've already ordered the greenery and calla lilies through a Hollywood florist they've got on retainer. They had them delivered to my shop late yesterday afternoon. The set designer came up with the placement and style of arrangements for the chapel. All I have to do is show up there in fifteen minutes and put things together as per direction, in time for them to get started with the filming around eight. It's not very hard."

Fletcher shot her a quelling glance. "Then why do it?" he asked mildly.

Lily had promised herself when her grandmother Rose passed that her days of answering to someone about every little thing she did were over. But something in Fletcher's eyes—concern or something deeper—had her wanting to put his mind at ease. Especially since she knew he was trying to protect her, not fence her in.

Lily tried hard not to notice how handsome Fletcher looked, lounging in the mussed covers of her bed, a coffee cup propped on his knee. "Because they've offered me a five-thousand-dollar fee for a couple of hours of work. All I had to do was agree to do it all myself."

Fletcher's jaw set. "So in other words you're going to be at the church alone," he deduced.

Lily did not like the hint of reproof in his low voice. "No." She turned to the mirror as she ran a brush through the still-damp layers of her curly blond hair, wondering if she looked as well loved to the uniformed observer as she felt. "There will be other people there," she stated firmly.

Fletcher's brow lifted. "Sure?"

Lily paused, lipstick in hand as the first inkling of doubt crept in. Carson McRue would not be doing all of this simply to get a chance to make a pass at her. Would he?

"It's not just the flowers that have to be done this morning," Lily persisted, even though she risked Fletcher's ire. "They have to set up the cameras, too." She spritzed on some perfume and bent to put on her shoes.

Fletcher stood and moved away from the bed where

they'd made love over and over through the night. He was clad in jeans, but his shirt lay open, baring his beautifully muscled chest, bronzed skin and mat of golden-brown hair. "Let me go with you."

Lily flushed beneath his quick but potent scrutiny. If he only knew how tempted she was to let him do just that....

"I don't need a bodyguard." *I'm a grown woman, capable of managing on my own.* "Besides, you were fired yesterday and escorted from the set, remember?" The last thing either of them needed was a scene. Lily might be trying to ditch her Ice Princess rep, but she did not want to be the focus of gossip. She had already experienced that the past couple of weeks. It hadn't been pleasant and she had no desire to repeat it.

"If no one else is going to be there, except the camera people, who's to know?" Fletcher asked.

Carson McRue, Lily thought. The arrogant actor would punish Fletcher. If for no other reason than Fletcher had publicly questioned Carson's ability to control that stallion yesterday....

Although tempted to accept his offer for reasons she couldn't quite understand, Lily shook her head. "You could do one thing for me, though," she said as she sashayed toward him and clasped the open edges of his shirt.

"Make love to you again?"

Lily went weak in the knees at just the thought. "If we were to start that again," she murmured, laying her head against his shoulder, "I'd never get to work."

"Yeah. But think of all the fun we'd have." Fletcher wrapped his arms around her and brought her fully against him. Tucking a hand beneath her chin, he delivered a long leisurely kiss as Spartacus padded into the bedroom to join them.

"I'm serious," Lily persisted as a sensual shiver slid down her spine. "I need someone to feed and walk Spartacus for me this morning."

"I'll do it," he murmured against her mouth, kissing her again.

"You sure?" Lily asked as his gaze ardently traced her face, lingering on each feature in turn.

Drawing back, Fletcher nodded. "Spartacus can come to work with me." A smile broke across his face as talk turned to their canine friend. Still holding her gaze, he inclined his head slightly to the side, shot a fond look at Spartacus then returned his attention to Lily. "It's about time I had a dog in my life again. Wouldn't you say?"

Two grueling hours later, Lily had Unity Church exactly the way the *Hollywood P.I.* set designer wanted it to look. Finished, she began packing up her gear in the toolbox she took with her on location jobs. She returned the leftover greenery, satin ribbon and calla lilies to the set designer's assistant, who immediately corrected her mistake.

"You're supposed to take those to Carson McRue's trailer."

Lily blinked. "Excuse me?"

The set designer shrugged. "He wanted a couple arrangements to brighten up the place."

A trickle of unease ran through Lily at the suspect nature of the request. "I didn't bring any vases."

"That's okay." The set designer looked distracted as she pushed a hand through her hair. "He's probably got a few extra in there. If not, he'll either send you out for some or make do." The set designer rushed off to help with the rolling out of the bridal carpet.

She could handle this, even if Carson made a pass. Hadn't she told Fletcher that? Well, now was the time to prove herself, Lily thought, as she dodged lighting and camera guys who were also setting up, and headed out to Carson's trailer. Holding the armload of flowers to her chest, she moved across the square and saw the crowd, who knew from reports on the local news that the wedding scenes from the show's November sweeps episodes were going to be filmed that morning.

It had stopped raining during the night, but the ground was saturated and the creek that ran through the city park across the street was swollen with rushing brown water. Out of the corner of her eye, she saw Fletcher standing next to his brother Mac. Fletcher had Spartacus on a leash and was looking her way. Mac was busy with his sheriff's duties, keeping onlookers back from the barricades. In the center of the square, was the horse trailer, the rowdy stallion and what Lily could only presume was the veterinary consultant hired to replace Fletcher.

She noticed Fletcher's frown as she hurried over to Carson's trailer. He didn't like this. Well, neither did she. And as soon as she dumped these flowers, she was out of there. Maybe in time to get some breakfast with Fletcher. As she neared the steps leading up to the trailer, the security person standing just outside looked at her with something akin to contempt. "Carson is waiting for you."

Taking a deep breath, Lily squared her shoulders and went on in.

Carson was seated on the rich leather sofa. He was dressed in a tuxedo shirt and tie and looked as handsome as any screen idol she had ever seen. "I was told you wanted floral arrangements in here?" Lily adapted her crispest, most professional tone.

Carson nodded. He gestured to several vases, filled with perfectly good flowers placed about the living room and kitchen area of the trailer. "You can use those. There's one in the bedroom, too."

"All right." Refusing to meet his eyes or make this situation any more intimate than it already was, Lily gathered them up, reminding herself all the while that there was a five-thousand-dollar fee attached to her work this morning that would go a long way toward making the redecoration of her home possible. "Is it all right if I work in the kitchen area," she asked impersonally, "or would you like me to take them out and bring them back when they're done?"

"Here's fine." Carson didn't lift his eyes from the script in front of him.

Maybe her imagination was running away from her. Maybe all he wanted from her were fresh flowers in vases.

Aware that the hair on the back of her neck was standing up, she was so on edge, Lily nevertheless got down to business and went to work. In ten minutes, she had all the flowers replaced, the old ones in a garbage bag she was prepared to take with her. "You're all set," she told Carson as she headed for the door.

He looked up from the page he was studying, then nodded his thanks. "Listen," he said, as she reached the door, "could you do me a favor?"

Uh-oh. Lily turned toward him, suddenly wishing

Fletcher were here, with her. "How can I help you?" she asked in the most impersonal voice she could manage.

"Run some lines with me. I'm having a heck of a time with this dialogue this morning."

She waved off the request. "I'm no actress."

Carson moved toward her in a way that suggested he was not going to take no for an answer. "All you have to do is say Sylvia's lines." He took the garbage bag of discarded blossoms from her, put it aside and thrust the script in her hands. "Right here." He gave her a brief, detached smile as he pointed where he wanted her to start.

Lily looked down at the script. It was the scene in the chapel where the two married. "Shouldn't your co-star be doing this?" she asked.

Carson shook his head. "She's not speaking to me. Hasn't been since yesterday. Actresses." He rolled his eyes.

"Right." Lily looked down at the page, lamenting all the while that Fletcher had been right. And wouldn't he just crow about that…? *Just get it over with. And get out of here.* She cleared her throat and read in a rote, choppy tone, "'Honestly, Rex, I do love you.'"

"'But?'" Carson stepped nearer, slid a hand beneath her chin. Lifting her face to his, he searched her eyes. Flustered, Lily stepped back, ducked her head and continued reading from the script in the most staccato robotic voice she could manage. "'I just don't know that this is the right thing for either of us.'"

Suddenly Carson's hands were cupping her shoulders. Startled to find him touching her again, she dropped her script and looked up at him.

"'But it is, Sylvia,'" Carson murmured, and then his head was lowering.

Lily had a millionth of a second and then he was going to kiss her.

So Lily did the only thing she could. She raised her sneaker-clad foot and stepped as hard as she could on the arrogant actor's instep.

"I'm telling you," Fletcher said to his brother Mac as he continued staring grimly at Carson McRue's trailer. "One more minute and I'm going in after her."

"Something tells me Lily Madsen would *not* appreciate that," Mac murmured, once again motioning spectators with cameras and camcorders back from the barricades.

Mac turned and gave Fletcher a hard look.

Guilt flooded Fletcher.

"Oh, man." Mac sighed, shaking his head as he correctly deduced what was really going on between Lily and Fletcher.

Fletcher lifted a palm. "Don't judge," he warned.

Mac did, anyway. Perhaps because his law-and-order personality would not allow him to do otherwise. "You're doing the stupidest thing you could possibly do, aren't you?" Mac grumbled, sounding like the head of the family he had become after their father's death twenty years before. Mac narrowed his eyes in obvious disapproval. "You're getting involved with her."

Getting? Fletcher thought. He and Lily were way past that. She was part of his life now.

"At least tell me you haven't taken her to bed," Mac continued sternly.

Fletcher never had been able to lie to Mac.

Conscience prickling, not for making love to her but for ever having involved her in a bet with his brothers, however unknowingly, Fletcher turned his attention to the horse being saddled up. Overhead, storm clouds were threatening once again. "That stallion is dangerous," Fletcher said, changing the subject adroitly. "You really need to get everyone out of here."

Mac looked at the nervous, prancing horse and took Fletcher at his word. "You really think someone will get hurt?" Mac asked.

Fletcher nodded grimly, just as the door to Carson McRue's trailer opened. "What in blazes…?" Fletcher murmured as Lily came storming out.

She looked exactly as she had when she had gone in, except her cheeks were bright red and she looked angrier and more upset than Fletcher had ever seen her. "That son of a bitch," Fletcher swore again as Lily crossed the square. Behind her, Carson McRue strode out, too, looking as debonair in a tuxedo as James Bond.

The director motioned to Carson and then the stallion. "We want to get these horse shots filmed now before it starts raining again!" the director said through his megaphone.

For once, Fletcher could have cared less about that. Taking Spartacus's leash, he moved to cut Lily off as she stepped around the barricades. "What happened?" he demanded.

Lily blushed all the harder and looked away. "Not here." She pushed the words through clenched teeth, refusing to look him in the eye. "Not now."

Fletcher caught her arm. "I swear, if McRue so much as looked at you funny, I'm going to go punch him out," he whispered furiously in her ear.

"Oh, please! I've had enough of stupid men for one

day!" Lily grabbed Spartacus's leash and wove her way through the crowd.

Fletcher stared after her, unsure whether to pursue her or just go and have it out with the arrogant actor right then and there. "Lily's right. Don't make a scene," Mac advised as the director called, "Action!" Carson took a running start toward the prancing stallion and jumped into the saddle with a stuntman's ease. Another actor rushed from the chapel, a fake pistol in his hand. Everyone gasped as the second tuxedo-clad actor fired repeatedly at Carson and the horse. And then, just as Fletcher had predicted, all hell broke loose as the stallion—unaccustomed to TV stunt work—went wild.

Lily was still cursing herself for her naiveté and winding her way through the hike and bike trails that ran parallel to the creek when she heard what sounded like gunshots. Startled, she and Spartacus both turned in the direction of the sound, and the screams of genuine terror that followed. She was shocked to find a thundering horse and ineptly out-of-control rider headed her way. For a second, Lily stood there transfixed by sheer terror, unable to move. And then she came to her senses and she and Spartacus both leapt out of the way.

Carson and the stallion that Fletcher had fought against using thundered past, knocking both Lily and her dog off balance. Lily had another second of mind-numbing panic, and then she and her dog were both slip-sliding on the mossy slope that lined the creek bank, losing their footing.

Lily knew she was going to fall—and probably drown, as well—in the rushing, churning brown water. She was damned if she was taking poor Spartacus in with her. So she did the only thing she could do. She let go of the leash. Made one last desperate attempt to save herself. And failed miserably.

Fletcher was already running toward her when Lily tumbled head over heels into the rushing creek. Dammit. Dammit! "Get a rope!" he yelled at Mac, his heart failing as he saw Lily bob up once, go back under, come up again and then go under and stay under.

Spartacus leaned over the bank, a lot more sure-footed than the sneaker-clad Lily had been. He was barking at the water where she had disappeared as Fletcher ran faster than he thought possible to rapidly close the distance between them. Still the seconds were ticking by and no Lily. Suddenly Spartacus was diving in after her and going underwater. Fletcher took off his shoes and dove in, too. Moments later, Spartacus bobbed up, the T-shirt of the unconscious Lily clamped firmly in his jaws.

Fletcher fought the current that was already sweeping them all downstream as Spartacus struggled to paddle toward him.

Please, God, he prayed, desperately. Please...don't take her from me, too.

Spartacus and Lily went under once again. Fletcher swam harder, determined to save them. And then a miracle happened. Spartacus bobbed up, Lily's shirt still clamped in his powerful jaws. Fletcher let out a shout of relief and gave a mighty push through the wall of water separating them. And then the three of them were locked together, he and Spartacus working together to keep from being swept under the swirling current as they struggled to hold the still-unconscious, gray-skinned Lily's head above water.

They got pushed downstream anyway, Fletcher's back scraping against exposed tree roots. Spartacus took a pounding, too. And then Mac was there above them, lasso in hand, yelling at them to hang on. Throwing them a rope.

His heart pounding, Fletcher held Lily all the tighter, praying it wasn't too late.

Chapter 12

Lily came to with the stormy gray sky above her, the hard ground beneath her and a rough canine tongue frantically licking her hand. As she struggled to focus, she saw Fletcher's face above her. He looked as if he had taken a dunking—his clothes were wet, his hair and face dripping with muddy water—and that quickly she recalled falling into the creek herself. Panicking all over again, she reached out.

"It's okay, Lily," he reassured her, his voice gruff with emotion. As she looked into his eyes, she saw they were filled with tears. And so, she realized belatedly, were hers.

"I'm here. And so is Spartacus. We've got you." Fletcher gripped her hand as two guys in EMS uniforms worked over her.

Realizing that she was indeed safe, Lily caught

a glimpse of Spartacus lying to the left of her. Also drenched, he had his handsome white-blond head on his paws, watching her, and indeed looked okay. Relief flowed through her, as well as the immediate need to comfort her pet as Fletcher was comforting her. She coughed, choking on the worst water she had ever tasted in her life, and struggled to sit up to get to him. "Just take it easy," one of the EMS workers told her, forcibly easing her back. "You had quite a tumble there."

Lily felt it in every inch of her body. And more importantly, she felt alive. *Fletcher,* she thought, locking eyes with him. *I love you.* And she could have sworn by the way he looked at her that he loved her, too.

"Dr. Hart and that dog saved your life," one of the EMS workers continued cheerfully as they listened to her lungs and checked her pulse.

Lily smiled weakly, watching as Fletcher reached over and petted Spartacus with his other hand, the gratitude and love she felt easing her ravaged senses. "No surprise there," Lily murmured with a weak smile, gripping Fletcher's palm even tighter. Those two guys were her heart. And then some.

A few hours later, Lily was being released from the Holly Springs Medical Center. Fletcher was there to take her home, and the still-shaken Lily had never been so glad in her life to see anyone waiting for her.

"You heard the doc," Fletcher said, still looking as wet and uncomfortable as Lily felt in her damp and dirty clothing. He held her against him and squeezed her as if he never wanted to let her go. "You need rest."

"And a shower." Lily sighed, knowing she must look a fright.

He clamped his arm tighter around her waist, looking

as eager to give her tender loving care as she was grateful to receive it. And that was a surprise. Lily had never
dreamed she would ever need—or want—a man this
much. And Fletcher, bless his courageous soul, seemed
to be struggling with the same wealth of feelings. Gratitude, that they'd survived. Anger, that any of them had
ever been endangered in the first place. As well as the
need to connect again, to reassure themselves that whatever this was that they had was not going to be taken
away. Not now, not ever.

"My place okay?" Fletcher asked, the emotion in his
low, husky voice counter to the studied casualness of
his words. He leaned over and kissed her temple. "It's
closer to the hospital."

"Sounds perfect," Lily murmured as Spartacus stuck
his head out of the open window of Fletcher's pickup
truck and let out a welcoming bark.

Fletcher helped Lily into the passenger seat, while
Spartacus hopped in the cargo space behind the front
seat. Spartacus smelled like creek water, too. And thank
heaven he did, Lily thought, since it had taken both of
them to keep her alive.

Fletcher still looked worried as he drove the short
distance to his apartment above the animal clinic. Lily
did what she could to lighten the mood and put aside
the close call they had all shared. "Well, you finally got
to see me in a wet T-shirt," Lily teased.

Fletcher shot her a look as she plucked the damp fabric away from her breasts. "Not the way I would have
ordered it up," he said just as dryly.

"I know." *God help me, I know…*

He parked and helped her out of the truck and up the
steps into his place. Lily leaned against him, appreciat-

ing his warmth and his strength. Once he had her safely inside, he sat her down at the table. Spartacus, satisfied all was well, collapsed in a heap on the kitchen floor and put his head on his paws. Fletcher walked over to get him a dog biscuit and knelt down to rub the Labrador retriever's head. "You're a hero. And you deserve more than this." He put the biscuit in front of him. "So it's steak tonight for all of us. Okay, buddy?"

Spartacus's liquid-brown eyes radiated understanding and love.

Fletcher grinned, rubbed the dog's head affectionately once again, then stood and came over to stand in front of Lily. "You want to get a shower? Or rest first?"

Lily's knees were still a little wobbly—whether from the accident or anticipation of the lovemaking to come—she didn't know. But she couldn't imagine climbing into the sheets with creek grit still clinging to her skin and hair. "Shower," Lily said.

Fletcher looked as if he had expected her to say just that. His arm around her waist, they walked into the bedroom. "You know," she quipped, trying not to think how right this felt or how easily she could get used to being cared for like this. "I think there have been days where we've both smelled better."

Fletcher feigned bafflement and stuck his nose in his armpit. "I don't know," he declared with a solemn face. "I might have smelled worse a time or two."

Lily supposed that was true, him being a guy and all. "Well, I haven't," she said primly.

She lifted her arms and let him help her take her long-sleeved T-shirt off. He narrowed his eyes at the angry red scrapes and purpling bruises on her shoulders, arms and rib cage.

"I'm okay, Fletcher," Lily reminded him. "Just a little banged-up from getting knocked around by the rushing water."

"No thanks to that jerk of an actor who mowed you down and knocked you into the creek." Fletcher looked as though he wanted to punch Carson McRue's lights out.

"Can we forget about him?" Lily pushed her hands through her hair. She had.

"Not until you answer me one question," Fletcher said, the calmness in his voice at odds with his hawk-like gaze. He moved in even closer. His voice might have been calm, but his eyes were hot. "What exactly happened between the two of you in that trailer?"

For a second, Fletcher thought Lily wasn't going to answer him. Then her expression changed and her guard lowered. "He started to make a really cheesy pass at me," she explained as if it were no big deal and happened to her all the time—and maybe, Fletcher thought, it did. "So I stomped on his instep as hard as I possibly could. He yelped. I told him what I thought of his manners—not much. Called him a few unprintable names. And took off."

Fletcher couldn't help but admire her decisive kick-butt reaction to the unwanted attention, even as un-accustomed jealousy roiled inside him. Lily was his woman, damn it. The sooner everyone realized that, the better. "That's why you left his trailer in such a hurry," Fletcher supposed.

"Yep." Lily toed off her sneakers and waterlogged socks. "If I'd stayed one second longer, I would have knocked him flat."

Fletcher watched as she shimmied out of her damp

jeans. She was wearing panties with flowers on them. "I'd still be happy to do it for you," he offered.

To Fletcher's disappointment, Lily did not look as if she found it necessary for him to further defend her honor. Her glance turned pitying as they continued to talk about the man who had nearly cost Lily her life. "I think he's suffered enough, don't you?"

Fletcher looked at Lily blankly. He had no clue what she meant.

Realizing this, Lily explained, "One of the spectators caught it all on videotape. Him losing control of the horse, looking like an idiot. While I was at the hospital, a reporter called, wanting to know my condition. The E.R. doc asked if he could tell the TV station I was being treated and released. I said okay to that but no to an interview with Trevor Zwick at W-MOL Action News. I imagine right about now Carson McRue is busy doing damage control and '*rue*ing' the day he ever tried to make time with me. Because this has got to hurt his suave hero image."

"Very true." Fletcher couldn't help but be pleased about that. The footage would probably be replayed endlessly on tabloid television shows. Repeated assaults on Carson McRue's pride would indeed be some punishment for what he had done. But not nearly enough, Fletcher thought, as he remembered all over again how scared he had been when he had watched Lily falling into the rain-swollen creek and going under...

"Fletcher," Lily warned as she stepped out of her panties and unfastened her bra. "You do not need to hit him on my behalf."

Trying to be gallant rather than lecherous—a pretty hard proposition given how damn beautiful Lily looked right now, standing there in the altogether—Fletcher leaned past her to turn on the shower and adjust it to just the right temperature for her. "I'll be the judge of that," Fletcher said, deciding a sock in the jaw was exactly what that pretty boy needed to make him think twice before ever needlessly endangering anyone again.

"Fletcher!" Lily warned, reading his mind as easily as ever.

"Fine," Fletcher relented, amazed to find himself taking the high road. "As long as Carson McRue never comes near either of us again, I will not punch his lights out." Although he sure would have enjoyed doing so.

"Thank you." Lily released a sigh of relief and stepped into the glass-and-tile-walled shower stall. Bruised and pale she was still the loveliest thing Fletcher had ever seen. He handed her a washcloth and looped a towel over the top of the shower door, within easy reach. "Anything else you need?" he asked, reluctantly preparing to make himself scarce.

"Yes," Lily said, hooking her hand in the front of his shirt and dragging him near. For the first time in two hours, the smile on her lips matched the one in her eyes. "You."

Lily had had a lot of experience being the Ice Princess of Holly Springs but not much chance to be a femme fatale. It was amazingly easy to get the hang of it, she discovered, when Fletcher Hart was her targeted male.

"Lily," Fletcher warned as she tugged him inside the stall with her.

"Yeah, yeah, I know." She watched the surprise come into his eyes, the desire. And knew even though he was bound to resist her out of some misguided sense of chivalry, that the battle was already won. Grinning saucily, she began undoing the buttons on his shirt. She let the backs of her hands brush the warmth of his chest and felt his muscles tense. "If you come in here and get naked with me you're going to want to make love to me."

"Exactly." Fletcher's eyes darkened to molten gold as she tugged the hem from the waistband of his jeans. Opening up the fabric of his shirt, she stepped inside it, bringing her body flush with his and letting her breasts brush against his skin. As her nipples tightened into tight buds of arousal, she moaned, a soft helpless little sound in the back of her throat. She smiled with satisfaction when she felt his lower body harden.

"Well, that's what I want," Lily said, already looping a hand around his neck and guiding his face down to hers. "You know what they say about near-death experiences." She pressed her lips to his, clinging to him and kissing him the way she had wanted to kiss him from the moment she had awakened and found herself lying on the ground beside him. She'd known in that instant that if not for his courage—and the courage of the dog she'd finally decided to adopt—she would not have made it. "All they really make you want to do is live," she murmured as one of his hands opened over her back, guiding her closer, and the other cupped her chin.

And live they did. As he passionately returned her kiss, desire wreaked havoc through their entire systems. But even that contact wasn't enough. Impatient to have him as naked—and thereby accessible to her questing hands, as she was to his—she stepped back, helped him off with his shirt...and saw his resistance flare.

He kissed her hard, but much too briefly, on the

mouth. "You know this is going to confirm a damning lack of chivalry on my part, don't you?" His voice was husky, his amber eyes bright. "Especially since the doctor said what you really needed to do was just rest."

"And I will," Lily persisted, helping him off with his jeans, making sure he knew by her look she really wanted this to happen. "Later."

"Lily." Fletcher groaned again as her hands slid inside his boxer-briefs and pushed those down, too. He continued to resist passively even as he kissed her neck, her throat, the top of her head.

"Fletcher." She playfully mocked his tone, his disapproving look.

When she had him naked, too, she straightened. She could see he was still having qualms about what she wanted them to do. He was still set on doing the right thing, especially where she was concerned. The old Lily would have just let the guy call the shots—even if they were the wrong ones. However, the new and improved Lily knew it was okay to have needs and wants of her own—and to act on those desires, no matter how inappropriate they might seem to someone else. Fletcher wasn't resisting her; he was trying to help her and would in fact do anything to help her feel better. She just had to let Fletcher know what the right thing in this situation was. Acutely aware of the myriad feelings running riot inside her, she gathered all her courage and took his hand, laid it across her breasts. "Feel my heart," she whispered urgently, still aching for him to touch her.

Fletcher's eyes darkened with a mixture of affection and awe. "It's racing."

"But not just any old way," she announced flirtatiously. She moved her lower torso in even closer until it rested against his, and she could feel the depth of his arousal. "With excitement."

Fletcher grinned, his knowledge of basic biology coming into play. "With unused adrenaline."

"Exactly." Lily nodded. She kissed him again, the kiss feeling like a commitment, a bridge to their future. "And can you think of any better way to work it off?" she finished triumphantly, looking deep into his eyes. "Especially after we all had such a close call?"

Fletcher didn't know what he had done to deserve a woman like Lily. He didn't care. All he knew was that somehow over the course of protecting her, he had fallen head over heels in love with her. To the point that he could no longer imagine his life without her. And as soon as things calmed down, he was going to have to do something about that. Something definitive, like propose. But for now all he really wanted to do, now that she had worked so hard to convince him she really was up to it, was make love to her as gently and thoroughly as possible. And the first thing they had to do in that regard was get the creek grit off of both of them.

"I don't know how good I'm going to be at this...." he murmured as he grabbed the bottle of baby shampoo and poured some into his palm. He had never washed a woman's hair before. Never told a woman he loved her. And the cynical side of him had to wonder how she would take the news. Would she immediately tell him that she loved him, too? As he hoped. Or get a panicked look and tell him she needed time. To be on her own. To live without comment or protection...

Not that it mattered, Fletcher reassured himself as he deftly worked the lather through Lily's damp curls. He knew he could be patient when he needed to be. The only thing that really mattered was what happened in the end, and about that he had no doubt. He and Lily were going to get married. And have a houseful of kids and pets and dual careers and make each other's dreams come true.

"Since the only person's hair I'm used to shampooing is mine," Fletcher continued out loud, already thinking about all the ways he was going to drive her wild. Because although Lily might look like innocence defined, at heart she was all passionate woman. And she needed him as much as he needed her, even if she hadn't quite come out and admitted it yet.

Lily grinned and closed her eyes as she sank into his touch. "Good thing it's tear-free, then," she quipped.

Fletcher chuckled, enjoying the anticipation of making love to her almost as much as he was going to savor claiming her as his. "You'll have your turn." He reached for the handheld showerhead and gently began rinsing the lather from her scalp, enjoying the way she surrendered herself to him. "'Cause I'm going to let you do mine."

Looking as if she could stay there with him forever, Lily pressed her lips to his damp skin, then rested her cheek on his forearm. "Then it'll be a first for me, too," she said as he soaped her body from head to toe, lingering on her breasts, buttocks and thighs before zeroing in on the most intimate place of all.

"Keep this up," she told him breathlessly as she reached for the shampoo and poured some in her palm, "and we'll never make it to the bed."

"Okay with me," Fletcher said, inclining his head to the left so she could more easily reach and shampoo his hair. He winked as she swayed toward him, wanting more. "I like you wet."

"Same here, bucko. Same here." Taking her time, she soaped him down and rinsed him with the showerhead. She worked efficiently at first. Then, a lot less efficiently, until they had a playful battle over the spray that ended with both of them getting doused liberally in the face and breaking into laughter. And then just as abruptly, playtime was over. His lips were locked on hers, her mouth pliant beneath his, her body soft and surrendering. Loving the way she responded to him— yielding sweetly to him one moment, ardently taking control the next—Fletcher put everything he had into the steamy caress, stroking and touching her, making her his. Until she was trembling, falling apart in his hands, moaning softly, urging him to love her then and there. Unable to deny her anything, he kissed her long and hard and deep, leaving no question about the depth of his need for her.

Love filled her eyes as he eased her back against the tile wall and settled between her legs. Their lips met and he kissed her again, until there was no doubt how much they needed each other. His manhood pressed against her inner thighs as he molded her breasts with his hands, teasing her nipples into pearling buds. Lily strained against him, undulating impatiently. Determined to give her everything he needed, he held on, making his way south, kissing her breathless and exploring damp silky flesh until she was clutching him closer and climaxing all over again.

Lily could feel the wildness in Fletcher matching the untamed part of her, and desperate to have him inside her once again—filling her completely—she went up on tiptoe in an effort to better accommodate him. He moaned, needing her, too, and sliding his hands beneath her hips, lifted her higher still. She gasped at the feel of him poised so hot and hard against her. And then, with one bold but gentle thrust, they were blissfully connected. The tile wall was against her back and he was as deep inside of her as he could be. Stroking and tantalizing, giving, taking. Demanding. Accepting. Engulfing her with tenderness and giving her his all.

Her eyes closed, Lily let her head fall back. She loved the feel of him. The scent of him. The way he was inside her, slowly, inexorably, claiming her as his, giving her untold pleasure even as he painstakingly sought out his own. She loved the womanly way he made her feel, the freedom he gave her just to be. She loved him. Just the way he was. And it was a secret that was nearly too much to bear....

Afterward, he dried her off and took her to bed. She knew he wanted her to go straight to sleep, but there were things she needed to say. Too much had happened to simply let it go without comment, she thought, as she cuddled close to him, resting her head on his chest and listening to the strong steady beat of his heart. "You were my hero today, you know. You and Spartacus, both." She shut her eyes, trying not to think about how near all three of them had come to death. Emotion tightened her throat as she pushed away the anxiety that lingered. "I wouldn't have survived without you."

Fletcher stroked his hands through the dampness of her just-washed hair, his touch as compelling and sure as his lovemaking had been. "No surprise there," he murmured huskily, kissing the top of her head, stroking her back. Tenderness filled his eyes. "No way were we going to let anything happen to you."

"Well, you didn't." Lily snuggled closer, inhaling the clean, soapy fragrance of his skin. *Don't rock the boat. Don't say anything that Fletcher might regret.* "And for that I'll be forever grateful."

Looking as happy to be there with her as she was to be with him, Fletcher rolled, so she was beneath him. He kissed her and they made love again, sweetly and slowly this time, before finally drifting off to sleep wrapped in each other's arms.

When Lily awakened, the alarm was going off. She blinked, disoriented, as Fletcher reached over and shut it off. The clock said six-thirty, and the room was filled with dusky light. Outside, they could hear the rain pouring down once again. Lily rolled onto her side, still trying to figure out what day it was. "Did we sleep all night?" she asked drowsily, rubbing her eyes.

Fletcher shook his head. He looked as if he could spend a lot longer in bed, too, but forced himself to sit up anyway. "Just all afternoon. I set the alarm because we have Janey and Thad's wedding rehearsal and dinner this evening." He searched her face. "Do you feel up to going? I'm sure they would understand if you didn't, under the circumstances."

"No. I want to go." Lily sat up, moving stiffly, stretched. She studied him, too. "Don't you?"

Fletcher nodded. To her relief, he looked as happy to be participating in his sister Janey's wedding, as Lily felt. "But I've got to go home," Lily continued. "Get my clothes and do my hair and all that."

"Give me ten minutes to shave and get ready myself and then I'll drive you," Fletcher promised.

* * *

"Don't you two look lovey-dovey," Hannah Reid noted as Lily and Fletcher entered the church where the wedding rehearsal was going to take place.

"Yeah," Joe's wife, Emma, demanded with a wink and a smile as she came up to stand beside them. "Who's getting married here tomorrow anyway?"

"Thad and me?" Janey continued the teasing playfully as she handed out "bouquets" for the bridesmaids to practice with. "Or Sir Galahad and the damsel in distress he rescued?"

Lily turned to Fletcher proudly and was shocked to see that for the first time that day Fletcher looked uncomfortable with the role he had played in pulling her out of the rising waters of Holly Creek.

He held up both hands in a gesture of surrender. "Don't go making me out to be a hero," he said gruffly, something akin to guilt flashing across his face before promptly disappearing once again.

"But you were one," Lily protested, frustrated that Fletcher still did not see himself as she saw him. As the bravest, most decent man in the whole world. "Because if you hadn't jumped in when you did—" she continued earnestly.

Once again, Fletcher couldn't quite look her in the eye as he cut her off with an abrupt shake of his head. "Someone else would have saved you," he told her curtly.

As the rest of Fletcher's brothers gathered around, Lily noticed all four of the Hart brothers—save Dylan, who wasn't there—and Janey's fiancé, Thad, were suddenly looking at Fletcher a little oddly. As if they all knew something she didn't. And perhaps should.

"Is there something going on I ought to know about?" Lily asked slowly.

More telltale scuffling of shoes. Looking everywhere but at her.

"No," every man in the room said abruptly and in unison. To Lily's dismay, Janey and Emma looked uncomfortable, too. Only Susan Hart and Hannah Reid looked as in the dark as Lily as to what could possibly be going on. And that was, Lily found, small comfort. Again, Lily felt a little niggling of doubt. Deliberately, she pushed it away. Nothing was going to ruin her blossoming relationship with Fletcher, or the feelings she had for him....

Fortunately, the minister arrived, and the rehearsal started soon after. To everyone's delight, it went off without a hitch, as did the catered rehearsal dinner back at Thad's home and the traditional giving out of gifts to members of the wedding party, by Janey and Thad. Fletcher was polite, funny, attentive to her every need. But whenever he thought she wasn't looking, he regarded her with something Lily could only identify as guilt or regret of some sort.

Was he sorry he had made love to her? Lily wondered. Sorry he had become so involved? Tired of her already and getting ready to dump her? Much to her frustration, she had no clue what was going on with him and could only pretend she was as cool and composed as Fletcher appeared to be.

Finally, it was time to leave. Fletcher drove Lily back to her place and walked her to the door. They could see Spartacus—who had been left with a pet-sitter that evening—waiting by the window. The pet-sitter, who cared for many of Fletcher's canine patients in the owners' absence, came forward to give them an update about the events of the evening. "He never stopped waiting for the two of you to come back," she told Fletcher and Lily.

"But he was otherwise calm," Lily ascertained, noting that it didn't look as if Spartacus had been chewing on his paws again.

The pet-sitter nodded as Fletcher took his wallet out and paid her. "Spartacus didn't seem to need any reassurance from me at all," she said.

Lily thanked her and the pet-sitter left to drive home.

Fletcher bent down to pet and praise Spartacus for his good behavior, then turned back to Lily and observed proudly, "He obviously considers this his home now."

Lily nodded, pleased by Fletcher's observation, but still feeling a little wary. Was it her imagination or was Fletcher still on edge? And if so, why? What was it everyone had not wanted her to pick up on?

Fletcher stood. "Something on your mind?"

The old Lily would have let it go, rather than risk doing something so unladylike as to make a guest in her home uncomfortable. And though the cowardly part of Lily was tempted to do just that, rather than risk discovering a problem that would jeopardize her feelings for Fletcher, the new, assertive Lily knew she couldn't just pretend that everything was fine when it wasn't. Or behave as though it was going to be okay for Fletcher to keep secrets from her that clearly made him and everyone else around him uncomfortable. If their love was true—and Lily acknowledged on her part that it was—then it ought to be strong enough to handle whatever difficulty came their way.

She looked Fletcher straight in the eye. "What's the secret between you and your brothers?" she asked.

Chapter 13

"You can't base a relationship on lies of omission," Joe had said. *"You have to tell Lily about the bet you made with us. Otherwise you risk her finding out some other way."*

Fletcher knew —as did his younger brother, Joe, who'd had his own problems caused by deliberately withheld information—that Lily would never forgive him if that happened. Fletcher could swear Thad and his brothers to secrecy, of course, but all it would take was one verbal slip or innocent but telling remark, by any of them, and then he would be in this exact same position again. So he had a choice. Either 'fess up and get it all out in the open and deal with the consequences now, whatever they might be. Or tell her it was nothing and have that lie and his guilt and fear of discovery continue to stand between them.

Lily was still regarding him expectantly. Aware it was time to own up to the reckless boast he wished like hell he had never made, Fletcher rubbed the tense muscles in the back of his neck. "You remember when you made a bet with your friends about Carson McRue?" he said with obvious difficulty.

Lily nodded.

Emotion choking his throat, Fletcher told her, "Well, I made a wager, too."

As soon as the words were out, Lily went so still Fletcher could almost feel the chill that descended over her heart. "What kind of wager?" she asked warily.

Guilt flooded Fletcher anew, as he looked her straight in the eye and admitted with increasing uneasiness, "The kind guys make to each other when they're at their most unruly. The kind I wished I could take back the moment the words were out of my mouth." But he hadn't, and now here they were.

Looking as if she suddenly needed to sit down, Lily moved to the living room and groped her way into a chair without ever taking her eyes from his.

Fletcher plunged on. "I bet Thad and all four of my brothers—"

"Or in other words, all the male members of the wedding party," Lily interrupted.

Fletcher nodded. "—that not only would you give up a date with Carson McRue but that you'd do it to go out with me."

"I see." Lily continued staring at him as if he were a stranger. "So all this attention—the rescuing, and making love to me—was to win a wager?" she asked incredulously. "That's why you refused to introduce me to Carson before he and the film crew hit town?"

Fletcher knew he could stop now. She already had enough to resent him the rest of her natural-born days. But then he'd have to worry about her finding out about the rest.

"No," he said, swallowing hard around the ache in his throat as she balled her hands into fists. "My protecting you in that sense had nothing to do with the bet, since it hadn't been made at that point."

"Then why?" Lily demanded furiously. Leaping from her seat, she trod closer. But not close enough that he could touch her.

Fletcher wished she didn't look so hurt, so betrayed. Knowing she wasn't going to take this next part well, either, he stayed where he was with his legs braced apart and arms folded in front of him. "I made a promise to your grandmother Rose that I would look out for you and keep you from getting involved with some guy who'd break your heart," he told her in a low, gravelly voice.

Lily smirked, a mixture of bitterness and disbelief lacing her expression. "But that didn't include you?" she guessed contemptuously.

"Actually," Fletcher said, forcing himself to be completely honest even as he tracked the moisture glimmering in her eyes, "I was exactly the kind of guy I thought you should stay away from."

Lily shook her head, as if that would clear it. "Which is why she went to you? Because it takes one to know one?"

He matched the biting sarcasm in her tone, knowing he had earned every bit of it. "I think that may have been the general thinking. She seemed to figure I knew the score, and since she had developed a rapport with me because I took care of your family cat, she must have felt she could trust me to do what she'd asked."

Lily threw up her hands and began to pace, her slender hips swaying gently beneath the delicate fabric of her dress. "And you just said yes?"

Fletcher shrugged helplessly. "She was on her deathbed, Lily. She needed, wanted, peace of mind."

Lily sat there, letting it all sink in, not knowing whether to erupt in bitter laughter or break out in gut-wrenching tears. So she did a little of both—simultaneously. "So what did you win when I refused to go out with Carson and went out with you instead?" she asked as she brushed her fingertips beneath her eyes.

"Nothing."

She glared at Fletcher, painfully aware that if not for the promise he had made to her grandmother Rose that he never would have felt beholden to stop her from going after Carson McRue or gotten so involved with her in the first place.

"I know guys," Lily said in a low choked voice. "They always wager something." She struggled to keep her composure even as she took another step closer, tilted her face up to his and demanded coolly, "What did you get if I rejected Carson McRue in favor of your swaggering attentions?"

Fletcher's golden-brown eyes gleamed with a mixture of displeasure and regret. "A hundred bucks."

Lily studied him as the words sunk in, feeling all the more devastated. Somehow she couldn't see him spending that much time and energy on her for that little payoff. Even if he had made a promise to Grandmother Rose. "That's all?" she echoed contemptuously.

Fletcher compressed his lips together grimly and admitted reluctantly, "From each one."

Now they were getting somewhere. "So if you lost it was going to cost you five hundred dollars. No wonder you went all out," Lily concluded sardonically as she turned her back and paced away from him.

If only she hadn't. Lily blushed hotly as she recalled how foolish she had been, letting her guard down so completely. How much better it would have been, she decided morosely, if she had given up her dream of experiencing passion and excitement and remained the Ice Princess of Holly Springs. She pivoted back to him with as much dignity as she could muster, trying to forget she had ever been so wildly in love and lust with him, she had done things she'd never thought possible—such as playfully tying him to the bed, and doing a provocative striptease.

Never mind that she'd revealed her most private thoughts and wishes and fears! Allowed herself to be truly and completely vulnerable with him. Shame flooded her from head to toe. "Get out!" She pushed the words through lips that felt frozen.

He held out his hands and came toward her imploringly. "Lily—"

"I mean it, Fletcher." Her voice was shrill, angry, unforgiving as she shoved him out of her physical space. "Get. Out."

His jaw hardened at the implacable tone in her low voice. "We're not through here," he warned determinedly.

"Oh, yes, we are," Lily shot back as she rushed past him toward the foyer. She stared right through him as she opened the door and held it wide. "I never ever want to see or hear from you again."

"So what's this I hear about there being trouble between you and Lily?" Fletcher's mother said when he arrived at the church Sunday afternoon, well in advance of the ceremony.

In the chapel, he could see the photographer taking pictures of Janey in her wedding dress. She was a beautiful bride. Glowing with happiness. Just as Lily would and should have been if he hadn't screwed up so badly.

"I don't know what you're talking about," Fletcher said, flushing guiltily.

Helen Hart grabbed him by the elbow and steered him into the currently unused church nursery. She shut the door behind them, looking every bit the practical disciplinarian and loving mother of six that he remembered from his youth.

"Fletcher Matthew Hart."

Oh, no, here it came. The use of his full given name. Fletcher winced.

"Don't even think about trying to shut down on me now," Helen continued.

"Now I really don't know what you're talking about," Fletcher replied stubbornly, casting yet another warning look at his mother.

Helen paused, obviously struggling to find a way to reach him. "I wish I could say you weren't always this way," she told him gently, all the love she felt for him in her eyes. "But the truth is you've always taken everything to heart."

Fletcher blew out a weary breath. He didn't want to be rude, but he didn't want to discuss this like some brokenhearted fool, either, even if that was exactly what he was. "Come on, Mom," he reminded gruffly. "I'm as cynical as they come. Everyone knows that."

"Hmm." Helen looked him up and down, her dissent with his assertion obvious. Reminding Fletcher that if anyone knew how vulnerable he was deep down, it was his mother.

His devil-may-care bravado worked on everyone but her. She'd held him when he cried as a kid. She'd tried to comfort him when he'd felt lost and alone—and refused to admit it—as an adolescent and an adult. For all the good it did either of them. Fletcher had remained unable to let his guard down completely with anyone but Lily. And now, because of his reprehensible, ungentlemanly behavior toward her, Lily had turned away from him, too.

His mother paused, still trying to figure out how to get him to confide in her and let her help him with his troubles. Finally, she said, in that soft, tender voice that always tore him up inside, "I've been trying to figure out how you got so cynical, Fletcher." Regret scored her expression. "What I did—or maybe didn't do when you were growing up—that made you this way."

"You didn't do anything," Fletcher declared impatiently.

"Then why don't you feel you deserve to be loved, heart and soul? Why won't you fight for it the way you fight for everything else? Fletcher, I've seen you work over an animal that everyone else has given up on. I've seen your confidence, your determination, when it comes to healing. I just don't understand why it doesn't carry over into your personal life. Unless..." She paused, bit her lip, then turned to him, as stubborn in her love for him as ever. "We've never talked about this. At the time, you wouldn't let me. And I felt maybe it was for the best to let it go and move on, forget that it had ever happened, rather than make it a regret you'd have to carry the rest of your life. But now I wonder if my attempt not to burden you that way really weighed you down even more."

Fletcher knew what she was talking about, even before she said, "You may not recall this, but your last one-on-one outing with your father didn't go particularly well."

Fletcher only wished he had been able to forget that evening. He had carried the burden of that unsuccessful heart-to-heart his dad had tried to have with him that night for nigh on twenty years now, not wanting to burden anyone else with his own self-centeredness—especially his mother, who had been so devastated by his father's death.

"He took you out for ice cream because he wanted to have a heart-to-heart with you," Helen continued, trying to jog his memory.

And I acted like he wasn't even there, Fletcher thought, as the failure to be the kind of son he should have been burned like acid in his gut.

Silence stretched out between them. His mother seemed to know she had struck a nerve, and simply waited. Fletcher searched his mother's eyes, almost afraid to ask. "What did Dad say to you about that night?" he demanded gruffly. *Please, tell me he didn't say anything that hurt you, too.*

Helen lifted her slender shoulders in an elegant shrug and kept her eyes firmly locked with his. "The usual. That he was worried you were taking too much upon yourself." Her eyes clouded with self-admonition as she recalled, "You were only ten, but already your father and I both could see you were way too hard on yourself, Fletcher."

"I deserved to be," Fletcher countered contemptuously, rejecting the forgiveness she was offering. "Lest you forget, my actions led directly to the death of our family's dog." A sin for which he would always pay.

Helen's expression was maternal as she reached out and touched his arm. "People make mistakes, Fletcher. We all do. What separates the grown-ups from the perpetual adolescents is the ability to forgive yourself, make amends to those you have hurt and move on."

And what if you couldn't do that? Fletcher wondered as he turned away from the compassion in his mother's touch. What if your actions had been too hurtful?

Fletcher felt his eyes begin to burn. "I know you mean well, Mom," he told her impatiently as he crossed to the window. "But you're way off base here." He blinked, said hoarsely, "You have no idea how stupidly and unforgivably I've behaved this time. Not that that's any surprise, either," he concluded bitterly.

He had a talent for making offhand decisions that somehow evolved into terrible disasters. And for the life of him he couldn't figure out why. It wasn't like he meant to get the family dog killed, or disrespect his father the very last time they saw each other, or crush every single one of Lily Madsen's heroic illusions about him and stomp all over her heart. But he had. And there was not going to be any recovery from this catastrophe, either.

Helen caught his arm, forced him to face her. "You are not unlovable, Fletcher, although to my considerable ongoing frustration, I know you have often deemed yourself to be." She paused, looking him up and down with the keen-eyed awareness only a mother had.

"Just tell me what happened between you and Lily," Helen implored again.

Fletcher had never been inclined to confide his deepest thoughts and feelings in anyone—save Lily. Now, she was gone. And heaven knew he needed to talk to someone. So, in halting words, Fletcher finally bared his soul to his mother and told her what he had done. "So you see," Fletcher concluded with disparagement, "Lily's grandmother Rose should never have asked me to look out for Lily. I was the absolutely wrong person for the job."

"Has it ever occurred to you," Helen asked with the patience of a saint, "that maybe there was a reason Rose did that?"

Fletcher threw up his hands in frustration. He didn't have a clue where his mother was going with this.

"It takes one to know one? And since she wanted to keep Lily away from guys who would hurt her—"

"That is not why Rose chose you," Helen interrupted sternly.

"Then why did she?" Fletcher demanded right back, mocking her highly exasperated tone.

"Probably because she saw the potential in pairing you—you, who are far too cynical and self-deprecating—with Lily, who up to now has been far too naive and ide-alistic. Being together has obviously helped both of you."

Had, Fletcher thought. Past tense.

"And it could help you even more if you'd just put

aside this cynicism once and for all and go after what you want, which is of course the woman you love."

"I never said I loved Lily," Fletcher stated.

Helen smiled with the wisdom gained by rearing six children into adulthood. "You don't have to. It's all over your face whenever you look at her or see her." Helen clamped a reassuring hand on his shoulder. "Even a fool could see that."

"Lily doesn't."

"Oh, Fletcher, haven't I taught you and your siblings anything? It is from adversity that strength is born. Painful as it was, your father's death forced us all to grow, to love, to be there for one another through thick and thin." She angled her head at him. "And we've done that, haven't we?"

The lump was back in his throat, big time, as he thought about how much his family meant to him. Gruffly, Fletcher looked at his mother and acknowledged, "You know we have."

"Well, Lily's had a lot of sadness in her life, too. But she deserves love, too."

Like he didn't know that? Like he didn't want to be the one to give it to her? Fletcher raked both his hands through his hair. He felt as if the starched collar and bowtie were suffocating him every bit as much as this conversation. "Did you miss the part where I completely blew it with her, Mom?"

"If you want to win Lily's hand in marriage, then go and do it. Because I'll tell you, Fletcher, I've seen the way she looks at you, and you've already won her heart."

Had he? His heart said yes. His cynical side told him that Lily never would forgive him, and she'd be right not to given the way he had behaved. His mother was still looking at him, waiting for that miracle to happen. Fletcher grimaced as frustration welled up inside him once again. "Easier said than done, given the fact she won't even talk to me."

Helen pooh-poohed that considerable obstacle with a wave of her hand. "No success in life is ever final— nor is any failure."

"Are you going to be able to walk down the aisle on Fletcher's arm?" Janey asked Lily as she and the other bridesmaids gathered in the anteroom at the back of the church. "Given the fact that you pretty much hate his guts right now? Because if you can't, we can switch the members of the wedding party around. Try to config- ure it some other way."

Heaven knew Lily was tempted to do just that. Every time she even thought of Fletcher, never mind caught a glimpse of him, it was all she could do not to burst into tears. She had loved him so much! Given him so much. Only to be betrayed and humiliated in the most awful way.

"There's no question he made a fool of me," Lily muttered as she attempted to apply her mascara with a hand that was not cooperating.

Emma and Janey exchanged concerned looks as Lily paused to remove the smudge of mascara she had just left under her right eye.

Since they were both ecstatically in love with the men of their dreams, they wanted everyone to be equally happy.

"From what Joe told me about the wager, it was just

Fletcher trying to put a spin on his attempts to protect you from Carson McRue," Emma said.

"Yeah, well, there was a reason for that, too." Briefly, Lily explained about the secret promise he had made to Grandmother Rose. So she'd either been a mercy date or a means to an end. Neither option appealed to her.

Fletcher's cousin Susan said, "For what it's worth, I've spent a lot of time with Fletcher since we grew up. He puts on a show, pretending he's the tough guy. And until you and Spartacus came along, his heart was in lockdown," Susan acknowledged seriously. "But once he started spending time with you, once he began to open up, he changed. To the point, I don't think there is any going back. And isn't that what true love is all about? Finding someone who helps you confront your own personal demons, whatever they are, and be the best person you're capable of being?"

"What are you trying to get at?" Lily demanded.

Susan leaned closer to the mirror as she reapplied her lipstick. "I don't think you should keep punishing him for a mistake he made before he really got to know you. It isn't as if he doesn't know he did wrong—he does. It's just that he can't take it back."

Emma, who had made her own share of mistakes in her romance with Joe, nodded. "Sometimes you just have to move on, Lily."

Janey agreed. "Otherwise you end up like Cal and Ashley."

"What's going on with them, anyway?" Lily asked. The two had only been married a short time when Ashley took off for a two-year fellowship in Hawaii, leaving Cal to practice sports medicine and orthopedic surgery at Holly Springs Medical Center. Both doctors insisted there was nothing wrong with their marriage, they were simply pursuing their careers to the best of their ability. But no one in town really believed it, including their own families. It was as if something had happened to drive them apart before Ashley left, and the rift was only getting wider.

Janey shrugged. "Nothing good, I can tell you that."

"Which is why we want you and Fletcher to be together," Susan explained as Emma helped Janey adjust the tiara in her hair. "Because true love—like what you share with Fletcher—might only come once. So you shouldn't let it go."

"How can you still be so idealistic?" Lily asked in frustration, wanting to believe there was still a chance for her and Fletcher, but not sure she should.

"When my own marriage ended in divorce?" Susan asked.

Lily nodded. She never would have said it, but now the assertion was out there.

Susan's expression turned reflective. She, too, had been scarred by a parent's death and knew what it was to grieve for all the times lost, the things not said or done. "I guess it's the romantic in me," Susan shrugged finally. "All I know is that when I saw Fletcher come into Wild Girls Only and take you out of there—there was something in the way he looked at you…so fiercely tender. Lily, I'd give anything if someone looked at me like that. My ex—Perry—never did."

The door opened and Helen Hart walked in, looking resplendent in her mother-of-the-bride dress. Janey took one look at her mother's face and knew, as did everyone in the room, that there was a glitch in the wedding. "What is it?" Janey asked her mother anxiously.

"Your brother Dylan isn't here yet."

Lily looked at the clock on the wall. "And the wedding starts in a little over an hour." Oh, dear...

Emma studied her mother-in-law with knowing eyes. "It gets worse, doesn't it?" Emma guessed with a wedding planner's aplomb.

Helen nodded. "He called Hannah Reid to pick him up at the Raleigh-Durham airport."

Lily had been wondering why the mechanic and part-time chauffeur, generally known to be perfectly on time, was so late arriving at the church. "So we're missing a bridesmaid and a groomsman," Lily concluded.

Helen sighed and looked all the more troubled. "Right."

Janey muttered something unladylike. "I'm going to kill that little brother of mine. Why did he have to wait until the very last minute to fly home for this? Wasn't it enough he missed the rehearsal and dinner last night?"

"Don't shoot the messenger—" Joe popped his head in, then seeing everyone was decent, strolled on in"— but Cal asked me to deliver the bad news to everyone."

The tension in the room increased tenfold.

"Let me guess," Janey said wearily as she found a seat. "His wife, Ashley, isn't coming?"

Joe shrugged his broad, hockey player shoulders. "Problems getting away. I guess that OB/GYN fellowship she's doing in Honolulu is pretty demanding." He walked over to lace his arm around Emma and give her a husbandly kiss.

"How's Cal taking it?" Susan asked.

"Not good." Joe's frown deepened. "He's outside on the cell phone, having words with his wife about her no-show right now. He's absolutely furious that she waited until the very last minute to give him the news."

"Oh, dear," Helen said as she collapsed next to the bride on the worn velvet settee. She fanned herself. "What else could possibly happen?" she asked in mother-of-the-bride distress.

"That's what I'd like to know," Janey muttered.

And then someone else was at the door to the anteroom. They all looked up. Fletcher was standing there. Tall, imposing. And more coolly determined than Lily had ever seen him.

Fletcher looked straight at Lily. "I want a word with you," he said. "Right now."

Lily's heart thundered in her chest as her spirits rose and crashed and rose again. She couldn't believe he was throwing down the gauntlet like this, right there in front of everyone. "This isn't the time," she murmured haughtily.

"It's exactly the time—" Fletcher drawled, crossing swiftly to her side.

When she resisted, he simply tucked a hand beneath her knees and swept her up into his arms, cradling her against the hardness of his chest.

"—since the nuptials are probably going to have to be delayed due to the late arrival of my younger brother."

"Remind me to thank Dylan when I see him," Lily muttered, excitement climbing into her cheeks.

Fletcher carried her past the approving expressions of the other members of the wedding party, out the door and up the stairs that flanked either side of the vestibule.

"The only one you're going to be thanking is me," Fletcher said as he continued past the door to the balcony, where the organist and soloist were warming up, down a narrow hallway, to an open doorway.

"Why would I be thanking you?" Lily demanded, trying hard not to inhale the intoxicatingly masculine fragrance of his cologne and skin as Fletcher strode into the supply closet, switched on the overhead light and shut the door behind them.

He set her down gently and raked her with a glance that brought forth a wealth of memories, both tender and erotic. "For refusing to give up on us."

The room—already small—got smaller, more intimate yet.

"What?" Lily prodded, stubbornly ignoring the tingles of desire he was creating, just being near her. She reminded herself that although she had given him her whole heart and soul, he had never once said he loved her. "Your brothers haven't paid up yet?"

Refusing to react to her needling, he gave her a look that said she was making this unnecessarily hard on them both. "I paid them."

That was news. Lily blinked, struggling to understand why he would have done such a thing, when he had clearly won his wager. Unless…? "I'm going out with Carson McRue?"

Fletcher scoffed and gave her that you-are-my-woman-look again. "Only when hell freezes over."

"Then why did you pay them?" Lily asked, trying not to warm at the fiercely possessive expression on his face.

He caught her hand and tugged her close. "To make a point."

She still didn't get it. "Well, it's completely escaping me," she said, mocking his droll tone to a T.

He wrapped both arms around her, and held her tenderly, looking deep into her eyes. "That my chasing you and courting you and protecting you was never about the promise or the wager, it was about what I was already feeling deep inside and was afraid to admit. It was about the fact that I love you," he said in a rough voice laced with all the affection she had ever wanted, and more. "Do you hear me, Lily? I. Love. You. Fletcher Hart loves Lily Madsen."

She looked into his eyes and knew he meant it, every word. And suddenly the mistakes they'd both made, the errors in judgment—and there had been plenty on both their parts—were negligible. Tears of happiness flooded her eyes. Knowing at last all her dreams were coming true, she rose on tiptoe, laced her arms around his neck and kissed him soundly. Once, twice, three times. When at last they drew apart, she felt peace in her heart unlike anything she had ever felt.

He lifted a hopeful brow, still holding her as if he never wanted to let her go. "I take it that kiss means you love me, too?" The smile on his face said he already knew the answer.

"With everything I have and am," Lily affirmed contentedly as their hearts beat in lovely harmony.

He smoothed a hand down her spine, bringing her closer yet. "Then marry me, Lily," he urged in a low voice, thick with emotion. "So we can spend the rest of our lives together."

Letting her actions speak for what was in her heart, Lily rose on tiptoe once again and kissed him again, even more passionately this time. Fletcher kissed her back. "Is that a yes?" he whispered as her whole world went right again.

"Most definitely," Lily replied, her heart pounding as she drew back to look him square in the face. "But only on one condition," she stipulated firmly.

"Anything," Fletcher told her, looking ready to make all her dreams come true, and then some. Not just for now, but for the next fifty, sixty years. "You just name it."

Lily grinned, aware she had never felt so happy—except for maybe when they'd made love and he'd shown her without a doubt all the woman she could be. She pressed a cautioning fingertip to his lips. "You have to swear to me you'll never make another bet concerning us with anyone but me."

To her delight, he didn't even have to think about it. "Done," he pledged firmly.

The happiness inside her bubbled up, lighter and more buoyant than ever. "And you have to promise me you will win this next one."

Interest flickered in his eyes at the possibility of another bet—this one made with her. "You need victory, Lily?" he promised cheerfully, kissing first her hand, then the inside of her wrist. "I'm your man."

"Good. 'Cause this is it." Lily wreathed one arm about his neck, smoothed her other palm over his chest. "I'm betting the two of us will last forever."

"Sweetheart," Fletcher said, taking her back into his arms, for another long, slow, incredibly tender and possessive kiss, "that's a wager we're destined to win."

* * * * *

SPECIAL EXCERPT FROM

Love Inspired.
SUSPENSE

*A K-9 cop must keep his childhood friend alive
when she finds herself in the crosshairs of a
drug-smuggling operation.*

*Read on for a sneak preview of
Act of Valor by Dana Mentink,
the next exciting installment in the
True Blue K-9 Unit miniseries, available in May 2019
from Love Inspired Suspense.*

Officer Zach Jameson surveyed the throng of people congregated around the ticket counter at LaGuardia Airport. Most ignored Zach and K-9 partner, Eddie, and that suited him just fine. Two months earlier he would have greeted people with a smile, or at least a polite nod while he and Eddie did their work of scanning for potential drug smugglers. These days he struggled to keep his mind on his duty while the ever-present darkness nibbled at the edges of his soul.

Eddie plopped himself on Zach's boot. He stroked the dog's ears, trying to clear away the fog that had descended the moment he heard of his brother's death.

Zach hadn't had so much as a whiff of suspicion that his brother was in danger. His brain knew he should talk to somebody, somebody like Violet Griffin, his friend from childhood who'd reached out so many times, but his heart would not let him pass through the dark curtain.

"Just get to work," he muttered to himself as his phone rang. He checked the number.

Violet.

He considered ignoring it, but Violet didn't ever call unless she needed help, and she rarely needed anyone. Strong enough to run a ticket counter at LaGuardia and have enough energy left over to help out at Griffin's, her family's diner. She could handle belligerent customers in both arenas and bake the best apple pie he'd ever had the privilege to chow down.

It almost made him smile as he accepted the call.

"Someone's after me, Zach."

Panic rippled through their connection. Panic, from a woman who was tough as they came. "Who? Where are you?"

Her breath was shallow as if she was running.

"I'm trying to get to the break room. I can lock myself in, but I don't… I can't…" There was a clatter.

"Violet?" he shouted.

But there was no answer.